A MATTER AMONG COWBOYS

A Matter Among Men
A Matter Among Four

Destiny Blaine

EROTIC ROMANCE

Siren Publishing, Inc.
www.SirenPublishing.com

A SIREN PUBLISHING BOOK
IMPRINT: Ménage Amour

A MATTER AMONG COWBOYS
A Matter Among Men
A Matter Among Four
Copyright © 2009 by Destiny Blaine

ISBN-10: 1-60601-351-3
ISBN-13: 978-1-60601-351-9

First Printing: October 2009

Cover design by Jinger Heaston
All cover art and logo copyright © 2009 by Siren Publishing, Inc.

ALL RIGHTS RESERVED: This literary work may not be reproduced or transmitted in any form or by any means, including electronic or photographic reproduction, in whole or in part, without express written permission.

All characters and events in this book are fictitious. Any resemblance to actual persons living or dead is strictly coincidental.

Printed in the U.S.A.

PUBLISHER
Siren Publishing, Inc.
www.SirenPublishing.com

DEDICATIONS

A Matter Among Men

This book is dedicated to every Tennessee cowboy I know—and I'm lucky enough to know a few!

A Matter Among Four

To Diana, my publisher.

I have an abundance of energy but can't keep up with you. Your shoes are far too big for any normal human being to fill—and that's a good thing.

I admire your energy and your dedication, and I thank you for your support. Without you, this book would not have materialized. The title and the idea for a sequel is all on you and I thank you for sharing your insights.

You're one of a kind.

SIREN PUBLISHING

Destiny Blaine

A MATTER AMONG MEN

A MATTER AMONG MEN

DESTINY BLAINE
Copyright © 2009

Chapter 1

I grew up with his kind. I knew all about them. They had tall hats, big ideas, and of course, they possessed the grandest of them all. Yes, I'm referring to a somewhat useless thing that on occasion finds some measure of purpose. The most treasured possession of every man alive—or obsession, which is often the case.

I rode horses with the best of them since I stood knee-high to where those good-ole-boys kept their prized assets. They bored me on most occasions, and since I had to listen to their tell-all tales from an early age forward, I *almost* decided to hold out for marriage. *Almost*— a little word, but it held a lot of meaning. *Almost* doesn't count when someone's trying to keep his or her virginity. I almost kept mine but didn't. Thanks in part to Finn McClanahan.

Finn changed my mind. Owing my gratitude all to him, I gained experience. He told me more than once 'a practiced woman' earns her place in a man's bed, and of course, I bought into such a line of bullshit. He claimed he also gave me treasured memories, but those are really up for debate.

"Darlene! Darlene! Are you in there?" The bathroom door was locked. I held the toothbrush to my teeth. I knew damn well she realized who stood on the other side of the door. I paused long enough to smile real big and grit my teeth in the mirror, making sure they looked pearly white. I did my best to scrub off any reminder that I'd had the better part of Finn McClanahan between my swollen lips the night before. My sister continued to bang on the wood separating us.

Looking into the mirror, I let out a sigh. I wasn't bad looking. A little on the skinny side but definitely top heavy enough to keep Finn coming back, and sometimes, I liked it when he did. Okay, so I loved it. Most of the time anyway.

The door came crashing forward and hit me in the forehead.

"Fuck! Can't you knock?"

She'd picked the lock. I knew she would.

She gave me her best "Bitch" for the morning and stared at my bare chest. Of course, I could count down what would follow from behind the closed bathroom door after she all but pushed me out into the hall.

"Darlene, you got no right to run around here topless. Stan spent the night, and it just ain't right…"

I could still hear her bitchin' as I strutted to the kitchen, grabbed an apple, and headed back to my room.

"Mornin', Stan." I smiled while brushing by him. Finn's older brother had a great ass and I took my time staring at it.

He liked me. A lot.

"Darlene." He nodded in my direction but never looked into my eyes. He closed the bedroom door to my sister's room and threw on his cowboy hat.

I loved to toy with men, especially those older than me. The very cowboys who chose to ride my sister for free were fair game. Believe me, there were a bunch of them. My sweet sister had become quite good at running men through a stable of a different sort. Most people in town called her a whore, but I don't recall seeing money on the table. I guess that made her stupid. With her body, she could've charged.

"Did you have a good time?" I took a bite out of the fruit and listened to myself chew. *Chomp. Chomp. Chomp. Chomp.* I looked over every inch of him. *Squirm, Stan. Squirm.* I wanted to laugh outright.

"Uh…" He kept his head down and his back to me.

I leaned over him but made sure my breasts never touched him. Still, a girl had to find her amusement somewhere. It was hard to find it in the middle of Tennessee. Whispering softly, I gave him some pointers. "She can hear you, so you better make it good. Say yes, Stan. Yes. Yes. Ahhhh, yes!" I giggled and turned to see my sister's gaze raking me over imaginary hot coals.

Stan's neck and cheeks stained a perfect shade of red. I could have a good time with Stan, and often, I wondered if I somehow ended up with the wrong brother.

My sister flew out of the bathroom, tossing a towel over me as she did. "Darlene, damn you. I warned about this. Are you forgetting how we were raised? Get on down there to your room and put some clothes on!"

I hadn't forgotten about our upbringing, but sadly, my sister wanted everyone in our small town to believe we had the best of it. What she didn't seem to understand was every woman within a hundred miles of our ranch feared us. They were scared to death their husbands or boyfriends would end up in our beds. The thing was, thanks to Kimbrell's reputation, I earned my own. It really sucked, since only one man ever climbed on top of me or slid in behind, which seemed to be a favored position.

"Bye-bye, Stan." Like a kid, I waved in slow motion. I couldn't help it. He was just so damn cute with his rosy little cheeks. "Do me a favor and tell your brother you saw me this morning. In fact, tell him I was just the way he left me in the middle of the night. He'll know precisely what you saw."

I gave the only thing covering me a quick fling and then turned around once more with my arms wide open. "Make sure you tell him now, okay?"

Stan nodded. "Yes ma'am." His eyes never left my chest. Oh, well. Sorry, Kimbrell.

The last thing I heard was a slap sound. I'm assuming his eyes lingered just a little longer than my dear sibling wanted them to, but either way, when I left the house about thirty minutes later, the initial smack had turned back into a familiar banging noise behind bedroom doors. Yep, he'd gone back for more. I guess all he needed was a little inspiration. My sister owed me big time. I doubt she would see it that way.

* * * *

The morning greetings sounded like wind chimes as I walked through the barn. "Mornin', Darlene." It was my favorite part of the day. Even the smell of horse shit had a different aroma in the morning. Okay, so it blended in with the coffee brewing on either side of the barn.

I sat down in the office and started to go over some of the paperwork I'd let pile up for over a decade. Really, it'd been that long since Momma departed with Daddy trailing right behind her. We were left to run things. Correction, I stepped in to manage the business, and my big sister was free to lie around on her back. That's not entirely fair. She did tell me she enjoyed *it* a lot up against the wall, too.

A long sigh escaped my lips before I called it a day. Two or three minutes was all it took to reach the decision. The pile accumulated for nearly ten years and it could continue to pile up for another ten or twenty more. A yawn followed a stretch before a few waist bends and I was ready to ride.

Three cowboys came in at about the same time my chair hit the back wall. They were strutting their stuff. I'd bedded one of them, blew two of them, and loved all of them. Yep, in my dreams. The one in the middle was mine, but the other two I'd never seen before. My loss, apparently.

"Morning, boys!" I called to them before I headed in the other direction. My farm manager was breaking in a colt, and I didn't need to be in the barn makin' small talk.

Finn caught up to me and grabbed me around the waist. "Now just where do you think you're going so fast?" His mischievous smirk told me he'd already let the others know he had me marked as his. Poor boy. If only he knew. Sadly, Finn only paid attention when another man gave me the eye. I looked past him at the two options. *Which one of you said something to Finn?* I didn't bother to ask. It was probably both of them. A pair of eyes stripped me down to a thong and I didn't wonder for long.

"Hell, baby, I know I'm good, but I'm not that good," I fired back at him and heard the laughter coming up on us. His sidekicks heard me loud and clear. It was all right. I didn't give a damn. Who the hell were they going to tell in Lewisburg, Tennessee? And with my growing reputation, why would I care if they told all two hundred people? Okay, two-fifty.

Finn sneered.

"What's wrong, Finn? Aren't you going to introduce me to your friends?" I batted my eyes. I was so glad I looked good this bright, sunny day. I had on a shiny red shirt, low-cut of course, denim faded to perfection, and a new pair of leather riding boots. I looked damn fine, and thank goodness for blonde hair. Men liked to sum me up in three statements. Big boobs. Tight ass. Dumb blonde. *Work it, baby. Work it.* I reminded myself to play it for all it was worth.

One of Finn's new friends gave me the once-over, and I propped an elbow up on a nearby ledge and threw a hip to rest my hand on it. That's a lie. I threw the hip to let him look over the curves I had in just the right places. Finn already knew all about them. He could look the other way if he was left unimpressed. He wasn't.

His brow gathered and narrowed. I swear it looked like it happened at the same time. See, I know Finn McClanahan better than he knows himself. What I was one-hundred percent sure of was the young and handsome Mr. McClanahan told these good ole boys in front of me some gal fucked him silly the night before.

He'd likely told them *this* "chick" also gave him the best blowjob he'd ever had or ever would have in his lifetime, because we both understood that much was true. I had a little mouth but could still suck baseballs, or mothballs, as the case would be with some men, through a water hose. Or yes, a straw.

I smiled sweetly, waiting for introductions, but Finn wasn't budging to make them. Then, the plot thickened. Actually, it sweetened. In walked Stan. Kimbrell didn't keep him from the work he needed to do. All four men stood there without a peep, exchanging looks and afraid to speak.

"Kimbrell let you go early this morning?" I turned away from Finn's older brother to stick out my hand to one of the new guys. "I'm Darlene. I'm the one he fucked last night." I pointed to Finn. I don't really think they needed verification.

The handsome one took my hand with some hesitation, but the other boy couldn't wait to shake it.

I gave Finn a daring glance. "That's about what I thought."

After our polite how-do-you-dos and the uncomfortable introductions, I turned to find a bucket and waltzed out of the barn. I tried to sway some, in case the handsome one found cause to watch.

I'm sure he did.

Finn, cute dimples and all, didn't have a lick of sense and once we were outside, I told him about it.

"What's wrong with you?" He leaned over the fence, staring straight ahead at the colt we were going to break.

"Not a damn thing," I coolly responded.

"Why'd you have to go and do that for? Embarrass yourself like that."

"Because, Finn, I told you no one should know about us. Just because you don't give out my name doesn't mean you can go and advertise what we do in the bedroom."

He seemed puzzled. "Darlene, you didn't have me in the bedroom."

I smacked him on the back of the head. "This I know. Hell, I still have a straw up my ass to prove I did you in the barn." I couldn't help but laugh.

He didn't think it was funny. Knowing Finn, he was still trying to reassure himself no one was in my bed and that the reference to one proved only figurative.

"Wanna tell me what you told them?" I challenged him some.

"Not particularly." He shook his head.

"Do you wanna see how quick they'll tell me?" My eyes held his and I waited for an answer.

"They ain't gonna say anything," he snapped. "I know they won't."

"Wanna bet?"

He was all over it. "You're on." The twinkle in his eye almost made me believe for an instant maybe he didn't tell them, but guys can't refuse bragging rights. I had a feeling boasting over me gave Finn just one too many tally marks. He happened to be the only one who knew what it was like to bed the sister of the town tramp. Even though Kimbrell's reputation still followed me around, only Finn understood me in the more carnal sense.

"What's the wager?" I hoped like hell he'd say a cheeseburger and fries from Betty's in Columbia, but I didn't get my wish.

"How about if I win, you owe me another night like last night?"

"Sure." I shook his hand. "And if I win?"

"I'll let you ride me anytime you like, even if I've got a girl."

I really didn't want his stupid bet, but the truth was, sometimes when Finn had a girlfriend, the need to screw did arrive. I guess it seemed like a fair gamble. We were tight friends, but he wanted those women who had the pretty bows in their hair and smelled all fresh like a baby's ass. It would only be a matter of time before I'd be left out in the barn for another frilly little lady with dresses and high heels.

"Deal." I decided it was a bargain after I thought of the lonely nights when he had another woman on his arm. Now, I really wanted to win.

We shook on it again.

* * * *

The sun beat down on those boys like it was the hottest day of summer. They'd already stripped off their shirts, and one of them was showing off some muscle with each hay bale he moved.

I knew which one happened to be the weakest link, and I went for the kill. I moved slowly in my pursuit, but I'm not sure I needed to since I was quickly called out on my game.

"So, you're a *real* cowboy?" I took my time drifting over him with a stare longing for more. Really, the one deserving of such appreciation was my next intended target, but he wasn't an easy mark. I was sure of it. I took the extra time to act real impressed with the one in front of me. *Exhibit A. Cowboy Up.*

I lightly touched his arm and then bit down on my lower lip. "I love to ride cowboys." Okay, so it was overdone to a fault. "I mean, I love to watch cowboys ride." I made the correction. "So tell me, *hon*...are you *really* a cowboy?" I purred with seduction, but my peripheral vision locked in on the other one. Call it instinct or something.

Behind me, I heard Finn grunt, and the one on the wagon shook his head. He did a cute little thing with his mouth, making me think he was chewing at the inside of his jaw. Still, it was kind of sexy. I don't think he bought the fact I might be overly interested in yet another man with a Stetson.

"Yes ma'am." He nodded. "I am indeed." He tilted his hat in my direction.

Stan stopped moving hay and jumped down off the wagon. He stood by quietly, ready to observe. I bet he did a lot of that with my sister. I eyed him carefully and returned my focus to the *game* I was running on the plowboy, waiting to earn my attention. Probably even my affection.

"Let me ask you something, cowboy." The words just rolled off my tongue with ease. "You like the same things Finn likes?"

The other guy was a little sharper. He stopped moving the hay around and looked at me long and hard. I think he saw right through me. "Don't answer her. She's roping you in like one of those young calves. Isn't that right, ma'am?" His jaw set, and for some reason, I felt like he'd already made a decision not to like me. "She's toying with you."

"Only with the pretty boys. Kind of like you, cowboy," I shot right back with nothing but total appreciation. "What kind of fun do you like to have with girls like me?"

Stan laughed and shook his head. "Ah shit. Here we go."

Finn looked like he'd just swallowed a toad.

I kept a keen eye on the good 'ole boys. Trying to sum up who would be most interested. Yes, that meant looking at the beads of sweat on their foreheads one minute and their cocks the next. Only one had a rise. And the one sporting it *was not* my weakest link.

I turned my focus to the man with the abs and arms. "So, Finn told you I could fuck for hours and on occasion, will even bend over just to take it up the ass?"

His expression showed a hint of frustration. "You got a smart mouth for a pretty woman."

"You didn't answer me." And I didn't thank him for the compliment.

He was every bit of six-feet tall and rock solid. Most men, even young ones his age, took a moment to get down off the wagon, but this one didn't. He didn't grab onto anything. Oh hell no, he had something to say, and he wanted to make an impression before he did it, I suppose. He bent both knees and jumped down, his muscular thighs gave way, and he landed right in front of me.

He bit the end of his covered fingers and pulled the work gloves off his hands. From underneath his cowboy hat, dark eyes dared me to make the wrong move, say the inappropriate thing.

"Yeah, I bet you know how to use your little body in a way to drive a man like that one crazy." He tilted his head in Finn's direction and then added more. He wanted to go in for the kill, and he did it well, I might add. "But not all of us are Finn."

Good damn thing. I smirked. I was, in fact, speechless. At least for a moment. "Then I won the bet." I turned to look at Finn, but he wasn't ready to concede.

My part-time lover wanted them to know all about us. He probably even hoped like hell to lose the bet after he saw the interest in his friend's face. He pushed for the loss. "I didn't tell them anything about what we did *or do*, did I, boys?" Oh, but how 'the do' gave it all away. He was jealous as hell and taking ownership now. How sweet. Well, not really.

The cowboy in front of me didn't move. His gaze drifted and rested at strategic points. Crotch. Tits. Neck. Lips. *Damn him.*

"Finn, the bet's off." There was something about this man, and I wasn't sure I wanted him to know too much about my personal life. My eyes couldn't move from the masculine focus intent on moving over me. He held onto me with some sort of invisible trance.

"Well, boys, hell. Go on, tell her. We didn't talk about much, did we?" Finn probed them for something. Anything. He wanted to break the connection I had with the new stud-muffin, or whatever he thought he was.

The cowboy's midnight blues zoomed in on one target—yeah, me. He slapped the gloves in the palm of his hand and then turned to Finn's brother. "Say, Stan, didn't you say she's got something every man in the county would sell out their home-places just to see?"

Stan blushed.

Hell, I blushed too.

Finn looked at his brother. "What are you asking him for?" Then he stared back at me.

The cowboy nodded. "Seems your girlfriend here is cleaning both your plows. That's about what I figured you'd get in these parts. Hell, do you boys take a wife and then let your brothers bed her for you? After all, this one here is probably a tiger to tame. It probably takes both of you to do it, especially with this ranch to run." He shook his head.

"Hardly, Mister." I grew tense and suddenly aware of everything. How I looked, how I held my hands. I even noticed when a speck of hay fell on my shirt. *Damn him. Again.*

"So, tell me something, ma'am, how much do you charge to give a real man a ride?" The newcomer slapped Stan on the back but Stan didn't budge because he was angry, and it was beginning to show.

"That's about enough," Stan cautioned.

Finn didn't say a word. Poor guy, he probably thought I was doing his brother since his sibling took up for me.

I shook my head and shot Stan a look of warning. We needed ranch hands, and I couldn't afford to piss another one off, especially one built for the work. "I don't know. I guess we could work something out if you boys could run on into town and find me a real man for the rodeo." I felt my mouth turn up in a smile. I must've done pretty well with the cut-down, because several of the boys started laughing.

"Got a sassy little mouth too, huh?" His feet parted with a stance determined to showcase his confidence.

"Darlin', you got no idea." I bit my lower lip and decided insults that turned into a game in my favor would be better than pissing off the man who quickly heated me to the quick.

"I have some." His focus went directly down the length of my legs.

Finn looked uncomfortable. "Darlene, let's get back to work. We've got a fence to fix, or we're going to have horses everywhere."

"Yep, we do." I acknowledged Finn, but I refused to back down from the hunk of flesh in front of me. Our eyes met again. I wanted to blink or move away from the lockdown of stares first, but there wasn't any way I was going to do it.

He spoke then and turned away when he did.

I won.

"So, what do you pay for mending a fence?" he asked.

"Depends on who's doing the mending," I told him.

"Got anybody in mind?" he asked.

"Several, to hear you tell it." Snapping out the words came easy for me.

Finn moved closer with a protective arm and he draped me in ownership—his. "I said, we've got work to do."

"Finn McClanahan, I'm well aware of the work we do around here, so why don't you go do it! Right now, I'm trying to sum up Mr. Dawson." I paused for effect and put a nervous hand on my hip. "It is Dawson, right?" I'd heard some of the boys call him Dawson, and I assumed it was a last name.

"Yes ma'am, it is."

"Got a first name?"

"Yes ma'am, I do." He stuck a piece of straw in the corner of his mouth and chewed a second before tossing it to the ground.

I waited. I could practice patience when it seemed to serve me well. "Well, are you going to tell me, or do I have to wait all day to hear it?" So much for endurance.

He slapped his gloves into his hand again and turned his back on me. I could feel my face heat as the big lug in front of me chose to ignore me, so I reached out for him and grabbed a solid arm.

Turning him around wasn't an option. He shrugged me off, tensing when I touched him. I felt it for a brief moment.

"Hey, buddy, I write the checks around here."

"From what I hear, the payment happens in there." He nodded in the direction of the house.

"Why you…" I wanted to slap the shit out of him, but the truth was, more and more men were coming to work for me because they realized if they did a good job and my sister found them interesting, they might just get paid for their efforts with some added benefits too. Hell, we should've just opened up a whorehouse. It would've been more profitable.

I stomped off and then stormed right back with both hands set on my waist. "Listen, I asked you for your name, and I would appreciate it if you would give it to me. In fact, if you'll follow me, I'll get everything I need from you in the office."

He followed me at a good distance to the tack room, and I paused there just so I could throw a halter on a nearby saddle. He was in the doorway when I started to turn back. "Not in here, in there." I pointed.

"Oh, is that where I get to negotiate the terms?" His eyes glassed over in a sea of blue. *Damn were they sexy.*

"Mister, there's nothing to negotiate if you can't give me your name."

"Oh, baby. I plan to give you my name, but it's not going to be a moment sooner than when you'll need to say it again and again." He took his time with a lingering once-over, and he did it twice more before he stopped to add, "Yep. You'll be screaming it by morning."

Chapter 2

"You like him." Finn held the fence steady, and I beat the nail into the board.

"I don't know what you're talking about," I lied. "Or who."

"Liar. You and him, you've got some kind of eye-thing going on." Finn didn't let me off the hook. Why would he? I was his girl in a twisted, messed-up sort-of way.

"What eye-thing?" I stopped the hammering and stared at him.

"The one where you both can't tear your gaze away from the other one."

"Sweet." I looked off to the distance.. "You're jealous?" It was definitely a question. I wanted to know.

"So, you're looking?"

"Maybe. Maybe not." I played Finn like a sport. He could handle it.

"So, when did you *do* Stan?" Finn had such an eloquent way with words.

I guess I was wrong. He couldn't handle it if he was jealous over his own brother. I glared at him. "You can't be serious."

"Yeah, I am." He took a deep breath and let it out slowly. "That's why Dawson can't wait to get you alone. Stan told him you had the best tits on any gal in the world. Not that his world goes much farther to the north or south of here."

I grinned. "Not that he would find any better if it did, so it doesn't matter." I bit playfully on my bottom lip.

"So, you're fucking him too?" Finn's voice stayed soft, but his face turned beet red. Damn good thing I didn't act like Kimbrell. Too much drama.

"No. I'm not fucking him."

"She will be." A masculine voice rang through the air. And it wasn't Stan behind it.

I turned around slowly and faced off with Dawson. The only name he wanted me to have.

Finn rubbed the sweat off his forehead with the back of his hand. "I wouldn't be so sure." He sneered. New blood was moving in on his territory.

"I'm pretty certain." He looked me up and down, staking his claim.

"Okay, Mr. Dawson," I began, but he cut me off.

"Not mister. Just Dawson." He smiled but barely sported a set of gorgeous, straight teeth.

I threw down the hammer and picked up the jug of water at my feet. After taking a sip to cure the dry throat, I made an attempt to put him in his place. "For the record, I wasn't talking about you. I was talking about Stan."

He snickered and took the bottle of water from me, turning it up and drinking from the same place my lips had only just left. That alone, turned me on. I was indeed losing it. After a few swallows, he wiped his mouth off on his bare arm and spoke in the most dominant, sexy voice I'd ever heard.

"Baby, I know you're not talking about me, because if you were, the words *no* and *not* wouldn't be in your vocabulary." He did his little mouth-thing again, and I decided he had a twitch. Not really. It was provocative as hell. That's why he did it. To drive women, specifically me, crazy.

Finn shook his head. "Never mind me."

"I'll try my best." He didn't look over at Finn, and he kept everything about me in his view. Visual sweeps, I decided, were something he enjoyed doing. They made me nervous. Sweet mercy. I wanted him right there just for lookin'.

I cleared my throat. "Dawson, I think you can help Finn, and I'll go get the mares turned out for the day."

"Finn can get the mares. I'll help you. How about it?"

I wanted to tell him I was the boss around there, but the words wouldn't form. Finn waited for me to tell him as much. I'm sure he expected it, but I just couldn't do it. Truth was, I wanted to get to know more about the mysterious man in front of me.

Finn kicked at the grass for a minute. "Fine. I'll get the damn mares."

I nodded. "Great idea."

He started to walk off, but before he could take two steps, he turned back to me and planted a kiss on my cheek. "We're still on for tonight, right?"

I couldn't think fast enough. It was kind of difficult when the sexy cowboy in front of me kept running the pad of his thumb over his bottom lip, just acting like he wanted to devour me whole with the very mouth he touched.

"Sure," I finally responded.

"Forget it, Finn. She already has plans." He quickly spoke the hell up but never looked over at the man he challenged. Quiet confidence ripped through the air.

Finn's face shaded nicely to a peach color, the middle of his cheekbones flaming with the brighter red tone in the center. The dead silence surrounded us and I swear, the only thing I heard then was the rumbling of leaves in the distance.

Once again, I could feel the tension rip through the man still close enough to touch me. His body looked straighter, and his eyes set with an element of danger about them. *Up-oh.* It was all I could think. He wasn't going to back down.

"Dawson," he began slowly with a cool temper in check, "You're new around here, and when somebody new comes around, me and

Stan like to set them straight from day one. See, Stan worked for Darlene's parents before Darlene and Kimbrell took over things here, and I've known them half my life. We look after them. Take care to keep them safe and all."

"Give me a break, Finn." He laughed and shook his head.

"What I'm trying to tell you is that um…" He paused and looked at me hard before he continued. He searched my face, and for the first time, I saw something in him I'd never noticed before. It almost scared me, because I sure didn't want to see it. "Well, um, Darlene here is my um…"

"Spit it out, Finn. She's your what? Roll in the hay?" He laughed and then continued. "From what you said last night, and with all due respect, Darlene, but I think you probably already know what he says about you, she's the tightest piece of ass a man can hope to find but not the marrying kind."

Finn's face brightened to blood red almost on command. "Damn you, Dawson. You know what I said, and what I said was…"

Dawson interrupted. "What you said was that many men would fight to have a woman like Darlene in their bed."

"So what if I did?" Finn lost the war of words before it ever really began.

A peculiar sound fell from Dawson's lips and it rang out like more of a grunt and a chuckle. "Well, from what I've seen of her, I imagine you're telling the truth. But I won't know about that, now will I, if I let you have her tonight? It's not going to happen. You don't have plans with Darlene tonight."

"Okay, boys. This is really nice to have you both biding for my attention, but I have work to get done around here, and I think we can save this conversation for another day." I really liked this Dawson character, but crossing Finn didn't make good common sense either.

Dawson turned to finally face off with Finn. "You ain't rolling around in the hay shed with her tonight, Finn." Dawson gnawed on his lower lip for a minute and then moved past Finn to gather up another board. Somebody needed to work and he looked ready.

"The hell I'm not. She'll be in my bed all night long, Dawson." Finn walked by me and didn't have the good sense to tread on out of there. He followed Dawson about ten feet to the pile of wood waiting to be put to good use.

"Like hell." Dawson turned on him with the first board, and I swear I thought he would use it to hit Finn, but he didn't. He just tossed it closer to the fence we were mending.

I watched all of this unfold in some kind of slow motion and felt like, in Dawson's presence, I didn't have a say so. Nobody ever took my ability to speak. *Nobody.* Not even Finn.

"You lost the bet." Losing with Dawson, Finn turned to me with his mouth of lies. "You owe me."

"I won the bet," I informed him.

"What damn wager have you two been rambling about all day?" Dawson asked the question, but I had a feeling he knew, and he probably had a good idea of what was on the line for the winner and loser.

"It was just a bet." I paused and then decided if Dawson really wanted to get rid of Finn, I could probably tell him about our little game and find out just how much Finn spilled about our romps.

Finn shot Dawson a daring stare.

"We were betting on what Finn told you and your buddy about me."

Dawson laughed out loud. "Huh, is that right."

"Who won?" Men just never listened.

"I think I did, and he obviously thinks he did," I informed him.

"Tell me more about this little wager." Dawson crossed his arms and leaned up against the fence. That's when I really noticed him. He was taller than I first imagined, and his body was hard and lean. Mercy hell, it was perfect. Six-pack abs or maybe even more. Was it possible for a man to pack a punch with a case of abs? I don't know, but his body could work someone into damnation and yeah, his stomach looked good enough to kiss. *Yes, mighty fine.*

His high cheekbones were enough to make a man beautiful, and his hair, while wavy brown, couldn't be viewed for the hat. What I did spot were dark, sexy, and inviting eyes and lips more than able to undo the best of moral women.

Stan walked up to save the day. "Dawson, I think you know enough about their stupid gambling to leave it be." He shot a disapproving look at his brother and then informed Dawson what should've inspired him to keep quiet. "There's nothing to what my brother tells you, so just leave it alone."

"Well then, I guess I did win." I shot Finn a hateful glare.

He didn't have the common sense to shut up. He never could be still. Especially in the sack, but that was beside the point.

"You did not." Finn always wanted to be right.

Dawson smiled at Finn and wrinkled his brow sort of in a condescending gesture. Then, he just spilled it all. "I think the lady should know what you've been telling."

"I think you need to keep your mouth shut," Finn smarted off to him.

"Tight snatch. Perfect tits. Better in bed than her sister. Hell, lots better than any woman had a right to be. Rides a man like a man rides a horse. Goes for hours or all night." He moved his palm to his lower back for effect before he added, "A man never gets tired of being on his back for this one." He then nodded at me, and a look of sadness or something similar filled his eyes. "I'm sorry, Darlene, but it goes downhill from there."

I couldn't really breathe well after he knocked the breath out of me. "You fucked Kimbrell?" I really had a hard time with the stated revelation. I looked at Finn and then back at Dawson and Stan.

Dawson shrugged. "You boys did her sister at the same time. Isn't that what you said?"

Stan swung first, and Dawson took the punch in his lower jaw. He set his lips in a thin line as his hand went to stroke the place where Stan's fist first hit.

"I'll let you have one, but either of you swing again, and it will be the last one you throw. I promise you." He then took me by the arm, trying to lead me away from them.

"Let me go." I moved my forearm a bit, trying to loosen the grasp. "You can't just come in here and start causing trouble."

He looked over his shoulder, and what he didn't say to the two men behind us said it all. He dared them to cross him. Sometimes a look of contempt speaks volumes, I suppose.

"I said let me go now!" I continued to twist and pull.

"Not on your life."

Chapter 3

Dawson damn near pulled me all the way back to my front porch. Once we were there, I was breathless. Exhausted from the squeals and tugging, not to mention the occasional kick.

Bending over at the waist, Dawson tried to catch his breath. When he straightened up, I was ready with an arm on auto-pilot, and he was just as prepared with one to stop the blow I wanted to bring down on him.

"What the fuck are you doing?" I screamed in his face. "You have no right to come in here and act like you own me!"

"But I do." His voice seemed calm. "I have every right."

I was, once again, without words. Oh, I had them, but the ability to form them and make some kind of logical sense didn't seem to exist in my immediate future.

I swallowed hard, trying to figure out why the man in front of me had my stomach doing flips and my heart running away with me even though I remained now at a complete stand still.

"Aren't you going to invite me in?"

"Sure." I managed a sweet smile while waiting for him to make the first move. I then held my hand up to stop him. "When hell freezes over and not one day sooner. And, Dawson, I hear it is mighty toasty down there. It's safe to say you won't be coming inside."

He laughed. Delicious sweet mercy did he laugh. It was sexy, manly, and seductive in every way. I was vanilla pudding on the spot. A limp dishrag and all of the stupid girly nonsense. Worse still, he knew it.

Before he gathered his thoughts, he ran his tongue over his bottom lip and then took the pad of his thumb across the layer he'd only just coated with sleek moisture. "You like me, don't you?"

"Yeah, I'm sure I've sent out those signs. What was your first clue? Was it the scratch, kick, or the raising of my hand to smack your stupid grin right off your face?" I took a deep breath in and let it out slowly. My heart really needed to slow down. I was pretty sure he could see it thumping in my chest. It's what I deserved for wearing a low-cut top.

A man can possess many looks, own various expressions, and even though I was still young, barely over twenty-four, I knew what it was to spot a man hungry with desire. I was facing off with one. He was all man and Finn…well, Finn was a young pup still wet behind the ears. There was no way to compare the two, and I quickly realized it.

Dawson's approach was so easy. Cool, manly, and possessive, which frightened the hell out of me. He took a few steps forward, and I backed the fuck right up. He smiled, took his hat off, and moved a few more steps in my direction, until my back was up against the siding of the house.

"You think you're going to slide behind the door and just make a run for it, don't you?" His voice left nothing to the imagination. If it did, when I glanced down and saw his lust bulging, the sexual promises his voice delivered without stating as much, left nothing behind to second guess. Nothing at all.

"This isn't right." The whispers of fear lingered in the air like the wind wanted it to stay in front of me. He knew he scared the shit out of me. It was written on his face when he touched the back of his hand to my chin, tilting it up just a bit, but pausing before he ravaged my lips.

I knew my mouth puckered and maybe even waited. Anticipated and wanted the kiss I felt sure he could deliver. It was in his telling eyes. Damn it, they were so fucking defiant. I wanted his kiss. Needed it right then but hell's fury, he wanted to see me crave him. He just looked at me.

Finally too uncomfortable, I swallowed fear and spoke first. "I have to go."

"You're not going anywhere until I'm through with you." His dominance almost spooked me. *I really had a problem with the almost-factor.* I ignored it and generally worked against the little variance that made all the difference in the world. The one between right and wrong—wants and needs.

I cleared my throat before placing my hands on his chest. Electric waves of shock seemed to surge through my body and while I intended to push him away, I could've just as easily pulled him closer.

"This isn't right," I spoke. *Imagine.* Not that he bought into what I was saying, but I spoke the words I felt compelled to share anyway.

A dimple formed in his right cheek. It was so cute and sexy and yep, truly intentional. He was good. "What's not right is that you don't think enough of yourself. You'll let someone like Finn tell all about you and what the rest of us are missing." He cleared his throat, but the words still came out raspy, full of lust. "Now, thanks to your boyfriend, I'll be damned if I'm not going to have my turn too."

I gave his body a quick push, but he didn't budge.

"Don't." I was firm.

"Don't what? Kiss you?"

I watched him with a burning gaze I couldn't move away from him. Hell, most boys would've kissed me by now. That was my true problem. Dawson was anything but a boy. He was a man. Rock hard and built for pleasure. There wasn't any doubt in my mind.

"Don't stand over me like you want me, unless you…" *Unless he what? Be careful.* I reminded myself, but it was too late. He was all over it.

He moved to my earlobe and lightly nipped the skin at the lowest point before his mouth seemed to cover the opening. "Unless I what, Darlene? Unless I want you? Unless I intend to have you? Unless I make good on what my body promises?" Hot words drifted from his lips right into my ear. They burned through my mind, spinning in a fashion nobody should be forced to define.

My breath caught in a dry throat. I couldn't swallow. Couldn't speak. Hell, I couldn't move. His lower body did enough to replace all of the above. Dawson moved into me, and I could feel his cock pleading for some kind of intervention. It must have had a mind of its own, and perhaps he thought using *it* to press forward with intent would leave me unable to make a rational decision. Something a man like Dawson probably enjoyed.

I tried to move against the weight of him. To the right. Maybe to the left. I couldn't budge. "Stop this. Stop this now." My eyes challenged him in a duel our tongues would be better off finishing if not our bodies.

"No way in hell." His hand moved to steady my chin, and he watched my expression. Trying to figure out if I would close my eyes and anticipate the close contact on the way, but I wasn't going to close them. It would leave me far too vulnerable.

"Why are you doing this?" I didn't recognize my own voice. It revealed a damaging, if not damning, weakness.

"I've been chasing your ass around since I was eight years old, and I'll be damned if I'm going to do it now." He smiled, probably thinking that I knew what he was talking about.

I felt my eyes narrow, but fixating on him wasn't helping me recognize whomever he thought I might see with his confession. "What are you talking about?"

He finally released me, allowing his body to move off to the side so I was no longer pinned under the weight of him. "I guess I should have figured as much. A gal like you can forget a guy like me until we grow into men to be reckoned with." He laughed, but pain seemed to move across his face.

I studied him longer than I typically would. I really focused on his lips and eyes. Yes, I felt there was some familiarity but couldn't quite put my finger on it.

Nervously, I sat down on the porch swing. "Okay, I admit it. I'm at a loss here. You do have eyes I feel like I've seen before, but beyond them, I'm at a loss. I give up. What's your name? Your real name? I take it Dawson isn't who you want me to remember? I don't recall knowing any Dawson since the age of five, but bear with me some here. Five was almost twenty years ago, and for some reason, I can't imagine why, but the details of my life then are shaky." I thought back to the neighbors who had lived right next door. The Dawson family had been dead for many years, and bringing them up then didn't seem right. There wasn't a connection there.

Dawson stood in front of me only for a minute and then took his seat on the swing. "I guess I had big dreams of coming to work here. I thought you would see me and just remember everything."

"Okay, this is starting to creep me out." I couldn't picture, for the life of me, how I might know him or where in my past he may have existed. "What's your real name?"

He put his arm around my shoulder, and slowly, his fingertips ran the length of my neck long enough to turn my head to face him. "What did I tell you in the barn today?" He spoke to me gently with a voice full of suggestion.

I knew damn well what he'd told me, and hell, I'd just about scream now to find out more. Yes, complete with the moans and groans, grunts and thumps. I just wanted to know who he was and why he felt so drawn to me.

I swallowed hard.

"Oh yeah. I meant every word I said to you earlier. If you can't figure this one out on your own, you'll be ready to scream my name before you'll discover who I am and why you've known me for a very long time."

"There are other ways to seduce a woman."

"Yeah, well then you can show me."

"I bet you would like that, wouldn't you?"

"Probably more than Finn." His dimples arrived again right on cue.

"You think so, do you?" I got up from the swing, and for some reason, found I was shocked when he pulled me back down. My ass fell into a perfect seat he naturally prepared with a solid leg beneath me.

I seemed to belong there, and it made me nervous as hell. We matched glances again. Solemn but excited, lust-filled, and very inquisitive; it was all there.

"I know I would. I've had twenty years to think about it. Think about you. About this." He leaned into me finally. A breath away. A kiss away. *Damn it, do it.* I wanted his kiss—just a simple connection. The chemistry between us was kicking my ass with a reaction of feminine heat I simply could not control.

His stare went to my lips, but he didn't move first. He wanted me to kiss him, but I wasn't going to start the dirty deed. I had a feeling one kiss and I would be bed-bound and in a hurry to get there. My mother didn't leave behind a promiscuous idiot. Well, scratch that. She left behind one, but Kimbrell had her own issues. They were excusable. I didn't typically sleep around with strange men. *Typically* being a choice word too. Kind of like the almost-thing. These issues were beginning to present a problem.

"So you're not going to kiss me." It was a statement. A true one. He wanted me to deliver the first one.

"You're going to kiss me. That's something you can bet on and it's a better one than the one you had with Finn."

"Depends on who you're asking." I smirked. I just couldn't resist. "Finn wouldn't agree."

"No, Finn wouldn't." Finn's voice broke up the sexual tension separating the splinters from the wood swinging under us.

I jumped up from Dawson's lap. "I didn't see you there."

"Would it really matter if you did?" Finn's words were ice. "Come on. We've got work to do. You can't start acting like your sister. You aren't going to whore around with every other guy who comes by ready to show you some attention when I look the other way."

Dawson stood up slowly. "From where I'm standing, I don't see it the same way you do, Finn. First of all, she's anything but a whore. Maybe she's been *your whore*, but a woman can fuck around with one man and be at his beckon call but it don't make her a whore. One man treating her like one won't make it true." He studied me and then Finn. "You're the one who's trashed up her name pretty good from what I can tell, and a damn shame you did, too. Look at her. I'll promise you one thing, you'll be the last man back in her bed if I have a say in it."

"You don't." Finn glared straight ahead. "Man, you have no idea the kind of history I have with this one." He nodded in my direction.

"With this one?" Dawson laughed loudly then. "Hell, you got it with both of them, according to you and your brother. Am I right?"

I swallowed hard and fast. The pain revisiting me with the truth being told. "Finn, we're friends. We've been good pals for a long time." I couldn't help it, but I was sad to know the truth, and what I wanted to say couldn't be said between so-called friends.

"Hell, Darlene. We've been more than good buddies. So I screwed up. I laid down with Kimbrell a few times, but damn, baby, who hasn't fucked her?"

The tears were going to choke me. Damn it all. I hated to cry. I rode horses and roped cattle. I damn sure didn't act like a cry-baby. Still, my feelings were hurt. "You're talking about my sister."

Dawson moved in front of me. "Call it a day, buddy. I'm serious, man. Call it one now and get the hell out of here. She's had enough and heard enough. Go on now, get out of here." His arm extended as he pointed beyond the porch. He wanted Finn to leave. The faster, the better.

I couldn't move. I watched Finn back down the first few steps leading to the porch. "You're going to wish you'd never seen this ranch, Dawson. I swear, you'll wish like hell you'd stayed down under."

"That's it, Finn. Run your jaw. Trip over it all you want, but I'm here to tell you this little gal's heart is never going to be beating next to yours again. It will be over my dead body."

"There's an idea. One I thought you might have had several years ago," Finn called back to him before he turned to hop in the jeep that pulled up to retrieve him.

Stan waved reluctantly from the driver's seat. He was probably still fuming, but Stan got over things eventually. Finn didn't always take things with a grain of salt. I had a feeling Dawson didn't either.

Chapter 4

The afternoon ended on a positive note. Dawson said he'd finish mucking stalls and then go home to clean up. He proposed taking me out on a real date—one where a guy picks up a girl in a car and they go somewhere. He pays. Imagine the concept. It wasn't something I knew anything about. Finn and I dated in the back of the barn. We fucked in hallways or horse stalls. I climbed on top of him in the backseat of a car, and that's just the way it was between us. I never stepped out in public with Finn and I never really expected things to change.

Kimbrell did go on dates, so she knew how to coach me. She helped me dress up in a nice pair of Levi jeans and a low-cut burgundy and crème top with a zigzag design across the waist, weaving a little line of glitter stuff around it. She told me it made my waistline smaller, but I'm sure I didn't need fashion to do anything for me. At least, that's what Kimbrell said. She knew about the fashion stuff. I did not. I knew about the price of feed and where to find the best bargains on saddles. It was the extent of my shopping abilities.

Dawson showed up at the door, and I heard Kimbrell talking to him in the kitchen. They were laughing. She was flirting her ass off but I didn't really care. Maybe sisters were supposed to share everything, even their men. Immediately, a twinge of pain crawled into my skin and settled there. Dawson wasn't a man I wanted to share. Finn, okay. Dawson, not a chance. The lone thought curled my toes. I grabbed my purse, which hooked over my shoulder like a sling-shot bag, and I headed down the hall.

"Look at you!" He immediately whistled and reached for my hand, giving me a twirl to check out my ass. He probably thought I was a bit on the stupid side, but my mother told me a long time ago when Dad twirled her, he checked out her sitter-downer. I laughed when Dawson twirled me the second time, hardly holding onto my fingertips. "You're sexy as hell."

I shot Kimbrell a look. "Did you hear him? Sexy as hell."

She nodded and smiled. "I heard him. He has good taste."

Her reaction wasn't expected. I looked back and forth between them, trying to figure out if they were already up to something, but if he was, or she was part of it, they didn't give it away by mere expressions. His gaze fixated on me and never left.

"You two kids have fun." She grabbed a beer from the refrigerator and headed down the hall, back to her room.

After she disappeared, I was ready to go but thought it might be rude if I didn't offer him a beverage or maybe even sex on the table. I opted for the soda. "Can I get you something? Anything to drink?"

He blinked twice, like I was pulling him out of a thought of some sort. "No. I'm only thirsty for one thing." He pulled me to him with speed, and I swear, a small thud could be heard when my body pressed into his with the sudden impact.

I should've offered the fuck-and-go option as originally debated.

"This is it, isn't it?" I couldn't help but smile big when I looked up at him.

"You tell me." He winked. "You want it. Take it." His lips moved across my cheek with a brisk kiss, and then his mouth closed in around my ear, like before. "And I know you want it."

His hand cupped my neck in a possessive hold, and when he moved his forefinger to the base of my neck, he forced a quick shift. I was forced to gaze into his eyes.

"You're confident, aren't you?" His sex appeal and charm played second fiddle to masculine arrogance.

"And you're not?" His back-at-cha approach irritated the hell out of me. He licked his lips and waited.

"Let's go." I moved away from him, and he laughed.

"You want me so bad it hurts." He grunted out the words with provocative meaning hid beneath every syllable.

"I just met you. I promise I have more self-control than what you might like." I wasn't sure if it happened to be the truth, but it sounded good.

"No, darlin'. You didn't just meet me, and it's why the chemistry is something you can't seem to get away from, but we'll talk about it later." He looked around the room like he seemed to be looking for something.

We moved through the family room and out onto the porch. Down the steps, we seemed to trot across them in unison before climbing into his sports car.

He opened the door for me and I damn near fell over. Finn generally walked through every door or gate first, especially if it happened to be a stall door. He was always waiting with his pants down by the time I caught up with him.

Sliding in behind the wheel of the car, Dawson's confidence and gentle ease around me still had me buzzing with curiosity.

He moved closer and spoke slowly. "Where would you like to go?"

"I don't know. Wherever you want to go is fine with me." I pulled the safety belt over my middle, and he caught my hand mid-stream.

"Allow me." He tugged the belt snug and secure before he latched it into the safety lock. He moved his body away from mine but his hand still trailed along the texture of the belt. He must have been fairly confident I wouldn't smack it away. He fingered the cloth and rubbed it from my stomach to my shoulder. His firm expression set off a new round of sexually charged explosives. He enjoyed touching what he allowed his hand to drift across.

"Smooth."

"Maybe. But it's not enough." He bit down on the inside of his jaw again, which allowed his lip to seduce me just a little more. I really didn't need the further encouragement.

I thought about that act alone. Someone, somewhere in my past made a similar gesture and they did it a lot, but for some reason, I couldn't remember who. It probably wasn't important and didn't mean anything.

"Probably won't be." I ran a hand through his hair. "I've been dying to do that too."

"Oh, I get it. You think I've been itching to touch you." He smirked before he pointed at the breast he'd only just brushed by with the back of his hand.

"Weren't you?"

He laughed. "Where are we going?" He also avoided the question on the table.

"It's your date. I'm just along for the ride."

He quickly moved closer and spoke into my parted lips. "Yes, and I'm still waiting for a first kiss. I promise you, it's going to be one you'll love, and you'll like it so much, you'll be an active participant." He was so close to doing it.

"Go ahead. Make the first move. You want to do it so pucker up."

"You first." He challenged me and probably knew I didn't move on dares alone.

"Meet in the middle?"

He let out a deep breath. It was hot air with a twinge of peppermint, and coming from him, smelled heavenly. He backed away.

"Okay, suit yourself." I looked out the window, and he put the car in reverse. "I like your car by the way. Sleek and beautiful. Corvettes are something else. What year is it?"

He slammed the car in park. "Damn you."

"What?" I know my eyes widened, because I was shocked. I thought we were going places and headed there fast. Little did I know, the man could slam on the brakes.

His lips pursed together in a line, and he grabbed my neck, only to pull me hard and fast to his lips. Almost. He was there, but he didn't move the inch or two forward to take it. Damn it, I didn't like this game anymore.

"Kiss me." His words were heavy and his body proved without reasonable doubt he possessed lust. His eyes flashed it even if his lips tried to control the fight for and against the meeting of mouths. I didn't make it easy for him.

I giggled. "No. I told you. If you want it. Take it." I threw his earlier words back at him before licking my bottom lip. I then held it captive under my teeth.

His hand moved to my face. Before I knew he planned to remove the lock my bite seemed to secure, he rubbed his thumb over my mouth, encircling it with the intent to ravage. Disabling me with what he wanted me to expect.

"I said kiss me, dammit." Apply pressure, his thumb massaged. It felt good—so damn good and so unbelievably sexy. I was putty in his hand. My body wanted to feel him touching every inch, claiming every part of it for his own.

A dumb blonde I wasn't, and I was smart enough to know myself. He was undoing me at the seams, and we were headed for one place only, regardless of where we went on our little date.

The more he rubbed his thumb over my lips, the more I thought about something else. I would love to have him sliding between them. It was the recognition of the carnal urges that forced me to fight them. If I didn't, I risked falling into the footsteps of Kimbrell, and my sister would love to tell me so.

"This is ridiculous." I moved away from him and grabbed the door handle, jumping out as quickly as I'd slid in to take my seat. The doors slammed behind me. First mine and then his. I was four steps away from the porch when he grabbed my free arm swinging closest to him.

"Don't. I'm not interested in whatever it is that you think I want from you." I tugged my arm away from him and marched in the house.

He came in right behind me. "You're not only interested in it, baby, you're in hot pursuit of it."

"Who do you think you are?" I screamed in his face, frustrated with everything going on and really mad at myself. I seemed to lack one ounce of self-control around him. Maybe I was more like Kimbrell than I cared to admit.

He leaned in front of me. "I am the man you're going to love waking up to tomorrow morning."

"Like hell."

"Like hell, huh? Well then, maybe I will." He practically yelled back at me. "That is, if you're there!" Before I knew what hit me, he bent down and threw me over his shoulder in one swift move. His palm firmly lay against my ass as we traveled through the kitchen.

"Which one is your room?" His strides seemed fast.

"Put me down, damn you!" I screamed, and moved my free hand around to the side and up his back, trying to slap him just once in the face. Maybe I could smack the smug look from his cheeks. The one I saw right before I was ass-up and hanging over his broad shoulder.

"I said, let me go now!" I continued to scream, and when we passed by my sister's room, she was in the doorframe, leaning up against it, smiling.

"I see you still get on her last nerve." She nodded her approval. "Short date, huh?"

"Nice. Really sweet. So you're in on this?" I shot her a glance. "Traitor! You sleep with my men, and then you connive with them! What have you turned into?" I wanted to go in for the kill by calling her a slut for sleeping with Finn, but I let it slide.

"Is she still in the last room on the left?" he called out to her in passing.

"Right. It's right," she told him. "You too have fun now, ya hear?"

"Urgh! Kimbrell, you're going to pay for this!" My mind raced. Who was this man, and why did everyone, even Finn and Stan, seem to know more about him than I did?

"You'll thank me tomorrow." She quickly added more. "I'm staying at Stan's. You two love-birds have the place to yourself."

"No! Wait! Stop! I don't know him! I don't want to be here by myself with him!" I tried to get her to stay, but she didn't appear interested.

"You're better off with him than any man in this town. Trust me. You'll see."

He kicked the door open. Well, that was a bit dramatic. As it happened, it was cracked a bit. So his foot just moved it wider and then we disappeared behind it in an instant. He seemed quite confident he wanted me behind closed doors as soon as possible. He never missed a stride as we practically sprinted across the threshold.

I was clear on one fact in particular. He planned on staying awhile. After the door slammed, it drove the point home a bit more.

Chapter 5

My back scraped over the light switch and somehow the damn light came on immediately.

"Just what I love, a woman who doesn't like to hide in the dark." His grin provided enough sparkle to the room, and it was the first thing I noticed when he tossed me onto my bed.

"I didn't turn the damn light on and you aren't staying!" I sprang to my feet and didn't waste time doing it. He pushed me back on the bed, and with his free hand, began to unbutton his shirt.

"This is so not going to happen." I threw my legs out to the other side, jumped up again, and failed once more.

He met me half-way and pushed me down on the bed without a second to spare. "We can do this all night." His tongue held a position of intent against his upper lip. "I promise, you'll begin to think of it as foreplay." The twist of words provoked a movement of tongue, and it ended up in the corner of his mouth. Damn if it didn't look downright inviting.

"You have no right." I jumped up again and again, found the mattress under me.

His hands continued to the last button, and he shrugged out of his shirt. "I have every right."

"Damn if you do!" I ran for the door, and he caught me there. He held me up against it with his thigh in place to my right side. His palm rested over my head to the left.

"But I do." His words were spoken as a whisper right above my heart, because his mouth rested below my neckline just for a second, maybe two.

"Oh gawd!" I cried out with exaggerated enunciation. "You really are full of yourself!"

"I drive you crazy, don't I? You shouldn't be surprised, really. You lost your mind and your heart to me from the moment you sat down one row behind me on the school bus twenty years or so ago. Now, it's time to surrender your body, and, baby, I've been waiting for this day. It's long overdue."

His eyes danced with his confession, and just as quickly as he spat the words out, his hand went to my shirt and unbuttoned the only two buttons holding my cleavage at bay. His voice took on another tone. "You always took the lead, and now turnabout is fair play, and, make no mistake about it, I do intend to play."

"What the hell did you just say?" I moved away from him, still unsure if I'd heard him right the first time.

"You heard me." His confession seemed too painful to repeat.

His back was to me. Now, suddenly, when he needed his confidence most it would seem, he couldn't find the words he wanted. Not that I planned to make it easy. Maybe he was afraid to see my expression. Maybe he was afraid he'd overestimated the impact he had on me in my youth, or perhaps he just wanted to take a moment to gather his thoughts before he saw the consequences of his admission.

I felt like the wind was knocked out of me. "*Jack Dawson* died in a very bad plane crash when I was fifteen years old." I was slow to speak. The pain of losing a friend came rolling back over me in an instant, and suddenly the emotions I'd kept bottled up inside threatened to spill over to the surface.

"Maybe the man I would've become died there, but the man I am walked away from it without a problem. Well, that's not entirely true. I did have to go through a few surgeries, which is what you see evidence of no doubt. But Darlene, it's me. I'm here. You're here. We're here. I'm alive. Very much so if you want to feel around for evidence." His voice took on a sensual tone and I'm pretty sure it may have won him sexual favors whenever he wanted them most.

My chest hurt. My tears wanted to fall. I sat down on the edge of the bed and I think I did so in slow motion. Jack Dawson had been a boy when I last saw him. He'd been our neighbor for years. His parents owned the acreage adjoining ours, and every morning I walked to the end of our driveway early, just so I could catch the same bus Jack rode. From day one, from kindergarten forward, he was the only love in my life. There wasn't a snowball's chance in hell he was alive, or a slight possibility that if he happened to be, he'd be interested in me. Not like this, anyway.

The last time Jack saw me, I was fourteen. His family decided to move south, due to some kind of scandal I never understood, because no one ever told me the details. Since Jack was four years older than me, he still didn't know I drew breath, or at least, it was the way I'd summed everything up. He did kiss me good-bye. A kiss on the cheek and I never wanted to wash my face again. I stayed convinced for some time after he left that his lips still lingered there. Finally, my mother threatened me with a spanking, or else I don't think I would've ever introduced soap to the area his lips met.

After he left, he sent a postcard or two every now and then but then the correspondence stopped. Last we heard, his whole family died in a plane crash. It was the worst of news. It was then followed by two more untimely deaths. Two I never even acknowledge as such. The departure of my mother followed Jack's death, and my father followed her soon after.

My parents *left me* when I least expected it, and while Kimbrell dealt with it in one way or another, through one man's arms or another, I found my love in the very business that kept my family afloat. It was enough Because it had to be enough—until now.

He sat down on the bed next to me and flashed his natural million-dollar smile. I remembered Jack's gentle smile. Those dimples he had were priceless, and the grin driving them into a devious little smirk reached into a forever I only wanted to find with him.

Childish, little, girly dreams began for me at around the age of five or six and they died with the news he wasn't going to come back for me one day. Jack wasn't coming home to Tennessee. They were just silly school-girl dreams and even included a happily-ever-after and a white wedding gown, but when news of his death reached us, I never dreamed them again. I didn't want them with anyone else—only Jack.

Every now and then, I thought about those fantasies, but they seemed to stay hidden in a dark area of my soul. I didn't permit myself to think about him, because then the haunting devastation came back with what-ifs and it all nearly drove me mad. I convinced myself long ago the kind of love I often imagined I had for Jack Dawson wasn't for the woman I'd become, only the girl I'd once been.

Dawson's mouth twitched, and he bit into his jaw, just like he did when I used to crawl under his skin and threaten to stay there if he didn't do what I wanted him to do. Four years older, Jack always tried to satisfy me or *pacify me,* if I told the truth. He tried to appease me with an unconnected emotion I wanted him to feel but I knew he never really would—until now.

"Fine way to re-enter our lives," I finally said. I was pretty sure, after closer inspection, my eyes were locked into a trance with *the* Jack Dawson. There were several giveaways, and it definitely started with his eyes. Even as a kid, he could scold me with a look or glance, or heaven forbid, a glare. Now, he was undressing me with those same haunting eyes. I couldn't wait to see if he could do it as skillfully as I'd imagined he could when I first watched him jump down off my wagon earlier in the day.

"Glad you approve." He worked his hand through the waves of hair.

"I don't remember you having this much hair." I started to reach for it and then stopped myself. Before I could bring my hand all the way back down, he caught my wrist and brought my fingers up to his lips. "Sweet Darlene. My sweet darlin' woman."

"I don't remember you thinkin' of me as sweet." I spoke the truth.

. "Hell no. You were the devil's child. I'd swear to it then."

"And now?" I had to ask.

"Now? Hmm…" He moved closer. "Kiss me, and I'll tell you."

"Not on your life." I jumped up, and of course, he caught me and pulled me back to his lap.

"I'm not going to ask you again. You know the truth now so everything has changed between us." He turned my face to look at him. He held my jaw firmly between his thumb and three fingers. "Do you understand? I'm serious. You owe me a kiss."

"I *owe* you?"

"You better believe it," he snapped back. "You threatened me with one for years when you were a little girl, and I didn't come all the way back here for a peck on the cheek."

"Why did you come back?" My words fell out barely above a whisper. .

"You know the answer before I tell you." He brushed the hair from my face.

"Hardly. I wasn't your favorite kid on the street."

"Are you joking here? You were the only kid on the street besides your sister!" He laughed.

"She was in on this with you, wasn't she?"

He nodded. "I couldn't have found you again without her, and I'm sure she'll be happy to tell you all the particulars, but I have other things on my mind. I've waited a lifetime for one little kiss, and I want it now." He moved inches away then and he was so fucking close. It was amazing how good it felt to go from believing someone was dead to realizing they were not only alive and well but sexy as hell. And hot for just one kiss! *From me!*

"I can't believe you're really here." I kissed his cheek and took his hand in mine. "I just can't believe…"

"Okay, I get the shock factor, and I get you are stubborn as hell, but I'm all out of words at the moment. I've waited for you longer than I ever intended to wait, and if you don't shut up long enough to smooch with me, then I'll just have to kiss you in between syllables."

He gathered me up, wrapping me closer than I ever thought possible without an intimate display of more body parts. Manly-man arms, with the biceps and strength to match, held me against a very masculine chest.

I smiled hoping he realized he was about to lose the wild little battle of wills we'd played over the passing hours. If he was going to lock lips with me, then he would make the first move.

"Fuck it."

"I'm sure you have that in mind too," I told him.

"You know it." He growled the words into my parted lips before a delicious tongue barely scraped by the small opening I supplied.

A sigh slipped from my lungs, chest, or somewhere within the same proximity. I wanted to speak but the way Jack Dawson's lips slanted over mine told me he would lick away all words. His dipping tongue and moist mouth provided a haven of bliss. I wanted it *all* now. I had tasted him. Now, I wanted him—all of him. I wanted to feel what it was I thought I'd never enjoy from him. I wanted him completely, and there wasn't a doubt in my mind. He planned to give me exactly what I craved and far more than I deserved.

Chapter 6

When our kiss broke, I was ready for the dirty deed. I needed him to just strip off, make mad passionate love until the break of dawn, and then start the process all over again. I didn't see the problem.

"Darlene, you need to know how I feel about you. From the moment I saw you, I wanted you."

I was in a daze. "You what?"

"I'm not talking about twenty years ago. I'm talking about today. Sure, I realized there was something there before I came back for you. I knew something pretty powerful tugged at my heart. Sure, I wanted to come back for the home place. I wanted to find my home again, but the pain of coming back here wasn't something I wanted to face alone."

"You'll never be alone here." Still without my breath or my senses, I rubbed a trembling forefinger over the lips he just deserted. *Mine.*

All the muscles I could see bulged, flinched. They reacted for him, and I'm sure he didn't like what they revealed. "I'm counting on it."

"I imagine you are." I said.

He stared across the room and his gaze seemed to settle on a chair in the corner. Candles were on my dresser, along with a lighter that stayed next to the five homespun jars of wax. I typically intended to light one or two when Finn and I were together. They never once held fire, because Finn never took the time to light them.

Dawson moved across the room and reached for the lighter. He flicked it twice. The flame burned high enough to light all of them, but the fire he lit in me as I watched him was incomparable to any burning wick.

He sat down on the chair and began to tug off his cowboy boots. His stare never left me. *Yes, Jack Dawson, I believe people change in appearances, but they can't hide their eyes, regardless of mature changes.* The eyes always stay the same. Thank goodness his did. I couldn't leave them as a kid, and now, I couldn't dessert them if I tried. I was afraid to look away. Afraid of what he'd do if I did, or maybe, I was scared if I left them, he would disappear and heaven help me, I didn't want him to leave.

"You might as well get rid of those clothes." If he wanted to seduce me, then I guess he was getting busy with it, but I wasn't sure I would be able to disrobe on my own. I wasn't sure I wanted to move at all. My focus was on the most beautiful of men, and every move he made to lose one more stitch of clothing was sexier than the previous second.

"I'm fine right now." It took a labor of effort to spit out four words.

His face looked rugged with years staining them in the form of one or two wrinkles. His handsome good looks and two-day-old beard undid me, but when he dropped all clothing and was down to his boxers, I really came undone. Most women probably did in matters of skin-on-skin.

A hard erection pressed into his shorts. It was visible, and even as he went to the door to lock it, I wanted him stripped bare. It wasn't fair for him to keep any clothing on after he took the time to discard most of it.

His stride across the room gave me time to watch everything about him. I noticed the entire framework surrounding his mouth. Something about his outer appearance gave off the impression of a man with stark determination. I saw existing heartache in his eyes. I imagined it was from a past he left behind somewhere or perhaps from everything he'd lost in his lifetime. His mother and father, his sister and brother. Maybe even his truer purpose. Perhaps it died with the rest of his family. Beyond facial features, I watched every muscle bend or tighten.

By the time he moved to the bedside to turn off the lamp, I was expecting his touch. Waiting for his kiss and ah yeah, wanting his body next to mine.

It didn't happen.

He did reach down and touch my cheek with masculine fingertips. No emotion drifted into his eyes. He was blank. Sort of empty, I thought. I expected more, but he didn't bring it with one simple caress. Instead, he returned to the corner and sat down again.

I brought my knees up to my chest and faced him. His legs were spread open in a relaxed position. With his handsome features and a body full of certain charms, he most definitely owned the look for the next Hanes commercial. He was all man—sexy uncovered.

"Undress, Darlene." His words demanded. It seemed like a true expectation he had. Perhaps he thought I made a habit of doing whatever the opposite sex instructed.

I cleared my throat. "No. You want them off. You take them off."

"No. I want you to do it. I want to watch from over here." He was as satisfied to keep his focus on me as I was to be the object of it. It remained evident in the tone he used with me, but there was something else there too. I didn't know how to react to it.

"No one has ever asked me to undress while they watch from across the room."

"I don't believe you. Finn watches you." His voice was filled with a man's appetite. "Now. Take it off. All of it." In the dimly lit room, I could see his strong features, and the ease he had with his own sexuality drew me to him.

I stood in front of him with the full purpose of doing whatever he asked. Everything he asked me to do, I wanted to do until something else hit me. He'd brought Finn into the very bedroom where Finn had fucked me more times than counting would confirm. I resented it.

"Finn doesn't watch me."

"So he fucks you and tells everyone about it, but he doesn't watch you?" he questioned me. I didn't care much for the snide remark either.

"You have no right to ask me about Finn, and you had no right to come back into my life, and in less than twenty-four hours get us to this…this place." I could feel my face heat with each word that left my lips. I turned to leave, and he didn't reach for me, but his choice of statements stopped me in my tracks before I reached the door.

"I have every right, Darlene." He was filled with possessiveness.

"No you don't." I fired back without turning around.

"If your father wasn't dead and cold in the grave right along with mine, you could ask them both. You belong to me and you always have." His words brought with it a truth I couldn't ignore, because I knew about the arrangement between our families. It was the agreement that didn't happen in the modern world. It did in mine, regardless of times changing and a cultural frowning on written documents.

The supporting of an arrangement of marriage seldom went down on paper. Instead, the families that wanted it most, families like mine, would make it damn near impossible to avoid. They sweetened the pot with money or land, and it was how our fathers designed it so they would get their way. Even in the event of their deaths.

I turned around quickly and went back to the exact location where I'd left Jack Dawson. He was still sprawled out in the chair, looking as comfortable as he did when I'd walked away from him. He was so sure of himself, so positive I wouldn't buck against my fate.

"You have no right to talk to me about my father."

"Fine, then I'll talk to you about your mother."

"Or her." I was angry. He'd gone too far. Way over the line.

"Okay, fine. I'll talk to you about mine and tell you what I know about you and yours. You think I don't know about you but you're wrong. You think I don't know you never came to terms with the death of your parents? They *are dead*, and you tell people you meet on the street, strangers, anyone who will listen, they've *left* or they've just gone away for a bit. Tell me something, Darlene. When do you plan to see them coming up the driveway again?"

I shook my head firmly, choking out the words beyond the struggle of inner cries. "You have no right to do this."

He continued. "I know this has been hard for you. Maybe life's been unkind, but I think…"

"I don't give a damn what you think." I went to the dresser, and in robotic fashion, blew out the most romantic moment I'd ever almost lived in. *Almost*. Damn the word, and damn Jack Dawson for making me do it.

"You need to start caring because, baby, I promise you, I'm not going anywhere." He didn't appear to be in a hurry. The very fact he didn't even flinch provided a sure sign he planned to keep his promises.

"The hell you aren't. You're leaving now!" I was boiling. The temperature in the room greatly compared to those found in the pits of hell. I wanted Jack Dawson out of my room, and I wanted him to disappear sooner rather than later.

He just wouldn't budge. The same cool confidence he had when he undressed still ran through his veins as he sat very still in the semi-darkness. I could see his shape, thanks to the porch light drifting in through the shades, but that was about it. Finally, I saw him stand and move closer. Slowly, he inched toward me. My breath caught in my chest, and damn it all, I couldn't catch it again until he touched me.

His hand smoothed over my cheek, and I wanted to cry. I wanted to bawl for the lost time I'd spent denying my parents were dead, denying I once loved one boy, a young man who'd lost his life in an accident long before his time. All the days I wasted away, refusing to love, because I only loved once in all of the years I'd lived. I refused to come to terms with things existing in the past, because it hurt to accept and was too painful to let go.

The first tear fell.

He wiped it away. It was perhaps a mistake, because the swipe allowed more to flow. They followed with ease, because he granted unspoken permission.

A rainfall of moisture flooded my cheeks, and his arms wrapped me in an embrace full of caring and understanding. His hand stroked my back while the other one continued to move over my face here and there.

"That's it, baby. Cry. Let it all out. I want you to cry. You need to finally let it all go." His words coaxed me for what seemed like hours, the passing minutes of unrestrained tears were long overdue.

"I…can't…cry." Through the tears, through the pain, I still denied.

"Yes, yes, you can," he assured me. The evidence supplied enough confirmation. "You need to finally face your grief."

He seemed to know too much about me. When we buried Mom, I never let the first tear fall. When my dad was buried six weeks later, I felt the burden. I knew, even as a youngster, my sister wouldn't be able to support us. The stress of running the ranch was all on me from the moment the casket lowered into the ground. There wasn't time to grieve. Little time to think about anything except who would pay the thirty men we needed to keep a running ranch profitable. I was a child, and I had to take on the role of an adult in a big way. I hardened but I did it so I could appear tough and manage a business well.

When the weeping finished getting the best of me, I dabbed my face with the back of my hand. Stained cheeks were so unattractive.

"Darlene?" His hand slowly moved down my back.

I froze in my skin.

"I'm going to take care of you." His words were final. So completely assumptive, he must have thought that I needed someone to do it, and his guessing proved accurate. I was falling apart, but denial offered me the chance to avoid the truth.

"I don't need handouts. We're making it here just fine."

His fingers moved to my chin, and he lifted my head up toward his in an instant. "You are? From where I stand, it looks more like surviving rather than living."

"What do you know about living?" I fired back and tried to step away from him.

His palm caught me and brought me back firmly to his chest. I was so aware—mindful of the hard cock pressing into his shorts. Occupied with how good it felt to be held by someone who wanted to hold me, and I wanted to hold.

"I know more about living…and dying than most. More than I care to know. What I don't understand is why a woman like you would settle for a man like Finn who has no use for you except for one purpose."

"You know nothing about me and Finn."

"Honey, I know more about you than you think. Finn tells anyone who will listen about you and your sister. He basically sells others on the fact that there's no other woman in the county or state who can do it quite like you can. From the oral sex to the wham-bam, thank you little ma'am, there's nothing he won't talk about. Hell, I'm quite sure if you were a little more open to the advances men make, you'd have several of them lined up on your porch right now." He moved away from me and went back to the dresser to light the candles again.

"Don't. We're not doing *this*." I didn't need to say it. *We're not fucking!* We were *so* going to do *it,* and I damn well expected it to begin within a few minutes.

"Oh yes we are. *This* we are doing." He continued to add fire to each wick without looking back for any nod of approval. He didn't need it, and apparently, didn't care if he had mine.

"You can't make me." I quivered to think about it. *Make me?* Damn straight. He knew I was almost begging for it earlier. We at least shared one mutual understanding.

After the candles took on a soft glow, he slipped out of his shorts and headed straight for me.

"Holy hell." I was completely in awe. If it was possible for a woman to be mesmerized by a man's natural packaging, then hypnotized best described my predicament.

"You know it—so don't fight it. I plan to raise a little of it with you." His face spread into a wide smirk. "And I promise you'll be screaming for more by the time you sink into the inferno I have planned for you."

Chapter 7

Protesting wasn't an option this time. What man with a hard dick revealed and yeah, more than primed and ready, even considers putting on the brakes? Not the one in front of me. As hard as he looked, a distress signal would be needed, and even then, a mayday wouldn't stop a man with an agenda for spicy satisfaction.

He took my hand in his, and in the most erotic dance of an uninhibited beginning, his lips trailed from my wrists to my elbow in slow motion. I was most definitely caught up in the moment. I really didn't realize he had unzipped my pants or his hand had slowly maneuvered my pants over hips and thighs. I didn't pay much attention until his palm cupped right underneath my intimate space. He pulled away long enough to stare into my soul. Forget my eyes, he bypassed them and went on a search for something more.

I swallowed hard. I wanted him to stop long enough to tell me more about him. How he'd spent the last few years of his life. I wanted to know why he'd taken so long to come home. I needed to understand if he knew all there was to know about the agreement between his father and mine. I wanted to find out, but with the look plastered across his face, there wasn't time now. No, not right then. There would be plenty of time for all of it later. Right now, his interests were somewhere far out of reach from the pillow talk later.

His free hand worked my shirt over shoulders and head. By the time he unhooked my bra, his palm shifted, the one he'd never bothered to move, and his fingers locked into place with a somewhat intimate dance he seemed perfectly capable of controlling.

Holding my lower back, he pressed his lips to mine before his foot kicked my stance apart. His knee firmly kept me parted for *his* pleasure. No, on second thought, the pending gratification seemed mine to own.

Fingers plunged into my pussy with full contemplation. "Damn, baby, you're so wet— incredibly wet and soaking ready, aren't ya?" His words were smiled into my mouth. It was wicked, deplorable. I wanted more.

I reached for him. Down his belly, my fingers moved fast until I had his cock fisted, drawing him into a slow hand-job I wanted him to ride.

His hips moved a little, giving a push and thrust of himself into the palm I closed only tighter.

"Ah, baby. I've waited so long to hold you." His words of truth were either going to be the death of me—or the life. At the moment, I wasn't sure which and if I'd thought much about it, how willing I was to be completely his, it would've stopped the hand motions.

He parted my lips again by thrusting his tongue into my mouth with a sweep of ecstasy. He tasted like peppermint and scotch. Divine, manly, and yep, completely mine. I imagined he'd never kissed anyone with so much passion. The kiss was something he mastered, and in my mind, I knew there was a lot that went with a kiss like his. I couldn't wait to find out just how well he could do the rest of it. Those thoughts scared the hell out of me. A man who could kiss and fuck with restraint should be feared. A man like Jack Dawson possessed the ability to strip a woman of her senses and control her by seduction. I didn't want to be one of those women.

I spread out before him like I was begging for it. Maybe I was. He stood over me, hovering for a minute. I fully expected him to lie on the bed next to me, but a woman who presumes too much often gets what she deserves.

I did—in a way.

He moved his hands over my thighs and hips before dragging my legs over his shoulders. He slumped down beside the bed while his hands moved under my ass, quickly raising me up to meet his lips.

"Sweet mercy hell." I looked down between my legs and liked what I found there.

"Yes, I'll take you there and back cause I promised you already." He made a few carnal sounds and dipped lower. "Baby, you're dripping…just waiting for me, aren't you?" He taunted more with kisses and those led him straight to the place I wanted him to go.

A truly skilled mouth covered me and he had a true desire. He wanted to rid me of need but the lust fueled strong and once his tongue reached inside, I never doubted his abilities. He could drive a woman quickly to the other side, or at least, out of her ordinary mind. I was that woman— his woman—at least for a little while.

He bit down on my clitoris and sucked gently before lapping at me like I was the only seductress in the world with needs so close to his own. He was talented in every way and hungry. Damn, if he wasn't begging to be fed. If he was thirsty, then he could drink from me any day of the week.

The lapping and licking of sexual stimulation wasn't enough. He had to take. He wanted to satisfy, and he did. Man, did he ever.

"I can't hold back," I warned him before I lost it but I didn't want him to move. My hand went to his head and pulled through his waves, bringing him closer, only pulling him tighter.

"Don't you dare stop!" I yelled. I screamed and hell's fury, I meant it.

He worked slower, completely circling me with a tongue driven to punish. My hips rose higher and higher, yet he slowed the fuck down. His tongue gave way with the flood of desire wracking my body. One hand stayed in his hair and the other gripped, clawed even, the sheets beneath us.

"Don't, Dawson. Please don't stop. More. Please. Oh hell, please give me more." I felt the surge of power go through my body, torturing me with selective gratification at the same time he began again with venomous licks. He understood what it took to make a woman scream.

"Jack…Dawson!" I cried, wept even. I rode the tongue driving me to the place I never wanted to stop finding. "Sweet mercy, baby. Sweet mercy."

"I'll show you sweet mercy until you can't find it anymore." He rose over me just when the last quiver subsided. His look of undeniable lust was more powerful than I'd ever witnessed in a man.

I pressed my lips to his before he mounted me, falling right into an age-old tempo every woman and man can seemingly find. Only, Jack knew how to work it for greater appreciation.

He was demanding. "Move up." My hips drove forward and then instinctively, I scooted up closer to the headboard.

He was divine. "You're beautiful, Darlene. Just tell me everything you want in a man. What turns you on?" He really wanted to know.

He was able. "Feels so good, doesn't it, baby. Doesn't it?" His cock found and stroked places I never knew a man could reach.

Damn if I could answer. Damn if he needed anything else to weigh in with his ego—or his cock.

Rhythmic sliding and gliding drove me to the point of no return. Looking into his eyes, I was lost to him, forever. He always had those fiery but sensual looks about him. I could not tear myself away from him, and in the moment, it seemed heavenly, almost like I'd waited my entire life to be in his arms again. Maybe it was possible. Maybe I'd saved a part of myself with the hope he would one day return.

I nearly ran out of air with each caress. Each heavy beat of his dick moving into me only made me wish, no pray, for more. "You're so damn big. Holy hell. You're killing me here."

"It's okay, baby." He pushed harder. "I'm there, baby. I'm already buried deep inside. Feel me." He grabbed a fistful of my hair and wrapped it around his hand. His hips gave way, and he drove into me in a frantic fury of need. The in-and-out moves seemed to find a tempo and the beat sounded out on the mattress under us and the headboard behind us.

His head bent down, and he bit at my nipple before going for a long, succulent exploration, massaging me under a competent tongue. Even with the pleasure, the pain existed. His cock retaliated against me for some reason. Perhaps it penalized me for ever being with anyone other than him.

I love you. I've always loved you. I wanted to tell him but didn't. It wasn't possible to love someone presumed dead for so many years.

A few more strokes and he pulled me up, yanked me, really, by the hair and gawd how he held tightly. His cock had a motive, and he explored it without apologies. Why bother. He was getting what he wanted, and I planned to help him take it all.

My legs wrapped tighter around his waist. He continued to pound hard and fast while looking into my eyes with true wanton satisfaction. Finally, it was more than I could take. I closed my eyes, ready to enjoy the place I'd almost reached again, with the pleasure winning out over the pain his cock deliberately delivered.

"You look at me now." He held me closer, tighter, and hell yeah, he fucked harder. Desperation lingered there. He apparently wanted no distance between us.

I couldn't open my eyes. Not yet. I was there—damnation, ready or not, it was time. The ripples came on slowly, but the waves. Damn if those waves weren't ready for us to take a willing ride.

His strokes came faster, pleading for more. His hips continued to rise and fall over me. His grip on my hair and head moved to my neck. "I said open your eyes, Darlene. Damn it. Now!" His demanding voice gained him the respect he wanted.

I looked at him just in time to see the sweat bead over his brow and his mouth twist in an expression of pure satisfaction.

"Say my name."

"Dawson…"

"No, damn you! Say my name. Say it like you want more of me."

In that moment I did. I truly wanted more than he would ever be able to give, because I wanted to feel him in my soul—in the pit of my gut, at the center of my universe. I wanted it like there wasn't another man who could deliver it.

"Jack! Please!" I would've been sarcastic as hell if only my orgasm didn't take me to a place like no other, but in the small window of opportunity, I was all over him for another reason. Tugging him closer, clawing at his back and ass. I wanted *it* more than any woman should ever desire a man –or what a man can offer. I truly desired the cock I couldn't seem to handle but couldn't quite escape. "Jack, please! Faster! Damn you!"

His groans and moans met mine as we danced into the climax our bodies were certain to find again. I rose up to meet him with each stroke he wanted me to feel, and never once did I look away from the hooded eyes filled with only me.

Chapter 8

"That was…" I didn't need to tell him. He felt the same way. That was something I did know about the man-and-woman thing. The connection, the chemistry if you will, either it exists or it doesn't. We had it. Damn did we ever have *it*.

"Perfect." He finished me and the sentence I tried to form before rolling off with one lingering stroke for good measure.

I curled up in his arms. His hand immediately stroked my hair, and his contentment shocked me. He wasn't in a hurry to move. In fact, I would have placed odds on the fact he planned to spend the night. Finn seldom stayed overnight. We typically got down and dirty, and sometimes he never even bothered to take his boots off for it. I guess it was why we never had a really deep connection. Pillow talk wasn't something he liked or anything I knew very much about.

"I came back here for you, Darlene." He sounded sincere.

"I imagine you came back to take care of some unfinished business." I let out a deep breath. "From what I hear, there's a lot of it. Kimbrell has been meeting with the lawyers about the family estate. We finally need to settle it."

"Kimbrell has been fucking the attorneys. Mine and yours." He laughed. "None of it really matters. I'm still here for you. I plan to make you mine. Make no mistakes about it."

I sat up on one elbow and gazed down on him. "Do you know everything about the agreement our fathers made?"

"I discussed it with Kimbrell." He told me what I really didn't want to hear.

"Kimbrell? Why Kimbrell? Do you think she cares about this stuff? She's only seeing the attorneys because I don't have time with the ranch to run. She's not really bright when it comes to business, you know."

"Really?" He playfully bit my nipple.

"What did she tell you?" I ignored the sexual insinuation.

"I know what we all stand to lose if I don't marry one of you." He smirked. I think he liked the idea.

"Well then, I guess she read you Daddy's will."

"She did indeed." Jack confirmed what I guessed before he bedded me down and tried his hand at making an honest woman out of me. Well, sort of.

"I'm going to just tell you like it is."

"Why don't you do just that," he teased and slapped my ass. I kind of liked it.

"Well, here's the thing, Jack. I'm not the marrying type. If you want to marry one of us and get the money the three of us stand to lose, chances are good you'll find my sister more suited for marriage." I tried to speak slowly because while my choice of words proved I could lie like hell my heart broke into a zillion little pieces. Finn betrayed me when he slept with my sister, but I could live with Finn and his lack of loyalty. I was sure I'd be sick all over if Jack slept with Kimbrell. If his lips touched her in the same places he kissed me, well, it would end the fantasy I started at a really young age. I felt confident I wouldn't find another one.

He just stared at me for a really, really long time. Finally, he pulled me in for a deep, need-ridden kiss. When he released me, he whispered his words right into my ear. "Tell me something, Darlene. Do you think your sister would like what I'm able to do for a woman?" His hand reminded me. He took the time to move my palm down to the sticky shaft. It still sported evidence of our romp. I didn't need a reminder.

"I'm sure she would," I snapped before rolling away from him and to the edge of the bed.

He laughed. "Believe me, I've had plenty of girls like Kimbrell in my life."

"I guess you have." *His confession* pissed me off. Without any warning, which only made me madder by the second, jealousy crept in and I thought it was rather ridiculous for me to have envy in my heart.

"I want you."

"Maybe you do, but since you've had your share of women, I can assure you I'm not as experienced as you might think."

Finn's words of wisdom crept back into my head right then and there. *An experienced woman earns her place in a man's bed.* I hoped Finn gave me plenty of it because it looked like I might need some.

"Baby, I believe you are far more competent *than you like to think*. Of course, I don't know everything. You still have a lot to show me but I'm willing to bet you can do things to a man with those hot little lips and your tight little ass—." His mouth fell open with a sigh and then a quick whistle to cover it up.

"I know where you're going with this." I realized Finn ran his mouth about my extraordinary talent with my mouth. It drove many men crazy just hearing him boast about it.

He tugged at my wrists and pulled me back. "I'm not going to play this game with you, Darlene. I want you. I don't care if you come with experience or without it. I don't care if you need a how-to manual on the nightstand or have the need to give a confession before you can live with whatever or whoever you've done in the past. I want you and you alone, and damn it all, I intend to have you." His grip loosened as he pulled me back to him.

"I have to think about this. You need to go."

"I'm proposing here."

I didn't see him down on one knee. Thank goodness. My eyes drifted upward, and I really was thankful. Because right then and there, I would have turned him down—flat on his cute solid ass.

"You're proposing what?" I spat the words out, and it was a difficult task with a dry mouth.

"I think you know."

"Marriage? Courtship?" I smiled, but I felt more like frowning. "I think what you are proposing is a partnership. If it is, you'd better go home and give it some thought, because I may look fragile on the outside, but when it comes to this ranch, I'm all business."

"I imagine you are, and I'm afraid, Darlene, when it comes to love, or maybe even lust, you're driven by this ranch and everything pertaining to it. That's what scares the hell out of *me*." Before he jumped up to gather his clothes, he shot me a look and it was telling. It told me we were going to end up in bed again within the next twenty-four hours. His slow, once-over glance held a divine masculine look of approval. One a man gets when he's just found the woman who can undo *him* just as much as he can get the best of her. *I've been watching too much damn television.*

"It's been years, Jack. Years of work, blood, sweat and..." *And too much drama. Watch another soap opera, Darlene.* I needed a horror flick. Maybe then I'd act sensible—or tough—or afraid of my own shadow. Never mind the man in my room.

"And what? Tears? No, I don't think so. From what I hear from Kimbrell, you buried me in your mind, your parents in the physical sense, and then you simply stopped living. That's not the way it's going to be now. I came back here for you, and I'll be damned if I'm leaving this ranch without you."

I expected more explanations. I wasn't quite sure what he meant by his chosen words, but I would soon find out.

"If you don't want me in your bed, I'll be on the couch, but the one place you won't be is back in Finn's bed or any other man's before you have a chance to give me and you a real fighting chance.

Now, if you want to sleep alone, suit yourself. Do you have an extra blanket and a pillow?"

"You aren't staying here." Finality. I spoke with it, but somehow I don't think I drove my point home.

"I'm not?"

"No." I don't know who I tried to fool. Me or him.

Jack walked over to me. "You've made it clear you don't want me in your bed tonight. Maybe you've got something against waking up in a man's arms, but I'm not, let me say this one more time so you're real clear on everything I tell you. I *am not leaving here* until you're ready to *go home* with me."

He kissed me on the forehead, grabbed a pillow off the bed, and before I could throw something at him, he was gone.

* * * *

It was two in the morning when I heard Finn's knock on the window. I rolled over to see him peering inside. Moaning, I threw the covers over my head and pulled them close around my neck. *Damn. Leave it to a man to ruin a wet dream he's not in.*

I was naked. That much I remembered, so I tugged the covers closer. Still, the window wasn't locked, and once my eyes met his, he raised it and climbed in.

He stood over me, undressing slowly. The look of lust was there but so was anger. He'd been man-handled by Jack, and my guess was he didn't think too highly of Jack or me at the moment. Maybe he wanted to sneak in and fuck until the anger went away.

"Did you have fun on your little date tonight?" His words slurred off an alcohol-saturated tongue.

The lights flipped on and Jack stood in the doorway. "She did. I did. Thanks for asking."

"What the fuck are you doing here?" Finn looked at Jack and then back at me. I was propped up on my elbows with the sheet wrapped over me, tucked in at my armpits. I could feel my nipples harden, and Finn's gaze went straight to my chest. He had to know I was completely nude, and I'm sure it only added to his fury. "What's going on here?"

Jack's bare feet moved him closer. I stared up at him with pleading eyes. I hoped to warn him off of a confrontation. He had his jeans on and zipped, but they were unsnapped at the top, and he didn't have his shirt on. With the picture we painted, Finn wouldn't have to call upon his imagination for much confirmation. It was right in front of him.

"What does it look like *went* on here?" He wanted Finn to know.

Damn the male ego thing. It really pissed me off sometimes—particularly during the wee morning hours.

Finn glared at me and then Jack again. "You bastard." The fury he barely held at bay came to the surface. "You think this is how it's going to be? Do you?" He shot me a look, telling me the questions were directed at me, before he continued with more of the same. "Do you want to know why he really came back here? Do you?"

"I know why he's here." I shrugged a shoulder away from him.

Jack spoke up with possessiveness clear in each of his words. "I'm here for her. Not the damn land. Not the money or the perks going with it. I'm here for her and the benefits that come along with Darlene. Those, I'm pretty sure, you know something about." His smirk was evil. He wanted to be sure Finn understood he'd already tried me on for a close, snug fit. Apparently, he liked the way it felt when he did.

"Darlene? He's what you want?" His anger was evident, but Finn wasn't the alpha male Jack Dawson seemed to be. He wouldn't put up a fight, or at least, I didn't expect him to duke it out.

Jack spoke for me. Maybe he didn't think I'd give an answer for myself. "Does she look like she's complaining?"

Finn's eyes narrowed. "I didn't ask you, Dawson."

"I answered you, all the same." Jack moved closer to him. Three more steps, and they would be nose-to-nose and probably smelling the anger the other one felt. Never mind the sex one of them had just had.

"Come with me, Darlene. Tell this son of a bitch to take a leap, and let's just go get married. We should've done it a long time ago. I don't know why it took me this long to see it."

Marriage? Why the fuck did everyone suddenly want to get married? Sure, Lewisburg didn't give a girl a lot of options, but for crying out loud, most of the females around here did have a few more than a quick sprint to the alter. Myself included.

"Married? You think she's going to marry you now? You said just yesterday you planned to fuck her until you married the girl of your dreams, and then you planned to keep her on the side. Now you want to marry her?" Jack moved another step. "You're a real piece of horse shit. You know this right?" He moved one more step.

This time Finn backed away. He pointed in the direction of the only person standing between me and him, or at least, that's the way he likely viewed everything. "You want him? You want a man who makes everyone in this town believe he's dead until he drives in to tell you something different?" He turned his focus back to Jack. "Dawson, I guess your attorney told you everything, huh? You must know you can't get your hands on your vacated piece of property unless you marry one of the sisters. It's the only reason you're here, right?"

"I don't have to answer you, but you…" He paused before he continued. "You need to leave right now, or else all of this is going to unfold in a way you don't want it to in front of Darlene. I promise you. I'm not going to hold anything back from her once I start spilling the truth."

"You're just dying to take your turn with *my girl*? Aren't ya? Well, she's got a sister, and unless you think you're too good to sleep with her, then I think you'll find she's the one who needs a husband. Darlene here isn't going to get married unless she marries me." He turned back to me, and for once, I saw the love. Or maybe it was jealousy. Okay, so the green-eyed monster seemed to win out over anything resembling affection.

I believe there might have been some love there too, though it wasn't really a deep-seated and romantic kind of love, it still existed. I could see it all over Finn's face. It didn't change anything. Finn and I had opportunities to build a life together, but it wasn't going to happen. We knew it years ago. Now, he wanted it because he couldn't stand to think of another man in my bed. It was driving him crazier by the second.

I cleared my throat. "Finn, Jack's right. You need to leave."

Jack moved closer to Finn, but this time he didn't budge. "You're not doing this, Dawson. I can promise you it's not going to happen as long as I draw a breath."

A smile formed on Jack's lips. "Buddy, look at her. Take a long look, and tell me what you see." He glanced back at me with a possessive nod of approval and it told me he was damn proud he could tell Finn he'd held me in his arms and pinned me under bunched thighs.

Finn's fists clenched at his sides. "This isn't going to happen. Not even on a dare, Dawson. Not now and not ever." His words were spoken slowly with a denial I was able to spot. I used denial as a key defense mechanism for most of my life.

"It already has." I told him for both of us. Maybe I thought it would sound better coming from me. Maybe I thought it would break up the dismissal of truth that seemed to slap him in the face. Finn didn't want to see the tangled sheets, my smeared make-up and tousled hair. It was hard to miss but apparently love isn't only blind when someone is intoxicated, but it's also arrogantly foolish to boot.

His jaw immediately dropped once he heard me admit the obvious. "You fucked him?" He wanted further confirmation. How malicious did he really want me to be? I could sling some cruelty if he wanted it. After all, his romps with Kimbrell certainly justified it.

I saw the hurt, and I hated it. But what did he expect? He fucked my sister and bragged about it. Heavens only knew what he told about me. Apparently, he revealed as much as he could to whoever wanted to listen because Jack wasn't short on details.

"What's it look like, Finn?" I all but screamed at him. "Sometimes you never stop amazing me."

"I promise to astonish you till daybreak if you'll tell him to get lost." Men always went back to their bedroom talents. Had to love the guy for trying, but the truth was, thanks to him, sex never impressed me much. Thanks to Jack, my opinion drastically changed.

Finn backed away from both of us with his hands held up in front of him. His skin took on an ashen appearance. "I'm not believing this."

"Oh, you can bet your last dollar on it. She's telling you the truth."

"You'll pay for this, Dawson." His promise was weak but there all the same.

"I'm sure you think I will, but here's the facts, buddy. She *is* mine and off-limits to you. Got it?" He pointed to me. "You and Stan can take your turns on Kimbrell. She's a grown woman. But let me catch you climbing in here again, and I'll take the time to teach you a lesson you won't soon forget. You understand me, right?"

Finn was never considered the smartest cowboy in boots. And he never understood when to keep his mouth shut. "You think because Dad…I mean *your* dad had some sort of old-fashioned will drawn up that Darlene belongs to you or something? Am I right?" The anger blushed across his face, reddening his cheeks and neck by the second. "I've got news for you, buddy. This isn't the age of arranged marriages and doing things by the book. Darlene has a mind of her own, and she can speak for herself. I promise you, her mouth has plenty of abilities, and telling you what's on her mind will come easy in the morning."

Finn started to turn around, but Jack didn't seem like a man willing to let another one have the last word. He wasn't going to allow Finn the pleasure of it anyway.

He spoke with a slow drawl. "I told you. Darlene belongs to me. You obviously have some unsettled business with her, but I can tell you this, it's going to forever remain as pending. You're through here, Finn, and on second thought, all of your business with these girls can be considered terminated. You and your brother have made a good living here, but it's time to move the hell on. Cut your losses, and go your separate ways, if you know what I mean."

Finn's fury got the best of him. "I don't think so, Jack." He drew his fist back and took the first punch.

"Stop this!" I screamed and jumped up from the bed, forgetting I was topless, not to mention bottomless, too. It didn't matter. Both men had seen it all before.

By the time I stood between them to separate the punches, Jack had two in and drew back to throw another one. "Finn! Jack! Stop now!" I screamed out the words and looked at both of them. Back and forth , one after the other.

"Get your clothes on, Darlene, and stay out of this. This is a matter among men." Jack didn't look at me. He was locked in on target, and he planned to go in for the kill.

Finn's eyes draped over me like a piece of cloth. "I've seen her more times like this than you can imagine, Dawson. It's what is driving you insane. Isn't it?" He wanted to know if Jack had an inch of jealousy in his veins.

I already knew he did.

"Then take a good look." Before I knew what hit me, Jack had me in a wrist-wrap, spinning me around twice for show. "Make sure to get an eye-full of her, because it needs to last you a cowboy's life since you'll never see her butt-naked again. My breasts bounced lightly, and Finn stared as if he believed what he heard. Maybe I even bought into it, even though Jack was beginning to try my patience.

Finn pushed me out of the way and threw another hook. "You don't tell me or Darlene what to do!" He threw a powerful punch but came through without a direct hit. Jack was able to retaliate, but instead of doing it, he decided to show Finn the window.

"I'll give you five seconds to crawl out the same way you squirmed your way in."

Finn dabbed at a bleeding lip. "This isn't over, Darlene."

"The hell it's not." Jack moved closer to Finn as if to say the groveling was surely finished.

When he was gone and the sound of his truck hummed away in the distance, Jack lowered and locked the window. He turned around on two heels and peered down at me. "So this is the way it's going to be?"

"What?" I pulled the sheet over me again.

"I turn my back for a second, and you allow Finn to sneak in?" He unzipped his pants and stepped out of them. His erection was beginning to shape the shadow of a man ready and built for all night satisfaction.

I wanted to tell him when hell froze over he could come back into my bed, but the truth was I didn't want to sleep without him beside me. Maybe hell was freezing already. If not, it should've been.

"Scoot over." His heavy voice weighed thick in the air. He wasn't asking for permission.

"I want you to go to the sofa." I didn't budge. My mouth continued to defy what my body wanted, and if my mind and heart didn't try to intervene soon, I felt confident I could find a way to piss him off.

He walked around to the other side of the bed and sat down. Before he said anything else, he stretched out beside me and let out a sigh of something. Relief? Exhaustion? Frustration? Maybe a simple combination of all three.

"You aren't welcome here in my bed." *Liar! Liar!* He could lie down next to me anytime he wanted now. Shew! Once I knew what he could do with his manly gifts, never mind the talent behind them, well I was just impressed all the way to heaven and back. .

"Get used to it, because I don't plan to leave it now." He closed his eyes. "Get the light."

"I said…"

"I'm not deaf. Get the damn light."

I stomped over to the door and opened it. "I said get the hell out of here." I pointed to the hall.

"Sleep on the sofa if you like it there, but I'm content here, and if you want me out of here, then you'll have to toss me out."

I seemed up for the challenge. I didn't like to be told what to do, and the man lying on my bed was beginning to like bossing me. It was obvious. I strutted over to the bed and bent down to pull him up. I grabbed both of his wrists and pulled.

"Argh!" I couldn't make him budge.

"This might work for Finn, but I'm telling you one more time. I'm not leaving." He crossed his arms over his chest.

I'm sure he thought he'd won some sort of battle of the sexes and truth be told, he did.

I grabbed the pillow from under his neck. The only one left on the bed. "Fine. Have it your way. Breakfast is at six." I slammed the door shut, wishing my pride wasn't left on the other side of the wood separating us. Wishing like hell I'd just joined him in another lip-lock and leg-hug. Knowing it was inevitable and would happen again, I just shrugged at the door keeping me away from Jack Dawson. It wasn't the first thing to ever separate us, and it damn sure wouldn't be the last.

Chapter 9

"You going to sleep all day?" I threw open the curtains as I called out to him. He was piled under a mountain of blankets. Or so I thought.

Nothing moved or stirred beneath the pile of cotton and flannel tossed on the bed.

"Do you think because you pretended to be dead for over a decade that you can come into my life and act the same way first thing in the morning? It doesn't work here. Nope, not here. I yanked the coverlet back, and to my surprise, found a bouquet wrapped in paper, with fresh picked flowers, and well, let's be honest here, weeds. Tied to the stems, a note stuck out to the side. I picked up the flowers.

From behind me, I heard my sister's voice. "You must've laid it on him good."

"Funny."

"What's the note say?" She probably wished Jack Dawson had been in her bed. If I told her of his skills in the sack, she'd make it her dying-day wish to get him there.

"It's private," I called back to her, but she stepped closer and snagged it from my hand.

"No secrets exist between sisters." She smirked and started to read. "Hope the couch was comfortable. I'll be back soon because I know you'll miss me. I'll also be in your bed tonight. Let me know if you need more blankets for the sofa." Kimbrell snorted a laugh. "You're impossible, little sister."

I grabbed the note and the flowers. "You're unbelievable. The note was private." I felt the woman hormones coming into play. Anger boiling, I simply turned away.

"Well, I'll let you in on a secret. Jack Dawson has lived through hell and back, and he didn't wait all this time for a woman who is dumb enough to sleep on the couch. And I can promise you, if you leave him out in the cold, he's a man worth fighting you for." Her grin widened, and then she added, "Take care of him, or I will." She pushed by me, and I just couldn't let it slide.

"Like you did Finn?" I snapped and then turned to face her. "I've loved Jack Dawson from the time I first laid eyes on him. Finn you can have. Jack and whatever it is I feel for him now is off-limits to you. Do I make myself clear?"

Kimbrell smiled. *"I'm staying home tonight.* If you don't want him in my bed, then I suggest you return to yours. A man like Jack knows what he wants, and he damn sure knows how to get it. If you don't think he'd be opposed to using me to get your attention, then you don't know men at all."

I couldn't believe what I was hearing. My own sister would betray me and would do it with the only man who'd ever held the keys to my heart. She would do it or die.

She must've been halfway back down the hall by the time I called out to her, but I know she heard me. "I guess I shouldn't be surprised. Since Jack's back, he's the only man within a hundred-mile radius who hasn't had a trip to my sister's bed. Well, don't let me stand in the way!" I shouted out the words, and the only reply I found was a slamming door to confirm she got the general underlying message.

* * * *

"Morning, Darlene. You're late getting out here this morning. Finn spend the night?" Stan asked me point-blank. It was a question he seldom had the balls to bring across his lips.

I opened my mouth to answer but was stopped short of it.

"No. I did." Jack appeared, leading my prized stallion from the back field.

"What the hell do you think you're doing?" I asked.

Stan held a puzzled glare too. "Where's Finn?"

"I let him go." Jack looked at me and then Stan. "With Kimbrell's blessing."

"You did what? Are you fucking out of your mind?" Okay, he had just earned a good, swift kick in the ass. I damn near delivered it but my foot only rose a few inches from the ground. One look at the man smiling down on me and I lowered it just as fast.

Jack slowly licked his lips. "You have the abilities to drive a man out of his mind. I'll give you that, sugar." He leaned over and kissed me on the cheek before he patted my behind.

I stomped forward and called out behind me, "Stan, would you please give us a second?"

"Sure." He wasn't going to say no. He needed his job, and I had a feeling even if Finn wouldn't be back, Stan wanted to stay on and work. He needed the money and probably even the perks my sister provided. Few women tried to claw their way into Stan's good graces. Let alone his bed.

Jack led my horse to the cross-ties and then went into the tack room.

"Don't you turn your back to me, Jack Dawson." I spat the words at him.

"Never bothered you before," he shot back.

"It bugs me a lot and now you know it.." He made a point. I used to love to sit behind him on the school bus but a lot had changed since then.

He chuckled. "Then let it eat your heart out." He turned around and faced off with me. Fire existed in his eyes, and red-hot passion began to rise in his jeans. I didn't have to strain my neck or anything else to see it. He moved closer to me and wrapped my waist tightly before drawing me in. His head lowered, and he kissed me lightly on the lips. "Good morning, darlin'. You look beautiful this morning."

"What I look like, Jack, is a woman who was rode hard and put up wet." I wiped my mouth on my arm.

"Well, there's an idea." He released me so I could stomp off in the other direction, which I would've done, but he swatted me on the ass with a hard hit. I just couldn't let it slide.

I turned back to glare at him with hell's fury behind me. "Jack! You have no right to come in here and disrupt this place! What is wrong with you?"

"You." He told the truth. It happened to exist all over his face.

"Then leave. If I'm a problem for you, get the hell out of here. I never asked you to stay."

He moved slowly toward me, reached behind me, and pulled the sliding door closed. He locked it with the latch and dared me to move it back in place. I saw it in his expression, and what I didn't see, I felt under the kiss.

A silver tongue masterfully told me of his goals. "I'm not leaving until you marry me, and then you and I will merge these two ranches into a place where we can raise a family. We'll have a couple of kids, a house buzzing with them if you want, and we will live happily ever after."

"I don't believe in happily-ever. You took all those little dreams away from me when you died." The thing was, he also gave them back to me in an instant when he decided to show up and prove he was among the living. "Now, move your ass while you still have one to move." I tried to get by him. Really I did. So maybe I didn't try hard enough. A woman deserves to have her own issues when the heat begins to rise between her legs. I had my share of them.

"I don't think so." His hand went to his belt buckle, and with a flip, it was released. The zipper followed, and he moved slightly, so he could hang out of his shorts. Literally.

"Put your pants on. Damn you, Jack." I was already wet with desire. Passion damn near stamped me with a *fuck-me* sign. It elevated my senses and refused to give me an alternative. I wanted him. Damn it all. I would take him. He was right there to have.

"I see it in your eyes." His nose tilted up in the air, and he took a deep breath. "I can't smell the desire yet, but I'm willing to bet you're dripping with a fountain of it. Are you soaking wet for me yet baby?" His mouth began to work its magic. "I bet you are." He kissed me into a new sense of understanding. I became instantly aware of the fact that I wasn't going to turn Jack down. We were seconds away from *the fuck*.

He worked his hand underneath my denim pants, only to confirm what he thought was, in fact, true. "Ah yeah, you're wet. Totally soaked." He smirked as he mouthed the words right under my ear. I could feel his lips turn up with a delicious taste of things to come. Heavy breathing followed sweet and spicy insinuations before a prologue of one wonderful suggestion. "Put me where you want me."

Eager hands went to my belt buckle and unlatched, unzipped, and unbuttoned what was left of a tight barrier to guard me from him. "Want it bad, don't you?" I teased him. There wasn't any question how naughty my boy could become or how quickly for that matter.

His mouth fell open, and mine took over kissing him wherever I could find exposed skin. I dropped to my knees, and he pulled me back up again. "No. I want inside of you *right now*." He raised my hips up, and before I knew what hit me, my legs draped around his waist while his cock demanded—and hell yeah—obtained, entry.

Jack possessed unmatched skill driving a woman against a barn wall. It only took a minute for the man to earn my vote. Once my legs curved over his sides, he quickly ripped the thong I wore to shreds. Victoria's Secret. Twenty-five dollars. It didn't really matter, but a girl thinks about these things to keep some level of sanity.

I came unglued in our moment. I also lost my heart to him once more. In those few seconds that consumed us, and the hour or so the night before, I belonged to Jack Dawson. But who was keeping a score card? I sure needed to, but with each new Jack-experience, it seemed to get a little tougher.

He slammed into me in one quick thrust and it left me truly breathless for the others that followed. In and out and in and out with a precise beat, all working toward a delicious performance, I found out what it meant to have more man than a woman's body could handle. I was sore from the night before, but he seemed to be unaware of it, or if he did know or realize the obvious, he didn't care. Hell, I wasn't ready to file a complaint.

"Damn, girl. You're so fucking beautiful." His hands ran over my hair as he pressed me farther into the boards against my back. He pushed into me as deeply as my body permitted him to be before splintering my ass with another precise thrust. "So fucking sexy." His body slammed against mine again and again. "Tight. So damn snug." He pushed into me twice more and those thrusts were slow and calculated—the two big ones. A truly fine erotic grind became a woman's undoing.

We were both almost there when the knock came hard against the door. "Dawson! Get your pants on, you prick! I'm not leaving here until I tell Darlene a thing or two about you!" Heavy fists pounded into the door. My back arched against the thud and ached with each blow the pounding fist on the other side caused.

"Oh shit. I can't move." Pain wracked through my body, so the exaggeration of hurt slipped from my lips before I thought about what it would do to Jack.

Sliding his dick from me, he zipped up quickly and barely waited for me to do the same. He touched my cheek and then whispered, "Go to the house. We'll finish what we started there." As soon as the gentle words left his lips, anger flooded his face and seemed to take up permanent residence there. He pushed the sliding door open to find Finn standing there with a man in a business suit.

"Darlene." The man nodded in my direction.

I didn't speak. My face was flushed from the sexual stimulation, and I was too embarrassed to try to trip over words I just really couldn't find the need to form.

"You better have a damn good reason for being back here." Jack's words were sharp, cutting off each of them one by one.

Finn grinned from ear to ear. "Oh, you better believe I do. Here, Darlene." He handed me a folder. "I'm sure you've seen your daddy's will, but in case you haven't, I have a copy of it and the Dawson will. Just so you know why Jack here is suddenly interested in claiming you for his own." Finn seemed to gloat. "I don't want to hurt you, sweetie, but I think it's only fair you know the man you're spending time with—since you apparently like the way your wasting your hours."

"You think I want to see a will?" I waved the folder back at him before moving in behind Jack. For the first time in my life, I felt protected, and I liked standing behind him.

He seemed to enjoy having me there too. "Darlene, go on up to the house." His hand reached behind us both and he stroked my hip for reassurance.

I started to protest but decided it might be nice to have Jack just handle things for me. It was time to let go of the tough act and just let someone look out for me. Jack seemed capable, and he was more than a little willing.

Jack stared straight ahead. "I'm not going to tell you twice. This is a matter among men."

Finn noted the obvious. "Same thing you said last night when you wanted to be sure Darlene allowed you to protect her good name. Is this some sort of ploy to keep the women in your life devoted to you, or do you use it on just the women you plan to marry?"

Tears threatened to spill. I caught the very pointed remark and how Finn said it. Jack had a wife somewhere. I'd put money on it. "What's he talking about, Jack?" I moved to the side and looked up at him. Of course, anytime I looked at Jack, it was generally up if we were standing. I was only five foot five. He towered over me.

"I *said* go to the house." His voice was firm.

"Finn?" I ignored Dawson and the fact he'd just been back two days and already had the ability to break my heart. *Time doesn't heal love or the ache it brings when Jack Dawson's the object of it.* I existed in a reality Jack Dawson controlled.

Finn definitely had the goods on Jack. He probably stayed up all night, calling in favors, to get them, and whatever he discovered, he was certain it was the truth and set in stone. He wasn't one to go around with rumors for ammunition.

Jack's jaw set, and a thin line formed to compensate for where my puckered lips had once been. He was mad as hell and Finn was going to push all the right buttons—or wrong ones. I knew him well enough to know he wasn't going to back down now. Jack came into town and took the one thing Finn thought he owned just as much as property—me. I'd always known it, and now I realized his feelings for me were real. Far deeper than he would've ever wanted anyone else to know.

"Your new lay has a history he doesn't want you to know about. Right, Dawson?"

Jack spat venomous words, "You should know all about them, buddy."

He then turned to me. "Darlene, please let me have the opportunity to talk to you about my past. Don't hear about it like this. Not from him. Not from a man who has detailed every intimate moment with you so explicitly that everyone who hears him swears they can see you by his description alone." Jack's eyes pleaded with me, but one thing I wasn't, and that was a woman who could be sent away with a wave of a hand when there seemed to be secrets driving the motive for doing it.

"Finn?" I waited for his response.

"Two wives, and how many kids is it now, Dawson?" Finn kicked his boot and twisted it around in the dirt.

"Why you son of a bitch." Dawson stepped up to swing, and I quickly blocked it by stepping in front of Finn.

"Not today you don't. I put up with this shit last night, and you're through." I kept them arms-away from one another. My palms settled. One against Jack's chest and one flat against Finn's belly.

"Both of them left him. One because of his violent temper and the other because he was in love with another woman, or so the story goes." Finn wanted to tell more, but he just didn't have it to tell.

I dropped my jaw. "You have kids?"

"No." He answered flatly. "I don't have kids of my own. Yes. I do have stepchildren, but I don't think they'd claim me."

He reluctantly continued. "I have one ex-wife, and I was engaged. She left me when she found out about you, but the truth is, I owe her everything. If it wasn't for her love, her need to let me go to find what it was that didn't quite tick with us, I wouldn't be here now." Jack's face took on an expression of regret. "Anything else you want me to clarify for Darlene?"

"You've been married." The hurt, for some reason, fell over me. I'd never married because of a dead man. Because I loved a man I presumed was down to skeletal remains. One who had the ability to breathe and live and be twenty feet under at the same time. One who kept me in love with a memory of what might have been. I kept my life on hold while he fucked around and lived in a marriage that possibly could have, or worse, most likely did, produce children.

"Yes. I was married, and yes, she left me," he snapped with the acknowledgement.

Finn crossed his arms. "See, Dawson, I understand *our* girl better than you do. I know that she's lived her life in the past. Wondering if you suffered when you supposedly died. Trying to imagine what it would have been like if you'd never moved away the year before the accident, She just lived out a fantasy of what it could've been like if only you would've been here to take care of her after her parents died.

You weren't, Jack. I was." Finn wrapped his arm around my shoulders and tried to move me away from the competition.

"No." I shrugged him off.

Jack moved toward me next. "And don't you take another step either." I pointed at him.

Hurt washed over him, and I could see he wanted to kill Finn, or at least bring him some well deserved pain. "Darlene, you aren't going to let him step in and ruin the only chance for happiness you've ever had. I won't let you do it."

"You don't have a choice. What was it you said earlier? A matter between men. Well, try this one on for a second or two. The woman in question has a deciding vote. One that will matter far more than anything the two of you can discuss. And I just want to be left alone. Totally alone."

I crossed my arms over my chest and walked back up to the house by myself. By the time I hit the door, I was sobs away from the only man I wanted in my life but damn mad I heard about his other life from the only man who really knew anything about mine. *He had a wife.* I didn't give a fuck if she was a current or past wife. He had one out there somewhere.

I went into the bathroom and washed my face in cold water, hoping to splash away the green envy existing there. The red streaks of pain etched into my skin, regardless of an attempt to dab them away. I scrubbed and rubbed but they remained. Finally, I slumped down into the corner and just sat there with my tears. They didn't keep me company. And that's when I finally accepted it—the hard truth crushed my heart and left me few options. I had to face it.

I loved Jack Dawson. I never stopped, and if he had a wife and twelve kids or five wives and thirty of them, I didn't care. He was mine to have. Jack Dawson was mine to love. I had to grow the hell up sometime. Might as well start now. I could start by facing the only love I'd ever known.

Chapter 10

I fell asleep with my truths and woke up with them too. I loved Jack Dawson, and he loved me. I saw it in his face, in those dark eyes he tried to hide under heavy lids burdened with a lot more secrets—the whole story. I wanted it, and if Jack and I were going to try to pick up where we left off, then this was something we were going to have to get out in the open as soon as possible.

When I opened the door, I was surprised to find Jack leaning against the opposite wall. He peered up from under his cowboy hat. His eye was swollen. His knuckles showcased dried blood, and I felt confident Finn had more of the same and likely even ended up with the worst of it.

I didn't say anything but instead moved to get a washcloth from under the sink. I dampened it with warm water and then began to softly touch the cloth to his skin. Looking into his eyes, I saw the love. And the pain. The regret existed there too, and I'm sure that's what he saw when he looked at me. I had plenty of it.

I dabbed his lip first. It had what appeared to be dried blood settled there but was more like mud. Then I cleaned his wounds. His eye, I rubbed gently before I did the same for his hand, where the rougher battle marks were more defined and obvious.

Deciding he could use an ice pack, I headed for the kitchen. "Don't." He spoke with authority.

"I think you need some ice on your eye."

"Maybe so, but I don't want any. I want you." He growled out the last part and readjusted his position to show me just how much he meant it.

I laughed. "Hmmm, I see, but we're going to have a long talk before there will be any more hanky panky." I touched his face softly, but I wanted to ravage his lips and just forget about the day or the work I tried to avoid while playing house with Jack.

"I figured as much."

"Are you hurting anywhere?" The question happened to be a serious one.

"Baby, you have no idea." He took my hand and helped me find just the place. "All I seem to need is a little TLC. "

"I'm serious." I stared at him in disbelief. Did everyone in the country think with whatever they had between their legs? I was beginning to think so.

"And I'm not? Baby, this is not a laughing matter." He moved into me with speed while his hands trailed over every curve. Anxious lips kissed every area of exposed skin. "Please, baby. Talking can wait. I swear it can."

I walked away from it all. Jack's lips, his hips grinding me into a heated inferno, and the promises of better things to come. I knew what the man could do to me, but what I wanted to know is how many other broken hearts were left waiting in some backwoods stable. There had to be more than what he wanted me to know about.

A long whistle was released.

I swayed down the hall, giving it all I could for a strut I wanted him to crave whenever he got out of hand. I looked over my shoulder, and with the best come-hither gesture I could muster, I purred out the words, "Be a good boy and follow me. Who knows, I may just lead you where you want to go if you tell me everything I want to hear."

His hand slid down the front of his pants, and I saw him. A hungry growl warded off any other call to the wild I'd heard from a man and it escaped the best of lips. It seemed to be inspired by half-man and half-animal. It screamed sex appeal. My body would've been well-satisfied to just go on and jump his bones. He would've appreciated it, and I felt confident the ride would be worth it.

But a woman always defies good reasoning when she fears there's someone else waiting in the wings. I wanted to be sure there wasn't, and if there was, I wanted to be sure we clipped the delicate wings and sent her flying in another direction. That was just me–the stupid woman in me, I guess. I had Jack Dawson and I didn't plan to share. If there were surprises, then I wanted to hear them.

We sat at the kitchen table.

"Can I get you anything?" I leaned over and placed my chin in an open palm.

"You," he fired back quickly almost before I finished speaking.

"In due time. Tell me about those years, Jack. I want to know everything there is to know."

"You want the short version or the long one?" His eyes hazed over, and it was the only reason I chose the shorter translation.

"The parts that count. I need to hear those. I want to know why you didn't come back here. I need to understand why you never wrote to me, and I want to know why you would marry someone else, because I know…" I swallowed hard. "I realize you never loved anyone else but me."

He leaned over the table and took both of my hands in his. "You know this how?"

"I know, because it's the reason you didn't come back."

"She told you." Jack confirmed what I believed.

"No. Kimbrell didn't tell me anything. But you just did." My vision already burned from the tears ready to fall. It was everything I'd suspected.

His eyes continued to question me with uncertainty, but he began to speak slowly. "I couldn't come back here. Without my mother and father and without yours here to guide us between right and wrong…"

"So you stayed away for my own good?"

"You're damn straight I did. Ask Kimbrell. She has the letters to prove it. I have the pictures of you and her letters to show you a lifetime of follow-up and follow-through but, baby, I couldn't come here before now. She didn't want me here, and I didn't want to come in and destroy you with my past and my own house of horrors. After the accident, I had plenty of them. I want you to understand. I stayed away because I...I..."

"Damn it to hell, Dawson," Kimbrell walked in and grabbed a beer from the refrigerator. "Tell her what's on your mind and quit dancing around it. If you don't, I will. I'm sure she'd rather hear it from you."

I glared at her. She'd been trying to one-up me since we were kids, and now it appeared she had long since been declared the winner. It was the more ultimate of betrayals. I was slow to speak. "You knew he was alive. You realized he was alive and well and you did nothing. You told me nothing at all."

The tears continued to threaten, but I choked on them, afraid to let them fall. Afraid to hear everything from the beginning but realizing I had to know or else risk a true crumble under an incredible house of cruel deception.

Kimbrell wanted to do the honors. I wasn't surprised. "You weren't able to handle the man he became when he walked away from his accident. He was ready to come in and claim you within months of Mom and Dad...leaving." She added the last part carefully.

Jack shook his head. "I was ready to come in and make an honest woman out of you at sixteen, and if your sister hadn't stopped me, I would have been back here for you."

"And it would've landed him in the State Pen, and you know it. With all the social workers buzzing in and out of here, I had to protect you both from each other." Kimbrell never had a wrong moment in her life, so getting her to admit it now wouldn't happen.

"Noble Kimbrell." My voice stayed barely above a whisper. "Such a loyal sister. So fiercely devoted."

She smiled, but it diminished by the time I was on my feet.

"Tell the truth, Kimbrell. The only reason you didn't tell me was because you wanted Jack for yourself. You always wanted the men who wanted me. Isn't that right?" I decided to let the crying begin. Tears defiantly streamed from my eyes.

Jack stood too. "I know what you're thinking, Darlene, but it's not true. I never slept with Kimbrell, and she never offered. It's not what you think."

"Really?" The hurt and lies consumed me, covered me with the looming heartbreak of knowing what I'd missed. What I'd put on hold for Jack Dawson.

"Well, don't worry, Jack. You hurt yourself more than you hurt me. Married someone else because you couldn't have me and then had another one on the line…for me? Is that right? Well, news flash, you missed out on everything I did and maybe even more."

"She's talking about popping her cherry. Not to worry, Finn took care of it." Kimbrell had a one-track mind. I swear she would have been better off living as a man.

"I'm talking about all of it. Not just who was in my pants first. Give me a friggin' break, Kimbrell."

"I'm trying to, but you won't let me. I'm trying to help you understand why Jack couldn't come back here. What was he going to come back to then? His family inheritance wasn't going to be his unless he decided to marry you, and I sure as hell wouldn't sign for you to marry at sixteen years old, heaven forbid, fifteen. If I messed up, then I'm sorry I screwed up."

I took a deep breath and let it out before I turned to Jack, refusing to give Kimbrell a real piece of my mind. "You messed up, alright. I could understand the years immediately following your family's death, but I'm in my twenties. It took you a damn long time to show up here."

"There's more." Kimbrell nodded and pulled out the letters from the cupboard. To think, just to imagine, evidence of Jack's life was hidden within my reach. Kimbrell pushed the box of letters over to me and I resisted the urge to shove them back.

Brushy Mountain Correctional Complex. "What is this?" "It's a matter of…"

"Don't." I quickly stopped him. "Don't you dare say it's none of my business or a matter to be discussed between you and someone other than me. I've heard it until I'm totally sick of hearing it. Do you understand? I want to know why you were in prison."

Kimbrell nodded, but Jack shook his head adamantly. "I'm not ready to talk about it. I may never be ready."

I searched their faces for anything. Something. Explanations for why he would be behind bars.

"Just know…I need you to know I wanted to be here sooner. I needed to be here sooner, but I couldn't get to you until now."

"What were you doing in prison?"

"His first wife was a nutcase." Kimbrell wanted to tell a twisted version of the story.

"Shut up, Kimbrell." He should've known my sister never listened to men unless they were seducing her with an animalistic nature. Then she was ready to crouch down all fours and purr if necessary.

"She claimed he tried to kill her and her son."

"He was my son. Well, he was and he wasn't." The pain flew across his face, and his neck tensed with the veins beginning to bulge. Whoever the woman was, she definitely left an inner wound or two.

Kimbrell continued. "She was screwing around with the kid's father, but he was a deadbeat, and Jack made a better public impression. He could support the kid, so she lied to him, and he stayed with her longer because of it."

"Kimbrell, I assure you this is something Darlene and I can talk about on our own." Jack's face turned red, but I think it was from the embarrassment rather than provoked anger.

"Fine, then you talk to her, but damn you, Jack Dawson, don't leave out the important stuff. After having a slime-ball like Finn in her bed for more than half a decade, my sister deserves an honorable man. Someone who can love her with honesty as well as his hard dick."

"Thank you, Kimbrell." I couldn't help but laugh outright. "I appreciate your ability to speak so eloquently about love and my affairs of the heart, mind, and body. You're quite good at putting things into perspective." Gees, the woman needed a dick of her own.

Jack pressed his palm into my lower back. "Let's go, baby. We have a lot to talk about."

I started to walk down the hallway toward my room, and he pulled me back to him. "No. I want you to go home with me. *Now.* We're going to be right next door, and I promise you if I don't give you a hundred good reasons to stay with me, I'll let you go. You can come back here to Kimbrell, and I'll let you make a life for yourself without me. But tonight you'll be in my bed, and with any luck, you'll like it well enough to stay there."

Kimbrell looked from Jack to me and back to Jack again. "I knew you two would be like this. I'm just glad you got here when you did."

Jack nodded and shot her a look.

"What now?" Did I dare ask?

"Finn." Kimbrell nodded to Jack.

"What about him?"

Jack looked down at the kitchen floor.

"He was Jack's ex-wife's lover. She met him when she came here, snooping around for information about you, and they had a few one-night stands."

I felt my voice box hitch with the sigh I wanted to release. "So…you're trying to tell me Finn knew Jack was alive all these years?"

"Yes. He knew too, but there's more to it." Kimbrell nodded again.

I shook my head with the disbelief. "No. He wouldn't. He wouldn't dare be that cold."

"Yes, Darlene. He would." Jack confirmed it. "Five years in prison. I spent the time for a beating she took from Finn, and then when I walked out a free man, anxious to see my son, I found out he didn't even belong to me. Finn and Stan paid her to stay quiet. It's a long story. We'll talk about it later."

Suddenly, breathing became an impossible task. It was hard to even contemplate. "What kind of deceptive webs have all of you been tangled in? And why have you remained there? Kimbrell, this was your idea of keeping Jack away from me?" I swallowed back nothing but my pain.

"Yes."

"It backfired in a big way." I stayed unbelievably calm.

"Yes." She agreed with me. There really wasn't room for a disagreement. It was truly obvious fate played out how it was meant to be anyway.

Jack was slow to speak. "I want you to have her letters. Mine are at home. You'll understand more then." He tilted his hat in my sister's direction. "Kimbrell, we'll see you tomorrow."

I shot her a look of contempt. She had her secrets with the man I loved, and yet her life was daily news when it came to the guys strolling in and out of her bedroom. She had plenty of men biding for her affection in one way or another but she decided to play Russian Roulette with the man I loved *and* the first man to make his way to my bed. Finn and Jack weren't bad people, but thanks to Kimbrell, they'd made bad choices. I was willing to bet all of the wrong ones left a trail leading straight back to me.

Chapter 11

I finally convinced Jack I would meet him a few hours later. I told him I wanted to change and get ready before I spent the first night of what he hoped would be many more in his family home. I wasn't sure he bought it, but he allowed it.

After I packed an overnight bag, I headed over to Finn's house. His mother was glad to see me and immediately sent me into the hayfield, where I found Stan and Finn baling hay.

"Stan, do you mind if I have a word with Finn?"

Stan shifted his weight back and forth. "Normally, you know I wouldn't. Typically, I'd tell you to keep him as long as you wanted, but things have changed here, haven't they, Darlene?" His eyes drifted over me, and for the first time, I saw what I knew was already there. He wanted me as much or more than his brother had. Not that I blamed Stan entirely. He'd seen me in the flesh more times than I dared to count. I liked to parade around in front of him just to have my morning jollies. He deserved a lingering stare. Still, his tone and overall demeanor shocked the hell out of me.

Finn pushed by Stan and stared a hole through me. "You have no idea what you're up against here." His words were bitter, and the way they were used burned with the intent to sting. The words didn't, at least not the choice of them, but the delivery of them was a different story.

"Ever wonder why you never met our father?" Stan began with a slow southern drawl, and Finn cut him off.

"That's not what this is about, is it? You're not here about Jack and the information I told you about him, are you, Darlene?" He moved toward me slowly, and before I saw him coming for me, he'd wrapped me in a tight embrace, pulling me closer before I could move away. "You're here because I kept him from you, and because I did, you were in my bed, so now all of this is my fault. Every bit of it, right?"

"No. It's not all your fault, Finn. Blame is oddly placed. Most of the time the only function blame serves is to benefit the one who can manipulate it best. Isn't that what you want to do? Manipulate just enough of it in another direction? Yet, what a loser, what a pathetic piece of flesh you are to have another man put behind bars for a crime you committed."

Finn shifted his weight. "There's more to it than meets the eye."

Stan agreed. "Yeah, you don't know the half of it, Darlene. Me and Finn, we took real good care of you and Kimbrell, didn't we?" He wanted to change the subject.

"What the fuck does that have to do with anything?" I wasn't sure I understood anything anymore. Now, everything just had to be spelled out for me.

Finn moved in behind me, and Stan stood in front of me. When Finn wrapped his arms around my body, I started to scream, but Stan put his fingertips to my lips. "You came here for answers, now let me give them to you. I have them. Every single one you want—and I'll give 'em to you with every stroke."

Finn whispered in my ear. "You love a rush, so here, feel the excitement." He pressed his swollen dick into my backside.

"Oh yeah, I feel it but it's so damn small, it's a struggle. Damn, why didn't I see you for the pervert you are?" I questioned him over my shoulder.

Finn sneered but didn't answer. He let Stan do the talking.

"I guess because you were too busy playing house with him when you weren't daydreaming about our other brother." Stan moved closer and then dove in for a kiss. Swift, sharp, and quick as a whip. His mouth hovered over mine while Finn held me tight so his brother could really grab a taste of me.

My lips formed a defiant and tight line. They wouldn't part. I kneed him in the nuts and kicked backwards, hoping to swing a foot in Finn's prized treasury department too. Before I could get away from him on my own, a gun shot fired into the air, and I looked up to find Jack standing about a hundred feet back.

"Let her go, Finn." He called out as he walked closer.

"No way, man. She's mine. You decided it when you didn't come back to get her. I will never let you have her. Never. You'll have to kill me first."

"Baby Brother…it can be arranged. I promise you."

Baby brother? I shot him a look. "Damn you, Jack Dawson. Is there anything else you want to tell me while you're at it?" My softly spoken rant probably wasn't heard because of the moans and groans coming from Stan.

Doubled over from my fierce attack on his manhood, Stan's fiery glare spoke as much volume as the words he used to hurt me. "You're just like the sister you keep trying to protect. Only there's a slight difference. You'll only whore yourself out for millions of dollars, and she's willing to let any old cowboy giddy-up for free."

"Come on, Finn. There's nothing left here for you. He's always going to come out on top. Just like Dad." Stan swiped his cowboy hat against his pant-leg.

Jack looked up and then back at the two half-brothers who had already decided a long time ago to hate him. "I know you two won't ever believe this, but somehow, I don't think Dad came out on top. Dying at forty-five doesn't make me believe he was a lucky man. You know?" Jack kicked the dust and dirt beneath him. "No, death didn't put him out ahead of anyone else, and it damn sure didn't leave us in a good place, did it?"

* * * *

We walked in the old Dawson home place, and Jack put his Stetson to rest on the coat rack next to the door.

I looked around totally mesmerized by what I saw. Everything was just as I remembered it. I couldn't believe my eyes. Right down to the rustic fragrance I always recalled when I thought of Jack's family. I took a deep breath, wanting to inhale the smell for as long as I could.

"I did the same thing. Candy apples and baked bread. The house will forever hold the scent of both."

I chose my words carefully then. "I remember everything about your mother."

He led me through the kitchen to the back steps, and we started to climb them together.

"She adored you." He probably thought about that a lot. His mother always loved me and I made sure she saw a lot of me so I could see more of Jack. It was possibly one of the reasons he wanted me. More than the documents that would forever bind us or encourage us to marry, it was his mother's approval he sought in her death just as he had during her life. The proof appeared to stare back from memories captured in photographs. My pictures were along the hallway, running up the length of the steps, right along with the rest of his family photos. I felt the tears begin to fall but swiped them away in a hurry. Family barbeques and horse back riding lessons, picnics and holiday parties, the pictures told of a history forever entwined. The years revisited there in solid wood frames were so long ago it seemed hard to remember the occasion captured in each.

When we reached the top of the steps, I immediately started to the left, but he pulled me back. "I moved my room to the guest room. I wanted the adjoining office, and since everything about this house still haunts me, a fresh change of scenery proved worth the effort. Besides, I thought you would be more comfortable there." He kissed my forehead.

"You're arrogant aren't you? Think I plan to stay, do you?" I winked and then batted my eyes for added effect.

He shrugged. "Never hurts to be optimistic. Besides, I don't remember giving you a final say-so in the matter. In fact, if you know what's good for you, you won't try to go home. I've become quite the stalker where you're concerned, and I plan to keep you now that I have you again."

"You never *had me* before yesterday."

His grin was downright scandalous. "There's no way you'll even think about leaving my bed after tonight. No way any woman in their right mind would dare think about it, if you don't mind my saying so."

I shivered with anticipation. No, it was forced and I wanted him to see it. "I hope like hell you keep those dirty little promises." I couldn't help but release a moan. "Tell me something, how does this work for you? The little thing you do with control?"

He stopped in the middle of the hallway and looked over at me. "You tell me. Are you already wet just thinking about it? Let's see, I'm willing to bet you are."

Faster than the speed of my prized horse, he pressed me against a nearby wall. Pouring into my mouth with a tongue skillfully able to divide and conquer, separate and totally devour, he had the art of kissing down. He mastered it, and I felt certain when it came to Jack Dawson, everything he did just improved with age. I hoped to find out. I planned to stick around long enough to enjoy the coming of matured improvements. Truthfully, he didn't need betterment—I liked him the way I found him.

His hand slid down inside my pants, and I moaned out with the pleasure it brought. He dipped into my intimate space long enough to see for himself. "Just like I thought. Drenching with a hurting need, aren't you, baby?" His words could make a woman cry out in agony and hope like hell for a stiff one sooner rather than later. Me? I wanted his kissing to move down south and I didn't want him to take his own sweet southern time either.

"I have plans of my own." I moved by him and he followed me. He sat down on the bed and acted really interested in hearing about them.

"Then it's your show, darlin'." His eyes undressed me before my hands had the ability to do it for us.

I swallowed hard, and he motioned for me. I moved to the edge of the bed, and he wrapped my neck with his palm bringing me in for a light peck on the cheek. *Damn him.* I wanted the tongue-thing.

"Can't wait? Hmm...I'm glad to know it." He snickered, and the moonlit room provided enough light to show off a flash of his sexy dimples.

I moved across the room, looking at everything. In the corner, an oriental designer print screen was set up to showcase tigers and lilies in a bold masterpiece. I'm sure his parents didn't purchase it, since a beautiful nude woman stood out in the midst of it all.

"Go over there and undress. I have something I want you to put on for me." A hungry, dominant growl followed, and damn if I didn't want to just do him in all the right positions. Yep, the man had the deliverance of sex gab down to a creative art form. A moan or growl and I was mush but a sexy request—hell, I'd fuck him just to hear him hand down the sensual orders.

A present, beautifully wrapped in gold paper with a purple ribbon, was placed on a little round table, along with a note and specific instructions. *Put this on, but don't step back out from behind the screen until you tell me you're ready, I have another surprise.*

I quickly ripped the package open. He could hear me, and his voice seemed closer when he asked the question certain to follow. "What do you think?"

There wasn't much there and I quickly realized it once I slipped the thong and high heels on.

"You're serious?" I called out to him.

"Very," he fired right back.

I peeked around the side of the screen. "You realize that there's only a thong and high heels?"

His wicked grin told me he wouldn't have it any other way.

With the hot red thong and screw-me-slow shoes to match, I was ready when he was. "I've never worn high heels," I confessed what he probably already guessed.

"First time for everything." He cleared his throat. "I figured I owed you the thong. There's something else too, so let me know when you're ready."

I sighed and resigned myself to the fact this was something Jack fantasized about. The high heels were as much a part of the fantasy as the thong. Pulling a clip from my purse, I quickly worked to secure my hair back in a cascade- waterfall of sorts. I eyed the heels, imagining how he'd see me in them. *Ridiculous*. I tried to sexy-up the goofy.

Still, the smile I wore by the time I was ready couldn't be measured against any other feeling. I was happy, and the joy alone would overcome any insecurity about being in heels and a thong, especially since the only man who would ever see me in them looked at me like I was the most precious of metals. And he did it every time he allowed his eyes to meet mine.

"Come out, baby." His voice was thick with desire.

I slowly moved from behind the screen, ready to show off the new panty covering very little of me, not to mention the heels I fought to keep on—not an easy task. "Ta-da." I threw my hands up in the air and pranced around like a showgirl on display.

He was on the bed, but he didn't stay there long. His hand reached for me, and he twirled me around in a spin that truly made me dizzy. "Gorgeous woman." He let out groans and whistles of true carnal approval and moved his hands around my waist to stop the spin he'd initiated.

His head immediately went to my breasts, and devour them he did as he feasted first on one nipple and then the other, tweaking them with teeth one second and a hungry mouth full of moisture the next. He was completely in tune with what I needed, and he gave a little preamble of what the night ahead guaranteed.

Music filled the room. It was the seventies. Something from the Bee Gees era but I couldn't peg the tune. It didn't matter. The only music I heard was humming through my body, driving me to a place I would never be able to define.

His lips were heavenly. Made for a woman's pleasure. I didn't doubt it for a minute, but when he gave me a glimpse of things to come, licking through the scant material, I was certain there was more of him I wanted to find. More of him I wanted to try.

Tingling sensations covered me when he sent my nerve endings into another experience. His tongue lightly maneuvered over the silk until the material was saturated. His finger ran over the creased area he deliberately made stand out. Now, the panties didn't even exist. "You're so wet for me, baby. So damn hot and ready."

Three fingers moved under the cloth. He was right outside the folds of a welcoming tunnel ready for his invasion. I wanted to tell him to stop, but there wasn't any way to turn him away when I already knew what his fingers were able to prove. And they weaved their magic. *Did they ever.*

His first stroke inside was one-handed, with a solitary finger, but soon three others were in place, working into me with a rough hand, massaging the outside of swollen pussy lips. "I'm going to come." Little did I know my words would stop the whole ever-lovin' show. *Damn it! I shouldn't have opened my mouth!*

"The hell you are. Not yet." He stopped abruptly and pulled out a toy from the bedside table. "All for you, baby. All for you." Not the surprise I expected.

I shot the box housing his little gadget a look of uncertainty. "I'm not sure about toys, Jack."

"You've never played with toys, sugar?" He worked at the box until he held it in his hand. It was…huge."

I looked at it for a long time—mere seconds maybe, but long enough to be uncomfortable. The vibrator he turned on cracked me up with the movement it made, never mind the sound.

"I can't do this, not yet, Jack."

"Sure you can, baby. I'm right here. If you don't like it, I'll move it." He smiled down on me and kissed me with more affection than ever before. Amazing what a man will do to get his way. *Fucking unbelievable.*

His hands moved to my cheeks while he made love to a mouth ready to wrap him into a divine instrument meant for a man's neverending pleasure. Yes, I knew I was good at a blow job but I wasn't so sure I could do my best with the toy in one end and a swollen cock in the other. Apparently, he didn't care because his confidence in my abilities showed all over his body. His nipples were hard and his dick? A sizeable improvement over the last time I'd had the occasion to touch it.

With a little lubricant, he moved the toy from the bed and into my vagina. "Oh hell. Sweet mercy hell. Jack…" He held my hands high above my head and began kissing me slowly before he moved down to massage my breasts with the same forbidden attention he showered on my lips.

"Damn you, Jack. Take it out. Please. Take it out." I pleaded with him, but the busy little toy didn't give it a rest. It jolted me one minute and massaged the next. I don't know how or when or where I was able to have the pleasure of another intrusion, but one or two seconds passed and Jack was in my mouth, stroking me with every solid inch of masculine thickness.

"Oh fuck yeah!" he screamed out as he drove into me. "Oh damn, baby. I'm so sorry. I'll hold back, I'll hold back." He made promises I planned to help him break.

The tip of his dick to the shaft was mine to explore, but the problem I had was keeping my teeth out of the picture, since the vibrator continued to call on me for an earth-shattering climax in the middle of the deep throat lock I had on the only man I'd ever loved. Nervous hands gripped the bed sheet when it took me the first time, but somehow, I managed to keep him positioned over me, straddled above me at just the right angle.

He held onto the headboard behind me and stroked the back of my throat. "Baby, baby…I'm going to lose it here." I certainly hoped so. I didn't want it to be said he couldn't, because I worked him over with everything I had to give. Tongue, teeth, sips, sucks, nibbles; everything I could give, he received.

Just hearing him say the facts, state them as I knew they existed, drove me into another time and place. He must've known I was going there, because he reached down my stomach and flipped up a switch. The vibrating sensation changed and so did his moves. I licked once more, telling him what I wanted while releasing the tip just long enough to ensure he paid attention.

"Come on, baby, give me all of it. I can handle it all." I pulled him in with a long, sucking motion about the same time the vibrator jarred me into yet another climax for the record books.

His body moved quicker, and a bead of sweat formed on his brow. "Oh sweet hell woman. Oh mercy hell, Darlene! I'm there, baby! You've…oh, baby. I'm…" He bit on his lower lip, and yes, it was more than a little obvious *he was there*. The proof glistened off the tip of his dick as I swallowed the last drop of the sweetest nectar a man's body ever provided. The salty remaining evidence of a mission accomplished—and hell yeah, a well negotiated deal.

Chapter 12

My body still felt depravation. It needed something more even as the last quiver and shake ceased to exist. Jack gently removed the toy from my pussy before replacing it with light strokes and a tender caress over the entire area the toy recently vacated. "You're so beautiful. So damn sexy."

He was perfect in every way. The cowboy he wanted me to know stayed dormant, just under the surface of a young man with a kind heart. The years obviously didn't show him their favor, because the evidence of a hardened man surfaced in his sexuality and oh gawd, how he used it. There was typically something hidden just beneath the surface of the manly men who demonstrated the true desire to dominate their women in the sack. Jack Dawson was one of those men.

"Roll over." He began his instructions as soon as he was sure I was ready for more.

"Are you kidding me? I have to rest." I slowly, reluctantly, rolled over, ready to follow his request.

"You can sleep later. Right now, you're going to know the feel of my hand on your sweet and sexy apple-bottom ass." He playfully nipped at my hip.

"The hell I will!" I was appalled and already cursing myself. I rolled over without question. I wanted to move back the other way, but his grip forbade it.

"You will. And darlin', you're going to love me for it." His husky voice brought with it the first slap of skin. Two more playful smacks and I felt the flinch in my muscle tissues. My soul entwined with his on the fourth and by the fifth, he owned me. Oh yeah, I truly experienced everything his hand delivered. My body begged for more and slowly my back arched with readiness. I anxiously awaited another one.

"More." I went ahead and asked for it while he smoothed away the sting with a gentle touch. The massage followed each slap against my skin and it was worth ten thousand more.

"I'm completely wet. Damn you, Jack Dawson. You're doing things to me that should have you tried and convicted of a major crime."

"You want to convict me, baby?" He was ready. His dick was already rising beneath me, and the way he'd moved his body to shelter and hold me with the next few slaps, there wasn't any question about it. He could position himself a bit better and then slide right on in.

I laughed at his question. "I want you to stop playing with me like this."

"Brutal honesty. Do you know why you like to hate it?" He smacked me again with the final slap before he kissed the same place his hand had only just left.

Before opportunity allowed me to answer, he found a way to make up for it all. He stood up and pulled me with him before he bent me over the bed sliding right in behind me.

"I hate it. That's all. I love it and hate it." I told him all about what I liked and hated about the spankings, the vibrator, and the cock driving me into an obscene orgasm. "You're ruining me for any other man. Doing these things to a woman defies any sense of law and order." *Damn you, Jack.* "More! Give me more!"

He whispered into my ear with primal need. "Consider yourself destroyed. Completely pampered but utterly wrecked of the ability to ever need or want another."

In and out. His cock drove home his point and a meticulous hand went to my side and held on for a tight, close ride.

"You like it, don't you, baby? Like the fact you can't get enough when I'm around." He pulled my hair back, and when he did, the carnal sense of being fucked just kicked in and with every slick stroke he allowed me to feel, I bucked against it. With every slow burning screw, I gave him cause to find another reason to push right back inside.

"Answer me!" His hips slowed to a calculated rocking motion.

I shook my head. "Just fuck me. Damn you, don't you dare stop!"

"Darlene, I will, and you'll like it." His body did. He stopped moving into me with an abrupt halt and it only encouraged me to buck harder against a cock unwilling to move in accommodation. Refusing to ratify my womanly requests for more of the same, he fucked like he never planned to stop.

"Oh shit, Jack. Mercy hell! Tell me what you want from me!" Begging didn't become me, but it sure as hell wasn't a disgrace. I considered what he was doing to my body and what he threatened to take away in an instant. Restraint was definitely his strong point when he wanted to use it.

"I want you to tell me how much you like it." His voice cracked into a hoarse plea.

"I like it, damn you!" I bucked wildly against his thighs, but the dick he continued to push into my intimate space slowed to a precision of claim. Once it did, he never showed the good decency to move. Refusing the propositions my body continued to make, Jack held my hips only tighter. Closer.

"You love it. In fact, now that you've had me, you'll hunger for more." His words were nothing but the harrowing cruelty of my new truth. He showed me what he could do to earn my devotion. He had it. He showed me how he planned to authenticate the loyalty he obviously wanted from me. Check. He earned it without any problem.

He was right. Cravings would only be satisfied by him. He now lived under my skin. Only a man like Jack Dawson would please me because I enjoyed a capable man. And he was capable. He was perfect and in bed—yeah— it made him a rare find.

The best part of it was men like Jack were seldom the kind to leave when they finally found their place. When they found their home in the arms of the one woman they could call their own, they recognized it for what it was worth.

It was more than lust, far more. It was the desire and passion that kept men like him alive. I was the woman for him. If there were any doubts, he settled all the old scores when he brought me up the stairs and into the room where the trial and errors could be kept down simply because they really didn't matter. If the smile on his face were an indication or the way he tried to resist the last buck of hips before he held on tighter for the ride, then I'd bet I earned my place in his bed. In fact, I felt confident of it.

* * * *

Breathless. It was the way he left me, and not only did he leave me in such a predicament, but he also started us off in much the same way. I rolled over to look at him, and he gave me a sexy little smile, with one eye open looking down over me.

"Now since we have the important stuff out of the way, I want you to tell me about Finn and Stan."

The smile quickly diminished. "There's not a lot to tell."

"I think there is. I've been trying to figure this all out, and since I never saw the side of Finn and Stan you seemed draw out, I think there is more than meets the eye."

Jack moved up to position his back against the bed. "You think too much, don't you?"

"Don't avoid the question, and don't think because you're a man you can wave a dismissive hand at me and I'll go away quietly. My mother didn't raise her girls to be silent."

Jack brought me in for a long kiss, and just as he released me, he said, "Maybe not. She raised a little screamer in you though, didn't she?"

We both laughed. I was pretty vocal with Jack, but damnation what an irresistible man he became when his hips began to move!

"Do you want me to go back and question Finn and Stan?" I cocked my head and puckered my lips into a pout.

"I want you to stay the hell away from them!" The anger he held inside for the brothers washed across his face in a country minute.

"Don't take your stupid superior tone with me." I jumped up from the bed and didn't realize what a picture I painted for the man I left behind.

A smile quickly replaced where the anger once existed. He reached for me. "Come here, *now*."

"No. I'm serious, Jack. I want answers."

"I'm serious too. You can't get up from my bed with tits bouncing and expect me to ignore such a proposition." He slowly lifted the sheet up to show off the swollen cock all ready for another go of it.

I moaned. "Not until you answer me."

Pointing to his perpetual hard-on, he licked his lower lip before running the pad of his thumb over it. "Baby, I have a feeling you can ask me anything right now, and I'll gladly answer in a rush."

I giggled and jumped back in bed, taking the time to sit Indian-style in front of him. His eyes immediately focused on my chest.

"Damn you." He took a long sigh but didn't bother reaching for me. "What do you want to know?" He seemed to draw a slight breath before releasing an exaggerated one.

"Did you know about them? I mean, did you know they were your brothers?"

"I found out about them when Sarah, my ex-wife, came here to find out more about you."

"How did she find out about it, you know about your family relationship with them, if I never did?" I was curious because I lived there my entire life. I grew up with Finn and Stan. I never knew about their father, and never asked.

"She stayed here and snooped." Jack shook his head. "It breaks my heart to know this, but my mother always knew about Finn and Stan. In fact, she paid their mother monthly to keep her quiet."

"Your dad knew."

"Oh sure, he did. But from what I can tell, he didn't support her very much. He gave her money when he saw her, but he just didn't send her money for the big things, you know, clothing and medical bills. My mother did but he didn't acknowledge those boys unless she made him, or so I gather."

My heart broke for Mrs. Dawson. I always loved and admired her. She was a true lady. Turns out, I pegged it. She was extraordinary to a fault.

"And this is the repayment you and your family get?" I questioned, still wanting more answers.

Jack reached for me. "This is why I've always admired you, Darlene." He smiled and brushed the hair back from my face. "You have no idea what we are or why the land we're sitting on is so valuable, do you?"

I laughed. "Of course I do. I know the value of an acre, and while property isn't at an all-time high in Tennessee, we still have two of the best-looking ranches from an aerial view." I shrugged. "Or so I've been told."

He raised an eyebrow. "By whom?"

"Finn and Stan took pictures of the properties awhile back."

"Figures."

That's when it hit me. "Oh my gawd."

Jack nodded. "Yes. Go ahead and say it. You're on the right track."

"They were playing me, weren't they? One of them would've eventually stepped up to marry me or Kimbrell?"

"They planned to step up and prove they were my father's sons, and with me out of the picture, they would've been able to get the same deal with Father's assets. They went to a lot of trouble to do it."

"I still don't know why they would need me and Kimbrell to do it."

Jack sighed. "Because, Darlene, they're after the same thing I am tied to through you, only there's a difference. I truly, and listen to me when I tell you this, because it's the truth, I *love* you. I always have."

My mouth fell open wide. I suddenly found the air a bit thick, and thinking seemed damn near impossible, presenting challenges of a different sort.

"This is the part where you tell me you love me back. After all, you've waited your entire life to tell me."

I inched closer to him, took his head in between two palms, and kissed him lightly on the lips. "I always knew you'd come to your senses."

"And…"

I couldn't help but tease him. He did deserve it. "You've waited too long."

The look on his face was priceless. He rolled over me and tickled me silly. "The hell you say."

Between laughter, I spat the words out again. "I'm serious. You stayed away too long. I'm a woman now. The silly, little-girl dreams are already gone." I moved my hand away from my chest and extended my arm to indicate those fantasies were long gone and all but sailing away.

He caught my hand before bringing it to his lips. "You think you're something, don't you. Tell me what I already know."

"Nope. Can't do it."

He tickled me again and then moved his lips to my chest, beginning with another full-chest massage. "Then if that's the truth, I'll just have to earn your love. Make you so crazy for me that you'll realize without a doubt you can't live without me."

I pushed my palm into his chest and stopped him in his tracks. "We're not through here. I still need to be told what the big deal is about these two ranches. There's more than you're telling me. Now spill it. What is it?."

Jack swallowed hard. "You *really* don't know. *Fucking unbelievable.*" His eyes locked with mine. "Really? You have no idea?"

"I know our fathers wanted us to marry. I know, according to my mother's journals, they felt like from the time we were children, we couldn't leave each other alone and *for some reason,* someone thought we'd be a match made in heaven…or hell, which is actually what my father thought." I swallowed back the pain I felt whenever I mentioned my dad. He was a positive force in my life and I missed him—a lot. I felt sure my eyes revealed a lot so I continued. "I know the two ranches joined together are worth double maybe even triple, since the properties together would be one of the largest working ranches in the southeast. Is there something more?"

Jack pulled me up to him and cleared his throat. "Well, there's also another minor detail." He paused for a minute and then continued. "The land we sit on has oil under it."

My jaw dropped. "It has what?"

"Once the drilling begins here, there will be more barrels of oil brought off of these two properties than what was ever found on any five random oil-producing Texas ranches."

"You're kidding." I just couldn't think quickly enough. "In Tennessee?"

"No, I'm not kidding, and yes, oil can be found in Tennessee. Under us now, a river of it flows with the crudest of oil." He laughed.

I swallowed hard. "You mean we're rich?"

"Baby, we're nasty with money."

"Are you serious? I can't believe this." I kept shaking my head. "No way."

"Would I lie to you?"

"Hmm…that's up for debate. You definitely did when you pulled your little disappearing act." I stared at him for a long time. "Rich? Mega-rich?"

"More money that you'll ever know what to do with, but the fact is, once the drilling starts, the land here as we know it is forever changed. It's why our fathers never began the drilling. They were content with what they had and wanted us to take care of the rest. Fact is, we don't really need the money. If we never decided to drill, then we'd still have plenty. You know all of this, right?"

"I'm aware of our finances." I really wasn't. The administrator still cut out our checks each month. One for Kimbrell and a check for me and we rarely spent a lot. I thought it might be time for someone like Jack to step in and take over. I needed a strong man to lean on—I needed *him*.

"You're aware of them, but you don't do anything with the money you were left. Hell, you and Kimbrell still drive around in beat-up cars and farm trucks." He moved closer. "That's what *I love* about you most. The simplicity of a complicated woman."

"I'll show you complicated." The smile he'd left on my lips only an hour or so ago needed to be refreshed. I reached for the ready cock because it always seemed eager to participate in bed gymnastics.

"I'm counting on it." He reached for a box on the bedside table and handed it to me. "Open it."

I closed my eyes, knowing what a box this size held for me. I slowly opened it as he moved to the side of the bed and dropped down on one knee.

"Oh, Jack." I smiled down on him. *Oh hell, here we go.*

"I've loved you for a long time now. It's time you did me the honor of becoming my wife."

I wanted to say yes. I probably even needed to say yes, but the truth had a way of haunting me. The man in front of me wasn't at all the man I remembered him being. He wasn't the kind little boy who sat one or two rows in front of me on the big yellow school bus. He wasn't the patient and kind son of a wealthy rancher who walked me home from school. He'd grown into a full, hot-blooded man, who not only drove me crazy but also scared the hell out of me. He was more man than I probably could handle. But I still wanted to try. *Cautiously.*

"I'm only able to stay in this position for a few seconds now. Give a guy a break, will ya? After all, there's a little something-something here rising up to celebrate the occasion." He looked down, and I couldn't help but laugh through the tears already running down my face.

"You're going to say yes. You are." He told me what he wanted to hear.

"I'm going to say yes." I couldn't say no. But the thing was, I wasn't going to march down a wedding aisle until I knew everything there was to know about Jack Dawson. History would not repeat itself, and men like the Dawson men were the kind who came with a lot of secrets. Even Finn and Stan had their share of them. It was in their blood. Their daddy was proof enough.

Jack slid the rock on my hand and naturally, it was divine. A ring meant for a lady. Something I wasn't sure I wanted to be. It made a strong statement. I was a woman who belonged to a man—one man. Sure, I loved Jack. What I knew of him and what I remembered about him. But did I want to *belong to him*? He wasn't going to grant me the time to figure it all out.

His palms rested easily on my knees as he spread me open to him. "You're going to marry me, but you still haven't told me what I really want to hear."

Moist lips began to kiss my leg before his tongue traced my kneecap. A lone finger trailed upward. "I love you, Darlene. Let me take care of you. All I want to do is take care of you."

I nodded, but I wasn't convinced. Men, something I knew from my own father, something I had only recently learned about Jack's dad, were capable of doing a lot of things for love or money. When the two collided, men with ambition would do whatever it took to gain what they wanted most.

The one in front of me wasn't much different. Sure, there was chemistry there. We had a history. But did we have love? We had the lust-thing down pat, but I was smart enough to know desire and passion didn't last. I wanted to know, needed to trust in something long term. I surely didn't know if we could have or already did have, true love. Jack reentered my life like a runaway stagecoach and I wanted to have a little time to let the dust settle and stir again before I made any kind of life changing decision.

My ideal of love would vary from his. I wasn't ready to profess it just because he seemed more than eager to hear it. I also wasn't going to sprint to the marriage bed when I already had everything I needed in the moment.

I thought back to his words. The heated exchange he had with Stan and Finn, his half-brothers. They seemed too willing to move me out of the conversation. It was, after all, a matter among men. The whole Finn-Stan-Jack ordeal was really just a matter of money. I wasn't willing to be in the middle of it. Unless, without a doubt, I was assured love existed there too. I was anything but convinced—at least not yet.

I told him the only thing I knew to pacify him. "I want you to take care of me." I moved farther up the mattress into the soft bedding surrounding us. His lips found their intended mark.

My head fell back as I drew him closer encircling his hips with my own. My hand trembled when I noticed the sensational rock he'd just placed on my finger. "And this seems like the perfect place to start."

THE END

WWW.DESTINYBLAINE.COM

Siren Publishing

Ménage Amour

Destiny Blaine

A MATTER AMONG FOUR

A MATTER AMONG FOUR

DESTINY BLAINE
Copyright © 2009

Prologue

I have to admit. My heart didn't shatter into a zillion pieces as I watched Darlene and Jack flee their wedding reception. I threw handfuls of rice and nearly tripped over Darlene's wedding train, only because I made sure her dress attached to the longest one in Tennessee wedding history. She cursed me under her breath and covered it up with a smile before she landed head first into the awaiting limousine. My foot kind of got away from me and one of those accidentally-on-purpose gestures sealed her fate.

That's my sister. Always lady-like and moving somewhere headfirst. As it happened, she landed in my brother-in-law's lap and he grinned really big before he shut the car door. I imagine he felt indebted to me. After all, I gave her the final shove, more or less.

Darlene never wanted to get married. She never planned to say 'I-do' to anything other than the dirty deed with Finn McClanahan. Then, her long lost love reappeared. Jack Dawson came back in town and stole my sister's heart away in an instant. Some said, he never wanted anything more than a move back to Lewisburg, Tennessee and Darlene on his arm.

Darlene's head appeared from the top of the car. She always loved a sunroof. "Hey! Kimbrell! Catch!"

I saw the small bouquet flying through the air. It looked like the darn thing propelled on a decided path. Somehow I think fate tried to intervene but failed. The silk streamers on the basket flew in the wind and rather than crash to the pavement before it reached me, the small basket kept a good speed and zoomed toward me. The wind showed the bride some favor and carried the flowers across the parking lot. I swear it tumbled right for Darlene's intended target…me.

I tried to back away from the crowd, run from the blasted thing, if you want to know the truth but some idiot behind me pushed me forward and well, the arrangement looked far too pretty to hit the ground. I'm particularly fond of roses, white ones especially, so I grabbed it. Nothing ventured, everything gained and I had a few cowboys waiting for my phone call. Why speculate if it meant anything when three men waited patiently to hear from me.

"Jack says you'll marry before we get back from our honeymoon!" She giggled, disappeared and popped back up again just as fast before the car slowly moved toward the stop sign and away from the church. "Kimbrell! Kimbrell!"

Doggone her, I almost got away and she reappeared like a decoration on top of the sleek, black automobile. She screamed at the top of her lungs. "Jack says to behave yourself!"

Jack says. Jack says squat. He set this whole thing in motion. I forced a smile, and remembered granny on *The Beverly Hillbillies.* I always loved how she waved during the credits on the show. Often Darlene and I did the same thing when we wanted the other one to move on along, like now, as a prime example. I grabbed my wrist with one hand and started waving my hand around wildly and just shooed them off on their merry way.

"Happy Honeymoon, Darlene!"

"Go find you a cowboy, big sister!"

Yeah, speaking of, a few of them were waiting to hear from me.

Chapter 1

The pounding continued with an uninterrupted pulse. I heard it sound off with a deliberate beat of a discontented drum as I reached behind my back and pulled another pillow over my head.

It didn't help and the damn noise continued. Darlene usually grabbed the door, especially bright and early in the morning. My sister typically hit the ground running regardless of the time. This body required a few inches of inspiration, more than seven or eight—anything less rarely proved worth the effort—to motivate these legs to move before high noon.

"Oh shit!" I sat straight up on the squishy, overused mattress, startled by the new day and a definite realization. Hangovers do a lot of things but the last time I checked, they didn't retaliate against the front door. The knocking there didn't subside.

"I'm coming!" I screamed out as I looked around the room.

Two more hard beats clobbered the thick wooden panels. "Damn it to hell, I said I'm coming!" *Shit, right about now, I wish.*

Another knock and then another.

Tossing the sheets back, I jumped up and hobbled around on the cold hardwood flooring as I shook out the denim shorts and more or less tripped into them before grabbing a sweatshirt. By the time I started down the hallway, the wiggling effect paid off and dressed in a great looking Dallas hoodie, my hand hit the cool doorknob.

Darlene and Jack gave me the Cowboys gear before they headed south on their honeymoon. They left it behind as a constant and enduring reminder. I needed to anticipate the arrival of my Texas guests because as expected, even with the damn sweatshirt hanging in my room, I forgot about the appearance of my brother-in-law's friends and my invited guests.

Jack wore around a lopsided smile for a week prior to his wedding anticipating these fellows almost as much as his own honeymoon. It was the only warning he offered, but enough to let me know an underlying motive existed in the arrival of a few cowboys.

After Jack came up with a brilliant plan to have his friends from Texas look out for me while he celebrated his union with my sister, I decided to get to know my future guests.

With technology and all, I felt like I already knew them after months of gabbing on the phone, sending emails and pictures back and forth, as well as a few letters through snail mail. I'd even told one of them—Dallas—a few of my fantasies. We were all good friends by the time they set a date to head my way. Some women might think of us as really tight since we had a chance to develop an odd sort of friendship several months in advance.

A few more powerful thuds fell against the door as I approached. One thing about it, patience and cowboys didn't form any kind of demonstrated bond.

"I said I'm coming! Jeez!" Guests or not, early morning callers should've known to wait patiently at a woman's door.

"Not yet, but I imagine you will be soon." I heard this very sexy reply the second I opened the door and recognized the voice behind it—Dallas.

I took a deep breath and pushed the door wider and there in front of me stood the best looking men I ever saw in my sweet southern life. I swallowed hard and then curled my fist to instinctively rub the leftover sleep from my eyes. Perhaps they weren't as handsome as I first thought. After one blink and then another, sure enough, they projected everything I first pictured, and more. It presented an unavoidable problem too. I didn't know which one to stare at first.

"Hello." I yawned. It was a fake one and far too obvious. I was anything but sleepy or bored now regardless of the time.

"Mornin' sunshine." One of them, the one with the turquoise eyes, extended his arm and more or less just grabbed my hand. He looked ready to snap me around the waist and just lay one on me. I tried to focus on those long eyelashes and his handsome face but there was something far too tempting lingering behind his denim duds. Call it instinct, a gut feeling, or just a woman's right to peruse the one who woke the dead. So help me, I took in the whole man. All the way down to his boots and up again before I dared to speak.

I'd stared at their pictures enough to know. This man, covered in nothing more than pure sex appeal had a name—Rex.

"Uh, yes. Good morning to you too. Awful early this mornin' for you boys." *Awful stupid mentioning it too when a woman is trying to flirt.* I glared at the clock on the wall like it was technology's fault my tongue worked off of a zipline. Six-thirty never looked so good. Who the hell cared about time when the morning callers were this good looking? I narrowed my gaze on the handsome hunks in front of me.

The first one released my hand. "I suppose it is, sweetheart but we couldn't wait to meet you. Kimbrell, I'm Rex." And a southern gentleman no doubt. I sort of expected a pawing hug after months of conversation and written correspondence.

"Your pictures, like I heard, didn't do you justice."

I felt my skin heat immediately. Wow, cowboys like these could talk to me all night or just look at me like they wanted to eat me right up which is how one in particular stared at me now.

Since they'd 'heard about me' from my brother-in-law, I felt confident they received spicy rich details. I continued to rub my eyes because the contact lenses prevented moisture. It was hard to take a good look at a well meaning cowboy with blurred vision.

"I apologize for driving in so early but since we just got into town, we decided to head on out here. You said to stop by anytime." He glanced over at the other two men standing next to him. "You know who these two handsome devils are too, no doubt."

Sure, they were handsome all right and the pictures they'd sent me of themselves didn't do *them* justice. One thing about it, *devils* sure didn't come to mind, more like gods, as in those found in Greek mythology or Lewisburg, Tennessee, for that matter. After all, they now stood on my piece of ground and our small town would never be the same after these three men graced us with their hunktified-beauty. Yeah, they were worthy of makin' up new words to describe them. Sexy never held a truer definition than right now.

Before I stopped to think about it, my hand flew forward in mid-air. Some might say I'm one on those gals who can do all sorts of things with body parts and then claim those limbs in question have a mind of their own. I waited for the next cowboy to properly introduce himself.

"This here is Corbin." Rex politely introduced his brother, the one he should have simply introduced as sex covered in denim thanks to a very obvious bulge in the front.

"Kimbrell, it's finally my pleasure." He tilted his hat and his midnight blues locked in at my chest. Incredulously, he held me in a complete stare and since gawking will lead a man, or a woman, everywhere, I saw no reason to keep my gape in one place. Yeah, I even opened my mouth wide and added the wow-factor, without the sound effects, of course. It was truly too early for those.

I kind of figured these kind gentlemen didn't come calling with good intentions and nothing else. After all, they showed up before an overnight guest would've typically made off like a bandit. I knew better. The proof, and probably the power, stood out in those tight pants, front and center. Shew, every gal dreams of waking up like this in a dead-end town. I was beginning to think the future looked brighter and we were only two-thirds of the way through the more formal how-do-you-dos.

Rex turned to the other one standing on my front porch. "And this is Dallas." Darlene once said he sounded downright orgasmic. I always agreed and every single time we spoke on the phone, I wanted to cup my ear and listen a little closer.

Dallas took my hand and brought it to his thick lips. "Ah, Rex, I think she's already feeling me against her skin. Look at her, she's running around here already marked as mine."

"Oh stop!" *Oh yeah. Stop it.* I didn't want to act all girly-girl now.

"We've talked about this, doll. I'm not a quitter, remember?"

Lord have mercy, I didn't know how sweet seduction sounded until one sentence all but invited me to jump-start a stranger. Not that I hadn't banged a few in my past but I committed myself to a goal and worked on my reputation in anticipation of the Carlisle men. I even tried to live a more sex-free lifestyle.

I wanted to try out the better kind of person, day-to-day normal kind of gig, someone my sister might like to call out as family. The type of woman who didn't lay around on her back all day. Then again, I reminded myself, my sister's new husband did the unthinkable. Jack dressed up temptation and called it cowboys. Then he led me straight to the Carlisles and God love his heart, he gave me three at one time.

Dallas tilted the rim of his hat and then with ease and mischief, he began rubbernecking, I mean there's no other way to put it. His focus fell right to my breasts and oh yeah, I felt him in places a woman wants to feel a man like Dallas. I knew from the moment I talked to him on the phone several months before, he was the one to avoid at all costs because if I had a betting nickel, I'd bet on him and I'd bet on me.

I started to fan myself like a woman with a pint-size hot flash or perhaps just overactive sexual tendencies. The Carlisle boys most likely understood the impact they had on women and I don't think they'd mistakenly believe I was having a woman moment, outside of fighting off female desires. They all stood there in front of me guilty of focusing on every curve. I rested my hand on my hip. I'd practiced the pose a few times.

"Great morning for a drive out here." Dallas smirked. "I prefer a morning ride but hey, can't complain about the views, or the mountains in Tennessee." He licked his lips and stared harder at my breasts.

"Good Lord, keep that up and you may get a closer view," I laughed. 'Course Dallas and I had shared a few good times on the phone late at night. We even almost had phone sex one time. Actually, after I hung up on him, I did have sex...with my vibrator.

Sure enough, Darlene had this one pegged. I felt a climax waiting just from the man's touch. My nipples came alive underneath the scratchy material. I looked down and saw them mark their place and press through the cotton. *Great. Just great.* I pulled my hand away from his because even after his mouth touched my knuckles, his grip didn't relax.

"Why don't you gentlemen come on inside and I'll start some coffee." I opened the door and moved against the wall, crossing my arms over my chest. I don't know why I was suddenly so aware of how I looked. Besides, what woman thinks about a bra in the early morning hours? Half the time, I ran around the ranch without one anyway. There was little cause for confinement since all clothing always found a way to hit the floor when the right man came along. Several regulars, men friends of mine, often came to call and in Lewisburg, none of them looked like these fellas.

Compliments of a great boob job, I didn't have to worry about looking flabby if anyone happened to stop by the place unannounced. Today, though, especially at six-thirty in the morning, I wasn't in the mood to have a man I'd just met face to face, staring at my breasts, let alone three of the sexiest creatures ever born. Actually, under normal circumstances, it wouldn't have presented a problem.

One by one, the handsome Carlisle men passed by me and one pair of eyes after the next, stared down at my arms now folded over beaded, hard nipples. I quickly debated what I should do first, put on the coffee or a bra. Since I figured these cowboys craved a little caffeine, Folgers won out and I imagine it was the only time it trumped Victoria's Secret.

They stood in the middle of my living room as if they wanted me to direct them from there. I pushed the front door back and left the screen behind it open. Cool and crisp, the wind shuffled around the leaves outside and the brisk signs of fall all but tumbled inside. Why not? The three handsome dudes who allowed for the first morning taste of it symbolized a breath of fresh air, one I certainly welcomed.

"Well, if you'd like to follow me into the kitchen, I'll get some breakfast started for you boys." Darlene would've done the same thing and well, since they'd driven all the way from Texas, I imagined they were expecting something for their efforts. Southern folk typically tried to make good on hospitality regardless of the time of day.

I reached into the cabinet and pulled out the coffee. I heard the chairs scoot across the tile floor as the cowboys grabbed their respective seats. Turning, I noticed how they tossed their hats aside almost in time. One thing about it, these boys had someone in their past who brought them up right. Another explicit thought arrived as assuredly as the last. *These kind of men probably didn't screw in their boots.* I quickly turned toward the cabinets to hide a big smile.

"So I take it you've been driving all night?" I questioned over my shoulder as I glanced outside, beyond the kitchen window. There, the three matching Dodge trucks and gooseneck trailers showed off the new gloss and shine. "Nice rigs, by the way."

"We've been driving *all night long*," Dallas said before adding, "Yeah, we like the same things in life—cattle, oil, women..." His voice trailed off and my imagination ran wild. After I reeled it back in a little, I took a deep breath, ignored the snickers behind me and returned my focus to their transportation.

Parked right next to their collective show of wealth, my beat-up truck appeared plumb tacky. Not that I couldn't have one of those fifty-five thousand dollar little jobs too, because I guess money wasn't an object for us. I found out, after Darlene and Jack started tying up loose ends and settling up momma and daddy's estate, money was pretty much a luxury spent at will. Maybe I'd start spending some of it. Nay, probably not, I wasn't the type to go spending money like I had plenty of it. I guess Darlene and I owned a lot of assets and we might keep them awhile if we didn't go around flaunting everything for others to see. Well, actually I tossed around a couple of my own but those were on my person. A woman had the right.

I curiously stared at the large boy toys in front of me taking care to notice their 'Three for One' license plates. Yeah, maybe I'd buy a truck like that sometime. Since the money was sitting there waiting for us to spend it.

Glancing over my shoulder, I checked out the new meat in town and the one closest to me extended his legs. Corbin's erection flexed into a nicely packaged bulge and all sorts of images came to mind. I glared back at the trucks. *Three for one*. What a delicious idea.

Rex joined me at the sink. "I told the guys you'd like our..." he looked over at Corbin and tilted his head before he turned back with a smile. "trucks."

Dallas quickly added. "Your brother-in-law told us, you need some new equipment around here." The other two chuckled at the underlying message in comic relief. "And while we're here, we're going to make sure you have everything you need."

I snapped back to reality realizing he remained somewhat focused on the conversation about their trucks rather than led my perverse fantasies. I cleared my throat and started to speak but I stopped short of saying something dumb.

"You'll want for nothing by the time we're through." Rex winked.

"That's what I'm real worried about."

They all watched me curiously as if they waited for more insight then. See, what I needed and what I wanted often was confused by the men in my life. I certainly didn't need one, two, or even three of them around to help complicate the differences, and I sure didn't want to let them know it all at once.

Dallas spoke up right then. "You can count on it, little lady. It's going to be our pleasure helping you out." He bit down on his lower lip and stared at my chest again. "I imagine you'll find some satisfaction in what we can do here too."

With the suggestive hints I found in the man's eyes, I couldn't stop the tremor in my hand and of all times, I dropped the coffee pot. Shards of glass slid across the floor in bits and pieces as three strong men shuffled around determined to help.

"Damn!" I immediately stooped over the glass and nervously began to pick up the shiny fragments of splintered glass. I tried to make excuses, like a woman has one, much less a few, when she's an outright klutz. "I'm not much of a morning person." Truth be told, I forever remained a night person because of what went on behind closed doors. I was quite fond of those things and beginning to discover, quite good at them too.

I reminded myself of a promise. I told Darlene I'd turn over a new leaf. *Yeah, right. Prior to the arrival of Studs in Duds.*

"Wait!" Rex called out with authority and it shocked me so much that I closed my fist around a handful of the broken pieces.

"Oh shit!" Pain shot through my hand and arm as a stream of blood splattered to the floor.

Corbin knelt down beside me. "Here, let me see your hand." He moved my fingers back and quickly picked the larger glass pieces away. "Do you have bandages and some antiseptic?" He glanced at Dallas with a condescending stare. "Don't pay him any mind. He's harmless."

He added more before he pulled me to my feet. "Well, most of the time." Snickering, his eyes followed mine. The length of Dallas's cock stoutly lay under his jeans and I nearly gulped with realization. The man, by all evidence showing, was enormous in size.

Returning to the blood on hand, I trembled against the pain and entertained the original idea of first aid. "It's in the bathroom." Darlene always said I was helpless to a fault when left in charge. I now kind of possessed a strange feeling the three in front of me were there to baby-sit as much as anything else. "I'll get it."

"I'm beginning to see why your brother-in-law felt so uneasy about leaving you here. Hell, I'm surprised he'd leave a sweet thing like you behind even for a little honeymoon time." Dallas slowly sipped and licked on his lower lip. Oh, he wanted to have some fun with me, no doubt about it.

"Knock it off." Rex looked around the room. "Where's your broom?"

I pointed to a small closet in the corner of the kitchen. Speaking through a woman's embarrassment didn't come easy. "I'll be right back."

"Here, I'll help you." Dallas offered.

"No, you've done enough. Really, trust me on this." I shot him a wry smile. "Leave the mess, I'll clean it up. Just give me a few minutes." I looked from one set of blue eyes into a sea of another. Drowning in baby blues of various shades, I swam forward in a sea of new beginnings on weak knees. I never liked the stench of blood, particularly my own.

In any event, my legs buckled without warning. The floor was unavoidable until six arms quickly snapped around me in some shape, form, or fashion. Rex took control then. "Dallas, grab the broom and I'll help Corbin with her. We know how to come rushing into a gal's mornin' and leave quite an impression, huh?" He peered down at me waiting for an answer, no doubt.

I think I nodded as I studied my bleeding palm. Before I realized it, Corbin scooped me up and cradled me against his large body. He carried me down the hallway. Following Rex, I noticed he kind of glanced in one room or the next before he found the bathroom. Once inside, Rex slammed the toilet seat down and then moved out of the way so Corbin could plop down with me.

The room began to spin. I halfway expected to faint, but then it suddenly occurred to me that Corbin still held me on his lap like a small child. Rex rummaged through my bathroom drawers on a mission for bandages and supplies. He searched in the right, and wrong, place. He wouldn't come up empty handed.

I swallowed back the embarrassment as he placed the tube of lubricant on the vanity followed by a box, a huge annual supply, of condoms. There was more. Yes, the crème of the crop—the mother wand of all vibrators. Rex slowly withdrew it from the drawer where we kept the first aid supplies. All three items remained there on the counter as Rex continued to search.

I shifted on Corbin's lap, uncomfortable as the blood continued to drizzle down my fingertips. This not-so-unfamiliar stranger, who I'd only just met face-to-face, continued to pull out things from my personal space. Most might consider these items as the kind of things men just weren't supposed to see or dig for within minutes of a first introduction.

Rex turned around in the tiny bathroom and grabbed a hand towel from a nearby shelf. "I don't know what I'm thinking." He glanced at the lovely array of a woman's promiscuous supplies and smirked as he turned the water faucet on and stared at his brother.

"I haven't a clue." Corbin shrugged and I just closed my eyes tighter.

"Oh, this is so embarrassing." I finally said. "I don't know which hurts worse, my wounded pride or these blasted cuts."

Rex turned off the faucet and wrung out the excess water before he wrapped the cloth around my hand. "Don't worry about it sweetheart. We never thought of you as innocent after drooling over all of those sexy pictures you sent, never mind finding you there in the doorway this morning in your Daisy Duke-shorts."

Drooling? Did he say drooling? I felt a hot flash coming on. Yeah, the kind of sudden heat a young woman in her prime finds.

"I don't have much company and I never worry about strange and handsome men going through my drawers." I held my breath and hoped he wouldn't notice the compliment, or for that matter—the fib. Plenty good 'ole boys visited my *drawers*. I giggled and they both stared at me.

Rex's lips curled into a deplorable smile. "Really?" He quickly looked over his shoulder and then back at his brother. "With 'drawers' like those I'd almost bet on a lot of company."

We all laughed and Rex applied too much pressure to my palm.

"Ouch!" I didn't mean to scream and I didn't take the time to tell my guest about my revolving bedroom door. In Lewisburg, with lots of satisfied visitors, I felt confident once one or all three of the Carlisles ventured beyond our boundaries, they'd hear enough about my wayward ways to form their own opinions.

"Sorry about that." He apologized for the deliberate squeeze.

Corbin shifted his weight some and I immediately moved because otherwise, his erection would've been right against my backside. He definitely had a rise. I guess the ten-year supply of condoms kind of did the trick or it could've been the size of the dildo because that often gave men a complex, unless of course they had one of comparable size. After he nudged me with his meaty cock, I thought of Corbin as a likely match.

He rippled against my bottom and I swear his body felt like it provided, by blessing of nature, more than any nine-inch dildo supplied. *Surely not.* I gasped with the thought and nudged him with my ass once more, this time acting as if I moved purely on accident. *Think again.*

"I uh…excuse me." I moved over to his thigh.

"Not a problem." Laughter lingered in his voice.

The way he said it caused a significant increase in my pulse. It raced forward and so help me, I wanted to slide over on him once more just so I could offer an apology and get another verbal response.

Rex provided gentle care. Initially, he wrapped the cloth around my hand to stop the bleeding but then he removed it to check for smaller pieces of glass. Sure enough, small little slivers of it broke the skin, just enough to serve as an irritating reminder. He began to pick at them one by one as Corbin held his breath. I didn't feel his soft wind against my neck.

"You don't care for blood either, I take it."

His pale skin gave everything away. "It's fine. I'm enjoying the company."

Corbin's gentle eyes were too pretty to watch. I felt a surge of heat in between my legs. I faced a lot of cold showers straight ahead. Either that or several hot and enjoyable nights. I felt like given my past record and undeniable passion for the opposite sex, the later held more accuracy and far too much appeal.

"Really, I can do this." I said as I continued to observe Rex.

"I'm sure you can but according to my brother here, what any woman can do, he can do better." Corbin whispered in my ear and I felt my nipples perk right up again. Damn, they liked to show off and for some reason whenever men like these two were around, they commanded center stage.

Rex smiled and I swear all of his facial features responded with it. His forehead gave a little bit as his eyebrows rose until gorgeous eyes just danced with mischief. "Knock it off, Corbin. Remember, we came in here unannounced this morning." His nod toward my nipples encouraged Corbin to look around then and the man, who first struck me as quite shy, didn't waste any time remarking on the obvious.

"Are you cold?"

Horny, perhaps, chillingly so, but freezing in the physical sense? "Uh, yes, as a matter of fact, I am." I shivered for a good show of drama. I mean what's a girl to do? I debated the sudden thought.

Maybe the sexual tension wouldn't kick my ass if I tried to flirt it off first. I batted my eyes too.

Rex snatched another large towel from the rack behind him. "Here." He draped it over me and as he did, Corbin shifted right as the towel drifted across my lap, and this time, his dick stayed mashed right against my ass. He wrapped his arms around my middle to let me know I wasn't going to move away this time. He wanted me to feel him pressing against me. I did more than feel. I memorized the ridges pressing through the blue jeans. Yep, damn straight. I'm just a somewhat civilized chick with a double-dirty mind so why deny it?

A quick exchange of glances between the brothers and Rex reached behind him to grab the antiseptic. He used some Q-tips to dab the moisture on the sliced skin.

"Any deeper and I think we would have talked about stitches."

"Is it going to scar?" I asked.

"Maybe a little, not bad. Besides what do you care? It's on the palm of your hand." Rex studied me for a minute. "Does it hurt?"

"Not now."

Corbin held on tighter when I started to pull away from his lap. "I think it's going to be fine." Corbin's arms flexed as he drew my back to his chest. The tip of his nose weaved through my mess of bed-hair. I held my breath and waited. Sure, I had a sleazy reputation around town but I'd never been pursued so fast by a newcomer, much less three of them. I wasn't opposed to it entirely. For several months, my ear stayed glued to the phone or my fingers lingered over the keyboard as I chatted with them. We were comfortable enough with one another on the phone. Darlene argued once that I knew them better than she knew her husband. Since a lot of expressions come through in letters, maybe so.

Rex stared at his brother and shook his head. "All right then." He pulled out a large patch-like bandage and ripped apart the adhesive covering before attaching it to the large area of open cuts. "We've got you fixed up." His lips formed a tight line and he used my knees to push himself away from me. "That one was on me. Next one will cost you." He picked up the tube of lubricant and released a sigh of pent-up sexual frustration. I recognized it. I'd heard it before in plenty of men.

"Corbin, what do you say we let Kimbrell here get some um…clothes on and we'll run out for fast food?"

"Go ahead. I'm afraid she might pass out while we're gone."

Dallas appeared in the doorway then. "If she does, I'll be here to catch her. You two run on out and get some biscuits and gravy. What do you like to eat, Kimbrell?"

"As skinny as she is, I don't think she eats much." Corbin's hips shifted upward and he reluctantly stood, careful to leave me in front of him with his hand catching the towel as he moved.

"I can believe it. Other than coffee, her cupboards are empty. Did you forget three growing boys planned on staying here for the month?" Dallas pulled out an aluminum-tinted wrapper and unfolded it before he popped a piece of gum in his mouth.

"I stocked their place for you." I felt my breath hitch and then run away all at once. I gave speaking another good shot. "I mean, Jack and Darlene's place, um…you're staying over there while you're here. I took the liberty to get some groceries in and stock their bar and such. I think you'll be more comfortable there."

"I don't think so," Dallas started.

"Me either," Corbin added before turning to Rex, "What do you think? Are we staying here or at Dawson's?"

"Depends on a few things, I guess," Rex replied.

"Yeah, I agree." Dallas took the opportunity to start at my ankles and slowly caress my skin with his gaze. If he thought I felt him earlier, he slammed right into me then. Good Lord, with a body like his and a voice to match, the man defined pure hell and danger all wrapped up snug in a pair of tight-fittin' Levis. I couldn't stand to watch him. He looked too damn pretty to be called a man and too hot and rugged to be called out as a woman. Shit. I stared into the face of pure trouble.

Trying to breathe again, I bridled my lust and scoured over his body like an appraiser ready to put a value on sex appeal. He stood there with an arrogant grin to let me know it wasn't the first time he gave a woman the opportunity, or the pleasure.

"Yes indeed, I think where we stay will depend on a few things." Dallas interrupted my body hike. He had the right since his body led the way.

"Like?" Corbin gave the pending conversation a little nudge. All eyes turned to the condoms and my little not-so-private toy.

"I guess it depends on whether Kimbrell here has a man around to keep us away from her." Rex slapped Dallas on the back.

"Do you have a man around here, Kimbrell? Because sweetheart," Dallas stepped closer and I backed up right against Corbin's hard chest where his hands fell comfortably to my waist, "I think it's going to take one hell of a possessive man to keep me away from you when night falls."

Corbin chuckled and moved around me then. "I second that." Rex and Corbin then stepped out of the bathroom and moved by Dallas who allowed enough space for them to slip away. Somehow, he refused the same favor when I started to follow right behind them.

"Not so fast, little lady." He turned his head to shout out a request to his brothers. "Bring Kimbrell a hearty breakfast boys because I have a feeling she knows how to work up a hefty appetite." He lowered his voice. "And food won't be the only thing you crave by the time I get done with the sexy likes of you."

Before I answered, Rex responded. "Yeah, I hear ya back there. You better behave. We have business to discuss and we don't need her panting through it." The slamming of the screen door assured of the obvious. Two Carlisles started out in pursuit of breakfast.

The one brother left behind began a hot pursuit of me.

Dallas and I were alone and since I had *his name* sprawled across the front of my sweatshirt, I couldn't deny that the man excited me on many different levels.

Where the legendary blue Cowboys logo lingered, the evidence of a woman's excitement remained underneath the material and his expectant eyes. Hard and perky reminders of the fact three very different men—brothers—seemed interested in me, throbbed for some individualized attention. My body wasn't opposed to the idea of one or all of them showing me some.

I pointed and my mouth moved. Words didn't spill. Dallas watched my lips as if he planned on waiting for some sort of sweet revelation.

Another attempt followed once I cocked my hip and practiced that come-and-get-me pose. I felt like a show of sassy attitude would bring back the confidence, and once again, I opened my mouth and nothing came out, not one solitary syllable.

He smirked. "Why don't you just give it up?"

"You'd like that, wouldn't you?"

He growled. "You have no idea."

"I bet all the women in Texas do precisely as the Carlisle men tell them."

"It's a safe bet." He shrugged, "A sure thing, really."

"My daddy always said there's no such thing as a sure thing unless it's—"

"Standing right in front of you?" He'd heard the saying too, apparently.

I swallowed back a small dose of fear when I saw the look of lust pouring into the man's eyes. He didn't look me up and down now, but instead, he studied me closely as if he wanted to search for something more significant. "I'm right here. Want me to tell you more about those sure things? I can, you know." He inched closer.

Blue eyes never blinked. I felt really uncomfortable with all of my goodies still spread out on the vanity. With the mirror behind the sink, it looked like I had two of everything so now, as luck would have it, a twenty year supply of condoms were boxed up and waiting for the call to active duty.

"You have pretty eyes." I finally said the first thing I thought of, outside of sex, which pretty much stayed on my mind all the time even without the evidence of it displayed.

"Thank you." His lips twitched and he added more, "I bet we'd have some beautiful children."

"Go ahead. Tell me." I laughed. "I've heard this line before. You aren't the only handsome blond hair, blue-eyed boy I've met."

"Boy, is it?"

"You're the youngest, aren't you?"

"I'm older than you and boy doesn't typically come into a woman's head when they're alone with me."

"Well, I'm sure that's true but..."

He reached out and tugged at my waist but instead of moving me closer to him, he gave me a spin so I faced the mirror before he twirled me again. "Look over your shoulder."

"What?" Instinctively, I glanced down at my butt.

With a growl, carnal in every way, he said, "Yeah, I bet you never tire of looking at that ass but I'm talking about the name on the back right here." His hand smoothed over the area between my shoulder blades and I damn near came on contact.

"Cowboys?"

"Yeah, darlin', cowboys. The kind that ride a worthy mare into the night without any restrictions or guarded rules, carrying plenty of rope just to ensure they tame the wild." His eyes twinkled before they dropped and his fingertip ran back and forth over the collar of my shirt. He continued, "Yeah, that kind of cowboy."

He stepped closer. I felt his breath whip around my face as his peppermint gum cooled the air I wanted to share with him, if only for a second. "And here you thought I meant those other good 'ole boys from the stadium in Dallas. I don't look like T.O., sweetheart but I can assure you of one thing. I'm after every touchdown I can get with you."

I gulped. Men didn't typically scare me. Dallas Carlisle terrified me.

His dimples were fully embedded in his cheeks now. He appeared ready to play and play hard.

"Besides, by the looks of this place, you planned ahead. You have a need for a few Cowboys, don't 'cha Kimbrell? When we walked in here, you wanted to look all sweet and sexy but down deep, there's more than sweet-n-sexy. I'm betting on hot, untamed, and totally saucy.

"As for the so-called line you've heard before, I don't waste my time tossing around meaningless statements. I said, 'I bet we'd have some beautiful children' and I can promise you, I meant it. 'Course there might be a few good reasons I seem to think you're ready for that kind of situation. I'm sure my brothers and me will find out while we're here."

My mouth dropped. I started to let it slide but somehow the point he wanted to make made my womb clench and not in the mothering way, like he implied. "Look here, Dallas—What kind of name is that for a man anyways? Never mind. Just because I have one of the most notorious and promiscuous reputations in the south, doesn't mean I earned it in hopes of one day seeing a farm filled with blue eyed children running around."

His eyes dropped to my breasts and his hands smoothed over my belly. His voice stayed shaded in sexual persuasion. "That's too bad, Kimbrell. See, I know a few fellows who are willing to take a risk and settle down. We all want the same things, the same kind of pleasure, and the same kind of woman who will enjoy what three can give just as eagerly as one."

"You're sick." And I loved the idea of it.

The thought of all three glorious men in my bed sent my knees to knocking and my stomach flipping. I gulped as I squeezed my legs tighter together. "Shit." I exhaled the air I gulped after I realized I released vocal proof the man in front of me got to me, in the worst of ways.

My legs crossed prohibiting the pool of desire from showing through my shorts again. My body responded without my permission and I felt the blush of skin.

Dallas's tongue tapped his lower lip and the moisture glistened from the tip of it, just enough to show oral lust. "What's wrong, Kimbrell? I think you like the sound of three men pounding into that hot little pussy, don't you? I believe it's the very reason you hung up on me the night we started talking on the phone about what kind of fantasies you had. It's the thought of three cowboys isn't it? That's it, isn't it, fancy hips?"

His eyes burned through mine. "You got no right to come into my momma and daddy's house and treat me...talk to me...like some common, whore." I didn't scream, just stated the facts as I saw them before I tried to push by him.

Before I was safely away from him, he took my hand in his and like a warm bolt of static electricity, I felt his grip in places a woman shouldn't feel a man she met only an hour or so earlier. The harder he squeezed my hand, the more I pressed my knees together.

"I bet that little snatch of yours is well trained and built to please. Tight like a fitted sweater," his finger trailed down the middle of my sweatshirt, right between my breasts, "I bet it's seen plenty of action but a woman like you takes care to choose her partners, and I'm betting on safe sex and boring men. Dull entertainment and one quickie here or there. How right am I, Kimbrell?"

I tugged my arm and he held it closer to his warm, hard body. I looked down at the intrusion. It provided an impossible guarantee that between Dallas and his brothers, I would know the fear found in a man's member, the entertainment found in target practice when the loaded guns aimed and fired all at the same time. Oh yeah, I needed to run from Dallas Carlisle and I needed to do it fast.

"I want you to let go." I feared what I might do if he didn't.

He finished his promises, or perceived threats. "Kimbrell, I don't beat around the bush. I don't have the patience to wine and dine a woman properly, though we've all agreed to try. Still, you gotta know where we're headed here. We're taking on a joint venture. My brothers and I feel like the little woman who settles down with us will want to deliver all sorts of bundles seeing as we're ready to supply loads and loads of pure joy."

He tilted my chin and looked into my eyes. Stiffly, I tried to swallow, an act that slowly became as difficult as breathing. I blinked, watched, and waited.

"I can promise you, Texas supplied plenty of women and if I wanted to dish out a bunch of bull-shit lines, I didn't have to drive to Tennessee to do it. We all had a purpose and a goal when we arrived and convincing you to give us a chance won't even present the first challenge. See, I know something more about you than my brothers, Kimbrell. I know who and what you are, something I chose to hide from Rex and Corbin just because after I saw your picture, heard your stories, and craved you from a distance, I decided—not Corbin or Rex—*I decided* you are the one."

The one? I didn't dare ask. I felt like this was a need-to-know basis kind of question. Since I didn't need to know one hour and fifteen minutes after meeting a man what intentions he had toward me, why inquire? *Shew!* I felt swoon-ready anyway.

His lips slanted and so help me I puckered. The kiss he wanted to give, I pretty much accepted prior to delivery. Only, that's just as far as it went. A slight movement from him, just a slow swipe of tongue and my mouth moistened, parted. He only needed to dip a little lower and since we were all alone, I was fairly glad he didn't go for it. Ever so happy, in fact, because I understood certain limitations and frankly, I didn't own a lot of them.

Rather than smooch with me, Dallas surprised me and kissed the top of my forehead before he planted his hands on my shoulders. It was hard to guess who seemed more surprised—me or him.

"I have self control, Kimbrell. Not a lot, but more than you, that's for doggone sure." He shook his head and then made a prediction. "You'll take my brothers to bed before you'll take me because by the time I go there, I want you starved for *it*—and ready for me."

I shivered when the chill started at the base of my neck and slowly ran down the length of my spine. I braced against it but it didn't work. The whole Carlisle situation held mystery. I realized it from the beginning but for some reason, I didn't try to figure it out at once. The truth was, from the moment my sister and Jack Dawson hooked up, I dreaded the day I would be left behind to fend for myself. My sister always ran the ranch and well, truth be told to one's self, I just ran a few good men through the house like all I had to do was stay in bed all day. It provided a few advantages, most of the time.

"Excuse me, I really need to um, well, you know—put something else on."

"No, you don't. We like you just fine like you are." His gaze didn't fall again to my chest but instead to my little zipper-zapper with the mushroom head. He picked it up and studied it real close before he waved it around enough to provide too much comic relief. I took a deep breath in and held it. Suddenly, I was real jealous. After all, my toy didn't move like that for me. My lips formed a tight line and I noticed it when I stared at Dallas through the mirror.

He smirked, showcasing those million dollar dimples again. "What's wrong, Kimbrell? Having a few dirty thoughts?" He patted my behind and then shook the toy again. His mouth went to my ear. "I'm going to use your little friend here to do all sorts of things to your delicious body. Keep him charged and ready to go. I'll make him rev right up for you."

I looked down at the floor and then glanced back up at the mirror. I was beet red now. "Really, I need to get dressed."

"You have on more clothes right now than I'll ever allow later. Trust me. You look just great to me. Short-shorts and a shirt with no bra, heavens to Betsy, cowgirl, you are everything a man wants to find in a woman." He didn't look at me as he spoke but instead studied my toy closer. "Is this yours?"

"Uh…" Now offered the perfect timing to say the dildo belonged to Darlene. Hell, she just got married. He might buy the fact she left it behind.

He moved the divine battery operated gadget underneath his nose and inhaled deeply before choking and really, almost dying from the fumes. "Alcohol?"

I laughed. "I keep it sanitized."

"With rubbing alcohol?" He snickered. "Hell, baby, now I gotta know what you do to your sweet little…" His eyes wandered south and I got the message.

I cleared my throat. "Actually, the last time I had it on the counter, I spilled a whole thing of alcohol over it. I'm a klutz, in case you failed to notice and I guess—"

"So it *is* yours?" he questioned. "I saw your twisted little mind churning earlier. You wanted to blame your sister, didn't you?"

"No, I… I believe I'm old enough to admit that these things here belong to me." My fingertips ran over the box of condoms and then the tube of lubricant. I'm sure if a sex show needed someone for commercials, the way I demonstrated handy little products would have opened doors to career options. I squinted for a second as I thought of those possibilities.

He moved into me and when he did, his cock settled against my pussy at a perfect angle. If I stripped off now, his dick was in perfect position to slide right on in. I tried to shift my weight and move my feet closer together to prevent further manipulation, something he mastered from hello.

"Tell me something, Kimbrell." His tone lowered and his lips did too. He did this crazy little thing with his neck like he resisted a forbidden urge or something. Once more, his lips hovered over mine but he didn't kiss me. Instead, he whispered the sweetest question I'd ever heard. "Are you woman enough to put these things here to good use? If you are, I know three good men who are willing, ready, and anxious to participate next time you decide you need any of these items for a satisfying good time." He slapped my battery operated joystick against his palm a few times and then tossed it back to the counter. "And I'm willing to bet we can teach you more than any toy you'll buy in a store."

* * * *

I leaned my head back and closed my eyes. I moved my hand behind my waist and locked the bedroom door before I slowly moved toward the full-length mirror across from the bed. Crossing my arms in front of my chest, I tugged at the hem of my sweatshirt and slipped it over my neck before my hair caught in the hood. Shaking it free, I held the shirt in front of me and stared at the back. "Property of The Cowboys" stood out in bold letters. I realized Jack Dawson and my sister probably got a pretty good kick out of giving me a sweatshirt that now held a lot of varied meanings. I felt confident my new brother-in-law realized from the get-go what he set in motion when he invited the Carlisle brothers to stay on our ranches.

Dallas was correct. I felt him against my skin the moment he entered my home. The same held true for his brothers. They all grabbed my attention long before simple hand-to-hand introductions.

Thanks to them, I now noticed other things. For starters, my nipples stayed hard, like rounded little tan pearls. I stepped closer to the mirror. They made several good points. I was too skinny, maybe because I drank too much and ate too little. It finally took its toll. I lived like a party girl and, well, if I didn't stop acting like the best celebrations started and stopped with me, soon I'd look my age. I shivered as I glared in the mirror. Thirty loomed.

My hands went to my breasts and I lifted them up as I tilted my head to examine myself closer. I had the boob job Darlene told me a thousand times I didn't need and now I wished I opted for a size bigger. My perfect C teetered along the lines of a D–size with a bra but more like a B without one. "I can't believe I'm doing this now." I stripped off my shorts and then turned around and checked out my ass. "Hmmm..." I slapped the skin to see if it wiggled. "Maybe a little." I realized what I saw may have been imagined. I tried it again and as I did, Dallas's heated words came roaring back to me. He liked my ass and I'd bet every dollar in the bank, he wanted a piece of it. I smacked again. Jiggle-jiggle. I decided it wouldn't hurt to lose a few pounds there. I hated my ass. Men loved it.

I turned back around and ran my hands over my belly. At least I didn't have stretch marks from children or from carrying around extra pounds for any good length of time. I walked over to the dresser and tugged the brass lever to release the lingerie compartment. Selecting a dry thong, since three gorgeous men in boots stirred enough desire to warrant the change out of a damp one. I stepped away from the peach lace and opted for a solid black one to match the low-cut demi bra.

I tossed the two items on the bed and then flopped down. It was too damn early for me to worry over lingerie. My immediate plans did not include strutting around in my underwear so no one would see my thong. Besides, it was plain odd to say the least, to be in dire need of a romp. "That's my problem. I'm a sex addict and completely addicted to cock. No one in their right mind would consider what I'm considering." I narrowed my gaze a little more. "Then again, few women enjoy sex as much as I do." I decided that must account for everything and explain it all well enough. I never said no to men because to speak the word defied what I wanted and I wanted to get laid—practically all the time—particularly now. I had a few good men in mind.

I let out a long sigh of frustration. Any woman crazy enough to talk to herself likely considered fucking all sorts of strange and sexy men. This kind of gal probably considered doing them at one time, something I now contemplated. "I'm not crazy by any stretch of the imagination, only cock-crazed." I studied the mirror again. I needed to move it closer to the bed. I liked being in bed with my lovers and watching as we moved across the mattress. I took a deep breath. "I wondered what it would be like to have three men like the Carlisle men…at one time."

Darlene would kill me. Her damn pussy-whipped husband would likely scold me too because, of course, my reputation needed repair, something those two continued to worry about since the land we all owned now had oil under it. "Well, I guess the oil has always been here and," I sighed, "so has the whore living inside of me." I shrugged and then turned around to retrieve my undergarments. I decided Jack and Darlene only invited the Carlisles to Lewisburg because they realized the men did not come with wife or commitment attachments. They most likely didn't know the men had a sick fascination for sharing. No, Jack wouldn't approve of such behavior, would he?

I started to dress again. "Oh my God." I whispered as I watched the three brothers move away from my window and up the front steps.

"That's it!" I tugged my thong on, the one with the pretty little rose right at my snatch, and then slipped back into the short-shorts that I knew drove every man who saw them completely insane. I stopped right in front of the mirror as a memory slapped me in the face.

I remembered a time when my sister paraded around topless in front of one of my bed partners. Jack's half-brother spent a lot of his free time with me but he stayed more than a little impressed with Darlene's boobs, which is why I decided on breast implants in the first place.

If the boys from Texas were going to act like Peeping Toms, I didn't see any reason not to taunt them more. I cleared my throat and decided to hell with it. I already shared some of my deepest fantasies with Dallas. Corbin and I communicated all sorts of desires in letters and Rex once told me what he liked most in a woman and the way he described it teetered along the lines of explicit.

So what if I had the well known reputation for being quite the seductress. "Why not seduce the willing?" I tossed the bra and shirt I planned to wear on the bed and prissed my ass over to the door and down the hallway.

Quiet conversation and the rattling of bags stopped me before I entered the kitchen. I stood outside the door and listened for a second.

"So help me, Dawson told it about right when he said we wouldn't be disappointed. She's a beautiful woman." It sounded like Rex sort of liked me...a lot. "I think she's kind of embarrassed though. We really shouldn't have spied on her."

"And she really shouldn't eavesdrop either." Before I had time to protest, Dallas clasped my wrist and dragged me with him straight into the middle of the kitchen. Topless, completely bare, I stood in front of them. He made sure I didn't back out on my original plans because he more or less helped me take the final surge forward.

"Damn, sweetheart." Rex's chin dropped and his eyes followed the lead.

"Dawson said this place is short on farm equipment. Apparently, you need some clothes too, huh?" Corbin caught his lower lip under his top teeth. "I'll be sweet damned if you don't have the best boobs this side of the sun."

"She does for sure, gentlemen." Dallas chuckled as he gave one a tight squeeze.

"Let me go!" I tugged my wrist from the closed hand gripping me and immediately covered my chest, wrapping my arms around my breasts, tucking my hands under them in the process. I glared at Dallas and then all of them as a consolidated unit.

Dallas rubbed his chin. "Don't look at me like you despise me. You ran out of your room with a feisty little sway, marched right by the bathroom door and hit the hardwood floor on some sort of mission. So what is it? What's on your mind, Kimbrell? Got something to say or everything to show?"

"What a dare," I quipped.

"Maybe so," Corbin grinned. "He's known for them."

I looked at the three cowboys staring back at me and pointed my finger at them. "You had no business watching me without my knowledge, or my permission."

Rex stood up and walked over to me. "Would you have given us permission, if we'd asked?" I summed him up pretty fast right then and there. The brains behind the Carlisle operations, Rex provided the truest bulls-eye for a quick no-strings romp.

I took a deep breath. "I might have."

"Then I'll ask right now. I want to see 'em." Corbin turned around in the chair and stared at precisely what he meant. "How about it, Rex? Wanna see her close up?"

Rex's skin blushed. "I've been thinking about it for a few hundred miles and I can tell ya, seeing isn't the only thing I've got on my mind." His hand touched my cheek. "But I'm not in any hurry and we have *a whole lot* of business to discuss. Go get dressed, Kimbrell. There's a biscuit and a cup of coffee when you're ready."

His gentle stroke encouraged me to move into his hand instinctively, like a dumb needy broad who wanted a cowboy's arms around her or something. The move of his palm against the side of my face and ear, inevitably guided the caress into a full fledged sexual hold. He gripped a little harder and stepped closer. My lips scraped by his palm and then I turned to leave, dropping my hands from my chest when I did.

"Holy hell." Dallas caught the whole show. He swatted my ass and I liked it, stranger or not. "Now *those*, I would've driven to Tennessee to see."

Corbin quietly turned back to his breakfast. I saw the look on Rex's face and translated it before walking away. The man looked hungry for something but buttered bread probably wasn't going to do the trick this early in the morning.

I slipped back into my room and walked over to the bed and retrieved my shirt and bra. I shoved my arms through the soft straps about the time he knocked.

"Come in," I snapped.

He stepped inside and shut the door. His palms moved over my shoulders and his hands then settled at the base of my neck. "I think I'm going to die if I don't do this so I apologize if it's a little presumptuous."

I swallowed hard as Rex lowered his lips to mine.

"No."

"No?"

"I mean, it's not that word you said—presumptuous—I mean. It's...Well, it's just that I wanted you to do it when you wrapped my hand earlier."

His lips curved and he slanted his mouth over mine. "Then come here and let me do it right."

Hungry for a good taste of what the Carlisle brothers planned to bring to the table, I opened my mouth and let the first one show me how business and pleasure, when appropriately mixed, offered just the right amount of sugar and salt to flavor the right negotiations.

"Hmmm…" His tongue tested for more as he kissed me right into a moan, and once I heard it slip, I knew danger lurked and waited for a full fledged invitation. For me, once a man initiated the moan, it was only a matter of time before the grunts and groans followed screams for more.

Rex's fingertips trailed over my bare flesh and he slipped the material off to the side. His right hand cupped the nape of my neck. "Damn you for being so impatient." He winked.

"I only wanted a kiss."

"Well, one kiss, darlin', is going to lead to this." His mouth moved down my neck and before I could say another word, his lips circled my nipple and suckled cautiously. His teeth lightly, just right really, scraped over the proof—my arousal—as his other hand began to squeeze and release my ass in some kind of sensual massage. It truly set every one of my nerve endings on a red-hot alert. I almost heard bells and whistles. Now if I could only see the flashing danger signs, just anything to stop me.

His hands moved to my sides and he backed up against the bed and sat down pulling me to him. "God, you're so beautiful. I saw the pictures from the engagement party. Jack sent them. But when I saw you this morning, woman, you're everything we thought we'd find and more."

The more is what I worried about and after talking it over with Dallas, I felt fairly certain there were causes for immediate concern. My breath hitched as I replayed another assumptive statement. Something was going on here and I guess the kissing bit needed to wait. "Let's put on the breaks before this goes too far. Um…Maybe you should go eat your Wheaties or something. Give us a chance to cool down and think things over."

"Sounds like an idea…for some, but not for me." He kissed my stomach and his tongue darted back and forth over the waistband of my shorts. "Tell me something sweetheart, why would I want to do that when I can eat right here?"

Oh God! Oh no, he did not just offer that, not that! Now, this man, certainly had mine name scribbled across his forehead. No doubt about it. Even if his brothers proved every bit as sexy and equally as handsome, Rex Carlisle belonged to me on a promise.

"Have you ever had a man eat that sweet little pussy for you? I bet you have but what I'm willing to wager on is that you've never had a cock in your mouth while a man drives you to one orgasm after another with his lips buried inside your tight little snatch." He glanced up before adding more with a truly twisted expression covering his tanned face, "And, Kimbrell, I'm talking buried here. A man's tongue and mouth completely drinking you in while devouring you like the meal you're meant to serve when you're marked as a man's woman."

I felt like something was stuck now in the back of my throat after hearing the intimate commitment to my kind of cause. The thought of cock-in-mouth took its toll because I definitely felt my pussy clench with the mental images Rex provided free of charge.

"I think this is inappropriate, considering we just met and all." Darlene warned me before she left. I had ranch to run. Darlene, or any other woman for that matter, most likely did not manage a multi-million dollar operation on their back. Well, actually, I kind of liked the idea of it now. *The Carlisle men are from good stock.* Darlene's words continued to play out in my head. *Impress them before you undress one of them.* Why not do both?

Rex's kisses landed as rough and centered. The first one at my belly button delivered by a quick tongue visited my innie with an insinuated sex act before he moved his mouth over the area where I felt certain he'd feel the desire even with the denim covering me. "God, you smell so good. I feel that predictable heat of a woman right under my mouth, sweetheart. It's spinning off of you. In fact, I smell sugar, darlin', and I'd love the sweet taste of your hot honey." His tongue swiped the cloth but since I wore tight shorts, I didn't miss the impact of the sudden stroke. "Only one sip and I guarantee your hips rise and fall with your pussy pushing against my tongue. Your cries for more would tug out the best promises I've ever made."

Breathless, I pushed away from him. "You've had your fun. I want you to go now." No, I really didn't. I wanted to strip and spread.

He watched me. "You want me to go?"

"Yes, I do."

"You don't." He chuckled, rubbed his chin and confirmed what I refused to tell him. "You absolutely don't. Trust me. I *know* what you're missing here."

"You still have to go."

"Kimbrell, can I be honest?"

Somehow I managed an answer. "Yes, please, that would be nice." I stepped back and dressed quickly. Rex kept his sharp focus on me.

"I'm real interested in you." His hungry growl certainly insinuated it but the close contact he made seconds before already left that very impression.

"That's nice."

He chuckled. "Come on, baby, is *nice* the best you can do?"

"Your brothers are too."

"Really?" He acted amused as he leaned back on the bed with his elbows bracing him forward. "You don't say."

"You didn't notice?"

"Can't say that I did." Outwardly amused described him now and he didn't seem surprised in the least. My talk with Dallas assured of one thing. The Carlisles fully understood the advantages found in numbers.

"Really?"

Rex eased up off the bed and stalked forward almost immediately. He reached for me and I moved away. "Okay, here's a proposal for you."

"I thought there might be one in you somewhere," I hummed.

"My brothers and I run one of the largest ranches in the country. We are shareholders in some of the most successful companies in the world and we've had it all handed to us on a silver platter, much like you. Still, we're busy. We have a lot of responsibilities and well, to put it bluntly, as individuals, a woman married or committed to any of us, isn't going to find her life fulfilling. However, as a package deal, we have a lot to offer and we'd like for you to consider us, as a package deal."

"You want me to date all of you?" I acted like it was the first time I'd ever heard such a ridiculous suggestion.

"Dating is a start, yes." Rex walked over to me and then touched my cheek. "And after we all get to know one another, I want you in my bed and I damn sure hope you aren't one of these women who like to take things nice and slow."

"In your bed?"

"Yours will work too, since it's closer than mine. Speaking of which, we really need to discuss our business here because, after the drive, I'll probably take a power nap later today. It's a long haul from San Antonio and with any luck, I'm expecting a long night ahead."

"I thought you lived in Dallas." I ignored the insinuation that he'd later join me in my bed for an all-night romp.

"Nope. We're south of Dallas and we're planning a move soon. Who knows, maybe we'll stick around here in Lewisburg."

"Here?" I don't think I sounded overly enthusiastic.

"Sure. Why do you think Darlene and Dawson wanted you to meet up with us? We're considering a move here."

"Uh-huh. Sounds like you've thought of everything. You have a move in mind, a plan in place, and obviously, you've thought some about recreation, never mind procreation." Ewe yuk, I so didn't like that word.

I was the sort of gal the boys took home to Daddy, in case he wanted to take a turn too—not the type to slap around with a warm body in hopes of becoming pregnant. The Carlisle brothers were in my hometown and they'd soon learn all of my dirty little secrets and they'd hear them fast in this town. The locals liked to gossip. A sigh of relief and a thought later, I decided it might be good if they found out everything. Then, they might reconsider blue-eyed babies and long-term commitments.

He licked his lower lip. "Don't worry, after seeing the way you've looked at all of us, you're going to like the idea. Your only problem is the obvious one. Which one of us will you drag off to bed first? I'm hoping you'll play fair and take us all at the same time but, if not, just remember what I told you about pleasuring a woman. I go deep then I settle in and stay awhile."

Chapter 2

The Carlisle boys went straight to work after breakfast. I dressed in jeans and a shirt without showing off too much cleavage, I started out there too. It took some doing, as the old folks say in the south, but I finally located one blouse that was anything but sexy. In fact, I resembled my former elementary school teachers.

As I started out the door, the phone rang. "Hello?"

"Kimbrell, is that you?"

"Yes! Darlene? I'm so glad you called! How's the honeymoon?" I walked as I talked and headed back to the kitchen to stare out at the trucks in my yard.

"It's great. Weather is nice but Jack wanted me to call and see if the Carlisles made it there yet. He's worried about you and how you're going to handle things if they don't get there today."

I released a loud, frustrated sigh. My sister was on her honeymoon and didn't have time to listen to me rant about a few good looking cowboys.

"Kimbrell? You there? Is everything alright?"

"Perfect. Yes, fine. They're here. They arrived this morning."

"Great. I'll let him know. Kimbrell?"

"Yeah?"

"What do you think?"

I pursed my lips. See, my sister and I were anything but real close. Sometimes I thought she resented the responsibility she took on at an early age and the truth of the matter was that if Darlene hadn't stepped in and worked like a man to keep the ranch, we would've been out on our asses as teenagers, right after Momma and Daddy passed away.

"Kimbrell? Come on now. I'm dying to know what you think."

"Don't you have a husband to fuck or a dick to suck or something?"

"Nice." She giggled then. "Actually, that's all I've done for the past few days. Now, I want to know about you and the Carlisle boys. What do you think?"

Right as she asked again, I saw Dallas rush over to his truck for something. He retrieved it and then looked up and tilted his hat with a smirk, realizing I watched him, no doubt. His words came back to me in an instant and I tried to explain to my little sister something she probably already guessed. "The Carlisle *men*, you mean."

"Huh? What are they—old?"

"No. I wish."

"Like 'em, do ya?" She pressed for more.

"I don't know, Darlene. They just got here this morning."

The phone went silent and then she reluctantly asked the dreaded question. "You haven't fucked one of them already, have you?"

"What?" I acted appalled by the inquiry. "Of course not! Darlene, do you think all I care about is sex?"

"Well, since you asked. Yeah, I do."

"I'll have you know that they only arrived here today, as in a few short hours ago and I haven't had the first notion to go to bed with one of them, let alone all three of ..." I stopped twirling my hair around my forefinger and froze before I turned around to face off with one of the handsome Texas cowboys. I knew he was there because the creak in the floor told me he'd crept up on me and now I couldn't quite finish my private conversation.

"Kimbrell? What did you say? I'm dying here. I gotta know what you think."

Corbin walked closer. He tugged at the work gloves and pulled them from his fingers one by one, casually tossing the pair to the table as he stalked forward.

"Uh, I…uh, I um…have to go." I watched his midnight blue eyes turn darker by the second.

"Wait! Don't hang up. There's something I need to tell you about the Carlisles and it's important. Jack didn't tell me until—"

"You'll have to tell me later."

"No! This can't wait!"

I disconnected the call. Darlene worried too much and if it really couldn't wait, she would call back. Right now, I had a 9-1-1 stare that really needed my undivided attention.

"You haven't had the first notion, huh?" His lips instantly curved into hard proof. Sure enough, he heard enough to take my proclamation as a challenge.

I swallowed. "We just met, after all."

Corbin reached for me and I started to stop him but if I had, stopped him that is, then it would've been like approving one brother and turning down another. I felt confident that Rex already explained to the other two what took place in my room. Now, if I wanted to remain impartial, and I did, taking Corbin up on his advances seemed like a must-do.

My right hand settled on his chest but my left lingered at his waist and how that happened was up for a little guessing. It must've been a go-ahead sign or something.

His teeth nipped at my lower lip. "Never had the first desire to go to bed with one or all of us, huh?" His tongue swiped at the spots his teeth might have missed. "A woman like you certainly has a lot better things to do than to think about sex, right, Kimbrell?"

I swallowed hard. If I'd been in doubt before, there wasn't any reason to second guess things now. My brother-in-law, the love of my sister's life, had described my reputation to these three and they knew exactly what they were headed for when they drove east to Tennessee.

Of course, some of the letters I exchanged with all of them bordered on the side of provocative.

"I..."

"You..." His hips moved and he pressed that divine cock of his, the one I'd already sat on earlier, right between my thighs.

"I think you and your brothers are lookin' for a little more than land and oil here."

"Do you?"

"I do."

"Really?"

"Yes."

"What else will you *do*, Kimbrell?"

"I don't understand."

He ignored me and my confusion. His lips possessed mine for a brief moment, just long enough for his kiss to linger there but not long enough for the fire of a lust-filled storm to sweep me under the man's spell.

From under hooded eyes, he asked me again, this time more direct, with a lot more sex appeal. "I want to know what a woman like you will do and can do with one or two cowboys like me."

"You'd like to know?" I whispered.

"Yeah, answer me."

"If you have to ask then I can tell you something for sure, you'll have the best time of all."

His lips curved up again, this time with recognition. "Rex got to you then. You know."

"You aren't just here on a favor to Jack Dawson. You're here for more than farm duty." I stepped away from his touch. "It was pretty obvious when all three of you came in here this morning wearing more than a smile. You're here for more than just business." I stared at his pressing problem, the hard-on I couldn't wait to see up close.

"You're right." He cupped his hands behind my neck and kissed me again. This time, a slow and easy tongue drifted between soft and gentle lips. He gave me one of the all-time best kisses I've ever had the pleasure of receiving.

His tongue uncurled inside of my mouth and in a stretch of effort, captured mine in a slow dance of entanglement. He gave some. I gave some. We both took it all and continued giving and taking the lead until he pulled away.

"Now." He closed his eyes and kissed the tip of my nose. "Now, I can get back out there and start working."

Now? Right this second? Heaven help me, I needed a cloud, just anything to float around on drifting from one cowboy to the next.

My hands gripped the countertop. I gripped the Formica top while my fingertips barely touched the stainless steel sink. I tried to catch my breath but as a gal who had been kissed straight through a short lifetime, it was pretty difficult to do. Harder still, I couldn't imagine a man walking away after a kiss like Corbin and I shared.

His knuckles scraped over my cheek. "Little lady, I'm going to fall in love with you while I'm here. You can count on it."

"You're going to what?" I'm sure my mouth fell open and I was so surprised that I never saw Dallas until he was almost standing right beside of Corbin.

"Don't scare her off, Corb. What's wrong with you, anyway?" He shot his brother a disapproving glare.

"He...I..." Shit, I don't know why I bothered. I didn't have anything to say and besides, he expected his brother to answer, not me.

"I kind of take your speech away, huh?" Dallas grinned.

"Yeah, I'm sure you want to believe it. After all, I'm sending out those flares. Glad you're around to respond appropriately." I rolled my eyes.

Corbin rubbed his lower lip with his thumb. "I guess I'll leave you for Dallas." He winked and then turned away.

I stopped him when I reached for his forearm. "Don't go." My voice hitched in my throat and instant regret washed over me. I feared being alone with Dallas and now they both realized it.

Dallas focused on his brother and Corbin's grin held a hint of mockery as he looked at both of us.

Dallas's lips twitched. "She's afraid to be alone with me. Mainly because while I've already explained to her that she'll wear the Carlisle brand, she's afraid I'll be the first to see her sear." He patted my hip and then stroked. "You should run, darlin', because right now, everywhere I look, I see me and you going at it."

"You have very vivid fantasies, I take it." I creamed thinking about them too. Many of them he knew all about. We'd talked about some of them too. I guess he probably thought my daydreams already included him and sure enough, they did.

His hooded eyes were as daring as his decisive nod. "Up against that back wall, splayed on the table there before breakfast with the smell of coffee hanging in the air, right here on this counter…" he patted it and continued, "and most importantly, buried tight between those shapely thighs—my dick, fingers, mouth."

I immediately felt of my cheeks. "Do you boys always talk like this around women because if you do, it may be the very reason why all three of you lack one!"

Corbin gave me a lopsided smile. "Oh I don't know. You like it. Others do too they just don't always admit it."

I struggled with what I wanted to say now because I didn't want to appear desperate to hear more, but I was, and apparently there was only one way to avoid Dallas and all of the sinful little exercises. I tilted my head toward Corbin. "I just…"

I wanted another kiss but how did a woman ask for a smooch when she didn't know how to describe it. I didn't think it was a mere meeting of mouths anyway. It seemed more like a meeting of hearts and souls entwined by something stronger than the sturdiest of ropes. When a woman hasn't had a man profess love or even the possibility of it, she tends to hold on to it. I grabbed on for dear life. And then there was the idea of that kiss—the best damn kiss a man had to give. I didn't want to forfeit another one because of an interruption.

He read my mind. "Kiss me, Kimbrell." Corbin's hungry voice sounded urgent, and demanding. He stepped closer but he didn't lay one finger on me.

"I...um, I can't right now." I turned toward Dallas and the hard evidence of an excited man pressed forward and threatened to pop a zipper from the denim jeans, along with every thread stitched across the front. Obviously, Dallas enjoyed his brother's theatrics, if that's what they called this charade. Then again, he proclaimed enough carnality to have all of us in a fine state of arousal.

Corbin cocked his head a little to the left. "Your loss."

You're tellin' me. I knew all about it. My loss, for sure.

"Do you know what I could do with your hot little mouth?" Corbin's eyes fell to my lips.

I do. I nodded. "I can imagine." *And crave.*

"No, I don't think you can." Corbin's mouth eased back over mine. He reclaimed his earlier position, with heart-shaped lips quickly twisting into a devastating smile, one that easily punished me for refusal. "But I swear to you, I'll dream about it until I show you."

His hot breath lingered behind his words, his poetic oath, an intimate lover's promise—and I lost it.

My knees mushed together like jelly and my lower back braced against the hard, rounded edge of the counter-top. "Screw it." I glanced over at Dallas and then hooked my fingers through two belt-loops. Before I had the chance to take control, his body slammed against mine and his piercing kiss and ready body only emphasized the lust lingering there.

"Promise?" His body began to slowly grind against mine.

"Huh?" In a daze, I played dumb. It came easy, almost like a natural reaction.

"You said, 'screw it' and what I'd like to know is if I can count on it today." He kissed me hard on the lips and then withdrew. "If so," his fingertips ran over the shape of my mouth, "then I want to know when and where because I don't want to be the brother left out in the cold when you decide to give it up for the main event. You understand this, right?" He kissed me again and then moved out of the way so Dallas could take his place, and maybe even his turn too.

I felt a peculiar emotional attachment to Corbin and I realized it even with the quick replacement Dallas offered. There was something about Corbin's gentle, but dominant kiss, his touch, his eyes, the whole package, really. I wanted him.

Rougher around the edges, Dallas wasn't without his symbolic attributes, one tented high enough to catch my wandering eye. It was every bit as inviting as Corbin's enticing kiss. These Carlisle men were here to change my life and one thing seemed certain. They didn't believe in wasting time, and I didn't possess enough self-control to withstand them.

Corbin sat down at the table and watched. "What do you think about her, Dallas?" They discussed me as if I didn't exist there in the same room with them. "She's built like a woman meant for lovin' three cowboys, isn't she?" Then they started eyeing me like I was the prettiest little filly to go on sale at auction. I shivered with the thought. I'd prance around for them any day of the week.

"That she is." Dallas lowered his head. "She looks pretty enough to fuck and smells good enough to eat." He licked his lower lip.

I turned to cream. Pudding and cream or maybe a soaking wet dishrag waiting on a good wringing. If it was the latter, then I wanted to choose, the right to choose one over the others for the first experience.

"Corbin?" I looked over Dallas's shoulder and Dallas jerked his head in a quick rotation as if to motion for him.

"Come over here, Kimbrell." He reached for me and I slid away from Dallas.

"I'll be damned." A cross between a snicker and a snort fell from Dallas's lips. "So you prefer the quiet types?" I declare, the man looked jealous, kind of cute considering the bold and straightforward conversation we shared hours before.

I teased as his earlier words came rushing back. "You'll take my brothers to bed before you'll take me because by the time I go there, I want you starved for *it*." I purred his statement with a flip of tongue. "What do you think, Dallas? Do I look like a woman who has too many lonely nights?"

A few seconds later, I allowed what I imagined was a truly despicable grin to form across my mouth. "Assuming I might have been coming out of or going into what you good 'ole southern boys consider a dry spell, I have to say I'm shocked a man like you wouldn't jump to the front of the line." My eyes narrowed and I waited. Darlene told me long before she left, the one most interested in me, the one who asked the most questions by far was the one who owned the sexiest voice we'd ever heard come across the telephone lines. Dallas was also the kind of man who would abuse a woman's body with his thick cock. Yeah, I shivered against the thought and glanced down for affirmation. It hung down his leg and I wanted to press on it just to feel it while it waited, imprisoned by the denim he wore. God help me, if it sprang free before I prepared myself to see it!

With a sudden scowl, Dallas barked, "Careful, Kimbrell, I've been known to change my mind when I'm provoked. Do you think you know how to handle a real man when he's ready to explode into a tight little cave with the roughest, rawest sex he can deliver?" He stroked the front of his pants. "What do you say we find out?"

Oh yeah, I'd had that kind of sex. Even if it was only once or twice, the puddle forming between my legs reminded me quickly how much I liked it too. I realized my face gave everything away as I looked down at Dallas's cock pressing harder and harder against his pants.

"Don't push me for it yet, Kimbrell. Let's get to know one another, okay?" He read my mind. "See, I know if you get a hold of me first, you'll be too sore for the others." He winked.

"Cocky, aren't you?"

"He is," Corbin agreed. "And a little honest."

Ouch! That had to hurt a man's pride. She let it pass.

So Dallas's act of restraint was some sort of generosity ploy. Yeah, right. Most men thought they possessed some sort of gigantic cock large enough to swing one way and please a woman while everyone stood to the other side in pure amazement. Dallas was one of *those* men. Grief, just what I needed. I rolled those blasted eyes of mine again before I thought.

"No promises, remember?" I recognized without a doubt that the dark side of the Carlisles, if one existed there, only lived within Dallas Carlisle. He was the brooding animal, the truest beat of the carnal heart possessed by all three brothers.

Corbin's dark eyes focused on his brother again. He actually appeared a little concerned when he heard Dallas threaten. I saw him wince once before he patted his leg. "Sit down here and tell me all about those lonely nights you don't have." His eyes flickered with knowledge and then concern. "Dallas likes it rough, scores of clubs are under his belt, memberships to the underground of BDSM clubs no one in their right mind would frequent."

"Is it true?"

"Wanna go?"

"Yeah, wait for me by the truck. I'll see you there." I huffed.

Both men chuckled and Dallas said, "We'll see you tied up yet."

Corbin nuzzled my hair. God, how I loved it when he inhaled me. It sent tingles, a powerful surge of electricity through my body. "Do you really understand what we want from you, Kimbrell?" His words were planted under my ear and then sealed with a kiss, sloppy and wet before he licked the same places his lips deserted. The electric charges surged through my body, up and down my spine.

"She ought to know." Dallas stood in front of me and at the same time, Corbin shifted my weight and moved his legs closer. I ended up sitting on his heavy cock again. Somehow, I understood if all four of us ended up in bed, Corbin's cock would have first dibs on my backside.

"Do you, Kimbrell?" His hand began to caress my shoulders. "Tell me, tell us."

Dallas's forefinger tilted my chin and he held me in his trance. "I hear Rex had a kiss earlier and I saw the two of you with my own eyes. It's my turn now."

He didn't seem to mind going last. He'd already predicted, perhaps even determined, his place in line.

Dallas's kiss wasn't anything close to Corbin's. His mouth hovered and his tongue dipped. His lips parted once or twice and then they snapped closed a few times to stop and delay a heavier pursuit. He left me hungry one minute and sated the next. I lost my lips in his just as I'd been lost in Rex's earlier but Corbin's left the deeper impression. The man knew how to kiss a woman and make her completely his. Dallas's kiss just left me completely wet and damn near desperate for a man's touch. My legs even parted.

His gaze fell to the obvious. "Ah, so you already want it, don't you?"

Hell yeah, I wanted it but the thought of him, seducing me with words and kisses and not touching me in the process just about inspired other thoughts too. I wanted to kick the man out on his solid, never mind great looking, ass.

It shocked me when Dallas's manly palms fell to my cheeks and he began a more thorough assault on my lips and tongue. "What do you like from your men, Kimbrell?" He searched my eyes for answers then kissed again. He didn't wait for a reply.

Why did he have to say *men*? Didn't he know how to keep a secret? Was it so important to bring up the past right now? Even if it was understood that he knew about mine, why imply it now? The

Carlisle men profoundly confused me, specifically Dallas. If he wanted to act the part of a gentleman, he could've asked me what I looked for in a *man*, as if to imply I'd only had one man to ever visit my bed. I got plumb tickled with that one considering my history.

As I kissed him then, I understood more than before. One woman couldn't have thought about the possibilities found in the Carlisle men if she was untouched. Maybe they knew it when they sought me out and I was beginning to think I was part of a some sort of deal my brother-in-law made with these sexual creatures.

I felt Corbin's hands on my bare stomach before I realized he'd lifted my shirt. Between moaning helplessly against Dallas's lips and moving into Corbin's palms, I kind of figured these two cowboys were ridged with enough lust to wrap themselves, maybe even their cocks, all the way around Lewisburg and maybe even back again. Before they did, I hoped to try one out for a long, slow ride.

Corbin's touch turned wicked. He inched closer and closer to my breasts and soon, his hands cupped over them in a sensual massage, an appreciative caress. Over the lace, his palms rubbed at my nipples before he whispered quietly and directly into my ear. The whispers I wanted to hear weren't easily translated for the kiss Dallas continued to claim.

Dallas's hands framed my face only tighter now and his mouth became more demanding, far more deliberate in a search for returned desire.

Corbin's fingertips scraped under the scant material of the demi-style selection. I reacted to the pleasure of having my nipples tweaked and they throbbed with acceptance.

Dallas drew me closer once more for a tighter embrace and a deeper kiss before he released me altogether for an observation. "Oh, she likes whatever you're doing under that shirt."

I bit down on my lip but it happened a second too late. A satisfied woman tends to do all sorts of things when she's pleased but one fighting off desires and pending diversions makes a lot of noise, and a groan, maybe half-laced with a grumble, slipped. When it did, it left me at their mercy.

Corbin's left hand pressed against my breast and his right fingertips rolled my hardened nub. He placed hot kisses against my neck and shoulder even though the shirt prevented full access of skin to mouth contact. "Ah yeah, that's right, let me work you into more need than you'll ever understand." His sweet breath traveled, then lingered, everywhere and I do mean everywhere.

The kisses from Dallas were hotter by the second with hard-spun interest and unstoppable passion as he kissed me better than before, sweet one second and sex driven the next. He caught my hand and quickly moved it to his cock.

I withdrew and he smiled. "No? Not yet?" He touched my face then and I saw the disappointment but didn't regret it. No, I promised Darlene to run things and so far, I proved I wasn't a manager of much. I couldn't control my own body much less seven hundred head of cattle and a working ranch. If I started fucking the help, as history would show as the norm, then the Carlisles might go back to Texas sooner than they needed to go.

"Kimbrell, I want to see you suck his cock," Corbin whispered in my ear as if he thought I'd do just about anything he suggested. My heart slammed against my chest with an uneven beat of defiance. I was ready to do just about anything but then he asked for one of the more personal acts performed. I choked on the idea only because it was followed by a little voice inside my head—thankfully, it overpowered the one in my ear—and I remembered while I'd chatted it up for several months with these guys, I'd only just met them.

My chest was tight. I tried to move away from him and his hands slid down my sides before he quickly pressed against my bottom once, maybe twice, and then God help me we were dry humping as he talked to me.

A dimple formed in Dallas's cheek. "Careful, Corbin, she's gonna beg you before you're finished if you don't watch it."

"I don't see a problem with that, do you, Kimbrell?"

"I...I...yes, yes...I do have a problem with it." I stopped moving my hips, by some will I never possessed in my life, so I'm not sure where I found it. Corbin mastered the art of seduction. He was the one I'd never guessed at taking the lead. Boy, did he fool me.

His shaft worked against the thin layer of denim and he held onto me with pure wicked intent. One minute he dragged me back and forth across his length and the next, he forced impeccable posture, for his benefit more than mine. Soon, he added another position too, one that ensured I felt all he had to give in a real nice body bump held outside the realm of intimacy by clothing barriers alone. He angled me forward then swiftly moved me back again and again. In short, we fucked with our clothes on.

"Kimbrell?" He reached around me, seriousness lay thick in his voice. Dallas stepped back. He held my chin with his forefinger and thumb. His middle finger stroked under my chin. "I have to ask you something."

It seemed like a good time to run for cover. Smarter than most gals with a reputation, I should have ran straight for the bed because at this rate, Corbin and I were going to be busy under a lot of tangled sheets. The moisture heating between my thighs offered the first of many clues. The way he looked at me provided another and then he kissed me again. After the intense smooching, I didn't need any other sign of things to come. My body fed off of them. His only guaranteed there were lots of possibilities looming.

* * * *

I don't know when Dallas left us alone. I imagine he believed Corbin had me right where he wanted me and since he seemed to mess up the ebb and flow of things, he vanished. I hated it and then again, I didn't.

Corbin kissed me into a senseless state of arousal and he took plenty of pleasure in doing it. His hand settled on my knees. I squeezed them closed, realizing I'd opened up for Dallas and my gesture proved I invited all unpardonable acts.

I wasn't born into this world a slut. I developed the trait over time and because of the experience gained through cowboys like Corbin, I wasn't completely naïve and yeah, sometimes playing hard to get held plenty of advantages for both parties.

His arm draped across my legs and he moved me forward before shifting upward. In an instant, we were on our feet. One of us—me, actually—didn't stand long. Corbin liked to haul me around. It wasn't a decision I reached immediately because I was actually in awe of our new position.

I faced him. His hands cupped underneath my bottom and my legs draped over his sides until he moved them into a locked position behind his back, or at least, I think he did. It was kind of hard to assume who moved what and when it happened since he didn't stop kissing me once he melded against my body.

Slowly, he carried me down the hallway. Right outside my bedroom, he stopped. He pressed my back against the wall and parted my lips more with his hearty kiss. No doubt about it, this cowboy accomplished what he wanted in a small window of opportunity. Corbin Carlisle was a man who recognized second chances only came twice if the quality of a first encounter warranted a repeat performance. He challenged those who stood in his way once he became certain of the end results. His quiet demeanor was an act of confidence more than someone who held himself in reserve. I recognized it too late. I couldn't help but wonder if I didn't fall into a well laid trap.

His body moved easily with mine. With trained fingertips and a soft hand, he swiped away the fallen hair from my brow. Then, he gripped my hips—mainly because positioning is everything—and began some of the sweetest grinding motions I'd ever experienced without moving straight into the throes of insatiable passion, of which I was certain he knew how to instigate without a lot of coaxing.

"I gotta ask you something, sweet lady." His lips temporarily vacated mine and his hot breath lingered across my cheek.

I shook my head, ridiculous no doubt, but it moved by itself. I didn't want to take responsibility for my actions but I had a feeling this Carlisle wasn't going to let me escape it. If he took me to bed, he'd do it without leaving me the option of later crying foul. Apparently, there was too much to risk and with the bar raised, the stakes flew higher than anyone dared admit.

A few beads of sweat covered his forehead and maybe even matched mine. "I want to know what happens in there. Are you going to let me feel your hot little body spread over me like warm honey butter?"

His mouth and teeth worked on me then. He waited. He pushed and pressed his dancing dick, and that's what it did—danced—thick and firm against my clothing.

I wanted to say no, but sometimes, no means yes and yes means no, or at least it did for me. I was one of 'those' women when it came to sex and even sexier cowboys. Apparently, those I only met hours before pulled an even greater effect.

"Tell me now because I walk in there," he moved his head toward my room, "and all bets are off. You're mine then and I'll make sure to keep you there from the time the sun sets and maybe even rises again."

He kept me grating against the wall with mindless lower body caresses until his hand moved from my ass to my inner thigh. A whimper left my lungs. "No…can't…not…" Speaking in codes, translation unknown, served the purpose. It delayed decisions and perhaps even quiet submission.

"Can't or won't, honey?"

His hand roughly rubbed against my denim-covered crotch, warm from desire and heat. "Tell me what you can't do, what you're willing to miss, if you miss out on this."

He released me then and allowed my body to slide against his. His hands cuffed my wrists high above my head and he looked deeply and directly into my eyes. "Tell me no, and that's the way it is. We've got time. I'm not going anywhere regardless. Tell me yes and you don't get to change your mind in there, because I'll convince you to try things even you don't know you're capable of doing."

I nodded.

"Is that a yes?"

Footsteps approached us. Two sets of them.

Rex cleared his throat. "It sure looks that way. Hell, little brother, if you're not up for it, then I can step in for you." He moved his hand to his belt and my admiration, along with my longing stare, followed too.

I decided right then. All Carlisles came equipped with long, loaded rifles, forget the guns. I was betting on rapid firing and a quick draw when the right woman encouraged them. I planned to learn what they wanted in their kind of woman.

Chapter 3

I tried to read Rex's expression and it proved easy enough. I wanted to see if he looked disappointed since his brother skipped a few steps ahead of him, if they were competing or wagering on who landed in my bed first.

Corbin mashed against my palm reminding me of a precious fact. He was waiting and willing… and by God, he was horny. By the expression on the men's faces staring back at us, they weren't lacking in desire.

"I don't think either of you will believe this," I stammered, "but I really don't know how my hand got there, I mean here." My palm, after all, still covered and stroked, Corbin's dick, something he provoked well as his fingers guided my wrist.

All three brothers stared at me while my hand spread over one, eyes caressed the other and my mind—God, my mind—did wonderful things to Dallas in three quarters time.

"You're not moving it." Corbin chuckled as he applied a little pressure to my forearm to further drive home a very good point made. Together, we fondled his thickness. My mouth watered one minute, dried right up the next.

Rex nudged his brother. "Dallas, what do you say we wait on Corbin and Kimbrell in the kitchen?"

"Good idea." Corbin growled but he didn't release me. His fingers continued to weave through and with mine as a gentle up and down maneuver turned rough in a hurry. His body responded favorably as the size of his cock pressed, into the grip I controlled as much as Corbin.

After his brothers turned their backs, Corbin pushed against my bedroom door and it gave way without much effort. He kicked it back and then questioned me. "What do you say we make my brothers jealous?"

"I don't think so, Corbin. I'm really not that kind of—"

"Oh but I think you are, Kimbrell. I think you're exactly the kind of woman we want and need." His lips smacked and he made sure he did it twice before his mouth brushed against mine. He moved us to the interior wall and closed the door. His hand went to his shirt and he unbuttoned it. I know I must've looked half confused and partly amused.

It only took a sensible second to decide that I wasn't going to do him or his brothers on day number one, or at least, I hoped for enough resistance. I held up my finger and then touched his lips. "Shh…you forgot something, didn't you?" I purred as seductively as I knew how. I typically earned my way with men because most of them gave it to me with a wide grin.

After he licked his lips, he tried to hush me with a kiss but I moved by him quickly. If we're going to play, I have to bring my toys too.

Okay, so I forgot the man in front of me wasn't like every man who strolled onto our farm. This one, actually all of the Carlisle men, were different and they probably wouldn't fall for every bullshit line I gave them. I moved by him and took the time to press into his dick, hoping to give him something more to think about.

He cupped my neck. I pulled back. "Oh no you don't. Your kisses are lethal."

"Oh yeah, I do." His lips crashed over mine and second thoughts began to creep in and change my mind. I wanted Corbin pretty damn bad but I also realized if I had one Carlisle in my bed, I'd have them all. I needed a few answers before anything like *that* happened.

"I'm easy," I confessed. Why I felt the need to tell him the obvious was the trillion dollar question.

"I know." His hands squeezed my ass and he lifted me up and down against the ridge of his cock. Damn I just wanted to feel it in the flesh, once—just once.

He lifted my shirt and started to push it over my head but I resisted. "I can't do this." I pulled away and nearly fled to the other side of the room.

Corbin's hand propelled across the front of his pants. It was something I enjoyed watching when I planned to fuck a man right out of his obvious pain and need. Right now, it disturbed me to think I left a man hungry for more because I didn't plan to take care of his growing problem anytime soon.

Biting my lip and probably my tongue and jaw, I started by him. He stopped me long enough to reclaim my mouth with a nibbling kiss. "You can walk now but it's only a matter of hours and minutes until I have you in my bed and so help me once you're there, you'll never want to leave."

"Your brothers seem to think the same thing," I quipped.

"Yeah?" He kissed me with more tongue than lips.

"Oh, yeah." I sounded convinced.

"Kimbrell, that's just one of the reasons why I'm sure you won't leave. Three on one kind of reduces your odds of walking away once we take you to bed. In fact, when you finally leave it, you'll crawl away with a tender reminder we've been in between those soft, sexy legs."

I nodded in acceptance. Why deny what anyone could see? Even before these three cowboys walked into my life, my body tirelessly anticipated the inevitable. I spent hours on the phone with each of them. They weren't exactly strangers, not really. I knew all about them and what I didn't know, I felt comfortable enough around them to ask. With the exception of Dallas, of course. I just couldn't look at him without wanting to fuck him.

I spent the better part of the last three months with my vibrator in one hand and a trashy novel in the other whispering at least one of their names as I zapped from one orgasm straight into the next. Sometimes, when I felt real saucy, I'd say them all at the same time. Since I started this long distance relationship of sorts, I changed. In some ways, they were so kind to me that they left me ruined for any other man long before they showed up in Lewisburg. Truth told, I feared what might happen if they took me to bed. Lord have mercy if they took me there and left me. Could I survive it?

Now, as luck had it, whenever I stepped close to any of them, my perverse mind pictured arms and legs entwined in the most pleasurable positions. Going to bed with them wasn't an if-matter, just a when-matter.

He tugged my hand and then opened the door, pulling me behind him as he walked. "Let them explain the rules of this game. I have a feeling you'll find it easier to win if you understand the terms and conditions."

We stumbled into the living room and Corbin stopped in front of the sofa. "Somehow I think Kimbrell still may have a few questions." He shot Rex a smirk and then nodded toward Dallas.

"What's on your mind, little woman?" Dallas studied me closer than he had before. "Come here and tell Dallas what you think we can do to help."

Okay, the 'come here and tell me' was starting to grate on my nerves. Still, his request fell from a sexy mouth with a raspy tone and I'd never forget the way he made me feel when I heard him use it with thick implications and the right enunciation.

The explicit tone, the illicit underlying meanings, and the way his chosen words flipped off a truly divine tongue would ring out through the night. In fact, when my little zipper-zapper came out to play later, I had a feeling the voice I'd hear somewhere in the distance would most certainly sound like Dallas Carlisle.

Darlene and I didn't do the man justice when we chatted it up about how he sounded on the phone. The man had a sexy voice—one

I'd love to hear whispering in my ear as I fell asleep at night—maybe even *tonight*. I pushed the thought out of mind, immediately.

Rex stood off to the side. I kept thinking to myself that he acted like the head of the family, the more sensible one, the one in control. So far, he explained things better than his brothers. He'd already offered a few explanations but I had a lot of questions, too many to ask when I was saturated with desire and completely in awe of at least one cowboy. The one responsible party moved away from me and Dallas took my hands.

"So Corbin couldn't keep his damn hands to himself and now you've got more questions, huh?"

"She knows what we want from her. She's woman enough—from what I can tell—to figure out the rest," Rex said.

"I take it you guys have done this before?"

Rex nodded. "We had one or two in mind before you. It didn't work out."

"Corbin didn't like the first one." Dallas watched me with downright hungry eyes. The eye thing, the way these guys stared at a woman—me—had to run in the family.

"Thank goodness Corbin spoke up when he did. She sucked in the sack." Dallas laughed and the other two shot him a you-can-shut-up-now glare.

"Or the second one," he gave me a lingering stare, a seal of approval in some ways, "I didn't like the second one either."

"We met her on a blind date through a dating service. None of us enjoyed her and she refused to take the time to get to know us, like you did. I mean, she didn't have time to talk on the phone or return emails, you know—she should've wanted to get to know us—so we decided to move on. She did like the idea of screwing three men so we realized we had a chance with her, but what we want reaches far beyond just sex, Kimbrell. We want a woman of substance."

Dallas placed his hands on my hips and moved me closer to him. "Thank goodness she didn't appeal to us." He pinched my thigh. "She lacked experience." He winked. "It was obvious when we had all three openings penetrated. She yelped like a slaughtered pig and growled like a man."

"Good grief," he painted some kind of imagine and I noticed they all watched curiously for a reaction. If they wanted one, they might get the one they wanted most. Three penetrations never sounded more enticing.

"She wasn't as good lookin' as you either," Corbin stated flatly.

Dallas patted my bottom and pinched again. This time higher. "We like our woman satisfied, but we'd like to know we're getting something for the effort. She didn't like to suck cock, which presented a truer problem." All three men glanced at one another and then back at me. Dallas went for it. "Do you like sucking a man's dick, fancy hips?" He gave me a hearty squeeze this time.

"Ouch, stop it." I moved away from him.

"Stop it? Darlin' after seeing you work your little body against my brother's there in the hallway, we're going to have to get something clear here. I'm not one for teasing. You get me all hot and bothered like you did him, and I'll have you stripped down to that pretty little thong and tongue-fucked silly. You understand what that means, right?"

I swallowed and then quickly turned around to check out Rex. He grinned. "He will. I will. Corbin went easy on you."

Rex made a similar promise about a gifted tongue only his way sounded far more appealing, and then again, maybe not. *Tongue-fucked silly?* Damn it. Yes, dripping wet now took on a new meaning. I needed dry panties again. Sexual promises and dry humping in the hallway, Lord have mercy, I should've stripped right then.

A hard knock or two crashed against the front door. I didn't have the chance to take off my clothes and ask for a more polite demonstration of what these men and their tongues could do.

I tried to release enough air to politely excuse myself. "I'll be right back." I walked around the half-wall in the living room straight into the small foyer. As light-headed as I was, I never paid attention when I tripped over the neatly lined-up boots there at the door. Regaining some composure, I kicked the dusty shoes to the side and looked up into the eyes of my uninvited guest. "Well, I'll be damned."

* * * *

"Finn McClanahan."
"You don't look happy to see me."
"The frown gave me away, huh?"
He only smiled more. "Darlene you missed me. I can tell."
"Yeah, like a migraine misses a dose of aspirin" He didn't get it. I wasn't even sure I did. "Why are you here?"

Finn caused enough trouble and heartache in my sister's life to last several lifetimes. Definitely cocksure of himself, Finn never realized he really wasn't all-that.

"How's my favorite little bed partner?" He never waited for me to release the lever and invite him in because most men who came to call there typically assumed they were welcome. Most, like Finn, either dropped their pants and dirty boots at the door or kicked them off as they headed down the hallway toward my bedroom.

I smirked. "You can't be serious."

He leaned in to kiss me on the cheek and his lips puckered right as Rex rounded the corner.

"Do we have company, sweetheart?"

I'm sure my mouth dropped.

Finn looked at me and then glared at Rex. "What did you just call her?"

Rex moved in beside me and draped a protective arm over my shoulder and then extended the other one. "I'm Rex Carlisle. Who are you?"

"Finn McClanahan."

"Nice to meet you, Finn. Are you lookin' for some work?"

Finn chuckled. "Yeah, you might say that." He winked at me.

Rex cleared his throat and then looked over his shoulder. Corbin and Dallas stood behind us. They looked confident and relaxed but possessive as ever lovin' hell. I reminded myself, once again, they'd only just arrived and just as quickly remembered we'd formed a lasting friendship, of sorts, over time. Maybe I needed to go back to bed and try to start this day all over again. *Like hell.*

"We could use some help around here. Jack Dawson is a friend of mine and he tells us Darlene and her sister here had to let some of the employees go, some kind of misunderstanding or something."

"Or something," Finn snarled.

"Oh, so you heard about it?" Rex grinned.

I leaned against the doorjamb and took it all in. Without a doubt, Rex realized who stood in front of him and Jack must have told him what to expect if he had the chance meeting. He understood what kind of scoundrel existed under the surface of Finn McClanahan.

"I did hear about it. Damn shame something like this happened to these *nice* girls too." Finn gave me the full body appraisal and Rex pulled me closer.

If he wanted me to feel protected, and hovered over, it worked. My heart even thumped out an extra beat or two just for Rex.

Dallas and Corbin stepped up and made their own introductions. Dallas held onto his hand a little longer than most would do. "You from around these parts?" he asked.

"Yeah, you might say me and Kimbrell go way back."

"You don't say," Rex sounded possessive.

"Well, I uh…dated Darlene." He might as well look for at least one escape. He must've forgotten his first declaration when he stepped inside.

Maybe the Carlisle men didn't hear him.

"Let me ask you something, McClanahan. Around these parts, do you date someone's sister and then refer to the other one as your favorite bed partner?" Corbin rubbed his chin. That cool demeanor in check, he smiled and then continued, "I'm just wondering how things are done around here, is all."

So much for assuming things, they heard Finn loud and clear. Someone informed the Carlisles, from what I could tell, about my history with the McClanahans.

Finn shifted his weight and didn't answer Corbin. "Kimbrell, can you step outside for a minute? I want to talk to you in private."

Rex stepped forward. "I think you've had years to talk to her and her sister, from what I've been told, McClanahan. Perhaps you need to go, and if I walked in your shoes, I wouldn't bother to come back."

"Uh, Rex?" I wiggled away from his grip. "I'd like to talk to Finn. We're old friends and I'd like to catch up with him. It's been awhile since we've seen one another."

Rex hesitantly released me. "It's your choice. We can't stop you."

"The hell we—" Dallas was stopped by his brother's automatic arm.

"Let her talk to him. They go way back. There's no harm in talking, Dallas. They sure as hell won't be moving forward from here." Corbin laughed and tossed on his cowboy hat.

Finn glanced from one Carlisle to the next. He probably tried to figure them out in a few slow Tennessee whiskey seconds and that wasn't going to happen. I'd already tried it and failed.

"Come on, Corb." He pushed by Finn and then turned back as he stepped on the porch. "Dallas, you too. Let's get some work done around here. Evidently, when Finn and his brother took charge here, they let the place go to hell. They had other things on their mind, I suppose."

Finn snarled. "Yeah, well just so all of you know, I've got a few of those same things on my mind now."

Dallas almost made it outside, but thanks to Finn's big mouth, he stopped short of hitting the porch. "Listen, buddy, I hear you gave Dawson a fit. Now, because you're his daddy's bastard son or whatever the hell you are," he paused and looked at him with pure disgust before he finished, "I'm not going to kick your ass today, but make no mistake, after the way you and your brother treated Kimbrell, I'd like to do it. And if I ever do, I'll make sure you remember it."

Finn's Adam's apple began to visibly respond as he swallowed a couple of times. He stared at me. "Want me to go?"

Dallas's lips went to his ear as he passed by him. "It might be in your best interest." He laughed as he snatched a pair of boots waiting for him by the entryway and met his brothers outside on the stoop.

"Kimbrell, we'll be in the barn. See you in five or ten minutes?" Rex asked.

I nodded but didn't take my eyes off Finn, mainly because to do so meant to look in the eyes of three men who'd driven me crazy with their looks, never mind the way they maintained controlling interest in my body since their arrival.

"Come on in, Finn." I moved off to the side with my back against the wall.

"I thought you'd want me to and I kind of figured you've missed me." He chuckled as he moved inside and closed the paneled door.

* * * *

"That probably wasn't a smart move shutting them out like you did." I told him as we stood in the kitchen. I looked out at the three brothers walking toward my barn. All three of them had on their cowboy hats. Dallas didn't have his shirt on and what I'd give if he'd turn around because I wanted to place bets on a washboard stomach. *Show off.* The nip in the air kept most of the farmhands clothed this time of year. *These boys aren't farmhands.* It didn't take a lot to remember it either.

Finn typically didn't waste time. Today, he wasn't in a hurry. He sat down at the table and then pointed to the refrigerator. "Got a beer?"

"Sure." I reached inside the fridge and pulled out a twelve-ounce can and handed it to him. "I guess a beer isn't the only reason you drove out here today."

He popped the top and nodded toward the window. "Who are the creeps in chaps?"

"Carlisles, from Texas."

"Uh-huh." He took a swig. "Are you fucking the possessive one—Rex, I think it is—or all of 'em?"

"That's none of your business," I snapped.

"Well, you see, Kimbrell, actually it is." He stood up and stalked forward.

My hand flew to his chest. "You don't want to do this right now."

His lips slanted over mine and his hands gripped the sides of my waist. "Oh yeah I do. I've had nearly twelve months to think about you and your damn sister. I promise ya, I drove out here this morning with every intention of doing *this*."

His mouth covered mine and I tried to push him away. He didn't stop.

"No, Finn. I said no." I gripped the counter behind me and looked away from him.

"You've said no before, baby girl, and we've had some of our best times when you've said no with my cock hanging in between your legs."

His small dick hanging anywhere drew a quick smirk from me. I stared down to prove amusement at his statement existed.

Chuckling, he reached back to grab his beer. Another quick swig and his lips went straight to my neck. "What I want to know is how many times you'll say that sexy little word to those guys while you're fuckin' 'em all."

"I don't think that's your business and I don't think we're going to hear it in the first place." Dallas glared at him from the back wall. I never heard him come inside and apparently, Finn didn't either. In fact, I didn't know how long he'd been standing there.

"So you *are* doing all of them?" He laughed hard. "Shit, Kimbrell, you never get tired of whoring around, do you?"

I felt like the wind was knocked out of me, not because of the insult, I lived through more than one or two of those. It was the look of possessiveness covering the face of someone I barely knew.

Dallas stalked forward. "It's time to go, McClanahan."

"I'm talking to an old friend."

"Then finish your chat. Say good-bye."

Finn took another gulp of his beer and then crushed the can in my sink. He took my hand and pulled me with him. "What we have to discuss is better done in the bedroom. I'm sure you boys can understand. Go play in the barn with your brothers. I've got a man's business to conduct here with Kimbrell."

Dallas didn't move out of the way. He crossed his thick arms and flexed his muscles. That part was for me, I think, and I really admired them, never mind those kissable abs.

I decided to gawk later.

Dallas grunted and I swear he must've known my dirty little mind churned faster and faster with all sorts of sordid thoughts. He turned his attention back to Finn and the only way to describe his look was cold and determined.

"Kimbrell, Rex is in the office and he asked me to send you out there so he can try to make heads or tails of the mess he found there."

"I um…I think I should…" I used my thumb and pointed at Finn.

"I think you should go out there and see what you can do to help Rex." That sexy tone pitched an octave and then held as condescending as hell.

"No, I'll wait for you." I tugged away from Finn's grip and crossed my arms.

Finn laughed. "Ah, so you *are* doing this one and his brother. I should've figured."

Dallas crept forward. I gathered he wanted an excuse to hit Finn, and now, he had one. I stepped in between the men and placed my hands on my hips.

I was ready to let him in on the fact I only just met the Carlisles. "For your information, Finn—"

Dallas swooped me into his arms and slanted his lips over mine, a hush-tactic I sort of liked so I kissed him back without thinking about it. With a smile he released me after our short meeting of mouths. "Now, baby, do me a favor and run out to the barn and see what Rex needs."

"I uh..." I'd do anything the man asked now. It took a second to regain my composure and then stand on solid ground. "Finn, it's good to see you but I think it's inappropriate for you to be here."

"You do?" Amused, he laughed. "It wasn't inappropriate when my brother and I looked after you and Darlene for all those years."

"True, but things have changed, you see."

"I can see. You went from one to two and now it's three?"

"Yeah, looks like it. I'm sorry about the way things turned out for you. I never got a chance to tell you and I figure I owed it to you since I knew all along Jack was coming back for Darlene."

"You knew?"

Oops. I guess he didn't put the pieces together. I helped Jack find his way back to my sister.

"You knew Jack was coming here to take Darlene away from me?"

"Pretty much." I nodded and I felt bad for him until I remembered the way he'd always treated Darlene. "But you know something, Finn. She's better off. I mean think about it. You never cared about her."

He grabbed me around the waist and his palms dropped to my hips. "Maybe I just always wanted her sister and now that Stan says I can have you, I've come back here to claim what's mine."

"Stan? Your brother doesn't own me, Finn and I don't care what he's told you. I'm not yours and never once did he claim me as his."

"Then, buddy, you need to check out those horse stalls out there. They need to be mucked and I swear, around here, the only thing you're going to take is a *whole lotta* shit." Dallas snorted and then pulled him away from me.

"Don't." I warned. I didn't want to clean up after two grown men threw a few punches.

"Don't worry, sugar. I'm not going to fight Flip."

"It's Finn."

"That too."

I giggled quietly as I recalled all the condescending names Jack gave Finn and his brother. Obviously, when he filled in the Carlisles, he left very little to chance. He wanted them armed with everything from name calling to past histories revealed.

"Trouble in here?" Rex asked as he entered with Corbin right on his heels.

Finn quickly saw the odds tilted in favor of the Carlisles. "No trouble. I'm leaving."

"Damn, what a great idea." Dallas sat down at the table and pulled me with him. I couldn't sit anywhere without a hard cock or muscular leg beneath me.

"Kimbrell, take care. I'll be at our place if you need me."

"She won't," Corbin growled as he followed him down the hallway.

"She might," he hissed.

"With the three of us? I don't see it happening," I heard Corbin respond.

With Finn out of sight and quickly leaving my mind, I turned to Dallas. "You shouldn't have kissed me in front of him."

"Kissed her? Damn, I turn my back and look what happens." Rex stepped forward and took his hat off. He grabbed my hand and pulled me from Dallas's lap. "You need to get used to kissing with an audience."

I should have seen this coming. The look Rex held for me had been one filled with lust since he took the time to tell me about his oral skills.

His mouth crashed against mine as Dallas smoothed his palms over my back and bottom. "Damn, Rex. She has a great ass."

Rex groaned, dipped into my mouth one last time and then complained. "Yeah, well, Corbin has claims on that sweet little tail first."

"I knew it."

"You knew what?" Corbin leaned up against the wall with his arms folded and legs crossed.

"Never mind." A searing heat surged through my body. Lust never felt so hot. Dallas pulled me back to sit with him while he softly stroked my back.

"So, now that we've ran off the competition, tell me something, Kimbrell. How many others should we expect?" Rex pulled up a chair.

"You've got to be kidding," Dallas said.

Rex studied me closer. "That many?"

"Uh…" I didn't know what to say. I faced off with the best looking men in the state, the world for that matter, and they stared back at me just waiting for an answer. I wasn't sure I wanted to give them one. I was afraid it might make or break a deal, and so far, I loved the attention.

"Don't answer him." Corbin saved me.

"I won't." My sass returned just in time. "Besides, if the three of you stick around here long enough, you'll hear enough gossip without me filling in the details to make it easier for you."

Rex shifted in his chair. "Maybe I'll go askin' around."

"If you want, then suit yourself. There's plenty of it to find if you know where to look for it. Some of it is true, and I imagine, some of it is just stockyard lies."

Dallas's fingertips began to ease under my shirt. "Don't even think about it," I snapped over my shoulder and started to get up.

"You're not going anywhere soon, fancy hips," he mumbled into my ear. His grip released only long enough for him to move me tighter against his chest with one hand while the other one guided those itchin' fingers higher. This time, he caressed over the material to prove while I might have said no to one thing, other options still existed and more than one way to turn on a woman. In my case, several offered inspiration, which forever presented a problem.

While Dallas rubbed around—all over me in fact—Corbin's eyes grew heavy and Rex, I think, drooled. At least, I think that's what happened since he continued to lick his lips and bite down on his lower lip.

"So, how many bedrooms do you have here?"

"Rex, I've already told you. The three of you aren't staying here. Darlene and I have everything in order for you at their house."

"We don't require much," Dallas chimed in and then added. "Besides, we want to get to know you better and how are we going to do that if we don't have quality time with you after the sun goes down?"

"For starters," I wiggled around and then slapped Dallas's hand away, "you need to realize the three of you are pursuing me like wild trains on runaway tracks bound to cross up in the middle somewhere and for the record, when they do, we'll all face disastrous consequences."

"We hope so." Corbin rubbed his upper lip with his forefinger.

"We're counting on it." Dallas's dimple showed up again to claim a spot in the swell of his cheeks.

"We didn't come out here for oil or land, Kimbrell. I promise Texas has plenty of both and we own lots of it." Rex studied me for a reaction.

"Then why did you come here to Tennessee?"

As if they practiced their response together, they all chirped at one time. "You."

Corbin stood and Rex moved forward. Dallas was behind me before I realized he took to his feet.

"I think maybe you've made a mistake. While I know I'm woman enough to handle any man, I've never given much thought to more than one."

"Stan and Finn pretty forgettable, huh?" Rex asked directly.

I smiled. "Let me ask you something. Since it's quite obvious you know too much about me, I have to ask this, you see. Did my brother-in-law pimp me out or something?"

"No, but he damn sure sweetened the deal when he told us about his lovely wife's sister." Rex's lips swept over me again. Damn it, these men just didn't know how to keep their wandering hands and sinful mouths to themselves.

His tongue swiped over my collarbone before he kissed his way up to my earlobe. "Tell me something, sweetheart. How long do I have to wait for you? How long do we all wait?" His mouth came back to a claiming position and his tongue lashed against mine until I saw stars and maybe even stripes—or in my case, maybe it was straps and ropes. Anything to bind me to these three held a lot of appeal.

Those large hands, his luscious kiss. No, it really wasn't a problem. So what if we'd only just physically met? I quickly felt right at home in their arms and I knew them better than most men I'd dated in the past.

I broke away from the kiss first. "Shew, what a kiss." As the recipient of more mouth to mouth than any one woman in Lewisburg, I had to admit the tongue taps given by these three left little to the imagination. "Have any of you failed to notice that since you stormed into my day, the only thing we've accomplished is kissing and talking?"

"You forgot the dry humping." Corbin touched my cheek. "I liked it but I think we can find better forms of entertainment."

"Kimbrell, you might as well just fuck us and let us get you out of our system." Rex stated what all of them probably thought. "

Dallas snarled as he glared out the window. "Damn him!" He jumped up and sprinted outside with the other two studs right behind him.

Chapter 4

"Man! You just made a serious fucking mistake." Dallas sprinted toward Finn. He grabbed his cell phone and threw it to the ground.

"Stop this!" I screamed as I followed them, tripping over my own feet, horrified to watch a grown man stomping a cellular phone into the mud but not so worried about the fact that Corbin and Rex pinned Finn against one of their trucks. "What do you think you're doing?"

Corbin smirked. "Getting rid of evidence, Dallas?"

"I'd say he has some," Rex added.

"Let him go," I demanded. "This is ridiculous."

Dallas's fists hung at his sides clenched into tight balls. He drew his arm back. I stepped in front of Finn and almost caught a left hook. "I said, let him go." I glared at Dallas, but then shouted over my shoulder at the two holding him.

Finn sneered. "Yeah, you heard her. Let me go. I imagine she's hungrier for me than she's been in a long time. After all, you boys can't possibly think Kimbrell would prefer the three of you to someone she's had in her bed on and off for several years."

"Ah shit, Finn…" I knew if I didn't throw that punch now, he'd likely catch one from three husky cowboys. I slapped him instead. As I turned to walk away, I decided I liked the way it felt so I turned around and smacked him again. "And that one is for Darlene. Lord knows she owed you a few of 'em."

I took Finn by surprise and it showed in his expression. "Tell me something, Kimbrell," Finn sneered, "How can you blame me without crooking that finger back at yourself? What kind of sister sneaks around with the only man her sibling's ever known, huh?"

I glared at him. "You're the one who came slipping into my room."

"Hell woman, we all slipped into your room, or should I say, your worn down bed? I wasn't the exception around here."

I swallowed stiffly.

Corbin reluctantly released Finn. "Come on, Kimbrell. Let's get you inside."

"I'm fine." I shook away his helpful hand. "I think I have some unfinished business with Finn."

"That's too damn bad because today you're not going to have the chance to close it out. I imagine he'll be around town and once you have time to calm down and think about what you want to say, then you can—"

I wheeled around far too fast. "*You* don't have *the right* to tell me—"

"Perhaps you're right." He interrupted me long enough to scoop me right up and over his shoulder. His hand immediately settled against my ass. "I may not have any horse in this race *yet* but it's high time one of us did and I think I'll just make sure I'm first out of the gate."

"Put me down on this blasted ground now!"

"Oh, I see how it is." Finn watched as I was carried away before he continued. "I thought only two of you were fuckin' her but then again, she's tried two out before. She'd have to go for three or more." Before he could laugh too loud, Dallas and Rex pulled him to the side of the truck and I heard a couple of punches delivered, followed by a painful moan.

Corbin began to trot across the lawn and he had too much of a spring in his step. He took long strides as he called to his brothers. "You two make yourself useful and get rid of him. Explain to Mr. McClanahan why we won't need him around here. Kimbrell and I will meet you in the barn shortly."

"You can't do this," I hissed.

He moved his hand over my bottom and took his own sweet Texas time doing it. "Kimbrell, I happen to know on good faith that you've had plenty of cowboys ride in here and take advantage of you only to ride on out. I'm going to see what these boys around here have to boast about but there's a difference. I'm not going to ride on out of here when it's all said and done."

"I'm not sleeping with you." I stopped wiggling against his broad frame.

"You're right."

I froze as he set me down right inside the kitchen. "So that was for show?" I asked.

"Oh no, it wasn't for show." His gaze dropped to my chest and his fingers curved over the material of my top.

"Then you must be out of your mind! I am not going to bed with you right now."

He picked me up and then put me on the kitchen counter. "You are right. We're not going to sleep and we're not going to bed." His hands grabbed the hem of my shirt and he tugged it over my head.

"Stop this," I whispered.

He stripped his shirt off and in record time, his belt separated from the hooks and loops. "Not a cowboy's chance on a long shot bull ride." Heavy lids threatened a dark desire loomed.

He cupped my neck and then kissed me with one of those smooches that ensured a fellow that a gal like me won't say no. "I'm going to fuck you, Kimbrell, and you're going to thank me for it." The words were spoken when the kiss broke but then he sealed them up all safe and neat again.

I pushed him back. "Confident, are you?"

"You'd better believe it, and for the record, you'll beg for more." His mouth covered my ear as his hands moved over the front of my bra. He pushed the material to the wayside and his lips covered my nipple. "Delicious, woman." His tongue soothed the ache of a fire the Carlisles started as soon as they said hello.

"I can't do this." Oh but I knew he believed differently. My good name in town all but assured it. I would end up spreading my legs for any man with the last name Carlisle, and fortunately, I had these three willing to help me. "I said I can't..."

The way his expression changed, the quickened pace when he rubbed his cock against me, the tenderness as much as the eagerness in his touch—all of it assured me I could and I would. He led me to his cock and then left my fingers unattended. I think I might have even been the guilty party to unzip him.

Corbin stood in between my legs like he'd done it a thousand times before. His tongue and then his fingers tweaked my nipples until the throb returned with a newfound desire. "I can't..."

"You're doing a fine job." He drew back from me and then stripped off his boots and pants.

He was right. The fine job happened to leave solid proof in front of me.

"Dear God." I stared at *it*. Why not? No wonder the man wasn't intimidated by my private forms of entertainment, my dildo was nothing compared to this man in length and width. Actually, Corbin had it by two inches, maybe more.

He was as well endowed as any man who'd ever visited my bed. It presented its problems. Damn shame a man like this could and probably would ruin me for all others.

A quirky smile curved the corners of his mouth. "I thought you'd approve." His hand overlapped mine and together we began one of those long hand jobs many men like to guide and control when they're afraid a woman's not going to stick around to finish the job. Whatever my lips said earlier could truly be dismissed once I felt the sticky evidence of pre-cum against my fingertips. Oh, I was going to do Corbin Carlisle in ways he'd only dreamed about and now I wasn't even going to fight it.

Corbin didn't have to worry. After a few hours of foreplay, I was fresh out of excuses or the desire to invent a few new ones. In fact, after that warm evidence of arousal touched my skin, it was all I could do to resist tasting the better part of him.

"Your brothers will shake with jealousy." I stated the obvious as he yanked me off of the counter and quickly pushed down my jeans and thong. I barely noticed the bra hooks because with the wave of a hand, the evidence of any coverage quickly disappeared.

"Let me look at you." He twirled me around and let out a whistle before he lifted me to him again. This time, he didn't set me down. The man understood how to twist and turn a woman when he wanted her legs bending like a pretzel around his mid-section.

Body heat warmed and invited. Holding onto the back of my legs, Corbin moved with me like we'd practiced this maneuver more than once or twice.

"They'll walk in," I whispered.

"Let them," he hissed. His mouth, hard at work, moved everywhere.

"You don't care?"

"They'll join us, and no, I don't care." He kissed me again before his hand went to my pussy. "Good Lord. You're one hot little number, aren't 'cha baby?" His fingers dipped beyond the folds into the slick heat my body provided. Plunging in, he pulled back to watch for my reaction. "Feel that? I bet you can come right now."

"Corbin." Breathless, I began to move into his palm. With his middle finger fucking my center, his thumb rotated over my clit. "I won't last…"

"Then don't last." One finger gained company and with the accomplice in place, I began to feel the hot juices gather. My hips defied all reasoning as I pushed my pussy against his palm again and again.

"That's it, lover. Sweet damn, you're tight." He worked his fingers through my folds and plunged into my core over and over again. "Hot, so fuckin' hot…" His mouth stayed against mine as his whispers drew out the kind of desire a woman only has with a man in full control. I liked those men, particularly the one in front of me.

Corbin opened and closed his mouth as I tugged at him and he touched, stroked, and adored me with his fingertips. "That's it beautiful, come for me." He bit his lower lip and held it under a restrained toothy grin.

Placing me back on the counter, Corbin spread my legs and stood in between them. "Tell me what you like, and what you want." He licked his lips. His fingertips softly touched mine with a driven caress, an unspoken request.

I searched my thoughts, gathered my reasoning and came up empty handed when I looked into his eyes. I didn't know. I wasn't sure if anyone ever asked me what I liked. Right now, I wanted him. In ten minutes or another day or two, it might change. Besides, no one ever stuck around long enough for me to think about it.

"You."

"You have it. Right now, you have it." He fisted his cock in one hand and his arm fell around my lower back as he drew me closer. "Now, take it."

I licked my lips and stared down between my legs.

His dark eyes dared me. "Oh yeah, you'll suck it too but right now, I need this. I want to feel your sweet pussy milking my cock and afterwards, you can have what you need."

His lips slanted over mine and he stole a hearty kiss as I shifted upward and just as he suggested, took all his body offered, all mine expected to handle. "Oh hell..." I tried to adjust to his size, tried to understand the length and width of a full and eager man.

"Damn, you're wet." His palms settled on my thighs. He spread them so I was splayed for his pleasure, receptive to a weighted man ready to take the final surge forward.

Closer, he drew me. Beads of sweat gathered in record time as he kissed, held and caressed me with lips, cock and fingertips. "Feel me, Kimbrell."

"I feel you." Damn did I ever. I couldn't imagine a woman who wasn't capable of feeling him all the way to places no other man reached.

His hips moved with an undetermined rhythm. Positioning prohibited some moves but he seemed to work with the problem. His head dropped to my breasts and he devoured them, evenly split the time between them, before he played favorites and sucked on my right nipple until I moaned out with unadulterated pleasure. "I'm going to…"

"The hell you are now." He withdrew and a cry of abandonment, maybe disappointment, escaped my lungs. "When I fucked you with my fingers, you had your chance. Now, you'll come when I tell you to come."

A carnal growl left his lips. He picked me up and carried me across the floor to the living room. Wide, never mind wild, eyes met us at the door.

"Dear God, woman." Dallas's mouth watered. Oh no, I didn't imagine it. He stepped inside and just gawked, with his mouth opened and a rosy blush tinting his skin.

"Wanna join us?" Corbin's lips curved and he motioned for his brother.

"I…" I was nervous as hell. "I can't. No, not yet."

"Then, can I watch?" Dallas sat down on the chair right inside the doorway.

I tried to squirm away from Corbin's grasp but he only retreated for a split second before he pushed his cock beyond my folds. He drove into me hard and fast as he pressed my back against the flat surface behind us. "Sweet damn boys, you're going to enjoy this." He reached around his back and locked my ankles but never broke his pace.

My fingernails dug into his skin. "Corbin, wait."

"Hell no, you want it as bad as I do. I'm not waiting, not stopping. Too late, baby and too damn good." His raspy voice was thick with desperation and whatever he thought he was going to find in me, he found with a quicker pace and without regard to the short journey it took to discover it.

I tugged what little air I bargained for into my lungs. "You're right. You're…so…right."

I wasn't going to win now. Hell no. Once I let the first Carlisle fuck me, it was all over. I understood it so why fight it? Why not become the slut they traveled to Tennessee to find? Why not slide into the role and become the woman they wanted me to be for them? Why not belong to them, at least for now? I braced myself against the wall and thrust into him.

"Ah, yeah. That's it. That's the girl I want." His heavy cock charged forward, with a penetrating push, he slowly began a side to side grind. "Wrap your legs around me," he ordered.

I stared over Corbin's shoulder and noticed Dallas's crooked, carnal smile. My eyes drifted to his cock and I almost felt sorry for the man. His erection pressed through his blue jeans and his gaze showcased splattered lust and thorough disappointment. I understood it to an extent because I shared the strongest chemistry with Dallas, even though I had plenty to around.

"Sweet hellish satisfaction." Corbin continued to fuck me. "That's it, Kimbrell. Spread your legs. Hang on…"

"Corbin…" Every time he spoke to me, I wanted to come. His raspy voice drove me to the brink before his cock retreated. He kept me on the realm of a flood, of desire I knew should break free and he did it deliberately. "Please…"

"Ah yeah, baby. That's it. Wrap me tight. Hold me closer."

Damn, I needed to come.

His hands cupped my ass and his cock continued pleasure's attack as he rocked into my walls with a motion meant to still a woman, quiet her long enough to keep her insatiable and yet begging for orgasms—yes, I gathered he made fucking into an art form. He moved in and out with a borderline abusive strength, and I wanted more.

"Don't stop." I closed my eyes as he came at me harder and stronger, the beats, calculated and the thrusts only deeper. I felt him unraveling inside. His strokes slowed and his cock hooked from side to side. He pressed my back tighter against the wall.

"Damn it, Corbin, don't break her." Rex walked in and acted like it was fully expected and completely normal to catch us fucking.

"That's it, sweetheart. Come for us. Let us watch you." Rex's hand moved up and down across the front of his pants.

"Corbin," I whispered.

"That's it, baby. Let me have your sweet pussy."

His cock twitched, his body began to move faster, and he let out a loud, satisfying groan.

"Corbin! Don't stop. You can't…stop."

He was going to stop.

His cock twitched more and more as my walls pulsed around his shaft and milked him one solid inch at a time. His hungry growl assured me he came before the jolt of our stupidity hit me with each jerk of his body. A spray of his semen reminded me first and foremost, I was in his clutches and his cock stroked at me without the use of a condom.

And it was too late to stop it.

"Come to me, Kimbrell. Now." His voice was eager but his body ran out of juice, in more ways than one.

My body felt plastered to the wall as my thighs squeezed and released. I arched for him. "Don't leave me yet. Just a little more," I whispered against his neck.

"I've got more." He gave a few harder thrusts and I fell against his shoulders.

"Corbin!"

"That's it, lover. Thank me like a woman should thank a man."

"Oh…God. This is…" It was erotic and sexy and so perverse I wanted to die right there. I needed to look at Dallas, feel Corbin and damn it to hell, I was dying to suck Rex's cock the more he stroked his hand over his slacks.

When Corbin finally released me, we slumped against the wall and his body covered mine, shielded me from the others. "Are you okay?" He whispered against my skin.

"I'm fine." I clutched him closer and glanced from Dallas to Rex. I wondered who was next. I wanted it to be Rex. I motioned for him. "Clean me up."

"It'll be my pleasure." He reached for me and pulled me from the floor. Before anyone said another word, I followed him down the hallway and into the bathroom.

* * * *

It was going to be a toss up between the brothers. I was betting on Rex as the soft romantic type. Originally, my money would have been on Corbin but now, I wasn't so sure. He had too many secrets, something I often read into the letters exchanged when we corresponded over the internet. After the wall sex, or hall sex, whatever the hell we just had, I saw another side.

Corbin's moves, once he got inside of me were diabolical and nearly perverse, like he tried to withhold ripping through my folds and simply claiming me, without forethought to pleasure and yet he pleasured. God, did he ever please and satisfy.

Rex moved around me in the tiny bathroom. He laid out two washcloths, two like-new bath towels and my joy toy.

"I don't think I'll need that," I teased.

"You'll need it," he promised.

He turned on the shower. Hot water spewed from the jets within seconds. Before he pushed back the shower curtain, he held out his hand and I took it. Stepping over the tub, I stood under the water faucet waiting for him, expecting him to join me immediately.

"So did you enjoy Corbin?" he asked from behind the half-closed curtain.

"I did."

"You'll enjoy all of us—individually and together." He answered one of those questions I had and I was glad he did it before he took me into one of those possessive holds.

"I know. It's what I'm most afraid of now."

"You shouldn't be scared, Kimbrell. We're not going to hurt you."

My heart continued to beat faster and faster. I was beginning to wonder if I needed to run like hell.

Rex stripped down to a cowboy's finest and within seconds, he joined me without hesitation. His lips claimed mine with a purpose and a drive I imagine was fueled by the show of carnality his brother displayed as openly as I did.

"Rex…I…we…"

His tongue lapped at my mouth. "I…we…are going to take care of you, Kimbrell."

"You don't understand. I'm not on birth control and I…we, Corbin and I didn't use a condom."

Rex's tongue moved in and out in a perverse insinuation. "And it was beautiful to watch."

"What do you mean exactly?"

"We want children. Don't you?"

"Uh, wait a second. I must've missed something here." I tried to push him back and he pursued more.

"Not now, Kimbrell. Later. We'll discuss it later."

"I want to talk about this now."

Rex's hands locked my hips against his body while his cock pressed into my ass again and again. "Let me have your sweet little ass. Can you do that for me, Kimbrell?"

"Rex?"

"Shh..." He pressed his lips against my shoulder and then lazily kissed his way to my neck and ear. "We aren't going to talk about the C's right now."

"The C's?"

"Sure—children, condoms, and Corbin."

"Right now, it's just me and you. It's all that matters. When we're all together, you can think about all of us, but one on one, I want your undivided attention."

Before another word passed between us, Rex reached for the washcloth and soap. Within seconds, I enjoyed the most erotic and mesmerizing shower of my lifetime. By the time, he dumped shampoo in my hair, I was ready for anything and I damn sure wanted Rex Carlisle.

Facing him, I knelt down in front of him as his hands massaged my scalp. Staring back at me was another larger than life reminder. I swallowed stiffly as I swiped the head of it. The small slit at the top reminded me of the finer things in life, the simple things too, the kind of relationships I'd had and the kind I craved for more than half of my adult life. I ran my tongue over his opening and savored the taste of a one hundred percent man.

Rex's gaze stayed on me. His palms worked the shampoo into a sudsy lather. "That's it, darlin', take me."

I sucked the whole head in between my lips, my tongue working back and forth over the tip. His hips shifted and I looked down to see the sides of his feet braced against the tub as he began to move with me. My head dropped over the shaft and the true fullness of Rex began to gather a little substance. His balls twitched and he moved one hand to mine as he quickly guided me over his sac. "Feel me, darlin', just feel me. Suck my balls and then take me in deep between those sweet little cheeks."

By the time I had a good idea of what he had in store for me, the shower curtain jiggled and another body stepped in behind me. It wasn't Dallas, like I sort of hoped. Not that I was disappointed to have Corbin, I already knew he'd be in between my legs before the end of the day and I understood why he waited, and held back some, at first. The man might scare a woman off with what I'd guessed he kept tucked away in his blue jeans.

"Couldn't stay away?" Rex teased.

"Once you get in between those sweet and sexy thighs, you'll understand."

With a pop, I released Rex and started to challenge Corbin with a seductive little statement or two but Rex was greedy and wasn't going to allow it.

"Where do you think you're going?" His head moved away from the showerhead and he reached above him for the wand there. He moved the water over and under my hair before he sprayed his brother in the face with a laugh. "Damn bastard. You want that ass, don't you?"

"I'm taking this ass." His finger ran down the middle of my rear before his hands worked into the shape of my rear.

Rex fisted his cock at my lips. "Here, sweetheart. Suck it good, for me, okay?"

My head bobbed up and down over his length and I showed sincere gratitude. For some reason, the only thing I had on my mind was how quickly Rex would come. I wanted him coming in my mouth, throwing his weight to the back of my throat.

"Damn, Rex. You're too generous." Corbin chuckled and then reached around the curtain. Lube was on his finger before I realized he wasn't going to let me take the time to prepare for him on my own. He wasn't a man who delivered false hope, he brought the best a man had to give and he did it with a smile.

"Spread those cheeks, sweetie." He moved his finger down the seam of my butt and my moans vibrated against Rex's shaft.

"Hell and damnation." Rex moved closer and closer before he withdrew and repositioned his angle. "Shit, she can suck a man through a hay straw." His breathing proved uneven and I glanced up just in time to watch the twisted expression of dire need take form.

Through gritted teeth and a partly open mouth, he bent down and yanked me up against him, into a heated kiss. By this time, Corbin's fingers were twisted deep inside of my ass, moving beyond the rings of skin, the pleasure principles no one dared to find. He had every intention of sealing it—filling it—with his cock.

Rex's fingertips rolled over my nipples before he set me on fire strumming his tongue with a brisk desire brewing, one I didn't know quite how to handle. "Drop that head back down low and show me what you've got, Kimbrell." His request was one I didn't take offense to at all. I wanted to show him how right he was. I could suck him into Neverland and he'd know who took him there. His mouth ensured with kisses, licking, and a few nibbles, it was time to finish what the two of us started only hours after our first meeting.

Corbin's teeth locked against my shoulder as I slid down his body and positioned my mouth over Rex's pulsing hard-on. The mushroom tip glistened with his excitement and suddenly, I was driven to compare. As my head descended over him, my fingers itched. Instead of dropping my head and opening my mouth more, I caught him with my left hand and stroked. Reaching behind me, I grabbed Corbin with my right palm.

"Sweet." Rex moved forward and back.

"Shit." Corbin pulled away and pushed back into my hand with force.

"Little vixen is comparing." Rex grinned as he watched.

I blinked my eyes innocently and then dropped my lips over his cock allowing my tongue to swirl around the veins and the width. No doubt about it. Size granted generosity and favored both men. Corbin was wide, perhaps longer than Rex but where Rex was shortened, stumped by maybe one inch, he made up for in true width. Most women ran from men like these. I swallowed as I compared them now only in my mind.

Corbin raised a playful hand and let it smack against my bottom. "You naughty gal, Rex is right."

"Mmmm…" I grabbed Rex's ass, my nails buried into his skin.

"Holy sweet…" He took a death hold on my shoulders and began pumping what I craved. I arched my back against Corbin's ready cock.

"You're ready now?" His raspy voice damn near choked out the question.

"Uh-huh." I managed two syllables when I slid back to the tip of Rex's dick and then lost my will to speak again as I filled my mouth and cheeks with nothing but the strength of a man ready to explode.

"That's it, Kimbrell. Suck me good, baby. Fuck me with that sweet little mouth." His body moved forward and back, faster and faster.

Corbin maneuvered me against, and then with, Rex's moves. Forward and back, in a teasing gesture, we rocked whichever way he thought it would serve the purpose. Before I realized it, he was controlling the entire situation in the shower. He decided when he'd take me and ultimately, he decided when we all came together. It was the more erotic of situations, the wicked part of being there with both men.

My hips pressed up and back. I begged as I moaned. I looked up at Rex's handsome face and blinked. He only grinned, drove harder and faster.

"Rex has the stamina of ten thousand horny men, Kimbrell. He loves the build-up." Corbin chuckled and I gulped, swallowed again and then once more. Rex only swelled wider and wider. Pride of knowledge, he took care to show me what his brother said held some measure of truth.

Corbin's forefinger ran down the seam and sank between my cheeks. He touched the entrance, just barely lubricated it again before he drove his finger forward and greedily sank deeper and deeper twirling around the entrance and then sinking into the rings of flesh waiting for the right inspiration to divide and conquer, part and accept. "Hello, sweet ass."

The tone, the seduction, the growl, the hunger, all of it was my sign but nothing prepared me for the breaking of flesh, the parting of wayward ways and the division of all circumstances that led us to this. I sucked deep but then by Corbin's force and the cock that refused to stand down and wait, I released Rex and cried out in pain and pleasure as my hips parted with understanding.

"Hurts…too much." I was able to get that much out, only a whine and a whimper.

"Good damn thing. I wanted to be sure no one else had this ass. No one deserved first dibs—just me, only me." Corbin's strokes didn't slow. His cock twitched and churned and Rex, while patient and considerate for a passing second, was ready now. Ready to come and apparently eager to do it on command.

His hand dropped to my breast. "Suck my cock, Kimbrell. You're not afraid of it. Show me what you can do to a man's world." His eyes drooped now. My fingers ran over his sac back and forth and back again before I dropped my mouth over the entire shaft. I fucked him as hard as I'd ever fucked a man with my mouth while I found out what it meant to have a man screw my ass without regard to whether or not I was a woman who might break. The one behind me didn't care if he split me in half so long as he heard me yelp right before he divided me in two.

"Damn it!" Corbin's pace gained some rhythm. I threw my head back to see, catch a glimpse of the pleasure I quickly figured out how to bring. Smiling up at him, he pulled my hair and twirled it around his fingers. "That's it. Suck him. Fuck me. Ride us both."

And ride we did, right into one sensational earth shattering orgasm filled with screams, moans, grunts, and yeah—all the confirmation Dallas needed to ensure it was definitely his turn.

Chapter 5

I woke up in bed. I vaguely recalled Corbin carefully positioning me in the center of it and then I remembered a strong arm around me as I slept. It wasn't familiar but then again, it was recognizable. Dallas cradled me while I slept and then at some point, left me.

I stretched as the morning sun came up over the barn and then blinked as I looked around the room. In the far corner, Dallas slept on a chaise lounger.

"Dallas?" I narrowed my eyes.

Immediately, he sat straight up.

"What are you doing here?" I studied him as he walked closer. There wasn't anything sexual about his pursuit.

"Your sister called last night and told Corbin where to find their key. Since you insisted we make ourselves at home there, we spent the night there."

"It's early. Did you even go over there?" Noting he'd changed clothes, I realized he must've left at some point.

"Sure." He brushed my bangs away from my face. "I'm not like those lazy brothers of mine. I generally work more than sleep, just four or five hours and I'm good to go."

"But you slept here, didn't you?"

His eyes danced with mischief. "Drove the other two crazy too, Rex even came over a couple times to check on us. I think he was afraid he was going to miss out on something."

I swallowed tightly and shifted uncomfortably. I'm sure I painted a picture of agony by the alarmed look on Dallas's face.

"Did they hurt you?"

Giggling, I tried to cover my morning breath and hide the growing embarrassment at the same time. "Are you kidding me?"

"Uh, no. I have a reason for asking."

I thought of the blood. The proof Corbin found far too much pleasure in between my apple shaped cheeks. I closed my eyes and winced with the easy reminder.

"Never took it up the ass, have you?"

"You believe in asking personal questions, don't you?"

"Just stating the obvious. Rex just about shot Corbin with your gun after he realized it."

"I wanted it." I also begged for more and all but threatened his life if he didn't thread each inch of himself beyond every guarded layer. Technically, I asked for and received raw sex and I didn't regret one minute of it.

A delicious smile replaced the worry evident on Dallas's face. "I bet." He touched my cheek with his open palm. "Can I get you anything?"

I studied him for a long time while he caressed my arms, face, and stomach. I liked this side of Dallas. I quickly reminded myself that his darker side, his deeply rooted connection with a side of sexuality that bordered on the absurd would somehow leave me stripped of my senses.

"Can I go get you some breakfast?" he asked. It was his question that made me realize I didn't answer him the first time.

"Dallas?"

"Hmm..." His fingertips trailed over my cheek, lips.

"You were here beside me last night and yet, didn't touch me. Why?"

"I touched you." His eyes focused on my lips and burned my existence and his into a kiss he didn't offer to give. My lips parted in an understood acceptance. I felt it even if he never delivered it.

"You held me."

"It was nice."

"It was..."

"Nice." He moved away from me.

Pressing upward on my palms, I looked out over the lawn. The sun appeared with a sweet announcement of a new day. I stared at Dallas's back. He seemed tense.

"Why didn't you join us yesterday?"

"Did you want me to?" He turned the question around on me.

"I..."

He sat down on the bed once more. "Kimbrell, I'm more man than you can handle right now."

A devilish thought or two came to mind. "That's in your head."

"No. It's not."

"It damn sure isn't in your jeans, cowboy." I teased.

A wicked growl, followed by a deliberate grunt eased from his chest. He leaned in and softly kissed my lips before standing again.

"You're afraid of being with me?"

"I'm afraid of feeling what I feel for you without so much as touching you."

His truth slammed into my heart. It stripped me of all senses and harnessed a new understanding filled with emotions and desires I didn't know I possessed.

"Say something," he encouraged.

"I don't know what to say."

"You look at me like you fear me. Maybe you should, but the way you look at me is exactly the way I imagined you would and it scares the hell out of me."

"Why did you stay here then? Why stay over here when you could've slept in a big bed with fresh sheets and a comfortable mattress beneath you?"

Dallas took a deep breath and slowly released it. "I'm going to go get some coffee and breakfast. Is there a Starbucks here?"

"Are you kiddin' me? This ain't Nashville, cowboy."

His eyes narrowed. "Nashville. There's a thought."

I loved going there. "I guess if you stay, I'll just have to show you around the big city. I love it there." I released a sigh and then tried to move my legs toward a new day. I needed to rise and shine, face the morning and manage some work.

"How about showing me today?"

"Oh, I…uh, I couldn't really. Not today, anyway. We have a load of cattle coming in from the feed yards in Texas and a couple of loads to sort for some fellows in Oklahoma."

"Rex and Corbin can take care of business. They've loaded a few trucks in their time." He rubbed his chin. "What do you like best about Nashville?"

"I don't know. I don't go much. I like the Opryland Hotel but I haven't been there in years. I enjoy the Grand 'Ole Opry but only when it suits me and I love to go to the Bluebird Café and hear the latest from rising stars."

"Get dressed." He marched across my room and flipped on the overhead light. "I'll be back in about thirty minutes. Can you get packed and ready to go in half an hour?"

"Are you crazy? Nashville isn't an overnight trip from here. It's up the interstate a piece and we never stay there when we go. It's kind of like a day out or something, a shopping trip or a nice dinner, but not an overnight stay." I laughed.

"How long will it take you to get ready?" He seemed hell bent on ignoring what I said.

"Dallas, I can't go to Nashville with you."

"Why not?"

"Well, for starters…I…"

"You don't know why you can't. You're just stubborn as hell. I said we're going."

"Look." I took a deep breath and wasted a few seconds trying to figure out the best way to handle him. "I'm sure this macho man effect you have on women typically wins you the chance to get your way, but you see, I'm not quite used to the idea of having three cowboys tell me what to do." I stopped chattering and that was my first mistake.

"Tell me something, Kimbrell. Have you ever spent the night in a hotel room before?" He moved close again and before I realized he was going to pick me up off the bed, I stood in the man's arms looking up at him.

"Sure I have." I gulped.

"With a man?"

"Huh?"

"It's not a difficult question. It's not one that requires a full declaration or even an open window into your past. I just want to know. Have you ever spent the night in a swanky hotel suite with a man catering to your every whim?"

"I...I don't..."

"Yes...or...no?"

"No."

"Then, pack. You're going to know what it's like to be treated like an adored woman."

"I thought..."

"You don't have to think. It might waste your energy and I promise, before I bring you home, you're going to need a lot of it. So, save it."

* * * *

The warm water oozed over my face and shoulders. The soft pellets against my body not only massaged, but soothed. In a flash, memories of the day before began to ricochet around my head in a format designed to make me dizzy. Around the same time Corbin joined me. "I hear you're leaving me." His hands wandered over my hips. He grinned as he scooted by me, taking care to let his member swing in between us. His stout cock pressed forward as he shook his head under the nozzle.

"The water pressure here sucks," he noted.

"Yeah, it does. It's one of those things you tolerate in the county, I suppose." I glanced down and then back up again. Breathing easy wasn't an option. Corbin simply took away the ability.

"So when do you and Dallas leave?"

"No. I'm not." I cleared my throat and then tried again, "I mean, I'm not leaving. Darlene and Jack would skin me alive if I took off without regard to my responsibilities here."

Corbin gazed at my chest as his wicked tongue traced the entire circumference of his mouth. "Would they?" He moved into me. His cock all but parted my folds. "Skin you alive, you say?"

"I'm serious. I can't go." I turned my back to him and then grabbed my facial soap from the nearby shower organizer. Lathering up, I closed my eyes and started to rub the white cream into my cheekbones.

"Let me." His hands began to massage my face with the silky smooth formula. "God, you have gorgeous skin."

"Thank you." I kept a stiff upper lip and pursed my lips together after the compliment.

His hands soothed the soap over my face before working down and around my neck. "Feels nice?"

"Mmm...hmm." I was in heaven. I didn't open my eyes for confirmation because I didn't need it.

He stepped aside and I moved closer to the drizzle. He massaged my neck and shoulders while I stood under the warmth. His cock loosely stayed positioned at my ass.

Corbin's grin turned wicked. "Can I give you a word of advice?"

"Any words you want to speak are welcome but I'm not going on a trip to Nashville with your brother."

"You don't know Dallas. If he says you're going away for a day or so with him, you're going."

I stood on my tiptoes and kissed the end of his nose. "You don't know me. If I say I'm not going, I'm not going. He'd have to tie me up first."

* * * *

"I'm not happy about this." I didn't bother looking to my left. I kept my focus straight ahead.

"No?" Humor laced his voice.

"I'm serious, Mr. Carlisle. This is nothing short of ridiculous. Never mind embarrassing. Do you know how humiliated I would be if the local cops pulled us over?"

"I imagine you'd explain things one way and I'd tell things from another perspective."

I gritted my teeth and continued to breathe in and out of my nose. "This isn't going to help move things in your favor, I hope you know." I was beginning to think the man next to me had a real issue with women, especially those he couldn't control, specifically me.

"Really? I'm disappointed to hear that, Kimbrell. Really, I am. I was bettin' on hot and bothered."

I glared at him. "Dallas. I am hot and I am bothered but the steam you see isn't rising from under this 'ole gal's skirt. It's coming from my ears and I am getting madder by the second." I tried to budge the bounds that held me and I couldn't get them to move. After a few yanks and tugs, I reminded him of the private party he busted up because of his impatience. "I'll have you know that I was hot, in all the right places, before you rudely interrupted one of the best oral pleasures known to womankind!" I thought back to that sinful tongue his brother possessed. The one parting my folds and going in deep before Dallas swept me into his hard arms and removed me from his brother's grasp, never mind his mouth.

"Give it a rest. You're not going to be able to loosen them until I do it for you."

I took a deep breath and slowly let it out. "When do you think you might consider that task?" I studied the man then—the whole man—the one who not only took pleasure in packing my suitcase and tossing me over his shoulder but also the one who strapped me in and tied my hands and feet together so I couldn't resist going with him on a romantic getaway. Some might debate whether or not the weekend was going to be a successful one given the way we left the ranch.

Dallas's eyes focused on the interstate. "Is the traffic here always this bad?"

"No. Sometimes it's worse, much worse." I tried to roll down the automatic window. It wouldn't budge.

"Child safety locks." He informed. "You'd know this if you didn't drive around in a beat-up pick-up."

When a person has met their match, they've met it. I wasn't ready to concede but I summed up my opponent. He was going to win in the end. "You always get your way, don't you?"

"Most of the time." He sang his answer and he did it to a smart-ass tune.

"Well, just for the record, I will call someone to pick me up the moment we arrive in Nashville."

"I believe you." He reached for his phone and pulled it out of his shirt pocket. He slowly dialed and then winked. "Thanks for reminding me."

My eyes bugged. Surely he wasn't going to have the hotel remove the hotel phones. "Hey, Corb, you were right. She's a feisty little hellcat with more energy than nine lives would ever supply. Call the Opryland Hotel and ask them to remove the phones. Remember, the story is she's always wanted to visit the hotel but due to her mental illness, we've been unable to travel with her. Have the phones removed." After a sideways glance, he added. "I will. I'll take real good care of her. Don't you worry."

"This is the craziest thing I've ever heard of in my life." I tried to stomp the floorboard but wasn't able to reach it.

"Is it?" He was too smug. "I think not." He reached over to the middle of the dashboard and turned the tunes up a notch. "Like country, I take it?"

"It's fine," I snapped.

"It is." His hand rested on my thigh. "Mighty fine indeed."

"What if I agreed to go willingly?" When you're beat, you're beat.

"Kimbrell, in case you haven't noticed, I don't give a shit if you go with me willingly or fight and claw your way all the way to our suite. You're going to be romanced, you're going to be courted, and you're going to be bedded in a grand suite at The Opryland Hotel. I don't give a damn if you fight me or love me because I've already made up my mind. We're going to have our weekend together and we're going to get to know one another the proper way so I can…" He deliberately cut off whatever he first intended to say.

"So you can what?"

"You'll find out." He accelerated then and began to weave in and out of traffic.

"What's the hurry?"

With a lopsided smile, he purposefully began to undress me with his eyes. "You have to ask? I listened to my brothers fuck you silly in that shower and you want to know why I'm in a hurry?" He coughed. "Let's just say I can't wait to show you what you were missing when you didn't scream out my name instead.

"I'm not fucking you."

"Suit yourself. I like it on top anyway. I'll fuck you. Promise to hold real still and not enjoy it?"

I felt a curve in my lips and unfortunately couldn't hide my smile. I quickly turned to face the window. "You're impossible."

"I try. You didn't promise."

"Cross my heart. How's that?"

"You mean there's a heart under all that armor?"

"Somewhere, I suppose."

"I thought so." He gently touched my cheek. "Slide over here."

"Will you untie me?"

A second later, he pulled off at a busy exit and then stopped at a service station. "If I loosen these ropes will you behave?"

"Depends."

"On?"

"What do I get for being a good girl?" I chuckled.

He began to loosen the ropes at my feet first and then rubbed my ankles. "Damn, you're going to have rope burns. Did you have to act like a double mule-headed woman? Those are going to hurt later."

"I don't like being told what to do."

"Get used to it."

"Not a chance." I huffed and puffed as I held out my wrists. "Untie me."

"Say please, master."

"Huh?"

"Please, master."

"You've got to be kidding me."

"Say it." His eyes were dark.

"When hell freezes over."

"Okay, suit yourself. Chances are you'll stay tied up for eternity."

He reached for the gearshift.

"I have a problem with that." My eyes threatened to spill tears because I called them out on purpose. "I can't…" I added a quivering lower lip for affect. "Please, Dallas. Untie me."

He watched the show of forced emotions and then slammed the truck in park again. "Okay, okay. Don't cry." He quickly untied the ropes and then gathered me in his arms and began to stroke my hair nervously. "I'm sorry, Kimbrell. I'd never hurt you. Never." He kissed the top of my head again and again. "I promise. It was only fun and…"

I froze against his chest and buried my amusement in his shirt. Fun and games. If that was the truth, then he should be able to dish it as well as take it. "Are you sure it's only fun and games, cowboy?" I peered up at him and slid my ass closer to his thigh.

"You don't have a particular objection to calling me master, do you?" His eyebrows gathered and his eyes narrowed.

"No, but you deserved it. You should've seen your face."

"Think you're slick?" His lips curled upward.

"I know I am." I bit down on my lower lip. "You just need to try and keep up, because if anything, you'll find we'll get along better when things go my way."

"Yeah, that's what my brothers said too." His eyebrow arched. "Is that what all the boys in town are going to tell us too, Kimbrell?"

I straightened up with the reminder. The sexual electricity in the air fizzled.

"I'm…uh, I'm…"

"Why do you do that?"

"Do what?"

"Remind me."

He seemed unsure of what I was talking about. "Remind you of what?"

"I know my reputation. I was there for every grunt and groan when I added a little more spit-n-shine to another cowboy's cock. According to you, there wasn't any question of who or what you'd find when you came here but you sure as hell like to remind me of it again and again."

"Yeah. I know I do."

"Why?"

He took a deep breath and slowly, painfully almost, let it out. "I guess I want you to realize what you're leaving behind for me." His eyes were serious, and the dancing devilment disappeared.

"What I'm leaving behind?"

"Yeah."

"I don't recall agreeing to anything permanent."

"No, you haven't. That's true." He tilted my chin and then looked deep into my eyes. "But you will. I'm going to make you remember your past in a way that will make you see it only prepared you for me."

"That's the craziest thing I've ever heard of in my life."

"We'll see." His lips locked over mine and he stole the moment with tongue and teeth. Then he left me puckered against the open air because of the fact he broke the kiss so abruptly.

"I think you like to play too many games," I stated flatly.

"This is no game, Kimbrell."

"Then what would you call it?"

"I'll let you know when I figure out a name for it."

"You do that." I crossed my arms over my chest.

"You'll be the first to know."

* * * *

"Do you know this place has five bathrooms?" I wheeled around on my heels and stared at Dallas. "Who can use five bathrooms?"

"We can find something different to do in each of them. How's that?"

"I think you wasted your money. Why not just stay in a normal room?"

Worry plastered its mark across his handsome face. "You don't like it?"

"Like it? I love it!" I nearly tripped over the oriental rug as I made my way to the atrium doors. Peering down at the indoor gardens, I simply added, "It's just a bit upscale for me, that's all."

Dallas moved closer as he helped me open the doors. "There's a neat trick to this." His hand covered mine as he whispered the instructions, "You have to unlock the deadbolt first." He smiled gently and then moved out of the way.

A Matter Among Four

"I can't believe you're paying over seven hundred dollars a night for this place. Do you know what kind of shopping I could do with that kind of money?" I laughed as I stepped outside and took in the beautiful greenery below.

"Kimbrell, you do know that you're just as rich as we are, don't you? I mean you're acting like you don't have a dollar to your name."

"I guess we have a good bit of money in the bank but Darlene and I always tried to get by on what we needed without makin' a big show of cash and such." I leaned against the railing and stood on my tiptoes before bending way over to look down. "I've never stayed here." I swallowed as I thought about why I hadn't. No one ever went out of their way to bring me and outside of the occasional night spent at a man's house or out in the barn, I slept in my own bed.

"It's time you start learning how to spend that money you and your sister hoard." He chuckled before he left me alone on the balcony, but quickly added, "Baby, if you don't lean back over this way, I may have you screaming at the visitors below. Damnation, what a position." A pat to my bottom and he disappeared back inside.

I let out a deep sigh of relief. It wasn't so bad being there with him. He wasn't making any unnecessary demands and the dark side I feared most wasn't something I detected in his voice or even saw in his facial expressions.

Giggles from another room drifted out into the atrium. A happy couple danced onto a nearby balcony, kissed, and then disappeared behind closed doors. Piano music began to play and I sat down to listen. It was familiar and soothing, distant but yet close enough to locate. I walked back inside.

"Dallas?"

The more steps I took, the louder the music. I kicked off my bright red high heels, the shoes Rex chose for me earlier since I was in the middle of a sassy southern fit and refused to dress myself. "Dallas?" I turned the corner and saw a sight to behold. "You play?"

"Some." His fingers masterfully ran over the piano keys. "Do you?"

I shook my head. "No."

"Darlene said you did."

"Darlene talks too much and apparently she talks too much to strangers. I thought I taught her better."

He raised an eyebrow. I shuddered. "I know, double standards. I can sleep with a few of them but God forbid if my little sister talks to anyone she doesn't know—especially domineering and handsome men from Texas."

The dimple I loved formed in his cheek and his hands slowed down while his gaze held me in a trance. "Some say you were a musical talent to be reckoned with prior to your mother's death. Play by ear, from what I understand."

"It's an overrated skill." I smiled and took a deep breath, preparing to change the subject.

"No, it isn't. It's a gift. One you refuse to use, apparently." His fingers worked from a rapid pace to a slow pecking of keys. He scooted over and patted the bench. "Sit down and play something for me."

"I don't play." I glared at the ivory keys of the grand piano. I hadn't played since I played at mother's funeral.

Dallas reached for my hands and he curved them over the center keys. "Play something for me. Anything at all. The choice is yours."

"Then I choose not to play." I stood up and looked around the room.

"Why do you run from everything that matters to you?"

"According to you, I don't run at all."

Dallas moved his legs and shifted his weight to the other side of the bench. With his legs stretched in front of him, he pulled me to his lap. "You run from important things you discount as trivial—money, your own God-given talents, life, romance, solid relationships, and Lord knows what else."

"You've summed all of this up in a little over twenty-four hours?"

"No. I've been drawing these conclusions for six months now."

"Six months?"

"Give or take a day or two." He bent his head and kissed my cheek.

"Sounds like you had time to conduct a little research." I bent back against the keyboard and startled myself and Dallas when I ran my fingers over a few keys, just henpecking around.

"Play something, anything you want."

"Maybe I will sometime." I shrugged. He didn't push the issue again.

"Are you hungry?" He stood up and by standing, forced me to do the same.

"Speaking of food, come here." I grabbed his hand and excitedly pulled him to the formal dining room. "Can you believe this place?"

He looked around at the furnishings but he didn't seem as impressed as I was or as I thought he should act. The long dining room table suggested many guests enjoyed the best of eloquent meals there and all he could do was glance around the room, unimpressed. He passed through another entryway, placed both palms on the doorjamb and leaned inside. After peering to the left and then the right, he moved back again.

"Nice pantry."

"The brochure says it's a catering kitchen." I smiled. "And did you know this suite can entertain up to a hundred people?"

"The suite can accommodate up to a hundred people? And there are only five bathrooms? I think I need to talk to someone about that. This could present a problem."

"Don't make fun of me," I snapped playfully and then gave a forced pout.

"Here." He handed me the hotel guest directory. "Choose one of the restaurants. Anywhere you want to eat."

I licked my lips and then stared at his cock. "You make for a delicious meal." I noticed because he'd provided enough to make my mouth water and my womb clench since I laid eyes on him. No one looked at Dallas Carlisle and asked 'where's the beef' because he sported it proudly, even in denim.

"No. I'm thinking food. Aren't you hungry?"

"I am." I licked my lips again and moved closer to him. "You act like I'm some kind of threat, a reminder of a sexual encounter you don't want, like you might even detest the idea or something."

With a grunt, he held my arms away from his body. "Kimbrell, that's not true. Nothing is further from the truth, but I want to teach you that life isn't all about sex and maybe by teaching you, I can help myself too." His control irked the hell out of me and some of the things he said to me about sex and sexuality, never mind my past, really pissed me off, not that it should, but it did.

"What do you mean help yourself?"

"It's a long story."

"I'm not going anywhere."

With reluctance and a heavy sigh, he provided a glimpse behind the darkness, only a quick look-see, but one nonetheless. "I crave the BDSM lifestyle. It's all I've ever known. Rex and Corbin, while they're strong men and dominating as hell, they weren't ready to share a woman with me if I brought my lifestyle into the relationship. It's not something they wanted to consider or will allow their woman to accept."

In that moment, I breathed a little easier. "So you're not going to put a choker around me and a chain?"

He laughed. "Not today."

"But you're not going to…you know." I moved into him, looked up at him on a dare, and licked my lips.

"Have sex with you?"

"I don't think you're attracted to me." Pushing away from him, I walked over to my luggage and tugged it into the bedroom. "I think you want me, maybe just because your brothers have encouraged this arrangement—the one you all seem to think you want—but the fact is…" I gasped as I stared into my luggage and saw proof to the contrary.

"Not attracted to you? Is that so? Well then sweet lady, the one with all of the answers, can you tell me why I bothered to pack your toys, lubricant and lingerie?" He grinned and then walked away.

I scooted my ass across the carpet and then turned around to face him with my legs cross Indian-style. "Games, you love them. I'm just a game to you, like I first thought."

With controlled speed and calculated moves, he walked over to the drapes and tugged them closed. He then turned back to me and that's when I saw he was absolutely horny as hell. His tented pants provided a sweet sampling of the man's truest endowments but his hooded eyes gave a certain personification to sexual heat. It scared the hell out of me—at least, at first.

Before I could stand, he grabbed my wrists and pulled me to him. With a grunt, I landed against his chest as his mouth slammed over mine in a heated exchange of desire- filled kisses. His knees backed up against the mattress, and in a second or two, we were on the bed and he pulled me on top of him.

In an instant, he rolled over me and pinned my arms high above my head. His swift moves, my overactive sex drive, and all of the fast-paced maneuvers challenged breathing again.

"I get lost in you." My breasts rose and fell with the declaration. Immediately, I regretted it. "I'm sorry, I have no idea where that came from and I…"

His tongue swiped at my bottom lip. "Shh…" He fought for self control. I witnessed it in his expression. He slowly kissed his way into my mouth once again. "If you apologize for that ever again, I'll spank your little ass until you beg me to fuck you and then I'll fuck you until you never forget that I've been between those gorgeous legs." The dark demeanor, the one that confused and frightened me, returned.

"Dallas?" I swallowed as he tugged me closer and closer but refused still to undress me. When I reached for his cock, his hand clasped around my wrist and he brought it to his lips. He kissed up and down my arm in no particular hurry or order. I tried again and he repeated the process.

"Will you trust me?" He held me against the bed with his thigh leveraging space between us but enough weight to pin me under him. One hand provided the strength needed to lock my hands against the soft bedding beneath us.

I studied his face, his handsome features and they way I recognized them were anything but shallow. Deeply set eyes were as dark as the lurking night one minute and light as crystal blue waters whenever he let his guard down and managed a smile. His chiseled cheeks led to perfect high bone structure and his lips curved thickly into a smile that many women would pay to see— sell out their home places to own. His moistened mouth curved into a mimicking natural grin which only invited the well defined occasional dimple to add substance to his natural beauty. Yeah, he was pretty boy handsome and sexy as hell but trouble existed behind his eyes and it stood out as the most powerful part of his appeal.

"I asked you if you would do me the honor of trusting me." He purposefully left a few butterfly kisses across my cheek.

"You want to tie me up again, don't 'cha?"

"Yes. That's part of it."

"And what else?" My heart hammered into my chest.

"Will you agree so you can find out?"

"I thought you were hungry."

"And I thought you were horny." He chuckled.

"I always am." I admitted it. "Why deny the truth when you already know it's part of my very existence?"

"Then let me teach you to control it."

"I…"

"It's the only way you're going to have my cock swell in between those sweet legs tonight."

"Then maybe I can do without."

"We'll see." He pointed to the guest directory again. "Better pick out your favorite. We're eating here at the hotel tonight."

"I hope so." I reached for his pants again fully expecting him to move away. This time he allowed me the pleasure of feeling him, the girth and length, the whole of his sexuality. I pressed up and down. Somewhat stunned by the sudden realization of one man's size, the acceptance only a minute or two away. Huge didn't quite cover it. The man had to be painfully aware of what he could do to a woman. Not only did I acknowledge it, I craved it more than a smart gal should. His natural gifts, if that's what I felt, had the ability to strip a woman of her virtue, whether she had it intact or not.

"Kimbrell?" He brought my hand to his lips after he pressed one final time into my palm. "Later, darling. I'll promise you this. If you can give me just one hour of total trust. Then, I'll show you how I can totally possess your heart and soul in one night. Right now, I'm going to take a cold shower. That leaves you four other bathrooms." He popped a kiss on my neck and then walked away, calling one final request over his shoulder. "I like the little black dress. Wear it."

* * * *

"I'll have what he's having." I closed the menu and then took another drink of ice cold beer.

"Didn't want to try the Tennessee Tea?" He winked.

The waitress waited patiently as I gave it some serious thought.

"No, the Single Barrel Barbeque Chicken sounds like all the excitement I need to find tonight." I closed the menu again and raised my glass to my lips.

The waitress disappeared and Dallas's hand caught mine. "You think so, do you?"

"Uh-huh. I do."

"Like the name of the chicken dinner a little much, huh?" He winked as he brought my fingertips to his lips and nipped one before sucking my middle finger into his mouth.

"Stop this, Dallas." I squirmed in my chair feeling like all eyes found me in the legendary Jack Daniel's Saloon.

"Make no mistake about it, you may have single-barrel for dinner but for dessert, you'll find a loaded shotgun."

"Promises." I sighed dramatically and pulled my hand away from his. "Do you like to tear a woman up with words or do you actually shoot off something other than your mouth once and awhile?" I reached under the table and stroked his kneecap. Before my hand trailed up his inner thigh, he caught my wrist and stopped me. I laughed and returned both hands to the tabletop.

"Ah you're good, aren't 'cha baby?"

"I try."

"Try, hell."

"Your brothers are already telling my secrets, huh?"

"Maybe."

"What did they say?" I leaned over the table and fully expected him to answer me.

"What does it matter?" He grimaced with the mention of my sexual encounter with the other two Carlisles.

"I didn't take you for the jealous type."

"I'm not. I share when I need to share and own when I'm all alone."

"Do you dance?" I nodded to the couples twirling around on the dance floor.

"Slow's all." His southern drawl caught up with him.

"I see." I winked and sipped. "Then I'll wait for a mellow song."

"Uh-huh. I thought you might."

"Tell me something new about you. Something we never talked about on the phone would be nice." I was interested in learning all he'd allow me to know and I imagined it wouldn't be much more than he shared through emails and phone calls.

"What would you like to know?" He reached across the table and stroked the back of my hand.

"I imagine there's a lot I want to know that you won't tell me."

"Fair enough, we understand one another. Ask the questions you think I won't mind answering."

"I've met your brothers. Got any sisters?"

"Nope, God help us if we'd had a sister."

"I guess it would be kind of hard imagining a sister putting up with cowboys like you, huh?"

"I'm not going to answer that one."

My eyes focused on his long, taut fingers. The man's hands were sizeable enough to draw a knowing woman's eyes to his cock. Since I already knew he had a large penis, I felt confident the man never fell short of finding several gawking women.

"Why don't you want to answer that one? Do you think what you and your brothers do to women is something of a disgrace? So distasteful that you wouldn't want your sister or perhaps even your mother to—"

"Kimbrell, you're headed in a direction you don't want to go. Change the subject." The darkness reappeared around the same time the waitress returned to check on us.

"Can I get you another beer?" She offered as she picked up my empty glass.

"Sure and bring me a screaming orgasm shot."

"I beg your pardon?" Her eyes bugged.

"Your bartender will know what I want." I shot him a sideways glance and he smiled as he rubbed down one of the bar glasses. "In fact, scratch it. You get the beer and I'll ask for the orgasm myself."

When the waitress disappeared, I patted Dallas's hand. "I'll be right back."

"Sit down, Kimbrell."

"I said…"

He stopped me with a firm grip. "If you want an orgasmic shot, then let the waitress bring you one. As for the screaming orgasms, you'll have plenty of those—maybe even a lifetime of them, starting tonight. What you aren't going to do is provoke a fight."

"Do you like to fight, Dallas? If so, and you stick around Lewisburg, you may find one or two." She sighed and then continued with a wide smile tugging at her lips, "I don't want you to fight over orgasms or to defend my honor, and frankly if you did, I'd like to remind you that you're too late. I don't have a lot left to defend."

"See, that's the problem. You've lost your self respect. Somewhere along the lines, you decided to screw your way through life and let any undeserving bastard have a go of it. Tell me, what made you think so little of yourself?"

"Don't do this right now," I whispered.

"Why not? No one is paying attention to us, and besides, you seem to be reckless with one beer in you. Why not try for honest recklessness and lay it all out on the table?"

He gave me the wrong idea and since I had actually downed two beers waiting on him to make a few phone calls, I was anything but sober. I'd always been what most considered a cheap date and an easy drunk or more appropriately, vice versa.

With a smirk, I stood up and walked around the table. Before he stopped
me, I planted my ass on the smooth surface of the wood, hiking my dress up right below my crotch in the process.

"Kimbrell, I'm warning you."

"Warn all you want. I want you to know what you have on your hands so you can quit analyzing me. I like sex, Dallas. I like fucking. I'm not going to apologize for something that is a big part of my life. I'll take it in the mouth, in the ass or in my personal favorite, and guaranteed to be yours too—my vagina. Now, we can dance around all night, flirt back and forth, have a nice dinner and make small talk

A Matter Among Four

but I can tell you, it's not going to matter in the morning. Tomorrow morning you're going to take me back to Lewisburg and then once Jack and Darlene come home, you'll be on your way. Men leave. People disappoint. Relationships fail. I survive."

Dallas glanced around the area. There were two couples trying their hand at a little saucy dancing and one couple very involved in tearing into three plates of appetizers.

A party crowd of about ten college-aged men appeared indecisive on whether or not to keep their gaping in check but they noticed me. Some looked on with pure lust in their eyes, some tried not to stare and others crooked their head as if they wanted to find out what they might miss. Yes, they seemed most concerned about what lingered under the dress.

"Hot, wet and ready." I smiled sweetly at the group and I swear three or four of them instantly ran their hands over the front of their slacks.

"Then bring it over here, sweetie," one called out.

"We'll take care of that little pussy one stroke at a time," another one added.

Dallas took a deep breath and slammed his hand down beside my hips. "Is this what you want to do?"

"You started it."

"No, darlin'. I didn't start it but I can clear out this bar without sacrificing as much as a minute of time with you, or you can get over there in your chair, pull your skirt down around those fancy hips of yours and try to behave like a lady."

I swallowed stiffly. "Or you could dance with me."

He growled as I slid off the table and onto his lap. Before I had the opportunity to grind into his cock, he held me at bay and forced me to stand on my own.

The song, one of my favorite, blared through the surround sound and Garth Brooks lured us closer with *The Dance*. Ironically, I thought Garth and Dallas probably would've been great friends in another lifetime. They each seemed to possess a deeply rooted dark side.

It's the eyes.

In Dallas's case, he was losing control. His half-hazy gaze seemed to defy it even though a small flicker of something greater, something threatening enough to ensure it might swallow him whole never allowed him to fully give up the long reins of control. I had a feeling Dallas's night to lose his grip lurked hours, maybe even minutes, away.

We began swaying to the music. The first few seconds defined awkward, but gently, he wrapped me closer to his warm body and soon we slid into a perfect tempo and a strangely familiar dance.

"You feel like a dose of heaven." He breathed a heavy sigh of relief into my neck and held onto me for dear life.

"You don't feel so bad yourself," I joked, and yeah, I pressed my lower half against his manhood. I liked, no loved, the feel of it twitching against me.

He gripped my shoulders and pulled me closer, tilting my chin as he did. "Look at me. Don't close your eyes."

"Okay." I smiled wider. "I like looking at you, for the record."

"Then you'll like kissing me with your eyes open." His hands framed my face and then he kissed me. His haunting, lust-filled stare held me captive in a deep gaze I wanted to break it because of a connection we established that I wasn't certain I wanted to have with anyone.

The group of college kids started to filter out one by one and the tallest, if not the most handsome, patted Dallas on the shoulder as he walked by him. "Damn, you're a lucky man. If you wanted to share, I'd leave those fellows to fend for their own ride."

Dallas's body tensed and I squeezed him closer. "You're staying right here with me." I teased him but I felt his animosity, the anger, and the spite. For a second, I feared he would follow the young pup out into the parking lot and teach him a thing or two about southern manners but thankfully he didn't.

"Don't ever do that again." He nodded in the direction of the table. "If you do, those who look will pay for indulging in your little display."

"Oh shut-up and kiss me again. I like it better when you use your lips for something worth remembering. Besides, I typically forget the jealous rants of a man I've just met."

"You know me better than most, Kimbrell, and it scares me to think of what you can do to me." He told me his secret on a whisper but he spoke loudly to my heart.

After the song ended and our kiss lingered long enough to turn into a hot war of tongues, our dinner was served. I took the lead when we walked back to the table and Dallas's hands stayed on my hips. Once or twice, he ran a lone finger over my ass from one cheek to the other. And thanks to the gesture, my chicken was nearly cold by the time I quit thinking about the cock waiting for me underneath the snug denim blues seated right across from me.

Chapter 6

"You're sure you don't want to go out dancing?"

"Positive," I called back over my shoulder as I stumbled into our suite. Stepping out of the pump-me-high or bend-me-over shoes, I left them at the door. I watched in a mesmerized state as Dallas picked them up by the straps and carried them into the bedroom closet. Reaching behind my back, I began to work with my zipper.

"Do you think I overdressed for that joint tonight?"

"It's not a dive and since we're at The Opryland Hotel, if anything, you dressed appropriately and the rest of us there looked too casual for where we're staying."

"This little black dress is too much." I started to dance as I worked after the first grip of the zipper so I could rip it down my back.

"Need some help?"

"I would love some." I smiled sweetly realizing what he'd find as soon as he permitted the dress to fall. The built-in cups allowed the backless dress to hold me in full support as long as the dress stayed on. After it started to fall, all bets were off.

"Turn around." As if he anticipated the outcome, he slowly whirled me around to face the mirror in the big bedroom.

"You're no dummy, are you?"

"Kimbrell, I'm probably the smartest man you'll ever meet. It's one of the reasons I don't talk as much as my brothers."

"I see. So if a man talks a lot, he's not as smart as someone like you, for example?"

He shot me a crooked smile and then swatted my bottom.

"Be careful, big boy. You might get more than you can handle tonight."

He caressed my rear and stared as he did before he lowered the zipper and kissed my back as each inch gained exposure. His breath hitched at the top of my thong and his hands stopped wandering further south.

"What's wrong?" I watched him through the looking glass.

He straightened his back. "Kimbrell, trust. Remember?"

I let the front of the dress fall, stood straighter and pushed my strawberry locks over my shoulders just as he touched several of my loose curls and lifted them carefully just to watch them drift behind my back.

"I trust you." My eyes felt heavy. Sureness in him came at a price and I understood what he might ask me to pay.

"Sweet fucking surrender." His gaze lingered directly on my breasts and his arms draped around my middle.

"I trust you," I whispered back at our reflections as he squeezed me closer and his mouth traveled across my neck.

"You shouldn't." His lips scraped over the nape before he nipped at my shoulder and smoothed his palms up and down my arms.

I watched him. "You want me to believe you won't hurt me and I do. I'm giving you what you asked. One hour of complete surrender and trust."

Startled, he looked back at me through the glass. "Hurt you? See there's the problem. Woman, I want to do things to you that most women would deem downright criminal given my size. Some might even demand imprisonment for a few years."

"I think you're concerned over something you shouldn't worry about." I reached behind my back and ran my hand over his front, stroking across him up and down, shocked at how much harder he seemed now, how much heavier and more erect than the last time I touched him.

I turned around to face him. "You're fighting a losing battle with me tonight. I don't want to go to sleep without knowing what you feel like, what you taste like," I unbuttoned his shirt and began kissing a trail of wanton desires down to his belt, "and I don't want to imagine how you'll fuck me, I want to know how you feel."

A hungry growl rose from his throat and domination took over. "Damn you, woman."

"Damn me all you want, but you will fuck me or you'll sit nearby and watch me do it for both of us."

Through parted lips and gritted teeth, he asked for the favor of watching me carry through with my threat. "Will you?"

"Will I what?" I kissed his stomach as I loosened his belt. "Oh dear Lord."

He took a deep breath as I worked to tug his erection from his shorts. "Hell and damnation, woman…" His thighs bunched and he pushed free and spilled right into my waiting hand. I swear it looked like the kind of thing National Geographic or The Guinness Book of World Records put on display.

"Shh…" I kissed the tip as I pushed his pants down his thighs and calves. "Will I suck your cock?" I breathed in his scent. Fresh, manly, rustic, and by all means, edible. I swallowed back the first fear as I watched his dick twitch against my lips. Rubbing both palms around his girth, I pressed my cheek against it and felt it harden against my skin.

"Damn you, that's erotic." He held his breath as I continued to massage him, cuddle against the thickness of a ready man.

If he knew the truth, he'd probably button it up and keep it in his pants. As I cradled him against my skin, I tried to think of where a man this size fit. I once read about a man with a similar problem and I wondered if Dallas compared in size. *Dream the hell on—he's bigger.* As I held it at a great distance from my body, I realized Dallas set records, whether he knew it or not. Every bit of thirteen inches, I considered it nearly lethal—almost deadly.

"Will you?" He chuckled and then gasped as my head bobbed over his stout member for the first time. "I've dreamed about this…and about you fucking yourself just so I could watch."

"I know what you want." I licked the head of his cock, the mushroom tip straining against the pulsing excitement and turning a dark shade of burgundy as it pressed against my chin. "I know you want to watch me run that vibrator in between my pussy lips and you will, I promise…but not yet because right now, I want to taste you, suck you, drain you." My mouth fell into place and my cheeks swelled with his sex. Of course, as great as I sucked cock, I had to realize one thing immediately, it would not fit all the way in my mouth. I hated it for Dallas.

His hands twirled through my hair. "That's it, baby. Suck it. Take what you can." His tone remained gentle and needy, crying out for attention and affection but desperate to hang onto the control he wanted to have over me and not the other way around.

The sounds of pending pleasure began to unravel after a few minutes of continued stroking and groping. My tongue tapped into the needs of a man while anxious fingertips stroked his balls back and forth.

"I'll come if you keep that up." His orgasmic voice, the one I grew to love long before we met, provided enough to set my clit on fire.

With a pop, I released the best part of him and managed to tell him, "I hope so" before wrapping my mouth around him once again.

"Oh God, Kimbrell. Be careful what you ask for." His hips moved with my mouth. His hard length slid across my tongue and tapped the back of my throat again and again, but I couldn't take it all.

What started out as a gentle act of giving oral sex turned rough in an instant. It happened so fast, I didn't see it coming. His hands tugged and pulled instead of the slight initial weave, the gentle touch of one strand or another. He held my hair off my shoulders in a mockery of a ponytail and guided my head with the pace he wanted.

"That's it, sweetheart. Take it. Suck it to the base and back." He continued to help me bob over his cock. "Drink me in, baby. I'm coming. So close now…slow down here. Ah yeah, that's it. Let me come."

His solid thighs pressed against my torso and he steadied his hands on my shoulders before slamming me against his groin. He drove against my mouth again and again as his dick filled my cheeks and his balls slapped against my chin. "Fuck me hard with that moist little tongue, baby."

His cock hit the back of my throat as I closed in around him and licked the underneath of his cock. A spray of his cum left him and quickly lavished my oral cavity with the sweetest tasting essence of a man. He drew back and then plunged forward as I allowed his semen to wash over my tongue in waves of satisfaction.

"Dear God woman, where'd you learn to suck cock like that?" Beads of sweat ran off his forehead as he began to slow down, pull back.

"I'm glad you approve." I tried to lick him clean as I slowly worked my mouth around his shaft going as far as he would allow and then back to the tip again.

"You're going to destroy me." He pulled me with him as he sank onto the bed and began to kiss my belly, drifting past my breasts for the first taste of what he and his brothers referred to as 'sweet honey' and somehow I was beginning to believe they had a true fondness for oral sex. They all spoke of it with such a gleam in their eyes.

"Let me have a taste of you." His mouth covered my pussy and his closed fists opened long enough to grab my calves and open me up for full display. "Touch yourself." He looked up at me and pulled my hand to my clit. "Here. This little button, right here." I swallowed hard.

"Who knew?" I giggled.

"I'm willing to bet you did." His mouth hovered over my entrance as his fingers twirled around mine to ensure we found some sort of favorable rhythm together. "Feel that, Kimbrell? What's it feel like?"

My blocked airway trapped words. I felt confident that someone sat on my chest because I didn't want to think about speaking, or even moaning. If I didn't need air, then taking a breath wouldn't seem important either. Not now, talking during sex was so overrated, or at least during oral sex.

Besides I needed to save my energy. The way the man whipped against me with his tongue made for preparation. I couldn't speak now but hell's fury, I'd soon scream.

His tongue lapped at the center as if the folds were never bypassed in the first place and then he came back to kiss the parted flesh over and over again. He licked, kissed, and thrust in and out on a divine mission.

My hips rose higher as I braced myself for the pending finish. I gripped the pretty pastel comforter and soon I clutched balls of the material in my hands as I rolled high on my heels and then up to my tip-toes. "Good damn. Please don't stop." I arched.

"Never." He kissed and sucked. "Not a chance." His lips covered my fingers and he licked them out of the way before he gently clamped down over the little button he first wanted me to control. Once his lips met the flesh found there, round one was over.

"Dallas!" I screamed his name and he ate like a sudden hunger slammed into his gut. The man had no mercy and certainly no shame. He sucked my clit and then parted my folds so he was able to go deep and long with a deliberate goal—to please an insatiable woman. For a stopped moment in time, I played the part of that woman—his woman.

"Please don't stop. Keep going. Keep…licking. Keep…fucking me with your tongue." A shudder and then a soft sigh, and it ended. It was over but…it was also just beginning.

* * * *

"You're beautiful when you come for me." He kissed my forehead and then moved over me. His cock positioned at my entrance, his palms on either side of my head.

"You're going to let me have you?" I bit down on my forefinger playfully as I waited for the penetration.

"Not yet, sugar. Not yet." His lips trailed over my neck. "I've showed you what I can do, now you show me."

He moved from the bed, leaving me in a nearly sated state before returning with my toy and handcuffs.

"Do you have the key to those?"

He dangled it from a keychain and then placed it on the nightstand. "I do."

"Okay, so have it your way. If I'm going to trust you though, you have to promise you won't leave me cuffed if I ask you to release me."

"Promise." He spit out the oath and appeared pained that I asked for his word. He started to move the fluffy pink cuffs to my wrists. "You know about safe words, don't you?"

"Safe words?" I smiled. "I read trashy novels but, Dallas, I don't want to live in that lifestyle." My air constricted. Did I want to live in that lifestyle? I shuddered then when I realized the answer. If Dallas wanted me there, I'd probably sign up for submissive lessons, if there were such opportunities, and I'd do it tomorrow.

"Dallas, you have to prom…" His lips covered mine to hush me, no doubt and as quickly as he did, my hands were behind my back and safely cuffed.

"Thought you were going to pin me to the bed."

"I am, but when I do that, it's going to have to be my body holding you. The posts are too thick for cuffs." His expression turned wicked. His fingers twitched and he turned his focus back to my favorite toy—the zipper zapper hummed as he inserted it into my vagina.

Licking his lower lip, he moved from the bed. His haunted gaze never abandoned me. By the time he took his seat across from me, I was already arching into my first orgasm with my preferred toy.

His voice hung in the distance as low, and completely sexual. "What do you think about when you're alone in your bed coming against nothing more than a man-made toy?"

"I think I'm going to die with the speed control you chose." My hips spread, my thighs splayed open and I began to shift with the dancing vibrator, my toy, and my loyal companion. Gyrating with it, my hips rose and fell with the magic of modern technology. One of the best vibrators on the market today, I moved up and down bracing myself against the balls of my feet one minute and my fists, bound and cuffed, the next.

Dallas watched. He slowly tugged at his cock. "You're a damn beautiful sight, prettier than anything I've ever seen in my life." His focus fell to my breasts. "Look at those pretty little pebbles. God, I love your nipples." He stroked his cock and his mouth watered. He continually licked at his lips.

"Dallas, please." I already needed his cock. The vibrator was doing the trick fast enough but the eyes of a hungry man, a cowboy starved for sex and eager to ride, was the undoing of my soul. "You said…you said you were going to leave…this…lifestyle."

"I'm playing, darlin', and this has nothing to do with my preferred lifestyle." With a grunt, he stopped stroking himself and then continued, "Pleasing you will be my first goal, always." He whispered the kind of endearments I didn't expect to hear coming from a tall, handsome rogue especially since I realized for Dallas, seeing me like this, only placed him in a brooding frame of mind.

The first climax hung in the air, I'd fought back taking it but now, it rode closer, encouraging me to snatch it while the getting was so damn good. I arched again and again as the slow buzzing sound began to rip through my flesh. I clenched my thighs together and held it at bay, but barely.

"Open your legs."

"I can't." Beads of sweat started down my chest, trickling in between my breasts. My back arched against the mattress. My feet pressed firmer against the mattress until my toes curled into the coverlet.

He stood, stalked forward, and came closer. "That's it. Kimbrell! Listen! Come for me. I want to see you drip, squirm, and yes come for me." His cock in hand, he watched as the vibrator twisted and twirled. Then, he tapped it on the end.

"Now!"

I swallowed back the fear, the loss of control, the dominance in his voice. Maybe I would, now that I had his granted permission because I knew he truly wanted me to wait for it regardless of his desire to leave his past behind. He wanted me to submit. He wanted me to obey. He wanted to control. I saw it in his eyes and it was the only reason I waited but now, oh God now, he gave permission—no, he ordered it. I had to come.

Grabbing my toy from the end, he jerked it out right as I pushed higher and allowed my thighs to open. "Oh God, no!" I glared at him. "I'm so…so hot and close. Let me come."

He slid it back in place. "You'll get there again, fancy hips." He rubbed his cock over my hips and thighs as he replaced and removed my joy toy.

"You're going to watch until all the juices drain from my pussy and then you'll have to wait to fuck me." I tempted him to come back to bed. I rolled over to ease the discomfort of having my arms behind my back.

As I curled on my side, my bottom flinched as the cool air in the room drifted over my naked shell. "Please, Dallas. This is delicious but so wicked, so hard to resist. Pressure and pleasure…it's building. You can feel it…I know you feel it… in your balls." I asked him something I hoped would draw him closer, urge him to come back to me. I watched his jaw twitch and his cock move stiffly forward as if in agreement.

"I feel you." His hand moved faster and faster. "I've felt you every night since the first time I saw your pictures, Kimbrell. I'd talk to you on the phone with my cock in hand. I bet you didn't know, did you?" He pulled his cock forward and the pre-cum came in a steady bubble, oozing just over the tip.

"Don't come yet!" I screamed. "Let me taste you while you jack off. Please don't come without my mouth."

He sneered. "Too late, darlin'." He rocked forward and back as his hand drew the first signs of a man's release and his body jerked. He yanked his shaft through his hand, kneading it again and again as his cream, nearly thick as lava, spilled over his fingers. "Damn woman, what are you doing to me?"

"Oh God, Dallas, please." My chest stayed tight. I needed to orgasm. I needed to watch. I had to taste. Good damn, I now understood want and need and how simply they blended together. "I…" Swallow. Breathe. Speak. "I want…more."

My hips swirled forward in a continual rolling motion. My pussy closed tighter around my little toy enduring as much pain as possible just to hold back the pending pleasure. I moaned, mumbled, and burned as the climax reeled closer.

"I need to fuck you." I begged. I watched him after he spilled his seed into his hand, confused and aroused as I saw the sticky remains of a man's excitement and finish.

A few moments later, I tore my gaze away from his cock. Glaring at the ceiling, I refused to look at him. I'd craved him since I'd met him and it was only going to get worse at this pace. "Please, I need…"

"You don't need to fuck anything, Kimbrell. That's the point. You can fuck yourself with that vibrator anytime you want. You don't need a man to get you where you need to be and you damn sure don't need a stranger telling you how to do it."

I swallowed stiffly, ignoring my toy and Dallas. "I want out of these cuffs now."

He sat down on the edge of the bed. "Don't be mad. I'm just…"

"I said I want out of these cuffs now."

He shot me a wicked grin. "You're still so damn wet, aren't you, baby? No matter what I say to you, that little pussy damn near drizzles with nothing but your lust for me." He yanked the toy from my vagina and covered my pussy with the hungriest mouth ever known in my world. He sipped in the juices the toy left behind and then plunged his tongue into the core of a woman again and again.

"Dallas," I whimpered.

"Tell me you aren't mad at me," he growled.

"I'm not mad at you," I purred. Damn it, I purred! I fell apart then and realized at this point, I'd bark, perhaps even neigh or moo every single time I heard his animalistic growl, if he'd just give me what I wanted. Ripples of pleasure, sweet satisfaction began to rake over my body in short waves.

"I'm sure you're not upset now." He glanced upward and then gripped my ass hard as he held my pussy closer to his face. "And you'll never stay angry with me long."

His tongue propelled inside my walls and he withdrew long enough to bathe the folds in his sweet moisture before going in for a lasting sweet time. "Now." He withdrew long enough to whisper, command.

"Yes, now!" I thrust against him. Throwing my hips forward as high as I could reach and every time I pressed higher, he held me there until he was on the bed with bended knees, holding my lower back so I felt him all the way to my neck and throat. "Pleasure, sweet mercy and pleasure."

He ate and sipped, drank and nibbled and my inner thighs framed his face as he brought on two wonderful, mind-destroying climaxes.

* * * *

Hours later, we were entwined in each other's arms. I woke up from a deep sleep, eased up on one elbow and watched him.

One eye quickly opened. "Not sleeping?"

"I can't."

He smiled. "You've been snoring softly so I think you can."

"You can't sleep with me, can you?"

"I told you before, I don't require a lot of sleep."

"But I mean you can't sleep next to a woman." I patiently waited for his answer but when I didn't get one, I tried again. "It's okay, you know. A lot of men don't want that connection and I don't mind if you sleep in the other bed."

With a grunt, he rolled over me. "Kimbrell, I am not opposed to waking up with you or going to sleep with you."

"That's good to know."

"Get used to it because you'll only wake up to me from here on out."

I gulped. "I think we need to talk."

"No, what we need to do is what you wanted to do last night. We need to fuck."

I felt a smile turn up the corners of my lips. "Have you been waiting all night to ask me for sex?"

"Darlin', I don't ask for sex."

"You're asking."

"No, technically, I'm telling you."

"Really?" I reached for his member and found him just the way I left him. Hard, ripe, erect and ready. The mushroom tip swelled against my fingertips as my hand wrapped him securely.

His mouth slanted over mine for only a second before joining his fingertips as they caressed my nipple. Dropping his head, he sucked in my full breast moaning with the pleasure surrounding us. "That's it…" He licked as he pushed his erection into my palm.

Moving lower with a wandering hand, I expected him to finger me but instead he shifted his weight, covered my hand, flipped his wrist and positioned the head of his cock at my vagina. "Move up."

I did what he asked. He rubbed his thick flesh over the entrance. My hips jerked forward as I tried to capture his cock and make him take that first dip.

"Ah, little siren. It's not going to be too easy." His hand blocked the intrusion and he began to stroke against my pussy with a deliberate need to arouse. "Scoot up." His voice stayed thick with his sexuality as he slapped my pussy with the back of his hand, just a love pat, but enough to know his cock wasn't there at my opening. "Watch me."

I did what he asked and angled my body against pillows, realizing he wanted us both to see him enter me. His eyes narrowed as he wrapped my fingers with his. "Now." He pulled his hand away and waited for me to take him.

"Sweet." I pulled away and arched for him. My legs moved around his waist and I locked my ankles behind his lower back pushing my body forward, capturing his cock in the process. He stared at my pussy, the vagina he planned to slowly penetrate.

"Slow and easy, baby. Take me slow," he warned and I needed to heed it. I wanted to do what he instructed me to do for both of us but I was too far gone to obey, too filled with lust to take his words to heart.

"I can't." I took a deep breath and pressed into him, my neck straining to see the show. He rolled back on the balls of his feet.

"Dear God, that's…long."

"Yeah, now you see the advantage." He chuckled but he looked more like pain struck him with a fatal blow. "I'm not going to last here, Kimbrell." Beads of sweat rolled off of him in a mesmerizing pattern across his forehead.

He pushed my thighs open, holding them apart and the move delayed the consequences. "Darlin', I'll rip you apart. Now, go slow, damn you. Take me slower. Patience, take your time." He swirled around my nipple with his hot, delicious tongue and a wave of lust poured through my body seeping around his cock. "Ah yeah, let me feel you." His forefinger caressed my lower lip. "Take it easy, we have all day, all night. Go slow."

"The hell you say." I became greedy with need, aching with lust I'd never known before. Taking things at a turtle's pace just wasn't going to happen.

I pulled him all the way in and with a yelp screamed in agony. "Oh God." He didn't move. He knew. I understood. I overestimated my ability to handle him and he realized he needed to withdraw but he damn well couldn't leave the snug cave he found in me.

"I can take it out." He started to ease back and I gripped him tighter with my thighs.

"Take it out?" I giggled and then moaned with pain. "Just give me a minute and don't you dare fuckin' move or so help me, I'll tie you to this bed with your own damn rope!"

"Kimbrell, you're not going to stretch that easily."

"I don't care. I just don't care. Just…give me two seconds. Please…two more." I tried to adjust but it wasn't happening. Damn it, he was right. My insides pulsed with him lodged between my thighs.

"I do." He started to move. "I know what I do to a woman."

"You have no idea what you do to *this* woman." I gripped his neck and brought him crashing against my lips. With a kiss in order, he gave me what I wanted and slowly moved out and then in again,, kissing me ever so tenderly.

I unleashed one of those pathetic woman pleas. The kind of statement I never wanted to have fall from my lips. The kind of request a woman who just met a man simply didn't make. "Please don't leave me."

"Like it that much, do you." His wicked grin was deplorable and enduring all at the same time.

"I love it. I love feeling you." I arched against him. "Now, move, damn you."

Hot heat began to surge through my body. He moved into me with slow calculation. A bit to the left, a tad inch forward, a swift move to the right and a deep penetration guaranteed to leave me screaming, arching and scraping my nails down his chest.

A fulfilling thrust and he went for the finish, waiting to begin. "That's it. Pull me in. Hold me tight. Never let go."

"Deeper." I pleaded for the impossible. He was as deep as any man hoped to go and I asked for more.

The bed moved with him as he tightened my arms around his neck. "Hold on, baby. Hold on."

I kissed his lips as he moved and thrashed against me. His hands dropped to my waist and with a slow grind, he fell into a new pattern, a new way to fuck a person silly. His hands held tightly to my waist as his gaze fell to our act. The sweet satisfaction covered his face. "Fuck me tighter, harder, more."

My intimate walls clenched and released, held and vibrated as he plunged his shaft harder against the folds, deeper into the realms of ecstasy. "That's it. Come for me. Let me feel you. Milk my cock, baby. Let me fill this sweet cunt with every single drop."

I was already there and he would get there—but it would take some time.

* * * *

I buried my head against his shoulder and released a fulfilling sigh. "I…but…you…" He didn't come. He didn't unleash his desires. They still existed, flamed almost completely out of control. The length of his erection impaled my flesh. I felt every vein then as I tried to prevent him from leaving me. I wanted to please him. I wanted him to know I marked him as mine as much as he apparently wanted me marked as his. None of it made sense but then again, nothing in my world did. Right now, only this mattered, and whatever he wished to give me, I needed to take.

"I will come. Don't worry." He grabbed something from the side of the bed. A plug of sorts, a cold stoneware with a defined impression at the top. A pointed tip, or maybe round. I couldn't focus. The orgasm I took still pulsed against my walls as he slipped completely away.

Before I asked questions or took the time to gawk, he dipped the small butt plug into the cool lubricant and inserted it into my anus. "Dallas…no."

His eyes were colder, harder, and much darker. "Yes."

"I can't. I'm…"

"Wet, ready." He jerked me to him. "Always ready. Always mine." His fingers dipped into my pussy as he watched me squirm away from his hand. His focus on our lower halves, he dipped and retreated with one finger, then two before he squeezed me tighter against his cock. He pushed me back on the bed again and with a groan, his lips attacked mine with a driven purpose, a new darkness lingering behind a haze of lust.

I knew what he needed. I even wanted it. I could submit to him. "I'll do anything you want." I swallowed.

"Careful, Kimbrell, I gave my word. I promised not to take you there." He referred to his oath, a promise between brothers.

"They're not here. This is you and this is me. Show me what they don't want me to see. Take me there with you. Let me have the real you."

"Damn it, Kimbrell!" Desperation came over him with a wash of untried desires. "No!" He clasped my hands over my head and I felt his cock press into me again. Hard and fast, he bit his lower lip and his upper lip twitched and curled.

I struggled against his weight, against the invasion in my rear. One hand closed over my wrists while the other held my hip, pinned me against him and the mattress beneath us.

"It hurts. Take it out." I made the request but didn't mean it, not really. To lose him or the stone plug made me stop and retract. "No, just…go slow. You're too…large."

He gave more of himself then. His thighs bunched and he thrust inside me with a growl and a groan. "Breathe, Kimbrell." He studied my face and continued to stroke.

"I…I can't."

"Yes, you can." He took a deep breath as if to mock me, show me. Each time he said something, his tone regressed and darkness trailed through his words. His movements changed and became calculated, and timed.

Lust and a thirst so perverse existed in his expression. His tinted flesh, the beads of sweat, all of it guaranteed he was a man in true heat. A man with a strong sexual hunger that not every woman appreciated, but this woman now craved.

My body stretched, as if he demanded it. I was wetter than before, the plug in place only brought about awareness. I imagined the feel of all men, all the Carlisle brothers and the heat rose. It paralyzed me with the sexuality Dallas claimed he didn't want me to have, yet it was precisely why he wanted me in the first place.

"That's it, move with me." He gritted his teeth as he nipped at my earlobe.

He was huge. His monster cock twisted inside of me and I felt like I'd die if I didn't come, but I wanted him to lose himself with me. My ass tingled with the pleasure, defiantly worked with the pressure as I rose up to greet his thrusts.

"Make love to me, Dallas." I wanted him to fuck me. Why I used the l-o-v-e insinuation slapped me with a dose of hard reality.

"God, yeah. Hell, yeah." His voice pitched. His pace increased and he released my wrists and spread my thighs open as blue-hot ripples began to tear through my womb. "Come for me, Kimbrell. That's it, baby. Work those fancy hips with me. Let me drive you crazy, baby. Let me…make you mine."

"Dallas!" I screamed his name right before his tongue parted my lips and moved into my mouth with the same pace as his cock.

"Good…so good. Milk my cock, lover. Milk it." He pushed his way forward as a spurt of his pleasure sank deep. Penetrating beyond anything I'd ever known, he bypassed my clenching walls only to cover me forever with his gratification and an undying sensation—one that would one day evolve into a truly forbidden kind of love.

Chapter 7

"Well if you two don't look like you've been rode hard, put up damp and ready to go again." Rex met us at the driveway and pulled me from the truck. I landed against his chest and his lips.

Corbin watched from the front porch. His eyes already undressed me one hundred and fifty different ways.

"What's his problem?" Dallas motioned to his brother.

Rex grunted. "He's angry as hell. That McClanahan fellow followed him to some bar in Columbia last night and then damn near beat the hell out of him."

"What?" I pulled my purse and a few shopping bags from the bench seat as I started to move by Rex. He patted my bottom as I ran to the stoop. Dropping the bags at Corbin's feet, I studied him.

"You don't look hurt to me."

"I'm not hurt." He studied me closer. "I'm better now, anyway. Get over here and kiss me."

I smirked and started to do exactly as suggested but then Rex stopped me.

"The hell he's not." Rex shifted his weight with the luggage he held. "Take a look at his back."

I gently laid my hand on his forearm. "Let me see."

Corbin stood up and his seductive tone changed in an instant. "I don't need a damn woman looking after me." He shook off my attempt to take a peek.

"Dallas?" I rapidly blinked my eyes, set my jaw and tilted my head in his direction.

"Shit." He dropped the overnight bags and some more shopping bags. "Corbin, let's see you."

The larger of the men, Dallas stopped his brother in the yard. "Let me take a look."

"Not in front of her."

I swallowed stiffly and glared at Rex and then Corbin. Before I could stop the tears, they swelled in the corners of my eyes. I understood his anger, the hostility, the vile reason he didn't want me to see. They were proud men. I related to pride but I also recognized my involvement if he took a beating from Finn and Stan.

"You defended me?" I asked.

"I didn't have to. They blind-sided me."

"No, they didn't blind-side you. They told you too much about me and you said the wrong thing to the wrong guys over a few beers. That's what happens in these parts. They may have gotten you from the back but if you weren't turning up a whiskey glass with the wrong group of men, you would've seen them coming."

"You're speaking that woman gibberish shit and I don't translate it well. Just go in the house and forget about it. We've got work to do around here." Corbin made his way to the barn and I felt like someone punched me in the gut a few times.

Rex turned his focus back to Dallas. "Did you two have a good time?"

"Great." He winked at me.

"Yeah, we had a fantastic time." I kissed Dallas on the cheek and then nervously walked over to Rex. After four days with Dallas, I still didn't understand our relationship or the one he wanted me to establish with his brothers. I kissed Rex on the cheek and then started for the house.

"Darlene called a half a dozen times for you. She said she needed to talk to you as soon as possible."

"Thanks. I'll call her now."

"Yep. And get dressed. I'm taking you out for supper," Rex said.

"For supper?" I laughed. "Local speak is getting to you, huh?"

He crooked his head and then winked. "Nay, but the locals need to see you out and about so I'm going to take you to a little place down the road."

I skipped up the front steps, walked inside and picked up the phone. I slowly dialed Darlene's cell phone and tugged my luggage down the hall. The rings finally subsided with instructions to leave a message. I started to leave one but quickly hung up when I heard the conversation in progress.

"So, what'd ya'll do?"

"What do you think we did?" Dallas chided.

"Not gonna share, huh?" I heard Rex's footsteps across the front porch and I held my breath waiting for Dallas's answer. Instead, Rex continued, "I can't say that I blame you—"

"No, we agreed. I'm not going back on my word."

"You're in love with her though," Rex said.

"Hell, boy, did you think we'd find a woman to share that we wouldn't love?"

"Sure, we all need to love her if we're going to make this thing work between us but I didn't expect you to fall so hard."

"I'm in love with her," Dallas admitted. "I loved her before I got here. Her sister made damn sure of it when she sent me all of those letters and pictures, everything she could think of, everything she wanted me to see so I would see the real Kimbrell but I gotta tell ya…" He paused for some reason and I released the breath I started to hold when I first heard the men discussing me, "She's more than all that stuff I received in a box."

"I know that," Rex agreed with a laugh.

I slumped down against the wall. My head barely scraping the top of the windowsill, I tried to keep my breathing in check and my runaway heart from thumping loud enough for them to hear.

"What happened here?"

"Dallas, it was awful. That Finn fellow ought to be shot in the back, especially after what he did to Corb."

I heard the crunching sound of gravel and realized Corbin was walking toward the house again. "I'm going to drive into town and get some horse feed. They're out here and Dawson's place is running low too."

"Come here and let me check out your back."

A few boards creaked and I realized Dallas stepped off the porch to check out his brother. I tried to see by raising my chin above the wood and peering outside. Corbin's back was to me and I squinted to see the evidence.

"Damn it to fucking hell!" Dallas screeched at the sight. I slumped down against the wall and held my cries by covering my mouth. The tears streamed anyway.

"What the hell did they do to you?"

"They took a cattle whip to his back," Rex said. "Three of 'em held him. McClanahan and his brother whipped him. Struck his flesh for every single day they'd thought about fuckin' her, or so they told him."

"And you didn't do anything about this?" Dallas's anger rose above the birds chirping in the trees.

"What the hell did you want me to do? Call you and tell you to come home?"

"It's over and done with and I don't want Kimbrell to know how bad it is. I'll heal," Corbin said.

"What started it?" Dallas moved closer to the house and Corbin must have followed. Their voices inched closer and I slumped lower, and continued to swipe at tears.

"I went to Columbia to a place called Betty's and they followed me down the road a piece to a bar. I went there minding my own business, looking for a drink and good conversation. They sent a few fellows in who asked the bartender if he knew where they could find some work. I started talking to them and before I know it one of them is laughing."

"Laughing?" Dallas questioned.

"Yeah. Fellow said, 'Oh, hell yeah, I'll come work for you. I know what happens when you work out there for Kimbrell and Darlene. Get paid up real nice in Kimbrell's bed. I'll damn sure work for you.' And the bartender grinned too like he agreed and understood."

"Then what happened?" Dallas pressed on and I closed my eyes tighter, fully anticipating more brutal tales of my tarnished, more like rusted, reputation.

"Back and forth conversation, some of the locals claimed it was a lie that Kimbrell and her sister were mainly used up by Finn and Stan McClanahan. Then, Stan McClanahan walks in and tells me he hears I'm 'doing his girl' and he wants to know if he can buy me off. Pay me to leave."

"He did, huh?" Dallas prodded for more.

"I told him you planned on marrying her."

"Uh-huh." Dallas didn't deny it and my heart stopped beating altogether as I listened closer. "What did he say to that?"

"He said if you married her then you'd take a piece of him and every other cowboy with you to the marriage bed. He said, 'he imagined Kimbrell would marry us all seeing as his brother had pictures to prove we were all doing her.'"

"He did, did he?"

Rex remained sensible. "He doesn't have pictures, Dallas. You know you got rid of those on his cell phone."

My phone rang and I bolted across the room and flew out the door with it in hand. "Hello?" I started walking down the hallway and ran smack dab into all three Carlisles who narrowed their gazes on me. They obviously knew I'd been eavesdropping.

"Hi Darlene!" I smiled and reacted with far too much enthusiasm as I dabbed away the moisture on my cheeks noting the black mascara all over my hands whenever I swiped at my face. "Can you give me a minute to talk to my sister?" I smiled sweetly at the men staring back at me.

Dallas gave me one of those heated stares that turned my knees to jelly and my insides, particularly the area that counts, churned into melted butter. "I don't think there's anything private around here. Go ahead and talk." He leaned against the wall with folded arms.

I set my jaw and turned around, headed back for the privacy of my room. I slammed the bedroom door and crossed over to the far wall. I waited until I heard the screen door open and shut. Once the footsteps sounded out on the front porch, I slammed the window down and crawled up in bed. "Now, tell me about this box you sent to Dallas Carlisle and talk fast."

* * * *

Dallas, Corbin, and Rex left in one of their expensive trucks while I chatted on the phone with Darlene. If I cared to guess, they headed into town for more than just farm supplies. Today, given the evidence on Corbin's back, they were also in search of trouble. I knew if they wanted to find it, they wouldn't have a problem. Everyone in town would point them in the right direction if they saw Corbin's back or heard the tales about the bar brawl.

"Come on now, tell me what you shipped to Texas."

"I sent him a photograph or two from every year you've been alive and a fact sheet, of sorts, that Jack helped me put together."

"Why would you do that?" I questioned.

"Why wouldn't I? These boys have been looking on dating sites for a match and Jack's the one who put it together that they were looking for one woman to share between them. We didn't figure it would hurt you any to consider it, seeing as—"

"Seeing as what?"

"Come on, Kimbrell, you and I both know you don't have the reputation as being as snow-white pure as a first winter snow."

"I'm not as bad as everyone seems to think, either." I finally admitted it. I was experienced, sure as the world, but not as cheap as some might think. In a short period of time, Dallas taught me that much. Most of the same men visited time and time again. Those in town might believe otherwise but who cared?

It was time I started believing that I was worthy of consideration and something more than a common whore. Just because I'd done a few men upside down and sideways didn't mean I ranked as the worst of my gender.

"I know that. Jack told Dallas and the rest of them the same thing. You're a good person, Kimbrell, a tad on the wild side, but you have heart and a lot of folks don't have heart."

"Jack said I'm not all bad?" Imagine.

"Yes, he did."

"I overheard all of 'em talking you know." I took a deep breath, weighing out whether or not I should tell her what I'd heard. "Dallas thinks he wants to marry me, or at least I think he does."

"It's what I hear too."

"You know?"

"Yeah. Corbin and Rex talked to Jack a few times after you ran off to Nashville. They said Dallas is obsessed with you and Corbin can't get enough of you." She laughed.

"And Rex?"

"Rex is smitten, but I don't think you'll ever wrap him around your pinky. In fact, don't take this the wrong way but he's the kind of man I imagine jacking off to a balance sheet."

"You might be right." I smiled as I stared out the window. I gave her first comment further consideration and then added, "Maybe he's not around my finger but I have something to keep him in check. It'll guarantee he comes back for more."

"Good grief, Kimbrell."

I smiled at the idea of my sister blushing and then thought of Rex again. He had the heaviest eyes I'd ever seen during sex. Oh yeah, I'd have him wrapped tight and I might even start tonight. "You're having a good honeymoon, I hope?"

"The best. Did you even see Nashville?"

"Yeah, as we passed through."

"So how's the sex?" She laughed.

"Hot."

"Did he talk you to sleep?" She giggled. "I told you a woman could come just listening to him."

"Darlene! You're talking about a man I might marry."

"Yep. And we've shared before. Maybe Jack will let him call me at bedtime or something."

"I don't think so. We haven't shared like what you're talking about, or how the Carlisles plan to share me."

"Ewe!" She let out a deep breath over the receiver. "Kimbrell, you're gonna take up with them, aren't 'cha?"

"Might."

"Move out west?"

"Maybe. They say they might move here."

"That'll work…well, maybe not."

"Why?"

"The locals and all."

"There are good people here in Lewisburg, Darlene."

"You better believe it. One of the best is on the other end of this phone with me. I gotta go, Kimbrell. Jack's got his one-eyed head in my face again."

I snickered. "I understand."

"I imagine you do." She hung up with a squeal and disconnected the call.

And I thought long and hard before I took matters into my own hands. Still, I came up with only one solution.

There was only one way to skin a cat or milk a cow in these parts. You had to get your hands on the animal if you expected to get the job done. I decided to pay a visit to the very beasts that made me look like a whore among men. It was past time to set the record straight. I crawled under my bed and pulled out a shotgun. I hoped I didn't need it but if so, I'd have it in hand.

Chapter 8

At one time, I might have loved Stan McClanahan. He was easy enough to touch and had a few good hidden qualities. A great ass and working hands, Stan hung around my bed more than most, and generally, when he came around, no one else bothered. Some in town thought we'd settle down but soon I realized if we did, that's what I would've done—settled.

I drove through the gates of the McClanahan property and pulled the shotgun from my front seat. Propping it up against the truck, I yelled for them. "Stan, Finn? Get on out here! Now!"

Momma McClanahan died several months before or else I wouldn't have dared to carry on like this on their property. Their daddy, the one they shared with Darlene's husband, died years ago.

Stan appeared first. "Well, I'll be damned. Some said you ran off to Dallas with a man named the same."

"Yeah, well, we didn't make it past Nashville."

"Miss me, did ya?" He checked out the gun behind me and licked his lower lip. "You know, I've been thinkin' 'bout you a lot here lately."

"Huh? Strange, but I don't remember you so much as saying good-bye after Dawson ran you out of town."

"I'm back now, Kimbrell. Came back here for you, if you want to know the truth."

"Where's Finn?" I looked around. I didn't want him sneakin' up on me.

"He's around." Stan took a deep breath as he studied me closer. "Got anything to share with a lonesome cowboy today?" His gaze settled at my crotch. Slowly, he stepped off the porch and as soon as he approached me, it was too late. I wasn't going to go for the gun. Too many memories came back all at one time. We'd shared some good times, some good fucks too.

"I've missed you." He whispered as he stepped forward. "Missed the smell of that sweet pussy under my lips. Damn girl, no woman has ever satisfied me like you do."

I swallowed hard as I watched his dark eyes twinkle with satisfaction. He slowly pursued me, crept closer. By the time I saw him nod to someone behind me, it was too late. He snapped his arms around my waist and yanked me against him as Finn tossed the shotgun off to the side.

"Finn figured about right." Stan's whiskey stench burned against my lips. "He said you'd come lookin' for revenge."

Finn's hot smelly breath moved across my neck. "I said she'd come lookin' for a fuck too and that's precisely what she's gonna get." I heard his zipper drop as my knees started to buckle.

"They'll kill you." I breathed in the trouble, feared the repercussions.

"They'll have to find us first." Finn slammed me against the truck and tugged at his pants.

"Damn you, Finn. Wait until we get her inside!" Stan screamed out as he tugged my wrists.

"Hell no. They've been in town all mornin' lookin' for us. When they come out here, they're gonna find my cock buried in her ass."

A shot fired in the distance and my neck jerked as Finn's cock twitched against my backside.

"Back away from her, now or I'll blow your little pecker to the wind." Dallas shouted out to them.

Finn's evil smirk held naughty intentions, the kind a woman didn't want to find out about. "I didn't know you swung your dick both ways, Carlisle but get on over here and I'll let you try it."

I sneered, "He at least has one to swing."

He fisted his cock and rubbed it against my ass. "If I don't get you now, I'll be coming for you. I will have you wiggling against this dick again," he hissed in my ear as Stan, the one I always believed had some sense, though it now appeared limited, backed away.

Corbin rose from the other side of the truck and peered in the window. "I'll blow you away and walk away with nothing more than a self-defense plea. You've got our girl and I've got the marks to prove you attacked from the back."

Finn grabbed me by my hair as he tugged his pants up with his free hand. Dragging me in front of Stan, he ordered Stan to back up. "Get in the house."

"Stop it!" I snapped. "Let me go damn you!"

Stan and Finn continued to hide behind me until they couldn't move anywhere at all.

Rex stepped out on the porch and took a seat on their stoop with a shotgun pointed at Finn's shrinking size. "Got a little pecker, doesn't he, Kimbrell?"

I stared into his eyes and gulped. He winked. "I want my woman and you two buzzards can fly free after you hand her over."

Finn held me closer. "Your woman? Your brother over there seems to think she belongs to him."

Dallas stalked forward. "I'm going to marry her. What we do with her after that isn't your concern."

I blinked. He looked me square in the eye when he said the five-letter dirty word. The one I believed should be washed and laundered before tossed about so freely.

"Let her go." He pointed his gun at Finn's cock.

Now, two cowboys lurked about with pointed guns, loaded ones—I was sure about that fact—and deadly glares in their eyes.

"Stan, go inside," I pleaded.

"Not on your life," he huffed as he grabbed me around the waist.

Corbin retrieved my daddy's gun and walked forward with it cocked and pointed.

Finn pulled a knife from his pocket and tried to open it. Before he had the chance, Corbin was on top of him. He shot the gun off in mid-air and tossed it aside. His fist crashed against Finn's jaw again and again. Stan stood by and watched for only a second before he tried to help his brother.

"It's between them." Rex pointed his gun at Stan's chest. "Get her home, Dallas."

"No! This stops here today! I'm not leaving without all of you."

"The hell you're not." Rex nodded at Dallas but he didn't budge. He was whipped, no doubt, and not likely to go against me since he'd had time to see the different moods I possessed.

"Shit! Stan! Do somethin'!" His brother whined as the strikes continued. Corbin pinned Finn under his broad frame and truly beat the holy hell out of him.

"Stop this! Please! You're going to kill him!"

Finn moaned with every strike.

Corbin shoved me aside as I tried to grab his arm. Scuffling around, I yanked the gun from Rex's hand and shot it in mid-air. Everyone froze. All cowboys stared at me. Corbin shoved another fist of anger against Finn's jaw and then left him with a toe in his groin. The agonizing moans whipped throughout the open air.

Pushing himself up, Corbin grabbed me from behind. "Damn you, woman!" He pulled me to the truck and tossed me inside. He then turned on his brothers and glared at them both. "If I have to fight for her honor, the least you two could do is keep her the hell out of the way."

Stan started toward us. Rex moved in front of him and Dallas held a gun on Finn. "No one move."

Pursing his lips, he stepped inside the truck. "Scoot over."

"No. You're not driving me." I glared at all of them.

"The hell I'm not. I'm going to drive you so far crazy that you'll know I've been between those thighs and those lips by the time the mornin' shines. Now scoot the hell over." His ass hit the seat and his hips nudged against mine.

I set my jaw and moved out of his way. The Carlisle men were beginning to piss me off. No, I bypassed pissed and decided mad as fucking hell more or less described my current stage of rage.

By the looks of things, Corbin had a few ways to lose some of his fury. His cock pressed tight against his jeans and he showcased just enough proof of adrenaline pumping. Boy oh boy, he was most definitely all man, all cowboy, and all hard male with emotions he was going to have to work out somewhere.

Lucky for me.

* * * *

"Get in the house." He opened my door, stood back and waited for me to get out of the truck.

"No. I'm not going to be ordered around by you or your brothers. Not today and not again." Although, looking at him then, I decided if someone wanted to make demands, I couldn't think of anyone who'd look any better doing it.

"Kimbrell, I'm not good at this and I don't want to fight with you." He dabbed at his lower lip. The only punch Finn got in left Corbin with a split lip, if it qualified as such. A dab of blood remained, nothing more.

"No, I know you don't. You want to fuck me. You and your brothers want to screw me until you can't feel anything at all when you're angry or tense, least of all horny—which is practically all the time—your brother told me it's a common problem for Carlisles. No, I'm not going to be that gal. I'm not going to bend over and take it up the ass just because you tell me to grab my ankles!"

"The hell you're not." He grabbed my hand and tugged me against him. I slammed against his chest and his cock aimed at a central position, pointed in my favor.

"Don't do this," I whispered against his skin as I held his collar in my hands.

Defiance and acceptance swept over his face. It left me to wonder which of the two stood a chance of winning out. He buried his head in my neck. His face brushed against my skin and he held me tight against him.

"Oh God, I'm sorry." He fought for control as he held me to him stroking my back and then my hair. "I'll never hurt you. I swear it. I only want to lo— "

"I know." I kissed the top of his head breaking off his words of endearment. "I believe you, but honest to God, I'm not going to have this kind of thing going on here in my backyard. You could've killed him, Corbin."

"They damn near killed me."

"They didn't. They wouldn't. Finn and Stan are a lot of things but they're not killers and revenge isn't going to make this go away. The way to beat them is to avoid them. Jack did and it worked out."

His eyes met mine and his palms framed my face. "Kiss me, Kimbrell. I have to have your lips on me."

I parted my mouth and swept him into a kiss with an eager tongue as he pushed me up against the truck. His hands remained on my cheeks as he carefully took the time to unleash some of his anger. The hostility he obviously carried, slowly unraveled as his tongue uncurled against mine. "Love me." He breathed the two simple words, breaking the power of oral pleasure between a lick, a swipe.

"I can't." I swallowed stiffly as I watched him accept what I was trying to say in more ways than one.

"Oh, yes, you can. We can all love you and you can love us in return." He pressed into me again and then bent his knees, gathered me in his arms and cradled me against his hard body.

My arms draped around his shoulders and I laid my head against his chest. When I heard the other truck pull in, I glanced over his back and watched the flicker of recognition in Dallas's eyes. Rex's jaw dropped and he nodded. "Today," I heard him say.

"Now," Dallas agreed.

My eyes darted between Rex and Dallas as Corbin carried me up the steps and across the porch. "You're going to love us all and we're going to take care of you. So help me we're going to protect you, Kimbrell," he whispered against my neck as he continued down the hall.

I heard the front door close and the heavy, weighted footsteps followed behind us. I heard the sound of running water, a bath drawn just for me. Corbin placed me upright on the bed. His lips went to mine and he gave me one of those sweet sensational kisses. Swallowing tightly, he acted like his will left him. I stripped from him. "Undress her and let her get cleaned up. I'll be back."

Dallas moved to my side and he silently plucked my boots from my feet. His fingers rolled my socks down my calves and over my feet before he balanced me against his broad shoulders. "Are you ready for this?" Concern in his voice, he kissed the tip of my nose before he pushed my pants down over my hips. His eyes sparkled with desire as he yanked the hem of my shirt and dismissed it as it fell to the floor. He clutched my head to his chest and kissed the top of it. He took my hand and led me to the bathroom and with a heated gaze, he started at my ankles and studied every exposed inch of flesh. "Are you?" He waited for my reply.

"I…I think I love you."

As if it pained him to hear it, he gritted his teeth and closed his eyes. I kissed him but he remained somewhat composed, defiantly withdrawn now. "Then, if you do, you'll love all of us." He closed the door and disappeared.

* * * *

I woke up in my room. Candles danced against the shadows on the wall. Dallas stretched out on one side of me and Rex, on the other. Corbin was in a chair directly across from us, gaping at the picture we must've created.

"How long have I been out?" I asked him. The heavy breathing of the two men beside me ensured they were napping.

"Long enough, too damn long, if you ask me." He stood up and approached, stalked. His mouth moved with only a whisper. "Come here and give me that wicked little body."

I watched him with an open mouth as he held his dick in his palm and walked toward the bed. His cock reached for me as much as his hand did. His member, stoutly erect, pointed my way. "I've gotta know what you feel like again."

"You know. Oh Corbin, you know," I mumbled against his skin, against his mouth, as he took me in his arms and greeted me with assurance— a tomorrow of kisses, a caress that warms the soul as much as the lips.

"Remind me," He pleaded. "Let me feel you under my skin."

I reached for him. My fingertips wrapped around his girth and with a tug and pull, I groaned against his tight kiss and whispered against his chin, "I need you, Corbin. I long for you in a way that does something to me I can't explain." I watched for his reaction and saw him flinch with my honesty.

I told him things that came as a brutal awakening because I acknowledged my feelings then, maybe a second sooner than the words were spoken.

My mouth devoured him as I trailed over his chest and shoulders before working my way to his back and the damage created by a cruel hand and several cattle whips across his skin. "Let me take all the pain away."

"Stop." He froze as my fingertips traced the lines, the evidence, the proof. He'd defended my honor, what little I had, like I deserved it.

"You took a beating because of me. I'm so sorry, Corbin."

He wheeled around to face me. "You're sorry?"

"I am."

"No, Kimbrell. I'm sorry. I'm sorry we weren't here for you when you needed us most, sorry we looked in all the wrong places before we found the only woman meant for us." His tongue darted between my lips and out again. "And most of all, I'm sorry I had to wait to do this." His mouth claimed mine in a hunger so perverse and delicious. Certainty guaranteed his kiss was designed for orgasmic wonder. "Love me, Kimbrell. Wrap your legs around me and love me the way I need you to love me."

I gulped when I heard those words again. The Carlisles had a way of gaining my attention with four letter words I once deemed as bad words. Softly spoken, whispered directly into my ear, against my flesh and at the wrong, or right, times. True urgency swept through me as he moved me to the bed. Dallas sat up, startled awake, rubbing one eye with the ball of his hand.

"Don't even think about it." A lopsided smile shaped Corbin's lips and when Rex woke up too, he must've read the expression with understanding.

"Come here." Corbin lowered his body over mine and with an open mouth and wandering tongue, he sucked in the first nipple before visiting the second. "I'm crazy when you're not around." His hands propelled down my sides and with an eagerness, a divine emergency, he flipped me over and maneuvered my body in a way to allow his palm to land softly against my pussy. His middle finger parted my folds and slid right in as the first slap against my bottom came down with a smack.

"Oh God, Corbin. No—"

"Oh yeah, you're spanked after your stunt." Rex scooted up against the headboard.

Dallas took a deep breath. "This is what it's all about, Kimbrell. We're going to enjoy you and make sure you never want anyone other than us in the process. Let him spank you."

"So damn sweet and wet." Corbin's mouth caressed and sucked every inch of flesh he could reach without vacating my center. His finger slid in and out in a precise time. A deliberate rhythm formed between sexes while his lone middle finger guaranteed our bodies forged ahead. Calculated strokes in and out, diabolical smacks against my ass, torturous licks—long and slow—ensured one thrust inside and my body's requirements would find fulfillment.

"Fill my palm with those sweet juices." His hand came down against my ass and the manual fucking stopped. It ceased to exist as he fisted his cock and ran it across my apple shaped bottom—the one I hated—and men loved.

"I can't. Not yet. You'll rip me apart."

With a growl, an apparent distaste for the word no, he turned me over once more. Straddled across my middle, he gave dire instructions. "Suck my cock. Take it. Damn you, I'm going crazy." His cock glistened with pre-cum as he pressed it against my chin. "Make me sane again, baby. Let me fuck that pretty little mouth."

I heard Dallas grunt behind us. "I'm crazy half the time when I'm with her." He moved back the sheet and made sure I caught sight of *it* in my peripheral vision. Long and stout, Dallas's cock was as ready as the one greedily positioned in front of me. I bit down on my forefinger because it was the only way to prevent myself from motioning him or Rex closer. They both waited, watched, craved. The lust in their eyes didn't leave anything to my imagination. I knew because I felt the same crazy hunger and it existed for all of them.

With his knees bent on either side of my body, Corbin's cock parted my lips. "You know how to please a man, Kimbrell. You understand what I need, what I have to have...right now." He pressed his cock against my mouth and rubbed it back and forth over my bottom lip. I sucked the mushroom head whenever he paused and when he finally released it, I sucked him from base to tip. "That's it, sweetheart. Pump me with your hot little mouth, stroke my cock with your tongue. God, that's good. So good, baby."

My fingertips lightly strummed across his balls and right as his pace slowed, I opened wider, knowing that he reeled forward caught in a clasp of suffocating desires, and yet he waited, just holding himself at bay long enough to surge forward with a newfound purpose, the goal of all hard men—getting off.

I blinked once and felt like my eyes rolled back in my head but I didn't shut him out completely. Still, I was shocked when his dick twitched at the back of my throat and then he pulled out and lowered himself over me. "Open your legs for me, darlin'." The head of his cock lay at my entrance. "Rex, Dallas." He grumbled as if inviting them to join the party wasn't what he wanted necessarily, but certainly what we all needed.

"I'm not going to share you often. I prefer the one on one to the song and dance Rex and Dallas like." With a moan he thrust inside, pushing in with the confidence of a well hung man and a man who took what he wanted. His fingers dug into my hips as he rose high enough to allow the suckling mouths that covered my breasts—Rex on one side, Dallas debating whether or not he'd stay locked in place on the other.

Dallas's lips tweaked my nipple into a hard bud before he knelt over me with his cock demanding oral satisfaction. I didn't wait for the invitation and I damn sure didn't want to chase his dick down while he rubbed it all over me. Grasping it in my hand, I pulled him closer, licked the underside and sucked him in while Corbin pounded his straining length into my tight cave.

"That's it, fancy hips. You know how I want you when I'm this horny." Dallas pressed his cock to the back of my throat as I tried to fathom the thought of Rex joining us too.

"Son of a bitch!" Corbin nearly jolted off the bed as he pulled my legs tighter around his waist. "Come with me, Kimbrell." His hips moved faster as my hands slid across his chest.

His muscular arms covered me like a jacket, pinning me against him and yet allowing me enough space to considerately finish what I started with Dallas. "Suck me, fuck him. "

"Do it right, do both of us, focus those fancy hips on Corbin and your sweet cheeks, ah sugar, these cheeks belong to me." Dallas dropped his dick more as he swelled in between my cheeks. Holy cow, I wondered if I'd ever think of his cock as anything more than an animalistic in size.

The first spray of satisfaction filled my mouth as Dallas rippled across my tongue. "Ah, yeah. Fuck me with your soft tongue." A few grunts later and I realized he was being far too kind and overly cautious. I wanted more.

I tried to raise my neck off the pillow and hold him closer, pull him to the back of my throat but he refused to give me what I wanted and he knew himself better than I did. Right now, maybe I didn't know what I was begging for but I damn sure understood the climax gripping me, taking him.

Corbin withdrew about an inch but an inch was all I allowed. My walls trembled with him and he stayed locked between my legs. I tried to capture him, keep him captivated enough to go in deep.

I released Dallas with a shout to Corbin, "Don't leave me!" I begged for mercy, screamed for the one in between my legs to finish the job of a well endowed cowboy. "Please!"

"Please? Ah yeah, sugar, I'll please." His hips began to work after a stiffer penetration, but even after he came, he didn't need to worry because he had more than enough to finish the job. "Come to me, now."

My hips rose and fell as I met his encouragement with a force so strong that I swore the earth began to spin. "So good, don't stop…"

"That's my girl." He swiped the hair from my eyes as he gazed into them. "That's it, darlin'." A thrust and I was creaming and screaming with his eyes piercing through mine.

Harder and harder he pounded his cock into my pussy and he was going for the multiple concept—the one all good men know how to give their women.

"I feel your hot heat seeping around my cock. Keep coming with me, darlin', keep it wet for me. Let me swim in you."

"God, I can't. I can't again." He pinned me under his weight. Rex moved over me next and drew me into a deeply passionate kiss. Dallas disappeared and returned with all sorts of goodies on a tray. Sexual goodies, damp washcloths, and a bottle of wine with several glasses filled the large tray.

I giggled as I watched him situate everything on my tiny nightstand. It was an erotic display of disarray, much like the way I felt right now with legs and arms tangled around me.

In an effort to leave me vulnerable, Dallas sat down at the head of the bed. "Here drink this." He offered a glass of wine but kept it just out of my reach. I rolled over on my belly and narrowed my eyes as soon as I felt Rex standing behind me.

Lips curved into naughty smiles all around the room and Dallas tossed Rex the lubricant he'd need if he wanted him to use if he planned to dive in from behind.

After a sip or two of what I believed to be the finest glass of homemade wine, I perched on all fours and rubbed my ass against the crest of Rex's cock. "You're waiting too long back there, handsome." I encouraged more than what I needed to do with these three, and soon, Rex's fingers tempted the spot he planned to take first.

Dallas's engorged head started forward again. "You're never satisfied," I told him with a smile.

"Oh I'm satisfied but I'll never get enough of you when you're like this."

I opened up for his tight shaft and orally stroked him with my tongue swiping all around him sipping him in once again. I still wanted him hitting the back of my throat and he took his own damn sweet time again.

"Dallas, please." I asked for more as I circled the mushroom tip and covered his tiny slit with a quick lick. "I want you to go deeper."

He tilted my chin forward with his forefinger. "You do?" His voice was thick with something—sarcasm—and a hint of anger. Only then did I understand why because I saw the pain in his eyes. He was pissed the hell off over the stunt I pulled, angry because I went to see Finn and Stan.

"Uh-huh." I dropped my mouth over him again and puckered against his dick with a kiss nearly twirling around the engorged head. "Give me all of it."

Corbin's hand came down against my ass as Rex began to finger the entrance he was now dying to take. I swallowed quickly, still trying to take all of Dallas, bring him in for a more satisfying blow job. He fisted a handful of strawberry locks and yanked me forward and back with a reminder of the man I thought I could control.

Rex's fingers worked with what he had and Corbin's palm cupped under my pussy. "Fuck her, Dallas. Let me have her mouth." He reached in between my legs. "A hot little pussy like this one doesn't need to stay empty long." His wicked smile turned into a pout and then he smacked again. "Yell for it, baby."

I swallowed the pre-cum from Dallas's tip and complained when he refused to give me what I craved. "I want you backed up against my throat, your balls slapping against my chin."

He brushed the hair away from my face. Beads of sweat formed on his brow. "I can't give you that right now. Trust me, I'd hurt you with the state of arousal you've put me in." He licked his lips and then pushed in once more, tapping the back of my throat for amusement.

With reluctance, I released him and Rex pulled me back against his chest long enough to let Dallas slide under us. Rex's sounded more sexual than before. "Straddle him across the middle and let me have that sweet ass." He helped position me for all of them. They were ready to join as one.

Dallas held my hands against his broad chest. Corbin moved to the side of our bodies and tilted my chin upward while Rex made all sorts of assumptions. "We'll rip her apart. She can't handle me and you both." He spoke to Dallas and Dallas watched me, ignoring his brother, making certain he owned and kept my attention. He had better things to do with his lips and apparently those sweet kisses he planted around my nipples took all of his concentration. His heavy cock stood erect and ready. Slowly, as if he didn't remain mindful of where his dick drifted, his penis began to move inside.

"Damn, what a tight little snatch." He released my nipple long enough to draw the other one into his swollen lips. Another inch and then another disappeared inside. He stretched me slowly and that's when a soothing hot moisture dribbled over my ass and down the tight seam.

Rex's mouth heated my earlobe with a lick, and on a promise, he pushed in, asking for leverage as he wrapped his arm around my waist. "Give me some space, Dallas." He joked. "Sweet sunshine, this is heaven." His cock tortured the forbidden rings and greedily found its own space.

Corbin's eyes flared as soon as I sucked his cock between my lips. He shifted his weight while I tugged him inside with a deep, satisfying suck. "Mmm…" I moaned against his texture, his salty taste.

"Ah, baby. That's good. So good." He pulled out and then pushed in again. Pulled out and then stroked against my mouth with a frightening beat. He found a true rhythm and I didn't want to break it because his sweet essence was going to be the first thing I tasted when I came. I was certain his release would find him and assurance only drive me higher.

"Is that good?" He watched me as I blinked my eyes.

Rex smacked my bottom trying to give a few more inches without making me sweat it, beg for it. "Come on now, sugar. Spread those hips."

"So good, Kimbrell. Suck it baby. You like it, don't you?" He swelled more and more, damn near doubling in size as he watched his brothers fuck me with an intent focus, mind-blowing sexual stare.

"Answer him!" Rex smacked again. Hot fluids flooded my pussy and I wanted to cry out and I darn sure wanted to come. Heat, red-hot warmth, devoured me and held me hostage. I never wanted this moment to end. I wanted them to keep me balanced on the realm of an earth-shattering orgasm. Right here, like this.

I moaned against the pulsing member locked in between my cheeks. "I'm dying here, baby. Your hot little mouth is badgering me, sweetheart. I burn for you, Kimbrell. Only you, there's no way you can even understand."

Oh but I did. His tense balls slapped against my chin. They were so taut, deliciously ripe. I wondered how a man lost his control with so much strength working with him to keep it?

Dallas's face was full of pride as he watched me. It was as if he thought he trained me for these unruly positions. "That's it, sweetheart, move those fancy hips good for us. I want you feeling my cock stretching you. You have to milk it, take me an inch at a time." His hands fell to my sides and he began to move me along his shaft. That's when Rex found his pace right along with us and at the same time, Dallas sank all the way.

I squeezed my eyes shut and moaned a muffled scream against Corbin's dick. "It's all right, baby girl. We've got you." Everything I'd ask from Dallas, I received from all of them at one time. One dick filled my mouth with the intent to strip my tonsils right out of my throat. One worked at wearing my ass out with dick and palm. And the other one, the most familiar, stripped my senses as my pussy clenched around him with a warning. It was tough going in, breaking through all barriers but I had enough strength to keep him there now that I had him easing his way into the depths of my cavern.

The muscles in my throat continued to constrict and expand as I sucked Corbin all the way to the back and the ripples between my cheeks began. Rex jolted as a sudden hot heat jetted forward, then filled my ass.

"Dear God, hold still." He gripped my waist and fucked my ass as hard as a man was supposed to fuck a woman when his orgasm began to ride in and claim him but what I didn't count on was everyone working together to come at the same time.

Dallas clamped over my nipple as his facial expression turned ravenous and Corbin flexed against the confinement of my compact throat. Faster and faster, he pushed into the back of my mouth as his semen sprayed over my tongue and washed down my throat in a sudden concentrated formula—his taste, his seed, his pleasure. "Good, baby. Suck and swallow. Ah yeah, so good."

Rex plunged harder and thrust himself into my ass with one explosion, and then so help me, it felt like another. His spurts of relief followed carnal, fulfilling moans and they were all anyone heard before the grunts of fulfillment began to course through another man's ride.

"Harder! Suck me harder." Corbin's balls softened against my chin as he came back one more time with a sudden, and now unexpected, second dose of his sweet juice. I swallowed faster and faster and then pulled away from delirious pleasure as he fell to the bed with my name on his lips.

Dallas grinned from ear to ear but his deplorable words were unrecognizable—harsh. "I took it like a real man. Now, you're going to ride me until I say the rodeo is over."

His body shifted. He pulled me off the bed with him sitting down in a chair right in front of my full length mirror.

Moving me in front of the reflection, I faced outward and my legs draped over his hard shapely thighs. He massaged my back and watched us fuck, heavy lids threatening the spill that lay right ahead. Beads of sweat broiled against my brow, proving once again I maintained a healthy sexual appetite and forever remained insatiable. I focused on the way his cock pierced through the saturated folds of my sex, and I remained wet, so damn ready for every inch of his steel, and his undeniable skill.

Closing my eyes, I refused to watch now, only because seeing us fuck made it impossible to breathe. Viewing what I hardly believed, I transformed into another person, another woman…yes, their woman. A Carlisle woman.

"Shit! This is too good to watch."

"Move those sweet hips, darlin'." Rex's turquoise eyes watched as Dallas fucked me for all to see. His enormous cock spread my pussy lips as it entered and then left me with an intoxicating visual experience. With a twist of his fingertips kneading my nipples, the fire he lit burned higher, tempted more, encouraged the unthinkable and the predictable—exploding around his thick cock. These men were my only basic need now. Right now!

"More! Give me more." I bit my lip and ground harder and harder against him.

"Easy, girl." Dallas watched me take him with the hungry, dominant male expression and winced as much as the rest of us as every stroke of pleasure brought with it some fair element of delusional pain. "More, sugar? More than what I have?"

"No, just you. Give me all of you. Harder, faster, come. Please." My palms gripped the underside of the chair as Dallas mashed his palm against my shoulder blades. His strokes came with a quicker tempo and the chair rocked us as I continued to lose the tighter grip working to gain some measure of twisted balance.

Corbin took pity on the situation. Dallas surged forward with all of his might. Corbin stood in front of me and braced me against his solid chest, holding onto my forearms as Dallas took as many as twenty strokes to start and finish his release.

When bliss ended, he picked me up and carried me to the bed only to leave me there with his brothers. He seemed angry or hurt, guilty or ashamed.

"What's going on with him?"

Rex kissed in his reassurance. "He's blaming himself because you went out to the McClanahan place."

"I thought so."

"You could've gotten yourself raped, Kimbrell." Rex stroked my back, tickled the skin above my tailbone.

"I know." I swallowed hard. "It was a dumb thing to do. Darlene had a similar experience with them. I took a gun but Finn—"

"Shh…" Rex's lips covered mine. "You're here with us now. We have you and we're going to keep you safe for as long as you'll stay in our arms."

Corbin sat down next to us and I glared at his back and the easy, if not permanent, reminders of what Finn and Stan did to a man. They were ruthless. They left the proof etched in my lover's skin.

Rex's massage provided a soothing sensation as he used a circular pattern to caress my skin. "I think I may just fall in love with you, woman." He kissed the top of my head and Corbin squeezed my hand as if to tell me he felt the same way.

Before either waited, or hoped for an endearment in return, Rex let out a sigh. "Go to him, Kimbrell. Give the devil his chance to throw a tantrum, or else it's only going to be worse for you the next time." His facial expression guaranteed he absolutely knew what he was talking about. He didn't smile or frown, but the tone in which he used indicated underlying concern.

On one hand, I didn't understand but on the other, I was totally aware of the reasons behind their request. Dallas fucked and loved as an obsessive lover. A dominating male, Dallas took what he wanted and understood he would do anything to get it but he was also a man who wasn't going to settle for his woman getting hurt.

An alpha male who protected his family, Dallas stepped in front of a threat to keep his woman safe and somehow, when he turned his back and looked the other way, I escaped the protection of a barrier he provided, one he now discovered as flawed.

* * * *

I walked on the back porch. He had his head between his hands sitting on the stoop. "Dallas?"

I pushed open the screen and stepped outside. "Come back to bed."

"I'll be there soon." He stared off at the barn.

"No, come with me now."

He gritted his teeth and looked up at me. "We were able to do that already, no thanks to you."

"What's that supposed to mean?"

Dallas stood up. Somewhere along the way, he must've forgotten that Tennesseans still wore pants because he was stark naked and his cock wasn't the only thing I noticed under the moonlight. His grim expression startled me too. I pulled my terrycloth robe closer.

"You shouldn't have to sneak off to see an old lover. You don't need to go around defending yourself with us here. You're lucky you didn't get yourself…"

"Say it." One brother had the balls to tell me, why didn't he?

"You're just lucky we got there in time," he snapped.

"Yes, I am." I sat down on the stoop, taking the seat he vacated.

"I should spank your ass."

"If it would make you feel better."

With a huff, he turned to go inside. "You're not going to run your game on us, Kimbrell. A woman like you can get a man killed."

"A woman like me?" I turned to face him and saw the lust in his eyes. The need apparent, the raging hard-on pulsing with tiny little veins of desire, and the anger—the kind a man didn't lose until he fought it out or fucked it out. I wanted either. I needed him to let go of it because this side of Dallas, truly frightened me. I'd known it since deciding on day one that he was the kind of man I needed to run from rather than hold close. Now, it was too late. I wanted to hold him close, and love him.

"I'm not going to share you with anyone other than my brothers, and so help me woman, if you turn back to your philandering ways, I'll leave your ass wherever most men found you, in the back of a barn somewhere."

"Thanks, Dallas. I appreciate the warning."

"I'm not kidding here, Kimbrell."

"No, I imagine you're not." I stood up, and then inched closer.

"Don't," he warned by whipping his palm against my chest.

My eyes were on fire now, burning with anger and confusion, blurring my vision, distorting all rational thoughts. "I want to ask you something, Dallas. Do you even want to share me with your brothers?"

I heard his teeth grind against an earth-shattering inner cry. "That's something you should never ask any of us."

"I imagine the other two would tell me they're okay with it, but not you. Never you, and I know it. I saw it in your eyes, felt it in your touch. God, Dallas, even your strokes were different, uneven and almost…tortured." I studied his expression, waited for his version of whatever truth he planned to reveal.

Corbin already readily admitted he wanted our sexual conquests performed one on one more than three on one but that was about sex. This was something entirely different. Dallas didn't want to share at all.

"Shut up, Kimbrell." His dick didn't shrink in size. It only stood harder, leaner, intent on making a statement. His fists clenched at his sides as he stepped closer.

"No, I won't. I won't because I think this relationship won't tolerate silence."

"It will if you'll learn to shut the hell up when one of us tells you to be quiet and leave well enough alone."

"Well enough alone is the problem." I dropped my robe and studied his rugged face, the colder demeanor challenging all other expressions, maybe even deeper feelings. I saw a slight twitch in his jaw, his gaze dropped and then returned to meet mine.

"Tell the truth. You can't stand it now. You're the one who orchestrated this whole thing from the beginning, but now, knowing your brothers enjoy me in all the ways you do…It's killing you."

"I said, stop." His tone held finality. "Damn you."

I gritted my teeth and pulled the robe over my shoulders again, taking the time to leave it open in the front. "No, damn you for doing this in the first place." I took a deep breath and started to walk by him and he snatched the tie at my waist and quickly drew me back against him.

His lips crashed against mine and he assaulted me with his fingers and his mouth while his cock sought out a firm obedience, a true surrender. "You push and push the men in your life. You make every damn man within a hundred miles of you crazy with need, and you get off on it. Tell me, Kimbrell, how long will it take before you can't get off on what you do to me? Huh? How long before I catch you in Finn's bed or Stan's arms? How long before the rancher down the street is lying on your sheets?"

My breath hitched in my lungs. "I don't want them. I only want you and—"

His lips slammed against mine, his fingers parted the folds of my pussy and he plunged deep the first time in. "Damn you, Kimbrell. You need me. You want only me. Right now, right here, I'm the only man you see. Tell me. Tell me now."

"Dallas!" I arched against him as I fought for some element of the same control he wanted.

Desperation tore through his kiss as his eyes closed and his brow wrinkled with a worry I didn't want to see brand his skin. "Let me feel you fuck my fingers, baby. Grind against them. Stretch for me. I have to get inside you. Right now." He whirled around quicker than multi-colored leaves spin around on a lovely autumn day and he pressed my back against the house siding. "Fuck!" As soon as he pressed my back into the louvers, his palm dropped from my pussy and his cock replaced it without a pause for preparation.

"Damn it!" I yelped as he drove into me with spite and anger, love and lust, dark ownership and true possessiveness. "Dallas!" I gulped for air but his cock funneled through my cave fast enough to steal it completely away.

"That's it, baby. Let me fuck you. Just me, and only you," he whispered against my neck as his hands gripped my thighs tighter. His short fingernails dug into my skin as his dick marched forward with a deliverance, a determination, one man's ultimate goal.

"Let me feel that tight snatch take it all." His lips were in a deplorable snarl but his eyes held love, remarkable adoration, no matter how weird and eerie the act itself brought about his inner consolation.

"Dallas." Oh yeah, I whimpered and almost cried because I needed this, whatever he wanted to give me, I had to take it from him just like this.

"Fuck me wild, baby." His thighs bunched and his forehead pressed against mine as he fought for dominance as much as independence. But he saw how quickly it diminished with the quiver of an orgasm.

His body slowed. "Oh, no you don't. Not yet."

"Please." I braced myself against his shoulders. "Harder," I whispered, pressed against him.

"No…no way." He withdrew in a diabolical fashion. Slowly, he pulled out. "Not again. Not until you…" His eyes widened and he stopped himself from finishing.

My own labored breathing matched his but he regained composure first, releasing me from his embrace as he gathered it.

Staring at me in a haze of too many emotions, too many undetermined feelings, he dropped to one knee and licked the deserted area with a perverse stroke. The spongy texture of his tongue swiped against my clit before he blew his hot breath over my entrance and then stood again.

"Dallas, don't." He hit too many tender places, crossed over guarded realms of pleasure, found spots that don't exist and to what? Leave me? No, I didn't understand the man in front of me and so what if I never did, just as long as he finished me here and now. "Don't you dare leave me wanting more. I'll…I'll…"

"You'll what, Kimbrell? Find another man to bed you? Two more are inside," he snarled.

"Yeah, I know. And you should've known from the first time you laid eyes on me, this is how it would be between us." I'd known. I'd recognized it. Through him, I believed in love at first sight. Because of the way he looked at me, because of the way he touched me, that first day, I understood. We were one in the same, a heart beating with the same desires, and the same pain and I believed we may have known long before he arrived in Tennessee.

"I can't get enough of you." He slumped against me, knelt in front of me. His hands spooned my bottom and he lifted me to his swollen lips. Softly, he licked the outside of my vagina, savoring my taste. Pools, no fountains, of desire gathered at my center and as the juices began to run free, he thrust inside.

I remained still against him, fighting the urge, defiant with refusal. "You're not getting off that easy." He didn't want to fuck me. He didn't want to feel me pulse against his cock. He wanted to take the low road. He wanted to ache for me, throb and burn, because with the aches and pains, he felt alive. I knew how that felt. I'd lived through plenty of those experiences.

He paused, looked up, and then responded. "No, I'm not getting off that easy, but you are." And as his teeth latched against my hard clit again right before his wild tongue drove in harder and faster, I realized—the man was right.

Chapter 9

"I'm marrying her." I heard Dallas inform the others as I walked toward the barn. The crunching sounds of gravel warned them I approached but I stopped with his declaration, frozen with the news I found impossible to digest.

"You are?" Rex asked.

"Yes. We decided before we came here if she was the one for us, I'd marry her and I'm going to ask her."

"You mean tell her." Rex released one hell of a huff with his reply.

"Tell, ask, what's the damn difference?" He certainly sounded determined.

"Tell me something, Dallas. How do you think she's going to respond since you haven't even looked her way since you fucked her up against the house with enough anger to start a war protest?" Rex sounded pissed.

"I did you two a favor, from the sounds I heard later."

"That you did," Corbin agreed.

"The hell he did. She cried herself to sleep that night."

"Only after you both fucked her, so you both owe me."

"Owe you?" Corbin's voice changed, his tone seemed tortured. "I love her. Fucking her isn't a problem. Seeing you take a first position in her life may present a few issues I'm not ready to discuss."

"You love her?"

"He does," Rex said.

"What about you, Rex? Do you love her?"

"I'm quite fond of her, yes."

"Hell, I didn't ask you if you were fond of her. Do you love her or not, yes or no?" Dallas pressed.

"Correct me if I'm wrong but wasn't that the whole idea here?" Corbin asked.

"Answer the damn question, Rex."

"I think you already know it. Hell, if you can't see it then I must've done something wrong somewhere."

"Well, I could've told you that much." Amusement sounded out in Corbin's statement.

"I'm with Corb, here. Dallas, we can't let you do it."

"You may not have a say-so."

"Oh, I think we do," Rex said. "I think we have about three hundred million say-sos or better."

"You're going to hold me by contract?"

"Damn straight. For Kimbrell, it's going to cost you and then I'll have to tell you, as for me, I'm still not letting her go."

"Me either," Corbin added. "We want her as much as you do."

"That damn contract isn't worth the paper it's written on."

"Now, Dallas," Rex began, "Do you honestly think I'm that stupid? I made damn sure I worded it in a way that we were all covered. I've never thought our money and women mixed together all that well. Besides, with you and Corbin here panting after her before you met her, I made darn sure we covered our asses, even if I had to be the one covering them all."

I heard Dallas grumble but couldn't make out what he said.

Corbin spoke next. "The legal stuff is in order, Dallas. We take a woman into our home and we all sign off in agreement. Then, the final part of our inheritance from granddaddy is released. That's just the way it is."

Dallas walked closer to the end of the barn. I heard his footsteps and ducked. "With what we were left from everyone else, if you think three hundred million dollars will keep me from taking off and marrying her, you're crazier than you look with your pants around your ankles."

"We'll see," Rex barked.

"I'm marrying her." Dallas spoke with finality. "You can still fuck her, love her, honor and cherish her but I'm the one she's going to marry and she'll sleep in my bed every night as my wife."

Rex stayed calm. "That's where we have the problem."

"Yep, it's turn about, like the agreement states. If we take one woman, we share her equally."

"Morning." I figured it was time to come out of hiding. I tried to pretend I didn't hear a thing. It proved tough since I had to walk right past the three men who openly professed their love.

"Kimbrell, we have to talk." Dallas called out behind me and I froze right there in a mid-air stride.

"I think we need a little more than words passed between us." I referred to the fact that he left me needy when I wanted him most. "And don't make me spell it out in front of your brothers."

"Told you." Rex smiled as he walked toward the feed bins. "You two talk, now. Ya hear?" Laughter shook his broad shoulders.

"Corbin, give us a minute," Dallas snapped.

I set my jaw. "I think for what you have to do, you're going to need more than a minute." I cocked my hip and batted my eyes.

"Talking, Kimbrell."

"Fucking, Dallas."

His lips curved in a smile. "You mean these two left you like a weeping willow and you're still mad at me because I didn't finish what I started?"

"I'm not mad but I will not be controlled with sex."

"Neither will I."

"Then we agree on something." My gaze held his for a second longer than I typically would have liked and I turned to catch up with his brother. "Corbin, wait up. I wanted to talk to you about that filly Rex said you think we should sell."

I might have taken four steps maybe, if they were long strides and I doubt they were. I was within an inch of Corbin's arm when sturdy limbs wrapped around my body and pushed me into a newly bedded horse stall. Without the proper warning, I was tossed in and the sliding gate snapped behind me, immediately securing a locked position. I stared at my captor through the bars of the stall my filly typically occupied. I heard the latch on the other side.

I know what little air released from my lungs came out as a true huff and puff. I didn't care if it sounded exaggerated or childish. I formed a new relationship with totally pissed off. It happened rather fast.

"I'm going to ask you once to let me out of here."

Dallas smiled. "I have some talking to do which means you have some listening to do. There's a bale of hay there so pull up a chair. I'll be back soon so we can get started."

"Rex! Corbin!" I screamed out for the other two men. "I know you both can hear me!"

No one, not even the man's blasted brothers, dared to go up against him when he took to one of his moods. While jovial enough this morning, Dallas still had a lot of answering to do and it was going to start where we left off. Plain and simple. I didn't plan to back down.

I thought Rex and Corbin might be in the lower barns so I decided to sit and wait until they came back. No point in screaming bloody hell if no one was around but Dallas. He sure wouldn't change his mind. "Stubborn old fart!"

Sitting on the prickly bale, I tried to think of something to provoke him, something to help him reconsider the childishness of the games he'd started to play. I thought of one or two ways but those would likely bring out the mad in his madness and I wasn't sure how far I wanted to push. The man did say he wanted to marry me and all.

I stiffly sat there and contemplated the idea of marriage and the idea of marrying three instead of one. Was that even legal? I assumed somewhere in this crazy world of ours, we might be able to get the deal sealed. Then again, politicians would never allow it. They typically didn't legalize the kind of marriages that made a handful of them jealous. I kicked up the sawdust and glared straight ahead. Hearing the clopping sound of hooves, I jumped to my feet.

"Corbin! Let me out of here." I fully expected him to comply.

He walked closer to my stall and peered inside. "What'll you give me if I free ya?" The filly on the other end of the lead rope snorted her disapproval. After all, I took her nice cozy space.

"Come closer and I'll show—"

"Touch that door and you're dead." Dallas entered the barn from the other end.

"Sweet damn, you've done it now. I can't cross him when he's threatening death." He rolled his eyes toward the ceiling.

I quickly tugged my shirt over my head. "What if I promise to send you out of this world in a way you'll never forget?"

His gaze fell to the proof that I meant business. He was tempted. "If I get you out of there are you going to let me eat that sweet pussy until first light of day?" A low growl, a slick swipe on his upper lip and I flinched against the desire rising.

Men. "Come on, Corbin. I'll keep my word. Make it worth your while. Me and you, no one else. I'll keep your hard cock twitching all night long."

"My mouth is watering thinkin' about it." He parted his lips and his tongue flipped in and out to insinuate a sweet sex act.

I reached behind my back and allowed my breasts to spill out into the open air. "And now?"

He glared at Dallas and then glanced back at me. "Come here."

I smirked. "Like these, don't you?" I pushed my breasts up and held them close enough for him to suck one nipple into his mouth. He released the filly but she didn't run off. She stomped and shook her little head like she'd ran out of patience hours ago.

"Shit!" His hand went to his cock and repositioned the weight under his jeans. "You're killing me here."

"Please, open up. I'll do anything you want. *Anything*." Right then, I really wanted him to comply. My womb clenched and my pussy dripped as soon as his sweet lips pulled me against the smooth texture of his tongue.

"She's lying. She'll be digging a large shallow grave. Touch it, Corbin, and I'll kick your ass until death looks like a long awaited invitation." Dallas propped up against the barn and crossed his legs. The bulge in his pants made me salivate. *Damn him.*

"Rex! Rex!" I screamed as loud as possible.

In a matter of minutes, Rex rushed into the barn. He came to a halt as soon as he saw me. With wide eyes, he addressed Dallas. "This is *not* a good idea."

"Did I ask for *your* permission?"

"No, you didn't." He tossed a feed scoop on the ground.

"That's what I thought." Dallas rubbed his chin thoughtfully.

"And you're damned-sure not going to ask for hers either. She's not your damn sub and she's not going to ask for your permission for anything. Period. We made a pact and that's something that isn't up for negotiations."

"Let it go, Rex," Corbin warned.

"The hell I will. You know him. You know this mood and the look in his eyes. You understand as well as I do what's on his mind."

I gasped and backed away from the bars. "You better be smart enough to know I will never play the part of a submissive." I happened to find the lifestyle fascinating but I found the way Dallas responded to it, or rather the memory of it, very disturbing.

"Playing?" Dallas stalked forward. "I never thought you'd *play the part*. I know you're going to slide right into your appropriate role as my submissive and live it. Count on it."

"Not a chance." I set my jaw and turned to Rex. "Get me out of this and I'll blow you all night long."

"Sweet offer, sunshine, but unfortunately..." He turned his gaze to Dallas and shook his head, "You started something with him that you may have to finish."

"No, it isn't. I get a deciding vote."

"No, Kimbrell. You don't." Dallas's crooked smile proved he believed in his abilities as a master or Dom, whatever the hell I was supposed to think of him as—I didn't know. All of this was new to me, and exciting. I shivered away the thought. No, I could not do it. This brought out too much darkness for Dallas.

Rex shifted his weight. "We discussed this, Dallas. You agreed to think it over before you'd introduce her to the error of your ways." Too much amusement lingered in his tone.

They're playing me. Thank goodness. I almost released a sigh of relief.

He grunted. "The error of my ways? That's bullshit and you damn well know it. The only way we're ever going to hold onto her is if we are able to properly discipline her and introduce her to the way I punish my women."

"Your women?" I saw green. Blue and purple too, as in the bruising effect. I planned to inflict pain on the man in front of me.

"He means the women he claimed before you," Rex whispered over his shoulder with an upturned lip.

"I got that part, but thank you so much for the confirmation."

"Anytime. Glad to be of service." He snickered.

I tried to think about the reasons why I didn't want to become anyone's submissive and after running through a mental list of pros and cons, I turned my focus back to Dallas. "This isn't going to work out." I glanced at Rex and Corbin and then informed them of my decision as well. "It's not going to work out for any of us, I'm afraid."

"You're that opposed to it?" Rex's amusement evident, he took a deep breath and then stepped closer to the sliding gate. "Thank goodness."

"She's not opposed to it—don't touch that gate—she liked the spankings. Wouldn't you two love to know what else she loves, craves?" Dallas's erection pressed against his pants. "I know I'm dying to know. I want her in position, kneeling in front of me, taking her orgasms when, and only if, I give her permission."

"Damn it," I whispered the words. I should've kept them to myself. I knew my face flushed with undeniable hard core lust. I needed someone to help me cope with it. Someone to teach me how to deal with it, maybe even punish me if I didn't. Jeez, Dallas made me wet just looking at him. Anything he wanted, I'd probably do without question.

"Shit, Dallas. Knock off the games. Kimbrell isn't going into that lifestyle."

I decided Rex first thought Dallas might have been kidding. Now, he wasn't sure. In fact, everyone was unsure.

"You promised, Dallas." I reminded him of our trip to Nashville. "You said you didn't break your word and you promised Rex and Corbin. What happened to that man?"

"I can't stop what I feel for you, fancy hips. I can't control what I want to do to you so I'll just have to make out the best way I know how."

"By having me submit to you?"

"Exactly."

"Hell no!" I held my breath and waited for Rex or Corbin to come to their senses and help me.

Corbin touched the lever. "I'm not going to let you tie her up and make her accept the ways of your darker side. I won't stand for it."

"Unhook that latch and you're in there with her."

"I'll take my chances."

* * * *

"Great." I stared down at the shavings Dallas dumped into the stall along with one pissed off Corbin, only a few hours earlier. At least we'd have a fairly comfortable stay if we spent the night there. "I was counting on you as my weakest link. The one guarantee that I wouldn't spend the night out here in the barn." I flopped down on my bale of hay.

"Darlin', I'm not your weakest link. Believe it or not, Dallas is. That's why he's so desperate to control you, pull you into his lifestyle."

"That doesn't make sense."

"It's the only way he'll ever be able to control his emotions when he's around you."

"Then if you realize this, why is it so important to you and Rex that you hold him to his word? Why not let him do it?"

"You want to be his—our—submissive?"

"Not particularly but I don't want to lose him either."

Corbin sat down next to me and draped his arm loosely around my shoulders. "You're not going to lose him, but if you take that step, you take us there with you and I have to be honest with you, I don't want that for myself. I don't want it for you."

With a saucy grin, I tried to tempt him, "You might like it."

A darkness lingered behind his eyes and I quickly gathered he already knew without reservations the lifestyle wasn't for him. "I don't think so."

"You've tried it?"

"Yes."

"And..."

"I didn't like it. It didn't do anything for me." His eyes lingered at my chest and he added with restraint and carnality, "As aggressive as you are in bed, I guarantee it wouldn't suit you either. Besides, I thought you were strongly opposed to the idea."

"I trust you. All of you. I don't have a reason to deny any of you something I don't know anything about. I can learn."

"The answer is no."

"Maybe you didn't have the right submissive. That's probably the reason you didn't like it." I pulled a piece of straw from his hair.

"Maybe I should give you a good sample of how it works." He latched his hand around my wrist and pulled me close enough to kiss me only he didn't steal one, didn't take what I felt certain he wanted.

"I'm willing."

"You just think you are." He quickly dropped my hand, stood up and walked over to the bars. "Kimbrell, what you don't understand is that there is so much more to being a submissive than what goes on in the bedroom."

"Teach me," I purred as I walked over to him.

"I…" His eyes darted down, covered me with a look filled with unadulterated lust. "You…"

"Please don't deny me."

Corbin's gaze grew darker. He clenched his teeth. "Kimbrell, honey, you have no idea what you'll bring out in Dallas if you ask for this. He is a powerful Dom and he becomes a force to be reckoned with—he demands, earns, and expects obedience. It goes beyond what you will do with him, with us, in the bedroom. He lives the lifestyle in a way that is much like a religion. It won't suit him to go back and revisit his past because it had such an incredible hold on all aspects of his life."

I grew wet just hearing him speak of it. "Tell me."

I took off my shirt, without a hint of sexual flavor and softly placed it over the thickest pile of fresh shavings. "Give me your shirt."

He loosened the buttons and shrugged it off with a growl and handed it over. I overlapped his and mine and then sat down on top leaning my back against the hay behind me. "Sit with me."

Corbin watched me now with nothing more than raw hunger. The itch was still there, I saw it. I wanted to scratch it, and force him back into the culture he claimed to have left behind.

Corbin began to pace like a caged animal now. I backed him into a corner and then provoked him out to play. He slowly began to come apart at the seams and I prepared to break them one by one.

"Please, Corbin." I arched my back. It was so ridiculous to be turned on by this.

With a sigh, he began, "Becoming our submissive wouldn't be an easy task for you. As a submissive you would serve and you would practice obedience. There are certain expectations. You are punished accordingly if you don't follow certain rules and guidelines."

I felt my nose wrinkle with such a thought. "In bed, right?"

"Not just in bed, Kimbrell. It takes a lot of self-control to turn your body over to someone else. In the true culture, you'll submit physically, emotionally, and mentally. You submit outside of the realms of sex."

"What are you doing?" Anger tumbled with each syllable found in the question.

My head snapped at the sound of Rex's voice. "I…um, I wanted him to tell me more about…"

"I heard. Shit, Corbin. We agreed. No more. I don't want our children raised in this lifestyle. Have you changed your mind?" His eyes held fury.

"Damn it, I can't win for losing. I tried to explain the aspects of the culture she seems so hell bent on understanding."

Rex glared at his brother's jeans. "I can see a little trip back into the past worked a fine number on you."

I heard the latch on the door and Rex stomped inside. He grabbed my arm and then held me tight against him. With an act of defiance, he asked me at once. "You think you want to submit to Corbin?"

"I…"

"Leave her alone," Corbin snapped at his brother. "I mean it, Rex. Nothing happened here. I only wanted to explain things to her, so she'd understand more."

"No, she wants to know, feels like she's woman enough to handle it. Are you, Kimbrell? Do you think I can tame that pretty little snatch into submission? Hmmm? Answer me!"

I swallowed as I saw the gray haze wash over his pupils. "You're hurting me." I tried to tug my wrist away from him.

"Let her go." Dallas stepped inside the barn stall.

A flicker of awareness inched over Rex's face. "Hell, I'm not going to hurt her. I'm trying to protect her from the foolishness the two of you seem to still crave."

"I don't crave that lifestyle anymore. For the last time, I only started to explain things."

"I asked him to tell me. What's the big deal?" I rubbed my arms as I glared at all of them.

"The big deal is I don't want a shared woman who wants to submit to one or all of us. It's my preference. I have a choice and you do too. All of us do." Rex glanced over his shoulder before adding, "I thought that's what we all wanted, and what we decided before we came here for Kimbrell." Rex appeared devastated, like he felt an unexplainable betrayal.

Dallas took a deep, ragged breath. "You're right." He kicked the sawdust. "I never had the right to mention it. I'm not going back on my word."

I narrowed my eyes on them then. "What if I want to submit? What if I want to learn more about it?"

Dallas crossed his arms across his chest and rubbed his chin with his forefinger and thumb. "Then, Kimbrell, we'll have to let you go." He didn't glance at his brothers but I felt like they supported his decision, even though it came as a shock for at least one of them.

Rex studied Corbin and then asked Dallas, "You're sure? If she's—"

"No, I'm sure. I've had enough time now to think about it. I think it would only hurt Kimbrell in the end." He took a deep breath and then turned to me to explain. "Kimbrell, I only wanted it for you after

I felt that loss of control. When you went on a search for Finn and Stan, I thought I'd lose my mind. When I found you there with them, I was ready to kill, taste their blood like a low-down vampire. I wanted death—theirs."

"I don't understand." I didn't.

Corbin tried to help. "If you'd been trained as a submissive, you wouldn't have gone there on your own accord. By going, you only brought about that awareness."

"I might be a wonderful sub and I want to try it. For you, for all of you." I hoped like hell I used the right term here. I understood so little and it probably showed the few times I tried to discuss submission and domination.

Dallas stepped forward. "Kimbrell, honey, you're craving something you've never had so how do you know what's best for you in this situation?" His fingertips stroked my lower lip. "Besides, you were adamantly opposed to it in the beginning. Why the change of heart?"

"I just want you to want me. If that means submitting to you—all of you—then I will. I just don't want you to leave me now that I've known the power of…" I stopped myself from saying it. They waited.

"The power of what?" Rex coaxed.

I didn't know if it was too soon to admit it, but if so, oh well. *Here goes nothing.* "Your love," I whispered.

All three men looked surprised, shocked really. "We love you too, Kimbrell." Dallas smiled at Rex and he nodded.

"I'll prove it for the rest of my life. These two will as well." Dallas dropped to one knee and pulled out a three stone emerald and diamond ring from his shirt pocket. "Kimbrell, will you do me the honor of becoming my legal wife?"

Tears. Damn how I hated to mess up my make-up at a time like this. It didn't matter. They came in droves in spite of twenty-four hour mascara that would indeed run down my cheeks. I threw my arms around his neck and sobbed.

"I'd love to be your wife." I held him close aware that two other Carlisles were left out of the moment, if for only a few seconds.

"How about mine?" Corbin dropped down next to Dallas and Rex dropped to one knee just as fast.

"And mine?"

I blinked at the three men in front of me. "I can't marry all of you!" Giggling, I tried to wipe away the tears of joy before those of confusion set in as well.

"You can. You'll marry Dallas legally, but become wife to all of us." Rex thought he possessed an answer for everything. Corbin shot him a wary look. I realized while I was locked in the barn with Corbin, Rex and Dallas must've agreed on the marriage issue. Corbin didn't get a final vote.

"Guys, it's like I'm choosing. I can't choose." If I stopped to think about it, Dallas was always the only choice, the right one. Dallas Carlisle was my heart. I loved his brothers, perhaps even as much as I loved Dallas, but it was different.

Dallas became, in a short period of time, my anchor. It had been years since anyone cared enough to support me on every level.

I framed Dallas's beautiful face, handsome in every physical way and looked deep into his eyes before I moved my gaze from Corbin to Rex. Kissing Dallas's soft, parted lips, I imagined at one time, women fought for him, wanted to become his submissive. Now, he was going to make a remarkable husband—mine. He'd stay with me for a lifetime, right along with the two handsome dudes beside of him. One of them now pulled me closer and nudged me with a stiff reminder.

"You owe me," Corbin breathed into my neck.

"And you owe me," I reminded Dallas playfully.

"Talking."

"Fucking."

"Bend over. Now." His husky voice held humor as three handsome rogues raced to drop their pants and they did it in record time.

Chapter 10

Everything was in order. I stared out the terrace door looking down on the Opryland Hotel gardens. My gaze twisted through the greenery below. In a few short hours, I would become Mrs. Kimbrell Carlisle. The day before, two handsome rogues reminded me why I couldn't marry into their family quick enough.

I took a deep breath and slowly let it seep from my lungs. Sweet memories, new beginnings, a whole new world waited for me in Texas but first things first. I need confirmation and someone planned to pronounce us men and wife. In so many words, I would marry one but belong to all.

"Are you ready to bolt?" Corbin came in and handed me a glass of white wine.

"Not a chance." I winked. "Wishful thinking, maybe."

Concern covered his face. "You want traditional?"

"Traditional?"

"Yeah, you know, one woman and one man get married and have a house filled with kids within the first year, that sort of thing."

"Hardly." I patted my flat stomach and smiled.

"You don't want children?" He studied me for a long time. "That would be a deal breaker here, I'm afraid." He patted my bottom and sat down on the bed.

"Can you keep a secret?"

"Hell no." Rex opened the door and stepped inside. "Neither can I but you can tell us anyway." He slipped a kiss on my cheek and added, "You look good enough to eat."

I decided secrets had their place and shared between these two wasn't the wisest choice to make. I turned around to face Corbin again. "The only thing I'm wishing for is that somehow I could marry all three of you legally and I guess I'm greedy enough to wish my sister considered cutting her own honeymoon short so she could send me away on mine."

Rex's smile turned devious. "What if I told you we can meet you halfway on those wishes?"

I studied him only for a second. The door flung open and closed just as fast. I blinked at the sight. "Darlene!" I ran right by my brother-in-law hardly noticing the large frame of Jack Dawson blocking her from my vision.

"I wouldn't miss this for the world." She kissed my cheek and hugged me again.

I turned to Jack. "Come here, you big lug." I embraced him quickly and then grabbed Darlene's hand. "Darlene, I want you to meet Corbin and Rex." I indicated who was who by pointing as I called them by name.

"Ma'am." Corbin smirked and tilted his hat. Rex took her hand and raised it to his lips. "Damn, there's two of you built for lovin' a man. Good damn thing Dawson didn't keep this one for himself." He pulled me close to him and kissed me lightly on the lips, truly on instinct.

Jack grinned, shook his hand and slapped Corbin on the back. "I forgot to thank you for picking us up at the airport."

I turned to Corbin and narrowed my eyes. "You knew she was here?"

"I know everything. I can keep secrets." His eyes pierced through mine and then he glanced at my belly.

Swallowing stiffly, I tried to return the focus to my sister and her husband. "Jack, would you give me away?" I shifted my weight from one foot to the other. "I mean, you have known me practically all of my life. If you wouldn't mind, I'd just be honored."

"You mean you couldn't talk one of them into giving you away." He nodded in Rex and Corbin's direction.

"Well, not exactly. It would hardly be appropriate considering."

"Let me guess. You're keeping all three of them?" Darlene winked.

I wheeled around and looked at Corbin, the only one who had opportunity to tell them everything. "I didn't keep that part to myself. I want your family to know where we stand so they don't have a problem when they have rugrats one day who rush into our room and find us all in bed together or something."

At the mention of rugrats, my hand instinctively fell to my stomach again. With all of the excitement, I felt queasy.

"I'd love to give you away. In fact, I'll sprint down the aisle with you just so I can push you in their direction, how's that?" Jack teased.

"Perfect."

"Darlene, did you meet Dallas?"

"I did. He reminds me of Jack." She grinned and then added with a true blush to her skin. "If Jack ever leaves me for a younger woman, Dallas promises to call me every night and have phone sex with me."

"Here we go." Jack rolled his eyes. "I've heard about that man's sexy voice for forty-five days."

"Well, if you don't watch it with your hands, big guy, you'll hear about it for forty-five more." Darlene shot back over her shoulder.

I glanced down and noticed his palms on her ass. He always kept his hands on her sitter-downer regardless of where they were. I imagine at times, she had to dish a hearty threat his way.

With a grunt, he shifted his grip upward and wrapped her in one of those tremendous bear hugs he reserved only for her. At one time, I remembered feeling some jealousy over the love they shared. Now, it was pointless. I had three men capable of wrapping me tight whenever I wanted a full body around mine.

"I'm sorry I didn't make it in time for the bachelorette party." She looked disappointed.

"Uh…" I looked from Rex to Corbin and then back at Jack and Darlene again. "It's okay." I shrugged.

Rex laughed and Corbin smirked before adding, "I don't think he would've let you join us." He tilted his head in Jack's direction.

"Oh!" She covered her mouth. "A private party, huh?"

"Yes. It was private and a party in every way." I bit my lower lip and threw my hip against Rex's side.

Laughter spun throughout the room. A heavy knock slammed against the door and Dallas stuck his head inside the door. Immediately, Corbin, Rex, and Jack stepped in front of me providing a wall to shield me from the groom.

"That's a sight to behold." He snickered. "I can't have a glimpse of the bride?"

"It's bad luck." Darlene began to push him away from the door. "But hey, you could sit and *talk* to me for a bit." She winked at me and nudged her husband in the belly before she followed Dallas into the hallway.

He whined in protest. "The thing is we're all marrying her. Why the hell can they spend time with her and I can't?"

"You're saying 'I do' and apparently they already did." I heard Darlene's laughter fill the suite.

Jack looked downright pitiful. "Damn. I swear, I used to have to worry about those sorry step-brothers of mine and now I'm going to have to worry about one of your husbands." He shook his head.

I liked the way he referred to the Carlisles as my husbands because after I said, 'I do' that's precisely how I planned to treat them.

"Let me go fetch my perverted wife so your brother can marry her sister and take her off our hands once and for all."

"Hey now, watch it," I chirped.

"Come on, Jack. Let's leave the bride alone. I've got a few drinks to swallow."

"Me too," Jack agreed. "Get dressed in your wedding get-up woman. You're going to be late for your own wedding."

"Not a chance," I called over my shoulder before I walked into the closet. When I returned, Corbin had a serious expression. "Does he know?"

"Does who know?" I paused and tried to decode his meaning. "Does who know what?" I tossed my shoes and dress across the bed.

"You're pregnant."

I swallowed stiffly. "No, of course not. If I tell him, it's going to spoil the wedding night for all of us."

"Or make it all the more special." He brought me closer and then kissed me. "I love you. He loves you. Rex…"

"Okay, I get that you all love me but not today. We're not telling him—or anyone else— today."

"Because the sex always comes first with you."

"No, of course not."

"Yeah, Kimbrell. It does. It's the only reason you'd postpone telling him, or Rex. We can't do the things we want to your body if you're pregnant but we can still make sure you enjoy it."

I shrugged. "Who knows? Maybe I'm not pregnant."

"Morning sickness suggests otherwise."

"So you know."

"I've known. And I also know that the baby could be mine, Dallas's or Rex's."

That's when everything hit me. "You have a problem with me marrying Dallas." I slumped down to the bed as the truth slammed against my gut.

"I have a problem with him having a stronger hold on you especially if you're carrying my child."

"What?" Dallas asked the question as he entered the room with Rex.

Both of our heads jerked when we heard him. "Dallas, it's bad luck to see the bride," I told him.

"You're pregnant?" His expression lit up the room.

"I think so."

"We're pregnant?" He slapped Rex on the back and then studied Corbin's expression.

"Apparently so," Corbin bit out.

Dallas wrapped me in his arms and lifted me from the floor, twirling me around the room. "God, I love you." His lips rested against mine, turning up in wicked acceptance while Corbin and Rex stood by and watched. Nervously, he put me down so they each could take their turn too but no one moved.

Dallas looked at Rex and then Corbin. "Something going on here that I need to know?"

Rex's lips pursed and he took a deep breath. "Corbin, I...well..."

"Damn it. Spit it out." Dallas glared at them.

"Alright, we don't like the idea of you marrying her when our feelings for her are just as strong, and every bit as real. We don't want you to have a solid claim on her when we want that same hold too. We want her for life, Dallas. We don't want to share her with you as the brothers of her husband. We want equal interest."

"You know it's not like that."

"What I know is that you can't expect us to love her less. She can't say 'I do' to you without saying the same to us or else what commitment does she have to us?"

I swallowed tightly. "I think I agree with them." I brushed my fingertips down Dallas's tightly placed arm. "You know how I feel about you, Dallas. You trust that, don't you?"

"Yeah." His gaze burned through his brothers. "I just wish they would've said something sooner."

"Corbin tried," Rex said. "We all discussed it once before but it didn't matter to you. After she was so excited over the ring we purchased, what did you want us to say?"

"Send the minister home. Let Jack marry us," I suggested.

"Dawson marry us? That's insane."

"No, it's not. Marriage is about what's in your heart. I don't have to have an ordained minister to tell me what's in mine. I love you all. I love you for the different qualities you possess and for loving me in the first place. I don't want to choose you over Rex and Corbin any more than I'd want to choose them over you."

"For once, she makes perfect sense when she's standing in her lingerie." Rex chuckled.

My eyes narrowed. "Very funny. For your information, I am most understood when I'm down to a thong."

"Sweet damn, I know that's true," Dallas agreed as he grabbed me around the waist and tugged me close enough to show me just how much he liked the idea. Corbin's eyes were already on my ass. I felt the strength in his gaze before I felt his hands on my rear, and Rex's lips scraped across my shoulders. He held out a silk burgundy robe so I could slip into some level of modesty.

"I'll pay the minister and send him on his way. Jack won't be able to marry us *and* give you away."

"Well hell, if you're going to go for the absurd, I might as well give my sister the final shove. I'm the next of kin, after all." Darlene peeked in at just the right time.

Jack walked in right behind her. Some said the man was pussy whipped. I believed it. So help me Darlene never left the man's sight for long. "Did I miss something?"

My eyes filled with tears as I looked back at my men—the three best looking men I'd ever seen in a tuxedo. "No. You didn't. I did. I don't have to choose. I don't have to say 'I do' to one while placing two in reserve. I can have everything I want and I can have it now."

Jack's brows arched and he looked at Darlene for answers. She only shrugged. "Don't ask me. She's the one who couldn't make up her damn mind. She wants to marry 'em all."

Jack smirked. "Why am I not surprised?"

"Jack Dawson, does my sister make your dreams come true?" I asked him pointedly.

"You'd better believe it." He pulled her close.

"Well then, if you had three of her, two more tiny little replicas of her and the love you share with her, could you chose?"

He thoughtfully responded. "I don't know. If I found one who purred like a kitten, I guess I might be able to place her at the front of the litter."

"Funny, very funny." Darlene cut her eyes at her husband before eyeing Dallas. "He's jealous."

"I know that feeling." He stalked forward and tugged me closer. "Damn do I ever."

Corbin opened the door to the terrace. "Hurry up, Kimbrell. You have a wedding march to play."

I took a deep breath and thought about the only request any of the Carlisles made. They wanted me to play my own wedding music on the big grand piano in the center of the suite. Maybe now I'd even play a lullaby too. I laughed out loud at the thought.

"Are you happy, sugar?" Rex asked.

"Yes. I'm happy." I moved close to him and wrapped my body around his in a tight embrace before sharing more of the same with Dallas and Corbin. "I'm the luckiest woman in the world."

With a growl, Corbin eased his hands over my ass. "Damn, I know it."

"Watch it." Dallas smacked his hands away. "You're not even supposed to see the bride before you get married."

Darlene stepped forward. "You're absolutely right. All men marrying my sister need to move on along. We've got a wedding to get underway." With an easy smile, she scooted my future husbands straight out the door.

I took a deep breath and watched Darlene do what she did best—manage the situation. Ironically, I was going to be able to do what I did best too. Only now, I wasn't going to be looked down on for it. My past only prepared me for a wonderful future.

My dreams overlapped with a beautiful reality. It was time to leave the past behind. I was going to love and be loved. Marry and be married. Together, we were going to begin a lifetime of happiness and I couldn't wait to start living my life as a Carlisle—wife and lover to the best of Texas men.

THE END

WWW.DESTINYBLAINE.COM

ABOUT THE AUTHOR

Destiny Blaine lives in Tennessee with her family. You can contact her through MySpace at www.myspace.com/destinyblaine or visit her on her website at www.destinyblaine.com for more information.

Siren Publishing, Inc.
www.SirenPublishing.com